T0326252

Dear Reader:

V. Anthony Rivers is very special to me; both as an author and a human being. Back when I first started Strebor Books International to self-publish my own books, a dear friend—Tee C. Royal—of RAWSISTAZ—asked me to read a self-published book by another author entitled *November Friend*. I found myself engulfed in the novel and fell out in tears by the time I read the ending. I had cried over dozens of films in my lifetime but that was the first time—EVER—that a book had made me cry. I emailed V. Anthony and told him how much I loved his book and asked if there was a sequel. There was and the combination of the two ended up being the first novel that I published by another author. It is entitled *Daughter by Spirit* and it is about a young woman who makes a big mistake that all women who have ever loved a man can relate to. His second novel, *Everybody Got Issues*, flipped the script on how women often sleep their way to the top of a corporation. In his novel, a man does the same exact thing and causes much drama and animosity between female co-workers. He is also a contributor to *Chocolate Flava, Sistergirls.com* and my upcoming book *Love is Never Painless*. As you can see, I am really feeling his work. So much so that I am publishing yet another novel by him this fall entitled *Until Again*.

This book, *My Life is All I Have*, is a moving story of a young girl caught up in the wrong things—like so many young women today—and it chronicles her journey to find her destiny without losing her essence in the process. I have no doubt that this book will catapult V. Anthony Rivers into the arena of bestselling authors and recognition of his work is long overdue. So I welcome you to read this book, written by the one author who inspired me to publish others. Now some 50 authors later, he truly spawned a dynasty and an imprint; all because he overwhelmed me with his talent.

I want to thank those of you who have been gracious enough to support the dozens of authors I publish under Strebor Books International, a division of ATRIA/Simon and Schuster. While writing serves as a catalyst for me to release my personal creativity, publishing allows me the opportunity to share the talent of so many others. If you are interested in being an independent sales representative for Strebor Books International, please send a blank email to info@streborbooks.com.

Peace and Blessings,

Zane

Publisher
Strebor Books International
www.streborbooks.com

OTHER BOOKS BY V. ANTHONY RIVERS
Daughter by Spirit
Everybody Got Issues

ZANE PRESENTS

My Life
IS ALL I HAVE

V. ANTHONY RIVERS

STREBOR BOOKS

NEW YORK LONDON TORONTO SYDNEY

Strebor Books
P.O. Box 6505
Largo, MD 20792
http://www.streborbooks.com

ISBN-13 978-1-59309-057-9
ISBN-10   1-59309-057-9
LCCN 2005937061

Cover design: www.mariondesigns.com

Distributed by Simon & Schuster, Inc.
1230 Avenue of the Americas
New York, NY 10020
1-800-223-2336

First Strebor Books trade paperback edition March 2006

10   9   8   7   6   5   4   3   2   1

Manufactured and Printed in the United States of America

For information regarding special discounts for bulk purchases,
please contact Simon & Schuster Special Sales at 1-800-456-6798
or business@simonandschuster.com

"I've been consciously researching this story for the past two years and unconsciously, all my life. It's been love from the start and a lesson every step of the way. This story is dedicated to the love that was down from day one. Welcome to my creative jungle."

—V. ANTHONY RIVERS

ACKNOWLEDGMENTS

This is by far the biggest dream come true to date. What can I say, I'm in love with this story and before I can go further with my acknowledgments I have to give special thanks to God above and departed family looking over me from heaven like guardian angels. I also have to thank two very incredible sisters who make this dream possible and also serve as inspiration for the awesome hard work that they put forth to make things happen not only for me but for many others under their wing. I speak fondly and with heartfelt sincerity when I say thank you to Zane and Charmaine. BIG THANK YOU!

Now it's time for some what ups, shout-outs, and heartfelt hellos. During my short time thus far in this literary arena, I've been blessed to meet some really cool people. A lot have become friends and quite a few have turned into angels, sisters, and brothers who have me smiling the moment I think about them. I have to say thank you to Darrien Lee for always being there and I mean ALWAYS because I think we email every single day except Sundays, huh? Ha! I always miss your Southern voice after we visit. JDaniels; another special sister friend that I've been blessed to know from the beginning of this dream-filled ride, helping me along the way and pushing my creativity. Shelley Halima; Ha! I've been waiting for the chance to give you a shout-out in such a very special way. I'm blessed by your friendship! D.V. Bernard; One of the deepest and funniest guys in the world. You've got words that can make a masterpiece reality. Eric Peete; Your kind spirit moved me right away, the moment we met. I always look forward to the next handshake. Stephanie Johnson; Issues brought us together, huh? Wink! Now we got friendship! Tina Brooks McKinney; All I can do is smile when I see you. I wish you success akin to sweet paradise sipping on your favorite cold beverage.

Glenys Colclough of Inspiremecafe.com; You definitely are an inspiration, a shoulder to lean on and great guidance. Danyel Smith; Inspiration from afar. A creative light I give the utmost respect to and yet never met. Shelia M. Goss; Thanks so much for the support, love, friendship, and inspiration. Carla Barclay; Many thanks, warm hugs and blessings for reminding me why God places true friends in our lives. Tell your mother I'm coming for that peach cobbler, aight! Charaine; You are an East Coast angel. Stay positive and keep the world tilted right with your positive spirit. Ardys Scott; Much love, remember true friendship...until again, nah mean? Layloni; Thanks for blessing this cover with your beautiful presence. The whole world should know about what comes from within you because as a young black woman, a friend, a good person—you got it going on! You are an amazing spirit. Keep your dreams and goals close to your heart 'cause you gonna be alright. Jamise L. Dames; Friend, inspiration, guidance, little big sister, magical connection that I thank God for. If I never made a dime at writing it wouldn't matter because I was paid in full when I met you thanks to this literary thang. I could write a book about how much I admire and respect you. Much love to your husband, Que, for keeping you safe and fabulous.

This book carries with it a lot of love and emotion so I gotta send out more thanks in the name of inspiration and life itself to the following: Malaysia; stay positive. Fantasy; big smiles and sincere respect. Kim Roseberry; endless love and friendship, keep that camera ready. Roberta Farwell; Keep that Southern spirit alive. Angela Schmidt; friendship and good shoulder...

In the essence of time and heart, I'll name more inspiration and thanks a little quicker with the most important coming last. Lexie Johnson, Hudson Kelley, Torrance Stephens, Shawnte' Paradise, Crenshaw Boulevard, Crenshaw Mall, Fox Hills Mall, Ladera Center meat market aka Magic Johnson's Friday's. The outside crew at Starbucks (Ladera Center). Tupac Amaru Shakur, The Jungle, Slauson Swap Meet, Jordan Downs, Nickerson Gardens, Imperial Courts, Starz, King Henry, RBC, Julio G.(Westside Radio), The Game, Snoop Dogg. Arnail Jackson; I remember back in the day when NWA and The D.O.C. had heavy rotation in our lives. Rockin' those beats in the mailroom. Vernice Lee, Liary Weathersby, the barbershop on Washington and

4th Avenue, King Tee, WC, Too Short, DJ Quik, The Dogg Pound, my blogging friends especially the Songbird ladies; BEG, Lambchop, Scorpio K, and Ja-me; all special, beautiful ladies. Lisa the bartender at Starz, Prince; my lifetime motivation soundtrack creator, Mathew Bragg (the coolest), Tyrone Griffith, Horace Farr, the Filipino Mafia at work (Edgardo, Vener, Rolly, Patrick, Greg, Art, Gilbert, Nestor et al), and the list goes on and on as I'm probably leaving out some folks but as they say, charge it to my head and not my heart. Everybody means everything, especially family... Tamer, Charles, Dee Dee, Bubba, Mildred, Vaughan, Natalie (RIP), Little Charles, Chris, Alzata (grandmother), Gloria (mother), and my hero Uncle Richard "Daddy Rich" Moorings who serves as inspiration in some of the creativity of this story. Thanks to everybody, especially the Strebor Books International Family! Atria/Simon & Schuster, Black Expressions, Cushcity, *Essence*, all the in-credible African American book clubs and sellers around the country. I'm running out of breath here but never out of sincere love. I leave you with the words of a cool brother and friend that I met at Starz by the name of Big E. "Peace and Love..."

PROLOGUE

Life to me is about the choices you make. I no longer believe in defining my life based purely on happiness. I'm more about freedom. I feel like I have to take a good hard look at the decisions I make first.

One of my biggest defining moments came on the day I met with my friend Scottie Franklin, aka "Blaze." He brought some fool with him who I didn't like from the jump. Together, the three of us, talked business. I was serious about what I wanted to do. I was ready to get the hell out of L.A. But for the change I wanted to make, I needed some serious cash.

I had ideas on how I wanted that to happen. It was simple and I imagined every possibility. The pros and cons were no mystery and the risks didn't scare me at all. The only shit that made me nervous was this fool that Blaze brought to me, saying he could be the one to help me out. He knew I only needed one person—someone who could think on his feet and not be an asshole, questioning me because I'm female.

We met at Sherman Oaks Galleria outside the Cheesecake Factory restaurant on Sepulveda and Ventura Boulevard. It was a hot day and I stood with my arms folded because Blaze was late as usual. His friend already didn't impress me with his fake walk, trying to look like he was all that wearing some baggy khakis and a Lakers jersey. Plus, he had this big-ass silver chain around his neck; he had to hold on to it because it kept hitting him in the chest as he bounced from side to side. It didn't look like his scrawny ass could take the pounding, let alone be good for what I needed him to do.

I instantly pulled Blaze to the side and asked, "Who you trying to introduce me to?"

"What you mean, girl?" he defended.

"You brought me some gangbanger from the hood?"

Blaze looked at his friend and then at me. "You trippin'. He aight. You said you needed somebody. I mean, what the fuck? You getting picky?"

"I know what I told you, but this is serious. I can't have somebody that I gotta be worried about at the same time I'm trying to do this. Come on!"

This fool started to get a little antsy, watching me and Blaze have a private conversation. He opened his mouth, which only convinced me even more that he was stupid. "Yo! Y'all not gonna show a brotha some love? What y'all whispering about over there? Bring a brotha way cross town and have him watch y'all whispering. Damn, I could be at the crib…chillin', watching some videos or some shit like that…what's up!"

I looked at Blaze with a see-what-I-mean expression on my face. My lips were poked out like a kid who got his bike stolen. I was ready to tell his friend to go back and finish watching his *Menace to Society* video with his wannabe O' Dog looking ass. I glanced over at him with the same head tilted to the side glare he was giving me. I started to say something, but I was interrupted by Blaze.

"Hey, let me introduce y'all, aight," Blaze said with his slanted-eye smile.

He always had a warm side to him that could be very infectious. He knew how to take control of situations, especially where I was concerned. He could make a potential bad moment sort of fade away, though not this time.

Blaze put his hand on my shoulder. "Uh, Leesha, this here is Stanley Broussard. Stan, this my girl, Leesha."

Stanley stepped forward a little like he was gonna hug me or something. He had a gold-toothed smile to go along with the colors in his Lakers jersey.

"What's up, mama? You just call me Stan. All my niggas know I be down for whatever…"

I didn't say a word. I just looked at Blaze with my arms still folded. I took a deep breath and broke my silence. "We gonna stand here and talk, or find someplace to sit down?"

Stanley smiled and started talking with his head tilted to the right like he was trying to get his flirt on. "I'm with you, mama. Anyplace you wanna go, I will follow, ya heard!"

I was about to accuse him of eating some fried chicken with his greasy lips and all that smacking he was doing while trying to impress me. I couldn't believe Blaze had brought a clown like him to introduce me to. The three of us walked into the mall and took the escalator up to the second floor. This mall doesn't have any stores. It has a huge movie theater, a health spa, and some restaurants so the place was packed with folks going to the movies or hanging out.

We found a spot on a metal bench as we walked past the Magic Johnson 24 Hour Fitness spa. Well, I sat down and then Stanley. He was seriously getting on my nerves trying to check me out. He sat his ass down right next to me. He was just rubbing his hands together and sucking his teeth. He was annoying the hell out of me. Blaze remained standing and paid no attention that I wanted to hurry up and get this over with.

Blaze reached inside his oversized Sean John shirt pocket and pulled out some cigarettes. He lit one and then took a long slow drag. I watched him looking all relaxed and calm, enjoying himself. Meanwhile, my peripheral vision was showing me this fool on my left undressing me constantly with his eyes.

Stanley decided to say something and wiggled while he talked. "So, what's up, y'all? First you was down there whispering and now we just gonna what, sit here and people watch? Y'all really trippin' now!"

Blaze smiled and watched as a couple of attractive sistahs walked out of the health spa. He took another puff from his cigarette and returned his attention to me and Stanley. "Yo, Stan, peep this. Ain't much need to be said except that Leesha need somebody to do a job with her." Blaze attempted to get right to the point.

"What kind of job, yo?" Stanley asked.

"Just a job, dude. It ain't like you qualified to do a helluva lot."

"Well damn, what we talkin' 'bout? Drive-by? I gotta shoot her baby daddy for messin' around? What?"

"Nah, fool... Hold up. Leesha, is it cool for me to tell him?" Blaze eyed me through the smoke he'd exhaled and waited for me to say something.

I looked at Stanley and spoke softly. "Let's just say it has to do with a bank."

Stanley started to laugh and that wasn't cool. "Oh shit! You trying to rob a bank? Yo fine ass need to either be at home playin' Mommy or showing yo booty in some magazine. Why you tryin' to rob some bank for? Shit. I know y'all trippin' now!"

I stood up and started to walk away. "Why you bring this nigga here?" I asked Blaze and had no problem pointing straight at Stanley.

"I honestly thought he was your man, Leesha." Blaze tried his best to remain calm. He looked at Stanley. "Yo, man, this ain't going down like it should so let's take off, aight?"

Stanley started grinning as he stood up, bouncing his head up and down. I could see right away he was about to talk some shit to me. He had that ignorant, up-to-no-good smile. "Maybe we need to start calling you Cleo with yo *Set It Off* acting ass, bitch..."

Blaze didn't say a word but he knew to step back a little 'cause he'd seen me in action before when somebody used that "B" word in vain. Shit, he'd seen me run across the street to slap this chick one time. I don't be playing.

Two seconds elapsed. *C-r-r-rack!* Blaze reacted.

I swung with all my might and connected with my intended target. Blaze tried to conceal his laughter as he watched me go off on Stanley. I socked Stanley square in his nose and he made the mistake of calling me a bitch again. Then before he could finish saying, "What you do that f...," I kicked my foot straight up in his nuts, sending him to the ground in agony.

"Damn, girl!" Blaze said with his hands no longer covering the laughter he had tried to hold earlier.

I realized a lot of people were watching and the attention alone would cause the security people, as slow as they were, to come see what was going on. Blaze realized the same and held on to Stanley while telling me I'd better leave. "I'll holla at you tonight, Leesha," he said.

I shook my head and walked away. I left the building and went home to my apartment in Studio City. On the way, my one-track mind kept thinking about who I could get to help me. I just needed one person, but it couldn't be Blaze because we have that understanding. He'd help me with the planning and anything else I'd need to pull it off, but he keeps clear of the actual work. He's probably the luckiest man alive. He's done so much dirt since he was a teenager and ain't never been caught. Now he say he's retired, but he will invest if he sees some potential for profit. He's been to school and taken economics courses. He still dirty, though, but he been like a brother to me for so many years, I lost count.

Once I got into my apartment, I kicked off my shoes, poured me some soda, grabbed a bag of potato chips, and sat on my balcony. I watched the occasional car drive by and listened to the birds. I checked out all this freedom that I'd lose if something were to go wrong with what I was about to do. I thought about my life. I am so ready to leave California and go live in the South—someplace like Atlanta or Augusta, Georgia. With some good money, I could buy a house real cheap and relax for a while before I need to do something else or start fresh with a new nine-to-five. I could do that once I'd get settled. I'd be cool with that. I just need something different, but I don't want to struggle while trying to make that happen.

My life was center stage in my thoughts while sitting on my apartment balcony. A name started to creep into my consciousness: Treyvon Williams. He's sort of a friend. We've kicked it on occasion since high school. It's cool sometimes to have a guy acting like he worships the ground you walk on. Blaze always jokes around because he says that Treyvon is in love with me.

Blaze would say something like "Leesha, that dude love you so much he done gave up dreams just to be near you."

I've always had a strange feeling inside ever since Blaze told me that. It seems like Treyvon could be so successful in life right now, but instead, he's working a cleaning job at Cedars-Sinai Hospital on the graveyard shift. Then he sometimes paints store windows for extra money during the day.

Blaze always hints at the possibility of changing or affecting Treyvon's life. His life would've been different if he had stayed away from me. I don't know. Maybe he's right. Maybe he's wrong. I just know that life is what you make it and you have to own up to the decisions, the mistakes, and anything else that comes your way. Maybe I'm wrong for not really caring but irregardless, I know what I'm doing and I know what I want. I can't worry about some guy. It's all about me and it always has been...Leesha Annette Tyler.

5

REMINISCE OVER ME

All my life I wanted to be free. When I got old enough to have attitude, I defined my idea of freedom in very simple terms. I wanted to be a bitch, a princess, and a queen all rolled up into one. Young ladies ain't supposed to be all hard. I keep hearing that if you living in modern times, you gotta be able to stand up to all the shit being thrown your way on a daily basis. You can't worry about being courteous or being a fuckin' "lady." Shit. I never once put in my list of dreams to become a part of the "in-crowd" and wear all that designer stuff. I can find just as good or better at the Slauson Swap Meet. I ain't stupid. I know what to do with my damn money. I learned how to shop from my mama. It was about the only thing she taught me that was worth knowing.

I started realizing Mama knew what she was talking about when I went to the mall one day alone. The only thing I could afford up in there was a T-shirt and a cute little belt. That's what I bought, too.

I felt so bad. I'd see other girls from my school hanging out and acting up. They was fast and I was just getting started. Teenage boys stepped to them left and right. I sat down in the food court area and watched the show. I learned a lot from watching. I liked the idea that females could have so much control. That's what I saw when I watched them. They had control over any male who tried to talk to them—that is, if they knew what control was all about. I noticed most of the girls collected names until they found themselves face-to-face with the most popular boys. Even though I wasn't part of any clique, I took notes until it was my time.

About every Saturday I sat watching inside the Crenshaw Mall. Mama thought I was either at the park or at some weekend school event. There was always something going on at my school so it was a good cover for me to be somewhere I wasn't supposed to be. What Mama didn't know didn't matter. She hardly went anywhere on the weekends so I didn't worry about bumping into her. Plus, people don't watch each other's kids no more so I was free and clear.

We lived on Buckingham Road, not far from the mall. I could walk there with no problem other than worrying about those men who hang out in front of the liquor store on Santa Rosalia Drive. I always walked on the opposite side to avoid hearing them talk shit to me. That didn't stop them, but at least it didn't hurt as bad as when I'd hear them say things that made it hard for me to swallow my own spit. They would say some really nasty stuff. I got used to it the more I walked past them. I learned to turn a deaf ear to all that shit though I'd never become completely immune.

I'd breathe a sigh of relief once I'd step inside the mall. I'd start smiling as soon as the cold air and bright lights hit me. Plus, it's always busy up inside there. People be loud as hell. Kids run all over the place. They got a beauty supply store where ladies go buy the freshest weaves and yell at the Korean owner when she says how much it cost.

I went in there with Mama one day and she was mouthing off because she was mad about the price of synthetic hair. She said, "How these folks who never been to Africa before know so much about the texture of our hair?"

I looked at Mama and asked her, "*You* been to Africa before?"

The two ladies who were paying attention to her laughed. Mama was kind of embarrassed and didn't talk to me in the car on the way home. I didn't understand at the time, but I figured it out soon after that.

One other thing that stood out in the mall was the police station. That was a trip to see. I stopped sitting on that end of the mall because I got tired of watching officers parade the latest criminal they caught. It gave me a bad feeling every time I'd see them holding on to somebody with handcuffs. They'd walk them slowly through the mall and most people stopped what they were doing to look directly at the person in handcuffs. I guess I was sensitive about certain things until I learned how to control what I'd felt and not really care. I exposed myself to so much from going to the mall on weekends. That place turned out to be my learning ground and my first taste of envy.

I was only fourteen years old and in the tenth grade at the time. I envied this girl named Janina Parrish. That was before I learned to call her a bitch and be done with her ass. She knew I was jealous of her. She could feel it. The look in my eyes was a dead giveaway and because we happened to be in the same grade, that gave her twice the pleasure of rubbing in her superiority over me.

Janina's parents had money so she got all her clothes from the big department stores on the other side of town. She wouldn't keep it a secret. She'd announce to the whole class whenever she went to the Beverly Center in Beverly Hills. Then she'd say some stupid shit like letting us know that she saw Keith Sweat or Da Brat up in there buying clothes, too.

Places like the Beverly Center were foreign to me. A thirty-minute drive to some store across town was like an international flight. Mama didn't see the value in going so far unless you were going to work, had a job interview, or a doctor's appointment. Her way of thinking only gave me another reason to look forward to independence. But in the meantime, I'd want what Janina had. I wanted to be the shit and even at her age, be able to walk around like it don't stank.

I watched her with a different outfit on every single weekend. Guys approached her, demanding her phone number, and she played like it didn't mean anything. That usually made them weak because she wouldn't give the number right away. It made them try harder to please her. She was only fourteen like me, so the best way to make her stop and talk was to offer to buy her something or take her to see the latest and most popular movie. Janina needed to be seen going places where others could envy her like I did. She wanted all of us to talk about how lucky she was and act like she some damn Queen Bee. After a while, I got pissed—not so much at her but at myself for falling in too deep behind the rest of the crowd, waiting to get popular like her. She had a stranglehold on her status. I had to put a stop to that shit.

Funny thing, though, was I found myself one day getting advice from my grandmother. I always called her "Grammy" and she was my heart. She didn't live too far from me and Mama, so it didn't take much to walk over and visit. She lived on the other side of Crenshaw in the Leimert Park area on 42nd Street. I liked her apartment a lot because it was so clean, which meant no graffiti. The neighborhood looked pretty much the same as ours but for some reason, people were nicer and you didn't run into a lot of thugs or drug addicts. That was another thing I didn't understand. Why life seemed so different depending on what street you lived on. Maybe deep down, I envied Grammy, too, but those feelings only came up when I was at home, listening to the muffled sounds of somebody getting their ass kicked. Or sometimes I'd all but jump out of my skin because we have this front gate outside that bangs really loud whenever somebody closes it. People go in and out all night long. It's hard to sleep sometimes.

Mama seemed used to all the noise. I think she got to the point where she'd block out everything including the sound of my voice because most of what I'd say to her, she wouldn't hear. That's why I wouldn't just walk to Grammy's place; I would run. Yeah, even though I was a freshman in high school, I'd still run to see Grammy as if I were a little kid. I hadn't built a reputation nor was I looked upon as being cool so nobody noticed me with my long hair trailing behind as I ran. They probably thought I was trying to hurry my ass through those rough streets. And when I'd get to Grammy's apartment, I'd be so happy. She'd open the door and instantly smile. Ain't nothing like being greeted by a grandmother's smile. That was something I never took for granted.

The day I asked her for advice was when I admitted my jealousy of Janina. Grammy was a little disappointed, but she tried not to show it. She sighed heavily, shook her head, and thought for a moment. I had to wait in her silence until she spoke. I sat nervously. I kept shaking my right leg and staring at Grammy with a puppy dog look on my face. Her silence grew deep. I could see she wasn't pleased at all by my confession, but she finally put aside her displeasure and talked to me as only a grandmother could.

She said, "Baby, you have nothing to be jealous of. Now whoever this other young lady is, I can't see how she can even imagine being better than you. Nobody in this world is better than my grandbaby—nobody. Don't you ever forget that. I know I taught you better than to want to be like somebody else."

I listened to Grammy as though my life depended on it, and in my mind, it did. Her words were wise, of course, but more so than that, she cared about everything I did, say, or thought about doing. I told her that what I felt wasn't because I believed Janina was better than me. I wanted for once to have some nice things, too.

"Leesha, you have to be patient. If you were a little older I'd say to you, go out and get those things for yourself. But, since you're still so very young, all I can say is that in time, you'll have those things and more. But, baby, you have to want for the right reasons."

I tried my best to take what Grammy said and use it to squash what I'd felt about Janina, but it wasn't working. I basically had to lie to her because she suggested that I stop going to the mall. She said it would be good because I wouldn't want what I didn't see.

"You're right, Grammy," I'd said, and she was beyond pleased to hear those words.

"I tell you what," she said, "pick out one thing that you really want and I'll just go into my little retirement fund and get the money to pay for it. It's not like I'm going on a cruise anytime soon."

I was so excited and then I felt guilty. Grammy was gonna take out money from her bank account just to buy me something so I could feel good about myself.

When I walked home that day, I got really mad. I even walked on the same side of the street as the liquor store where folks be hanging out. My mind was on an island of guilt somewhere faraway. One guy said something to me and I told him to go fuck himself. He laughed. Maybe I was lucky that he didn't take me serious, but I was so mad that I didn't care where I was or who I'd encounter.

When I got home, I went straight to my room, closed the door, and sat on my bed. I stayed there until nightfall, listening to the noise outside and thinking about everything Grammy had said to me. I didn't like disappointing her and I really didn't want to take her money.

That night as I stared out my bedroom window, I saw some guys standing around, drinking, messing with this girl and listening to music. They all looked like thugs, even the girl. I watched for a while and listened. My concentration was so focused on them that I twitched a little whenever that noisy gate would close. Then simultaneously as the gate slammed, I saw one of the guys slap the girl in her face. She went down instantly and didn't get up. She stayed on the ground, holding her face. I could see her legs moving, but she wasn't trying to get back up. My heart was beating like crazy because I didn't know what else to do besides watch. I thought about telling Mama so she could call the police, but it was late and she'd probably try to hit me if I woke her.

Finally, one of the guys helped the girl up. I could see her bleeding from the nose and she could barely stand. They acted as if what happened was okay. Nobody seemed to care. The guy who helped her stand opened the back door of the car that he and the rest stood around, and she got in. Another guy followed and got inside the car with her. Then they closed the door. I knew what they were doing because I'd heard about females who wanted to join gangs, but I thought they'd just get beat up by other girls. I kept watching as one guy after the other got inside the back seat of that car. They were taking turns. And the more I watched, the less scared I became. I watched as though I understood. It was normal. It was a part of life in my neighborhood.

When the girl got out of the car, her spirit seemed taken from her. She looked ashamed. She was so unlike how she was before. She got beat down in more ways than one and those guys controlled her like a dog on a leash. She walked away clutching her shirt with her head bowed. I didn't like seeing that at all and never wanted to experience what that felt like—again. I say "again" because I felt like all my jealousy over Janina translated into a mental beat down of my very own and I was the one walking home with my tail between my legs. I was the one afraid to look up whenever men or anybody else talked shit to me. I was the one jumping out of my skin every time that damn gate would close. Things needed to change and I'd planned to take my first steps toward making that happen.

One day in English class, the teacher announced that she had a very special project for us. Nobody was excited and most of us worried that whatever it was gonna be, it probably meant we had to stand in front of the class and read something. I hated that shit and most times nobody listened, they just looked at you. If I was gonna stand up there and do something that I hated, I at least wanted people to listen.

My English teacher was alright. Ms. Stafford was cool most of the time. She didn't tolerate anyone who sat and did nothing. You couldn't just sit there and expect to pass her class. You had to speak up and speak *clearly*. She'd stop you in mid-sentence if you said anything that sounded like slang. I actually learned a lot in her class. I hated that she kept on our asses all the time, but at least you knew she was serious about teaching you something.

When she announced our special assignment, my mouth dropped open. She called herself doing something out of the ordinary in order to bring honesty to the classroom and get past any hidden feelings that might exist among students. Ms. Stafford was going to school herself during that time. She was taking child psychology. I think a lot of the assignments she'd give us were things she could use to satisfy her own educational requirements. In a funny way, I respected her for that because she was doing her *thang*. She was killing two birds with one stone, teaching us shit and doing her home-work at the same time. She was yet another example of a woman in control and I loved that about her.

"Okay, class!" she announced. "The assignment I have for you is to do a report on someone in the class that you don't know and, or don't like."

When she said that, the class started buggin' out. Chairs were moving around, students were moaning, and as I said, my mouth dropped wide open. Ms. Stafford had to keep telling everybody to be quiet so they could let her finish.

"In this assignment,"she continued, "you'll be able to express your true feelings and in the end, perhaps you'll find that this exercise will bridge the gap that exists between you and this person that you claim to dislike."

Ms. Stafford said so many of us in this world tend to make up our minds about people without really taking the time to know one another. She felt that by teaching us to recognize this condition now would make us better people when we became adults and had to face the world every day. She had me thinking about Mama and all the shit she'd say about people she don't even know. Mama be pre- and post-judging all the time. She can talk non-stop even about Grammy. I don't like it when she does that and I guess that's why I'm always asking her a question that belittles the comments she makes.

After the students in my English class settled, Ms. Stafford asked us to write on a piece of paper which person we chose to write about and why. I couldn't believe she put us on the spot like that right away. I thought she would at least let us go home and write our reports.

Funny thing, though, it didn't take me long to do what Ms. Stafford requested. All I had to do was look toward the third seat in the second row from the door and find the subject of my report. That's where Janina sat. I stared in her direction the whole time Ms. Stafford was telling us to write down the name of our subject. I smiled and then while in mid air of my devious thoughts, she caught me looking. Janina had turned her head to the left and seen me staring. I sat in the fourth seat of the fifth row. She saw me and she looked at me like I was nothing. She'd never made eye contact with me long enough to even say hello before so this moment was a rarity. Then as she returned my stares with her *what-the-fuck-you-lookin'-at* glare, she began to write something on her paper. I kept my eyes on her all the while writing her name: *Janina Parrish*. And then I listed why I hated her.

"Okay class, make your answers honest. As I said before, I want an honest portrayal of your true feelings. Think out your answers, people. Don't just give me simple ones. You can do this!"

Ms. Stafford forced me to really think about what I was writing so I had to disconnect from the cold hard stares that I was locked in to with Janina. I hated being the first one to look away. It felt like I'd let Janina get the best of me and even worse, she might've thought that she did, too. Bitch.

I thought hard and began to list my feelings. I wrote about how I felt Janina looked down on others and anyone who called themselves her friend, really meant nothing more to her than her personal cheering squad. Then I let my bitterness show. I wrote, *Janina is nothing more than a bitch. She acts like she's all that but I bet when she gets home and is all by herself with no audience around, she don't do shit but mop floors and take out the trash for her parents. They only send her to the mall all the time so she won't be around and they have to look at her ass. Janina is nothing but a fake, wannabe ho and I've got no love or respect for her. She ain't earned shit and don't deserve shit.*

I sat for a moment, thinking to myself, *What the hell?* Then I started trying to write down something else to turn in but the school bell sounded. Ms. Stafford was already in my row, collecting papers. She didn't care what was on the page. She snatched pieces of paper off desks as she walked by. I tried to fold mine so I could hide it, but by the time I made the first crease, she was standing at my desk with her hand out.

"I'll take that from you, Leesha. Looks like you had plenty to say in such a short time," she said.

I nodded. I felt so embarrassed and couldn't believe how I'd gone into a whole 'nother zone when thinking about how much I hated Janina. Ms. Stafford glanced at my paper. I noticed her reaction as she read over what I wrote. I started to get up from my chair and leave like all the other kids had done as she collected papers. Then she said my name.

"Leesha..."

I looked at her and began apologizing before she'd even questioned me.

"I'm sorry, Ms. Stafford, I just—"

She stopped me in mid-sentence. "Leesha, I'm looking for honest feelings so I can't fault you for what you wrote. However, I'll have to really think about whether or not I can have you read this before the class. Words like these would get us both in trouble, don't you think?"

"Yes, ma'am..."

"When you bring in your paper tomorrow, I want to read it first. What I may do is simply have you and Janina meet with me in private. There seems to be some deep-seated anger in your words, Leesha. Does Janina know how you feel about her?"

"I don't know..."

"Hmm, I'm really curious..."

Ms. Stafford had something serious on her mind. She turned toward the door and noticed Janina about to exit the classroom. "Janina, can I see you a moment?"

Janina turned and walked over to us. We made eye contact again for a moment. She gave me that look like before. I couldn't stand her, either. She had me wanting to write down some more shit about her.

"Yes, Ms. Stafford?" Janina said.

She acted completely different when she approached the teacher. You could tell she was one of them spoiled kids who know how to play the game and then once they're out of their parents' sight, they do all kind of shit to fuck up your life.

"Janina, I believe I picked up your paper, correct?" Ms. Stafford asked.

"Yes, you have mine already."

Ms. Stafford thumbed through the papers she'd collected until she came to hers. She smiled to herself and then began to nod her head as if she'd made some type of discovery. "Thank you, Janina. I want to have the two of you in class alone tomorrow. I'd like for the report that you write to be read to each other, rather than to the class."

Janina and I both asked why simultaneously. Then we looked at each other. She probably had the same *I-hate-you* thoughts going through her mind that I did.

"Just bear with me. You both appear to have issues with one another and I think if we recognize those feelings now, perhaps we can do something about them. So, I'll see you both here tomorrow, early."

Janina and I moaned with displeasure. She left the classroom first. Actually, Ms. Stafford held me for a moment and waited until Janina was gone. Then she allowed me to leave. I guess she could feel the tension. She should have since she stood between Janina and me. Ms. Stafford was good at recognizing potential problems, but she had no clue that this one would never be solved. At least, not the way she'd want it to be.

I'd made it to Ms. Stafford's class early the next day, thinking that I'd beat

Janina and be able to have the upper hand on her ass. But then, as soon as I walked in, there she was waiting. I'd felt like I couldn't win. *Is she for real?* I thought. I couldn't believe she had beaten me to class, and to make matters worse, she was carrying a really big folder. Deep inside I'd reached the panic zone. The paper I'd written was folded and stuck in my back pocket. Janina had her shit in what looked like a leather or vinyl organizer. I hated her even more and was mad at myself for letting her get the best of me in more ways than one.

When I stepped inside the classroom, Ms. Stafford spotted me immediately. "Come on over, Leesha!" she said.

My eyes quickly focused upon Janina, standing with that look in her eyes again. She didn't say a word to me and I didn't say shit to her, either.

"Okay, who's first?" Ms. Stafford asked.

"I'll go first, if it's alright with her," Janina said with an air of conceit in her voice.

"She has a name, Janina, so I think we need to be more respectful of each other."

"She does? And what is it because I forgot."

"Ladies?" Ms. Stafford warned as she'd seen the look in my eyes go from anger to boil in less than a second. I was about to kick Janina's ass.

"I'm quite sure you know her name, Janina, so please, ask if there's no problem with you going first."

Ms. Stafford was trying her hardest to keep things civilized. I couldn't tell if she was in denial of how things were between Janina and me or if she really thought she could make us like one another. That wasn't happening.

Janina glanced over at me briefly and then spoke after turning her head to look forward. "Is it okay with you...um, Leesha, if I go first?" she struggled.

I responded without any hint of struggle in my voice. "Yeah, bitch, go 'head on!"

Ms. Stafford was so shocked by my response that she'd frozen in her tracks, giving me time to lunge at Janina. I knocked her to the ground with my open hand to the side of her face. I think her ass was stunned, too, but she tried to get up and defend herself. I kicked her ass, literally and figuratively, before Ms. Stafford got herself together and pulled me off Janina. I kept on kicking my legs because I didn't want Janina to think she could take advantage of me being held back by Ms. Stafford. I quickly realized that wouldn't be a problem because Janina was too busy checking her bloody lip and holding her stomach where I kicked her a few times.

"Have you lost your mind, Leesha!" Ms. Stafford said.

I never answered, nor did I say too much at the principal's office. They sent me home after about thirty minutes of interrogation. I was told that because it was my first time getting into trouble I would be suspended for two weeks instead of being expelled. I would also be responsible for making up any assignments that I missed. That didn't bother me because my classes weren't that hard. I felt like they gave me two week's vacation and when I went home, I was celebrating. Mama was still at work and it was only me, the television, and some leftover beef stroganoff.

My celebration lasted for about an hour. Mama came home early. She had this look on her face as if she knew something. Either that or somebody at work pissed her off so bad that she had to leave. She confirmed my first suspicion as soon as she shut the door behind her.

"Leesha, have you lost your damn mind! Girl, I got a call at work saying my child was fighting and using all kind of foul language! Is you crazy? You ain't learn to act that way in this damn house!"

Mama went off. She threw her purse down and took off her shoes. There she stood in her blue polyester dress suit, screaming at the top of her lungs. One moment she had her hands on her hips and the next moment, she was pointing so hard at me, I thought she was gonna stab me with that finger of hers. I never responded. I sat there and listened. Her voice was so loud they could probably hear her down the block. I'm pretty sure everyone in the building knew I got suspended from school. Mama was giving me a verbal beat down but not once did I have feelings of regret. If Janina had been standing in my living room, I'd kick her ass again, right in front of Mama.

I can't even remember how long the verbal assault lasted. However, it did come to an abrupt ending when she told me that I sickened her, which hurt my feelings and got my attention. I looked up at her, standing over me and breathing hard as if she were completely exhausted behind all the yelling. We both had eyes filled with tears.

Mama said, "Leesha, it really hurts me what you did today. While you're on suspension, I want you to go live with your grandmother. I called her from work already. I'm so ashamed that I don't think I could look at you for these two weeks. You stay with her and do me a favor…Think about what you've done and see if maybe you realize how wrong you were."

I never responded verbally to the things Mama said, but when she pointed for me to go to my room and pack some things, I had no hesitation in my step. As much as it hurt me to be yelled at, I was really happy to stay with Grammy. My earlier thoughts of being on vacation had returned and the more clothes I grabbed from the closet, the more I felt like smiling again.

MORE LIKE LOCKDOWN

My two weeks with Grammy were a far cry from being on vacation. She put me through a serious guilt trip the whole time and never let up on me about my behavior in school. Actually, it seemed like before I arrived at her apartment, she'd transformed her place into a school with prison-like conditions.

As soon as Grammy opened her door, I knew I was in trouble. Gone was her smile as I had to endure the sternness of her voice. She showed me to the room where I'd be sleeping. It was a lot like mine and had a window with a view. But unlike mine, the only thing I could see was the alleyway on the side of the apartment and the garage area for the apartments next door. It wasn't much to see but it sure felt good to know that the alleyway poured in to a world that was waiting for me once my two-week sentence was up.

Grammy had me hang up all my clothes before she sat me down and went over the house rules. I made a remark that I quickly wanted to take back, but of course, I couldn't once it slipped from my mouth.

"Rules?" I asked with a smirk on my face.

Grammy turned around with a look that meant business. I could see her whole body tense up.

And before she could let me have it in any kind of way, I quickly apologized. "Sorry, Grammy."

I received no response as she turned back around and continued to walk toward the living room. "Okay, Leesha, have a seat," she told me.

I sat down and made an attempt at another smile. I tried to show my cutesy face that Grammy always liked. In the past she'd respond with laughter and a smile that could light up a dark movie theater. But on this day, she had nothing for me but rules to follow and emotionless words to convey her message.

"First, I have to say that I just couldn't believe the things I heard about you, Leesha. I mean, fighting, cursing... I'm almost speechless. For a while as I listened to your mother, I kept saying that there must be some mistake and that this wasn't my baby she was talking about. But she kept repeating over and over what the people at your school said. I kept thinking she had to be talking about somebody else's kid, but it broke my heart to know that she was talking about you. Do you have anything to say?"

During that moment, I'd felt a sort of disconnect from Grammy. She was so angry and disappointed in me, but I continued to feel no regret for what I'd done. I couldn't relate to the notion that my actions were wrong. Kicking Janina's ass had felt good. It was almost electrifying. I even wished I had had more of an audience, though I knew the kids at school probably had enough gossip traveling among them to fill in all the blanks.

My silence was met with more disappointment from Grammy. I had nothing really to say—at least, not anything she'd want to hear. No apologies. No regret.

"Fine, well, these two weeks won't be any sort of picnic for you, Leesha. You will still be expected to study every day as well as do chores around the house," Grammy said.

She then laid down the rest of her rules and let me know that sleeping in late would warrant severe punishment. I didn't ask what she meant by "severe" so I nodded and promised to get up every morning.

"First thing I want from you when you get up is to take a bath, brush your teeth, and fix your hair. Around this house, you're going to be a lady. After that, then you can come in here and make your breakfast. If there are any dishes that need to be cleaned, you'll do those first before cooking. I'll expect you to always clean up after yourself and to leave the kitchen spotless after every meal. Do you understand?"

"Yes, Grammy."

"Good. After breakfast is over, I'll have some things for you to read and occasionally we'll discuss it. I'm also gonna have your mother find out what your assignments will be at school during these two weeks so you don't fall behind. I don't like feeling this way, Leesha, and hopefully you'll learn your lesson. Maybe this experience will allow you to grow into a better person. I want you to grow up to be a lady…"

"Yes, ma'am."

"And Leesha?"

"Yes?"

"Don't think that I love you any less. It's just that right now, I'm feeling very disappointed."

"Okay, Grammy."

When Grammy left the living room, I took a deep breath and rolled my eyes. *Is this the kind of shit I'm gonna go through?* I thought. I love my Grammy more than anything in the world, but the guilt trip she was giving me made me tired. I know that's a disrespectful way to feel, but going through her punishment was like a game of survival. All I needed to do was put in my time and then get back to the real world.

Day three of my punishment turned out to be an interesting one. I felt Grammy beginning to loosen the noose she'd had around my neck. I mean, the first two days were so tense that I tried not to make any kind of noise that would cause her to look in my direction. I even found myself memorizing where the creaks in the floor were. I got pretty good at tiptoeing around all those soft spots, on my way to either the kitchen or the living room. Those are about the only places I was allowed to go besides the bathroom. Grammy's room was off limits. I could only talk to her outside her door if I needed something. But on the third day of punishment, as I sat on the couch in the living room, I felt as though I was being watched. Every time I looked up, I saw Grammy's shadow, floating against her white living room walls. I never turned around to confirm my suspicion of her presence. I figured she was making sure I was there, doing what I was supposed to be doing. She always checked on me every hour anyway, so why should this time be any different? That's part of the reason I didn't turn to look at her. But despite that, I could sense something else going on. Nevertheless, I continued to read the book she'd given me.

Grammy was a book fiend. She had a library inside her apartment of mostly books by black authors. To me, I thought it was only her way of decorating because there were bookshelves in every room. I never imagined that she actually read everything. Sometimes she talks about it but not really that much. She ain't the type to brag about anything—except me. I don't think she'd been doing that a whole lot lately.

I did my best to read what she'd given me. At first, I skimmed through most of it and only stopped on things that caught my attention. It was some hard shit to read with old words and strange ways of talking. Even the slang was a trip. I'm thinking it was supposed to be ghetto, but I couldn't relate. I got easily distracted. When I heard a car driving by bump'n "Funkdafied" by Da Brat, I wanted to run to the window. I knew if I did, Grammy would come running to the living room because she'd be able to sense that I was out there having fun. The thought of me enjoying myself during these two weeks was something she didn't encourage at all. This time was all about punishment, education, and thinking about what got me there in the first place.

I continued to read and I focused even harder whenever I felt Grammy's eyes on my back. It was a strange feeling to be watched so closely and even more strange that Grammy was being so hard on me. As I continued reading, some of the words kind of drew me in. This one scene in particular had me scratching my head and then I thought to myself, *Shit, maybe I do understand this stuff!* This man in the story used to be some kind of musician but he was walking around acting like his life used to be better than what it eventually became. It's like he did something to mess up his game. Probably drugs or some chick he couldn't handle. He keeps talking about this Leona chick; a white girl. Maybe she screwed up his mind.

I couldn't believe that Grammy had me reading this stuff but she probably had her reasons. Like the day before she had me reading something about being young, gifted and black. By the time my two-hour reading sessions were up, I was tired as hell. Seemed like Grammy was trying to turn me into some kind of black historian or something.

I wrestled with the words on the page. I read sentence after sentence and tried to figure out what was being said. They kept calling people "squares" and it was a trip to me that Grammy gave me a book with so much foul language. Then, before I could turn to the next page to see if this guy named Rufus finally has sex with Leona, Grammy walked up behind the couch I was sitting on.

"What do you think about James Baldwin's writing, Leesha?" she asked.

"I don't know. It's kind of depressing. Very sad, but it's okay, I guess."

"Well, I wanted you to see a side of life that I pray you avoid and never have to witness on your own."

"It might be too late for that, Grammy. Me and Mama live in a place that people sometimes call the Jungle, you know."

"I hear things about where you live, baby, and I know your mama can't afford to move you to a better area. But good people can still come from bad conditions."

"You come from bad conditions, Grammy?"

"Well, quite honestly, because there was so much love inside my house, anything bad on the outside had no effect upon us. We'd hear things, and rather than focus on being sad, we'd try to see if anyone needed help. Times are different now. Young folks grow up faster. Young ladies are exposed to way too much and I think that's partly why you got into trouble, Leesha."

"Maybe, Grammy…"

Grammy walked around the couch and sat down next to me. She removed the book from my hands and placed it on the coffee table. Then she told me to move closer to her. Grammy held me in her arms and laughed. "I guess I've been a little hard on you, huh?"

I shrugged my shoulders and I tried to be careful. I figured if I said she was too hard on me, she might take that as criticism and become even harder. "It's okay, Grammy."

She laughed and rocked me back and forth. "Now Leesha, I can never excuse what you did to get in trouble, but I may ease up a little on your punishment. But one thing, while you're here, I do want you to do your studies and I want us to talk to each other. Your mama stays busy and I'm not so sure she's giving you enough attention. I noticed that when you come over here, once I get you started talking, you just go on and on. I so enjoy that, but I can't help but feel like it's the result of you not being close to your mother. Is that true?"

"Me and Mama don't really talk that much. She has her room and I have mine."

"She has her room and you have yours? Chile! You talk like you grown. You're a fourteen-year-old young lady and this is a time when you need some guidance, not separation. I'm going to speak to your mother about that."

"Were you close to your mother, Grammy?"

Grammy started smiling before I could even finish my question. "Chile, yes. I think she'd probably whoop all of us if we tried not to be close to one another. You know I had a brother, your Uncle Horace; and a sister, your Auntie Ruth. We were all so close. We may have had one or two instances where there was some fighting among siblings but that's about it. No, we had a close family. I'm pretty sure it comes from Mama's upbringing in the South. She always told me about the closeness of her family, and Papa said the same about his."

"You close to your father, too?"

I asked Grammy that question as if it were unusual anyone could be close to their father. I had no image or recollection of mine. I used to dream about him, but I could never see his face. It would only be like a smell or something. I think I'd just mentally held on to a scent of cologne that I smelled one day at the mall when walking through the men's section. Something about that smell stuck with me like it belonged to an older man—a father figure whose hands would smell so nice and feel so strong when he held you.

I lost myself inside my memories. Grammy's voice faded away like cigarette smoke in the air. I only paid attention to what was going through my mind. I smiled. I closed my eyes as I leaned against her chest and held her tight. I forgot for a moment that she was even talking.

"Leesha, you okay, baby?"

"Huh?"

"Baby, you supposed to be listening to me. You just drifting off to only God knows where."

"Sorry, Grammy…"

"Where your mind go to just now?"

"Nowhere…"

"Uh-huh…Nowhere my foot!"

"Grammy, did you know my daddy?"

Grammy laughed to herself. I smiled because at first I thought she might pull away from me if I asked about Daddy. He ain't been around and didn't raise me so I figured he'd be on Grammy's shit-list, for sure.

"Leesha, your mama never talk about him?" she responded.

I shook my head and then I tried to remember if Mama said anything about Daddy. If she had, it was something I'd overheard rather than it being something she'd told me.

"Well, I suppose I can tell you something about him. It's been a while since I've heard anything. I tried to keep tabs on him and make sure he always knew how you were doing, but it got to be real hard keeping in touch. Your daddy felt really bad about not being able to see you."

"Why didn't he try?"

"Your Mama run him off…"

"But, he a man."

"That he is and I can't sit here and find an excuse for him 'cause God knows we have enough fatherless children running around. Your daddy moved to D.C. a few months after you was born. I had a friend out there that would talk to him. They worked together. That's how I was able to know where he was and what he was doing at the time. I didn't dare tell your mother about it but for you, I just had to keep in touch with him."

I looked up at Grammy with the saddest expression she'd ever seen on my face. I think it broke her heart, especially after I'd asked her something which brought home her point about fatherless children. "Grammy, what was my Daddy's name?"

"Aw, baby, you don't know your daddy's name?"

Grammy got very upset and started toward the telephone. She cursed underneath her breath so I wouldn't hear what she was saying, but there was no hiding her anger. Grammy stood with the phone in her right hand, next to her ear while her left hand was on her hip after she'd dialed the numbers. I knew she was calling Mama. It wasn't really a big deal to me that I never knew my daddy's name until now.

"Where is your mama?" Grammy asked. "Seems like since you been over here, she been constantly in the streets. I'm gonna have to have a talk with your mama 'bout her behavior."

"You don't have to, Grammy."

"Chile, it ain't right what your mama done, but let me sit down and finish telling you about your daddy."

Grammy hung up the phone and took a deep breath. She brushed her hands against the top of her thighs as if to suggest she was done with her feelings about Mama. She sat back down next to me and held me in her arms. "Let's see...His name was William Tyler. He was a sweetheart, too. That man smile so much till I was afraid some bugs might fly in his mouth. Chile, he was really nice. A gentleman...The kind of young man you don't see too much of these days, but you know they're out there, somewhere."

Grammy seemed very fond of Daddy and that was a good feeling. She went on to describe him as medium-brown skin, with a small Afro and a mustache tapered off at the sides of his top lip. But most of all, she kept returning to the fact that my father would smile so much. It was nice to hear but it didn't excuse him for not being around.

"Your daddy tickle me. One time I was standing with him when he heard his name called. Somebody said, 'William!' He turned around and smiled but come to find out that the person was calling somebody else. William just shrug his shoulders and kept on smiling."

"So, that's my daddy, huh?"

"Yeah, I wish I knew where he was. All I have is an address that was given to me when he first moved to D.C., but I don't know if it's still good. I tried sending him a card with your picture in it, but I don't know if it got lost in the mail or he just didn't respond."

"You never heard from him?"

Grammy shook her head.

After that, we both sat quietly and listened to the silence between us. I could hear Grammy's heart beating. I felt mentally drained after reading some of that book she had given me and then hearing about my father. The rhythm of Grammy's heartbeat mirrored the heaviness of my eyelids. The sound was so intoxicating that I'd soon fall asleep in her arms.

Time sort of flew by after Grammy let up a little bit on my punishment. I was still under house arrest and couldn't go anywhere, but she seemed a little more lenient about me staying up late or sleeping in longer. It drove me crazy that I couldn't leave and go outside but that was my punishment and I had to deal with it or suffer more disappointing looks from her. I didn't want to do that. All our little talks really brought us closer together and it was nice to see Grammy walking and smiling again.

During the second week, I developed a fondness for Grammy's kitchen window. I could see the street from that spot and it became my source for watching the outside world. Television was boring. All them soap operas pretty much looked the same. And you know I got no life when the television guide becomes my personal calendar. I found myself counting the days before the *Fresh Prince of Bel Air* came on. That's real sad. So, needless to say, I learned how to survive without the television.

I continued to read some of the stuff that Grammy had on her shelves. I couldn't believe some of what I found. Grammy was the last person who I thought of as being militant. I mean, she had books about Angela Davis, Assata Shakur, and the one about the Soledad Brother. I couldn't believe my eyes at the time, but then I got to thinking that maybe that's the side of Grammy that rubbed off on me. That wanna-be-in-control side where you don't want anybody having a whole lot of say in your life—except yourself. Grammy had other books on her shelves and most was what you'd expect. You know those nice stories or those uplifting, all-God's-children type of books.

Grammy's collection had me straight-up trippin', but despite being impressed by what I'd seen, nothing pulled at my curiosity like the outside world. I'd check to see what was going on at least once every hour. Sometimes there would be cars driving by and other times I'd see people walking and not paying attention to anything around them. It wasn't the same as where I lived with Mama. Anyone walking by there always checked to see what's around them. If you didn't, you might've gotten robbed, beaten or both. In Grammy's hood, you didn't have to worry about that so much. Her place was like an oasis compared to the jungle that me and mama lived in.

The countdown I'd started after the third day of the second week felt real good. I wasn't really excited about going home, but I was anxious to return to school. I'd promised myself I would be cool, do my thing in class, and stay out of trouble. I figured that I'd already proven my point by kicking Janina's ass so there was no need for me to continue to trip about her.

Grammy could feel my excitement so much that she never bothered to ask if I'd done all my school assignments. To be honest, I didn't do any of them. I figured I could just BS my way through that stuff on Sunday night when I was back home in my room. I only had to do some math problems and a couple of book reports—some typical shit they have you do just to keep you in check at school. Nobody really learns anything from that stuff.

Grammy defends the educational system by telling me that they teach us to think so we can make good choices with our lives. Mama went to school. She said Daddy was really smart. Look at the choices they made. I didn't know what Daddy was doing, but Mama never proved to be the shining example of Grammy's philosophy. Education...Mine came from the streets, listening to Grammy, and watching the stupid choices my mama made.

When Saturday morning arrived, I was up bright and early. I stopped and thought to myself, *I'm going home!* But then I realized where home was. My excitement went away. Mostly I was relieved because at least I'd be able to go outside and see more than what Grammy's kitchen window allowed me to see.

I hadn't brought that much with me when I started my punishment. All I had was a bunch of T-shirts, a few pair of jeans, and some pajamas, so it was easy to carry my stuff home. Grammy gave me a hug that I thought would last until nightfall. She kept saying how proud she was of me and how much she enjoyed our time. The way she'd said "our time" was sort of eerie. It messed with my mind for half of the time I was walking home. But then, once I got to the stoplight at Crenshaw and Stocker Street, my whole outlook changed. Grammy sort of faded to the back of my mind and the whole vibe of where I was started to take over.

The action was on and poppin'. Crenshaw Boulevard was alive! It was a trip to see so many folks so early in the day, but I guess everyone figured they'd get an early start on cruising before the police shut things down like they typically do. Once they put up roadblocks and direct the flow of traffic, niggas start overflowing into the side streets and neighborhoods. That's the part that pissed off the community. I don't think they really cared when everything stayed confined to the boulevard itself. That was the politics of life that never changed, year after year.

When the light changed and the walk signal illuminated, I strolled like a dude rather than strutted like a young lady. I was toting my black bag that felt a lot heavier than it did when I went to Grammy's. I bobbed my head to all the different jams coming from the cars and trucks. Mostly I heard Tupac's music. His stuff seemed to get people pumped up with the courage to act a fool and start fights. "Holler If You Hear Me" was like a jungle cry in my neighborhood. But besides Tupac, you might hear some "Bump N' Grind" from R. Kelly booming through somebody's system. That kind of electricity made you want to sit on the corner and watch the action go by.

Once I got about a block away from Crenshaw, the noise started to die down a little bit. I took a deep breath because it was nothing like smelling gas fumes combined with the heavenly aroma of the International House of Pancakes at the entranceway of the mall. I walked past with an extra pep in my step as I cut through the parking lot on my way home. I started to see some of the tops of the apartment buildings in my neighborhood and began feeling a little sad. It was like I got there too fast.

Maybe I was going through some kind of withdrawal. I mean, reality hit me in the pit of my stomach because I would be back at home, listening to all the shit that made me pissed off in the first place. I wasn't ready to hear that front gate slamming shut all night but I had no choice. When I got home and stood for a moment, in front of my building, I decided to get used to the noise in my own way. I opened that front gate and slammed it really hard behind me. I put so much strength behind what I'd done that it caused me to fall forward to the ground. I was a little bit embarrassed, but then I got up, cursed the gate, and went on inside the building.

When I got to the front door, I didn't have my key. I'd left it at home because I didn't want to lose it at Grammy's. I regretted that decision because Mama's ass took forever to answer the damn door. I had to knock five or six times. I could hear the television on so I knew she was in there. I could even smell some food through the door. It smelled like she must've poured a bucket of hot sauce over whatever she had cooked.

"Mama, can you open the door!" I yelled.

Then I heard some footsteps coming in my direction. The floor started creaking, she was walking so hard.

"Hold on, Leesha, I be right there!" Mama shouted.

"Aw, Mama!"

"Just hold on, girl, I'm doing something right now."

I kicked the door really hard to vent my frustration and then I sat down on the steps and waited. I must've sat for ten minutes before I could hear the lock turning and see the door finally open. I spoke without turning my head to see Mama.

"It's about time!" I said while picking up my bag.

Then I heard a sound that almost sent me falling down the stairs. It was a man's voice. "'Bout time for what?" he said.

"Who are you?" I asked.

"Ain't you hear your mama tell you she was coming? You gotta clock in or something like you late for work?" he said to me with his funky-ass breath.

I looked at him real hard and tried to use some kind of mental telepathy to tell his funky-breath ass to get out of my way. I didn't want to go anywhere near him as he stood all up in the doorway *Who the fuck is this?* I thought.

The man turned to look toward Mama. She was standing over a pot on the stove, stirring and adding more salt and pepper to whatever she called her-self cooking.

"Yo, baby, this your daughter?" he asked.

"Yeah, that's Leesha, honey!" Mama responded.

She was in her nightgown, acting like the only company she was expecting and planned to entertain was funky-breath man.

"Yo daughter cute! She get that from you or her daddy?"

"Neither one," I told him before Mama could answer.

"Oh damn, she got attitude, too? Her little ass must've got that from you, huh, baby?"

"Whatcha say, Victor?"

"Nuttin'."

Mama couldn't even take the time to say hello to me since she was so busy preparing food for her and this man she called Victor. She didn't bother to introduce us and I didn't give a damn since I'd seen her return to her cooking rather than display any signs of missing her daughter. I could feel Victor's eyes on my backside as I walked to my room. I turned to look at him before closing the door. He waved at me like some filthy-minded fool who was about to start slobbering any minute. I thought about how Grammy wanted to talk to Mama about her lifestyle, but I think she was too late. Mama was stuck on stupid and self-absorbed into her own world; no one had any say but her.

I could hear her laughing through my bedroom door. The walls were already thin in our apartment, but hearing her and Victor reminded me of that fact even more. I could hear him talking shit nonstop.

"Damn, gurl! What you made over here?" I heard Victor say.

"Just a little family secret recipe. You like it?"

"Shit, you got my mouth on fire. I'm about to scream so loud that your little family secret gonna be out there in a minute!"

Then they both started screaming with laughter. Maybe Mama was happy but they was both making me sick. I cracked my door open a little bit so I could see what they was doing. I couldn't believe how silly Mama was acting. She was feeding this dude and he was acting like he couldn't chew without slobbering because food kept falling out his mouth. That shit was nasty but Mama was all into it, wiping his mouth after she'd feed him. Then she'd have the nerve to kiss him. Mama was sitting all up on him at the dining room table and he was steadily eating and running his hands all over her thighs. I closed my door and sat on my bed in disgust.

The noise and laughter got worse. I was mad as hell and trying to adjust to being back at home. I emptied my bag and noticed a couple of books tumble out. Grammy had put them in there and that explained why my bag seemed a little heavier on my walk home. I missed Grammy already. The time we had spent together was real cool and it was nice getting to know another side of her.

Memories of Grammy were constantly interrupted by Mama, Victor, and the noise outside. Mama and Victor were more irritating, though. I looked out the window and seen a police car cruising by with its lights on. Then when I stuck my head out and looked in the opposite direction, I could see a bunch of guys sitting on top of a car, smoking and drinking. My neighborhood ain't changed and I don't know why I even thought things would be different. Shit, it had only been two weeks.

I decided to go for a walk to escape the noise. When I opened my bedroom door, I saw Victor and Mama on the couch in the living room. He was on top of her, pulling up her gown and trying to get between her legs. I guess they didn't give a shit that I was around. I watched them for a couple of minutes. You'd think they'd felt me watching, but they never noticed. I didn't bother to make my presence known, either. I stood there and got a filthy taste in my mouth like I wanted to get a bucket of ice-cold water and drown they asses in it. But rather than do that, I walked out the front door and closed it quietly behind me. There was no need in me letting Mama know I was gone since she didn't care that I was back home in the first place.

As soon as I stepped outside my building, I took a look in both directions and decided against walking anywhere. That didn't seem like the wisest choice since it was getting dark outside. Instead, I sat down on the front steps and watched my world go by. The guys down the street became louder as the night progressed and there were no signs of any patrolling police. Seems like LAPD fades deeper into darkness once night falls and since I didn't hear my name being called, I figured my so-called Mama didn't give a damn about me or where I was.

Whenever our street seemed calm and empty except for one gang of niggas hanging out, that's when you knew something was gonna happen. This night was no exception because shit happened whenever there was alcohol involved. I wondered why they didn't get it. Just like clockwork they'd start to get really loud, somebody says the wrong thing, they get louder, and then punches are thrown. That's what happened except this time it got out of hand. They started throwing those big forty-ounce bottles at each other and breaking out windows of cars that they hid behind. I didn't see anybody running outside to see about all the noise, but there was plenty of people in their windows watching those fools hurt each other. And then like always, somebody's got a gun. Three sporadic shots rang out and then they all scattered like birds taking off in different directions. It didn't appear that anyone got shot, but when all those guys disappeared, all you could see were damaged cars with busted windows. The police came about ten minutes later, standing around with puzzled looks on their faces trying to figure out what had happened.

I watched them off and on for about thirty minutes. Every so often another police officer would drive by, wave, and then keep going. I felt sorry for the one lonely police officer. He had to stay behind and talk to the car owners who finally came outside, way after the fact. I got bored watching the sideshow. I figured it was time to take my ass to bed, which is a weird thing for a young person to say, but since I didn't have a mama who made me go to bed, I had to do such things myself.

Walking back upstairs, I worried that I might walk in on Mama and Victor doing something nasty in the living room. I really wasn't ready for that. Being a young woman and still a virgin at the time, I didn't want my ass to be traumatized so I took each step slowly. I held on to the wall with my right hand and tried to walk as quietly as possible. I listened for any little noise I could hear. Mostly I heard the television.

In my apartment building, it seemed like a competition going on between who had the loudest television set. Somebody's *60 Minutes* was overlapping our BET. And in between all that noise was Mama and Victor.

I opened the front door and there they were, on the couch and going at it. Victor was doing Mama from behind and she loved it. She was gripping the couch. Her eyes were closed. She was biting her bottom lip and then without stopping his movements, Victor turned his head toward me. He knew I was standing there all along. He looked at me in a way that turned my stomach. I think he figured I was either frozen where I stood or was about to run to my bedroom in a state of shock.

At that moment and because I didn't want that nigga to get the best of me, I snapped back to my own reality. I wasn't gonna be the one feeling traumatized. I slammed the front door as hard as I could, which immediately broke the rhythm that Victor had going. Mama let out a scream like I'd never heard before and then she'd seen me, smiling, but I didn't have a full smile. It was a half-smile like I was up to no good and proud of it.

Mama tried to grab something to pull over her, but she was so shocked out of her mind that she couldn't figure out what to do. Victor seemed mostly pissed off that he didn't get to finish. He acted like I upset his plan to get off to me watching him with Mama. He had the nerve to ask Mama if she wanted him to handle things. She was speechless. At first she struggled to say my name; it came out like "Lee..." instead of Leesha.

I looked at Victor and said, "Yeah right!" Then I walked to my bedroom without looking back. I could hear Victor talking about how he could handle me or put me in my place, but Mama kept telling him to let me go. For once, she was thinking right.

I tried going straight to bed. I bypassed taking a shower because I was scared Victor might make some kind of excuse and come walking in on me. I put on some pajamas rather than my usual oversized T-shirt because of that nigga. I even jumped in bed without making my usual detour to look out the window. That's how anxious I was for the night to turn into morning.

I never did eat. There was no way I was going to the kitchen with those two out there on the couch. How could I possibly sit at the kitchen table and have dinner while Mama was getting fucked by some man? I can't believe Mama would do that knowing full well that I'd returned home. It's like she didn't care at all. She didn't have any respect for herself or for me. Thinking about it made me want to vomit.

After only a few hours of sleep, I got out of bed feeling really restless. I checked the clock. It was one-thirty a.m. Sleeping wasn't very comfortable to me with a strange man staying the night. I knew he was Mama's man and all but to me, he could be anybody and the little cheap-ass lock on my door couldn't keep out a small kid let alone a grown man.

I got up from the bed and opened my door. I peeked out and noticed a flickering light in the living room. I took a guess that they'd left the television on, but I was wrong. Actually, when I walked all the way into the living room, there he was. Victor was smoking a cigarette and watching something on television. I couldn't tell what it was, but he was looking at it so hard, it seemed like he was trying to learn something. He looked stupid to me, though. I tried my best to walk past him as quietly as I could so he wouldn't notice me. I did pretty good in that I'd made it all the way to the kitchen and was able to look inside the refrigerator without hearing his voice. I guess I learned a lot on how to walk quietly from being over Grammy's during my punishment.

When I looked inside the refrigerator, I shook my head in disappointment. There wasn't shit inside. Mama must've tried so hard to impress that nigga that she cooked him everything we had. We didn't even have Kool-Aid or any kind of soda. I couldn't believe she had let his ass drink up everything! Mama would yell at me if I did that. She always tells me I need to learn how to conserve some shit. I'd look at her and say "Mama, this ain't no gasoline, this Kool-Aid!"

Mama would give me one of her mean looks and say, "Don't make me repeat myself, girl. You heard what I said."

So, my mama and her cheap ass be making me ration some damn Kool-Aid. Sometimes she don't even realize that I'm the one who stops by the liquor store and buys some of those little bags, especially the grape-flavored ones.

It didn't look like she made her man conserve on the alcohol he brought over. There was plenty of Budweiser and even a couple of bottles of Old English in the refrigerator. I also seen some drinking water and some stuff to make sandwiches, but I couldn't see myself fixing a sandwich so late at night. I had to settle for a glass of water and some Ritz crackers. That was good enough for me, plus I didn't want to push my luck for too long with Victor sitting on the couch. I didn't want him to see me and I sure as hell didn't want to talk to him.

After I got my water and crackers, I tiptoed out of the kitchen. I kept my eye on Victor as I walked slowly on the balls of my feet. I only looked away once to see if Mama's bedroom door was open. It wasn't. I guess Victor must've made her happy for the night so she went to bed. I turned to look at Victor again and there he was, staring right back at me with his dark eyes. I reacted as if I'd seen a ghost. I didn't scream or nothing like that, but I wanted to. Victor's eyes were like daggers going into my heart. I felt paralyzed so I stood there. My legs were really heavy for a moment and I didn't know what to do but stay where I was and look right back at him.

"What's up, girl? You shoulda ate with us earlier..."

Victor's voice sounded scratchy, like he hadn't spoken for a long time. He didn't even bother to clear his throat. He just kept talking, puffing on his cigarette and blowing the smoke in my direction. You could look at him and tell that being rude was a part of his natural personality. Plus, there was something about his eyes that instantly had me feeling violated.

From the jump, I didn't like this man. He probably knew it but figured he could charm me like he done my mother. He didn't know that Mama ain't got no appealing habits that intrigued me. Our only similarity is the blood flowing through our veins.

"Come over here and sit with me," Victor said.

Victor patted his hand on the couch, gesturing for me to sit right next to him. I quickly refused and told him that I was headed back to bed.

"What for, you up now..."

I didn't respond further. I continued walking to my bedroom with the sound of his laughter trailing right behind me. I guess he got a kick out my uncomfortable reaction. I wished I was big enough and able enough to kick his happy ass all up and down my block. I thought about it after I closed my door and locked it behind me. I thought about it long and hard. I hated that Victor was around. Then I'd begun to question why and how Mama could be with a man like him. He probably had ways to fill Mama up inside with compliments and promises. I'd bet all the money Grammy ever gave me that any promises Victor make to Mama, he ain't never gonna keep. Mama is just that kind of lady. She'll believe anything a man tells her. Anything...

The next day came and Victor was still there. I was so disappointed that I screamed at the top of my lungs, "Shit!"

Mama yelled back at me. "Leesha, girl, what the hell did you just say? You don't be cursing up in my damn house! Since when you get grown all of a sudden?"

I didn't pay Mama no kind of attention. I knew she was just trying to front and show Victor that she had some kind of control over her daughter. I could hear Victor laughing like he approved of the way she'd talked to me.

When it was time to get dressed, I grabbed all my clothes that I would be wearing to school and took them into the bathroom with me. I couldn't walk around so freely with Victor being there and watching every move I'd make. After I closed the door, I placed the clothes hamper right in front of it. I wasn't taking any chances. Mama might turn her back for one second and then before I knew it, that grown-ass man might be trying to get in the shower with me.

I pretty much ran up under the water for a couple minutes and then I was done. I figured that maybe after school I could go over to Grammy's and take a real shower at her place. Plus, I was gonna tell her about Mama and Victor. There wasn't no shame in my plan. If Grammy could help me get Victor out of the apartment and even better, out of my life, then I'd be one happy young lady. I'd scream for joy and owe Grammy a week's worth of chores without moaning and groaning like I usually do when she'd ask me to do something.

It was a trip walking on the school grounds again after two weeks of so-called suspension. I was happy and nervous at the same time. I felt a tingle in my hands. If I tried to write something, my hand would probably have been shaking all over the paper.

As I walked down the hallway, headed for my homeroom class, a few guys gave me strange looks. It was like they didn't think they'd ever see me again. Not that I really knew them, but I'd seen them around before and sometimes I'd seen them with Janina and her girlfriends. I started to get a little scared when I noticed them begin to follow me. That made me even more nervous than I was before. The first thing that went through my mind was revenge—not for me but for Janina. Those guys might've been following me so they could kick my ass.

I had about three options running through my mind as I picked up the pace of my walking without being too obvious. I'd pass on my first option, which was to walk nonchalantly into my homeroom class and dare those guys to follow me inside. Niggas is bold these days. Meaning, they might've followed me and kicked my ass in front of the class. That ain't a good way to make my return to school. Any reputation that developed in my absence would be erased completely.

My second option was to run into the girls' bathroom, but at this school, females be fighting all the time up in there. No so-called adults ever look inside to see what's going on. I passed on that option because I might've run into more of Janina's friends.

I chose option number three. I walked upstairs and seen those guys still following me. I hurried up and got to the top and then I waited next to the trash can that you had to walk around in order to continue up the next flight of stairs.

They started walking slower as they approached the middle of the stairway. There were only two guys rather than the four that first started following me. We made eye contact and neither of them smiled. I held my head up so they couldn't see that I was trippin' over them being after me. Then soon as they got about three steps away from me, I placed my foot behind the trash can and got ready to push it in their direction.

"What's up with y'all following me, huh?" I asked before knocking the trash can down the stairs, sending it flying in their direction.

"Shit, girl!" one of them shouted as they both stepped over the mess I'd created.

I'd made more noise than I wanted to as a few kids down the hallway started laughing. This brought the kind of attention I didn't need or want on my first day back at school.

"Damn, Leesha, we just wanted to talk with you, girl."

The cutest one of the two guys spoke to me and the other one just looked around nervously. The cute one had his hair in braids and looked like he wore about two T-shirts underneath his triple XL T-shirt. His black khakis sagged low and he had on some Air Jordans. I didn't look at his friend too hard, but he spoke before I could say anything.

"Yo, dude, them teachers gonna be coming in a second cause of all this noise she made."

"I heard that, damn. Hey, Leesha, we wasn't trying to do nuttin' to you. Just wanted to talk, girl…"

I looked at them and felt really embarrassed.

"You better go since you knocked the trash can down. We out, too," the cute one said.

I stood there for a few seconds and watched as they disappeared around the corner. Then I snapped back to reality and took my ass to class. When I walked in, nobody paid much attention to me except for my homeroom teacher, Miss Bentley.

"Leesha, come here for a moment, please," she said.

The other kids started whispering and the room got so noisy that Miss Bentley had to stand up and show her mean look to the class. "Excuse me everyone, please!"

They got quiet but I could pretty much read everyone's mind so it didn't matter if they were talking or not.

Miss Bentley welcomed me back to school and gave me a few tips. Actually, they were rules but she called them "tips." I listened and I tried to be respectful. A few times I caught myself before saying something that I knew would get me into trouble again. Miss Bentley was always cool with me. I had to look beyond all the stuff she was saying because I'd heard it before. She ended by asking me, "Are we clear?"

Miss Bentley put some volume in her voice when she'd asked that question. She did it more for show than anything else. It seemed like she wanted to let the class know that she was in control. I played along.

"Yes, ma'am, we're clear," I responded.

"Wonderful then, please take a seat, Leesha."

As I walked to my desk some of the kids were mocking Miss Bentley and repeating her question to me. I kept my cool and didn't appear fazed by all the comments. The ones who were talking shit only did it to make themselves feel popular. I didn't care. It was gonna take a lot more for me to lose my cool and get in trouble again. After I sat down, I ignored everyone and waited for the bell to ring since homeroom didn't last that long.

My first day back at school went pretty fast. I was spared an embarrassing moment with Janina because she was absent. The rumor floating around school was that she didn't come in because she knew I was returning. Then somebody else tried to say that Janina didn't want to be around while I got my ass kicked. Those were rumors that I laughed about and then continued my business. Keeping my promise to Grammy was more important than worrying about what everyone was saying. I'd kept my promise for the first few days, but then something changed when I started spending more time with J.T. around school.

Jessie "J.T." Thomas was the cutie who I thought was gonna kick my ass the first day I returned. He's the one with the braids. He had my heart skipping a beat. He wasn't that big but because he wore so many layers of T-shirts, it made him look bigger than he really was. A lot of the other kids were afraid of him because they said his brother was a well-known drug dealer who could make you disappear. They always said Jessie was a Crip and did some stuff for his brother, but I never believed it. Every time I'd mentioned it to Jessie, he would smile and then I'd forget my question.

Jessie was cool. He'd wait for me during lunchtime—always at the same table. If he had money, he'd buy my food and have it ready for me. It wasn't like we were going together or that we decided to do things for each other. It just started happening. We became cool and because of that, we did shit for each other, no questions asked. The other kids would watch us and then they'd get to talking. As soon as his buddy Tyrell would let him know the latest gossip, they'd approach whoever they thought was talking about them. All of a sudden, you wouldn't hear anything else.

Tyrell was strange to me, though. He was lanky and dark skinned. He always stayed close to Jessie but if I was around, Tyrell would keep some distance between us. It was like Tyrell was learning how to be a bodyguard. They said he was a Crip, too, but neither Jessie nor Tyrell would admit to being one. I couldn't figure out why it would be such a big secret if they were really into it. But then again, I didn't care as long as they didn't get me involved in any kind of crazy mess. Besides, I enjoyed that the other kids seemed afraid of them.

I loved walking with Jessie and having everybody stare at us. It was my way of enjoying the kind of notoriety that Janina had before, but I'd done her one better because I was linked with a thug. Jessie would never admit to being a thug, but because everyone believed he was then that's all that mattered to me. I laughed whenever somebody would say hello and I could hear their voice change pitch because they were so nervous. As mean as it may sound, I loved being close to that kind of power even though it was only in the mind and not reality. If I'd gotten crazy and went off on Jessie, I could've probably kicked his ass. I think most at my school could but he was pretty smart. He had everybody so afraid of him that they never considered the possibility he really wasn't who he claimed to be.

One day, our friendship reached a point where Jessie wanted to test the boundaries, so to speak. He didn't want us to get serious or anything like that. I mean, we were only in the ninth grade and his reputation didn't include being serious about a girl. Actually, Jessie was a grade higher than me. Still, neither of us was talking about a deep commitment. Jessie asked me about something else. Despite my desire to grow up fast and leave my mama's house, I'd never wanted to rush into it. I mean, some of the other things that go along with growing up could wait as far as I was concerned. It was bad enough that I'd seen Mama with her man, but Jessie asked me.

"Leesha, I wanna have sex with you."

"Huh?" was my initial response.

He asked the question while I was stuffing my face with a honey bun that he'd bought me. He had a boom box sitting on the lunch table next to us, so he turned it on while waiting for me to respond. Jessie acted like his question was no big deal. I struggled to answer and then my first attempt was drowned out by the sounds of the Wu-Tang Clan coming from his boom box.

"Sex?" I asked.

"Yeah, what, you don't think about it?"

"Not really, I mean…"

"Shit, Leesha, I be thinking about it all the time. I figure we down like that. We ain't like going together, but it's like I got your back and you got mine, right?"

"Yeah, Jessie, but sex?"

Jessie looked around the lunch area, bobbing his head to the music and mouthing the words to the song.

"Dollar, dollar bill, y'all!" he sang, thrusting his fist in the air like he in a hip-hop trance.

"Jessie!" I said to get him back in the conversation.

"You gonna do it?" he asked.

His one-track mind didn't need much help, I found out.

"Sex ain't something you just do, Jessie. It ain't the same as you buying me food or us going to the movies. You expect me to just say it's cool, you can fuck me? What if I get pregnant?"

"What you talking 'bout, I'll bring a jimmy. It ain't about all that anyway. I'm just thinking we can do this…"

"But why, Jessie?"

"What you mean, why? What's up with you, Leesha?"

At that moment, I didn't feel like I could talk to Jessie. His mind didn't seem to grasp any kind of common sense and even though I was a young girl who could easily be impressed by a so-called thug, I wasn't about to open my legs for any nigga. Being stupid was not a character flaw for me. Somehow, some way he had gotten this idea that he and I needed to have sex. And as much as I liked Jessie, I just couldn't see myself going through with that.

It was another example of how I was so much like Grammy and so unlike Mama. I just couldn't be with Jessie even though I knew it meant there would be no more friendship between us. What we had ended right there at that lunch table and I walked away feeling used as if I did have sex with him. My little heart was broken because I'd enjoyed the friendship we shared and being down for each other was cool to me. But as I walked away from Jessie, I couldn't even feel him staring at my back. It was like our connection instantly disappeared and he no longer gave a fuck about me, whatsoever. He turned up his music and kept singing that one phrase over and over as I walked far enough until I could no longer hear him.

"Dollar, dollar bill, y'all!"

SUMMERTIME FLAVA

The song that was bumpin' pretty much everywhere I went during the summer of '94 was "Flava in Ya Ear" by Craig Mack. It was a trip how everybody and they mama would start dancing even if they only heard that song for five seconds. The first day after school was out, I can remember sitting on the front steps of our apartment building and hearing a car drive by with that song playing. It was hot that day, too. Mama was upstairs being lazy and as usual, begging her nigga to come over and see her. That mean't one thing to me. I would either stay home and hear her acting stupid or I'd go spend the night with Grammy. My choice was obvious, but I was getting to the point where I didn't always like having to leave home because of Mama.

I remember one time when she went overboard, talking all loud to Victor on the phone. She was telling him how she loved all the wonderful things he did for her. But I never recalled him doing anything. His routine was to come over, give her a couple kisses, and then ask her two questions.

"What you cook, baby? I hope you got some beer to go along with that 'cause a brotha had a tough week," he'd tell her.

I could see he'd be lying. Victor never talked about what he did to bring home some money. He always made Mama spend hers. It seemed like Mama's second job was kissing his ass. I stopped feeling sorry for her after a while, but I never stopped watching how he treated her. When Victor came over that time, I followed him right up the stairs.

"Where you going, little mama?" he asked me.

I looked around to see if he was truly talking to me but of course, I knew he was. I didn't answer until he asked me two more times. The third time he sounded frustrated and I liked that.

"Damn, girl, you need to respond when folks older than you ask you a fuckin' question! Where you going?"

"I'm going inside."

"Inside?"

Victor tried to mimic the sound of my voice. I secretly wished he would fall down the stairs and break his neck. He tried to stop and turned around, thinking I would stop right behind him but I kept on going.

"Shit. I'm trying to be alone with your mother. Why can't you just go somewhere?"

"'Cause I live here. Why don't you take my mama out somewhere?"

"I don't need to take her nowhere. She love cooking for me. You could learn a little something from watching yo' mama."

"Learn something?"

I'd made it to the top of the stairs and turned to look at Victor who was two steps below where I stood after I'd brushed past him. His eyes had a sparkle in them, but it was the kind that just warned you that something stupid was about to be said. To me, Victor was gifted when it came to talking shit that earned him a ticket to get his ass kicked.

"Leesha, when you get older, you gonna look good as hell! Fellas gonna be after your ass all the time so maybe you need to be taught a little sumpin sumpin…"

That's when Mama opened the front door and poked her head out. She gave me a half-smile and then noticed Victor in the stairway, too. She gave him a full smile which let me know she didn't hear her man trying to flirt with her daughter. Mama looked so sprung that I knew if I tried to tell her about Victor, she'd throw me out of the house and have him move in for good—five minutes later. They hugged each other and Victor acted like he was being bashful. In reality he almost got busted. If Mama had opened her door a few seconds earlier, she could've heard what he'd said.

I walked inside and left them in the stairway. They was kissing and Mama was asking him if he was hungry in between all the smooching. That was a dumb question. I could hear his answer echo long enough to make its way inside the apartment.

"Hell yeah, baby! Shee-it, my black ass is always hungry!" Victor said.

Before they came inside, I made a quick dash into the kitchen to try and grab myself some food. I knew once Victor sat down to be served, Mama would start acting like I was a piece of old, out-of-place furniture. She'd only glance at me a few times and step around me if I got in the way.

Mama had cooked a lot of stuff that I liked. She had some mashed potatoes, greens, hot water cornbread, and some baked chicken that had our apartment smelling like the best soul food restaurant in town. Mama cooked so much for Victor to the point where she got really good at it. Thing is, as long as he was around, all her cooking was meant for him to enjoy—exclusively. If I even thought about touching any of it, she'd give me one of those mean looks you give dogs when they about to do something wrong. That's how I felt, too—like a dog searching for scraps after everything was gone.

Eventually, my situation with Mama only made me stronger. I taught myself to look elsewhere for what I didn't get at home. I'm talking about everything from love to respect, to just being able to talk about whatever. That's something that's unheard of when it came to Mama and me. If I ask her any kind of question, she'll answer by asking me why I wanna know. I can't stand it when she does that. Mama don't do nothing that might have me believe that going to her would be a good thing.

I remember once she sat down with me in the living room, looking all serious but at the same time smiling as if she wanted to make sure I was prepared for whatever she was about to say.

I asked her, "Mama, what's wrong?"

"Ain't nuttin' wrong, Leesha. Why something gotta be wrong for me to talk with you?"

I shrugged my shoulders and poked my lips out before responding. "I don't know."

"Well, I know I been busy lately and haven't spent much time with you. It's hard, honey. I mean, I got a man who really needs my attention and besides, you almost grown."

"I'm just in the tenth grade, Mama. How can that be grown?"

"Don't be smart, Leesha. You always gotta cut me off and say something smart. That's why it be hard to talk to you sometime! You do that at school, too?"

I rolled my eyes and didn't answer. I stayed quiet and wondered what Mama was up to.

"Anyway, like I said, I been busy with Victor, which by the way, it would help if you be nice to him and at least smile a little more often when you come into the room. You be lookin' all mean like you somebody else's child."

"I thought we was having a talk, Mama."

"See, there you go again, cutting me off. Leesha—"

"Mama, is Victor moving in with us? Is that why you're having this talk with me?"

"Victor might move in but I ain't sure yet. We kinda just talking about it right now. We even talked about you, too, Leesha."

"Me?"

"Yes. If Victor does move in, I'll probably spend even less time with you so I'm going to give you the option to go and stay with your grandmother. I think she be happy to take you in."

I could see something like that coming a mile away but for the most part, I chose to ignore it. I knew Mama would have a talk with me about Victor moving in. Actually, I figured I'd one day come home and learn that he was already living with us. The possibility made my stomach turn. Mama was totally blind about Victor. She couldn't tell he wasn't shit. And the first chance he got he probably would start feeling all over my ass. If I spent one day off from school, I'd probably be fighting with that nigga, trying to get him off me.

Mama ended our conversation by saying, "That about does it for our talk, Leesha. I just wanted to let you know and then you won't be surprised if you happen to find Victor here when I ain't home yet."

As soon as Mama finished, I stood up, walked across the living room in the direction of the front door, and wasted no time leaving. I could hear my mother call out to me, but I didn't answer at first.

"Where you think you going, Leesha?" she asked.

When I reached the bottom of the stairs, I screamed, "Nowhere!" I was pissed and really wanted to curse her out for being so stupid over some man who didn't do shit for her. Only thing Victor ever brought over was beer and that was for his ass to drink.

Mama didn't seem too concerned over where I was going because ten minutes after I stormed out, she was on the phone with Victor. I could hear her because she had the window open. She was giggling and saying his name like he was the love of her life.

It's nice to be happy and all, but listening to Mama made me feel like being in love, turned you into nothing more than a silly bitch. It pissed me off to have those kinds of feelings about my own mother. I'd always wished she would change and be somebody who I could respect. Sort of like Grammy.

In my neighborhood, there weren't too many people who you could truly look up to. It seemed like most didn't give a damn when something happened. They'd just look the other way or hurry up and run inside. Then they come out later when the police got a body covered up or a young person in handcuffs. They'll come out when they see the yellow tape stretched across the street. That's when they want to know how long they gonna have to wait before they can move they car. And me, I'd just sit on the steps watching everything and how people act. That's how I learned because other than Grammy, there hadn't been anyone around to teach me what I really wanted to know.

One day, that changed and my life along with it. The summer was flying by. Each day felt like the next because nothing really different was going on. Mama was loving on her Victor and trying to decide whether or not to let him move in. And I spent most of my days sitting on the front steps of our apartment building, watching the ghetto tumbleweed roll down the street. That's just a fancy name for trash that I made up. I'd get lost in my own thoughts as I watched it blowing down the street. I'd hear the clanging sound of an empty soda can and follow its journey as it moved further along whenever a car would pass by. It's not like I wanted to be that can, but for whatever reason, I just couldn't take my eyes off it until I heard these guys across the street talking. When I looked in their direction, I could barely see them. They stood underneath a big tree with branches that hung very low. It was probably the reason why the apartment building across the street had such green grass all the time. That tree kept the whole front area really shaded and dark.

After a couple of minutes, two guys walked from underneath the tree almost nervously and never looked back. I could tell they were doing something they shouldn't be doing. They were probably buying drugs because they looked like they took that stuff for breakfast, lunch, and dinner. I sat curiously waiting to see what the third guy looked like, but he didn't move at all, except for his hands. He was counting his money. Then as he moved forward, a little bit into the light, I could see a big grin on his face. He seemed very proud of what he'd done and then I noticed how young he looked as compared to the two who walked away.

I could tell this guy was older than me but not by too much. He had a bushy Afro and a caramel complexion. He was cute but I wasn't really checking him out like that. He looked too thuggish to me, but not so much where you would run from him or cross the street to avoid his ass. He was wearing the typical clothes that never seem to go out of style in the hood: a black T-shirt over some baggy, gray khaki pants. It's funny because as long as I sat there watching the guy he never looked up from counting his money. I started to worry that somebody might come up and take it so I glanced around for him. I couldn't believe he was taking that kind of a chance, but maybe he was bold that way.

After he finished counting the money, he stopped, reached into his back pocket, and pulled out a pack of cigarettes. At the same time with his other hand, he stuffed his money in one of his front pockets.

I think my curiosity got the best of me and I turned a little bold myself as he lit up his cigarette. "Ain't you kind of young to be smoking?" I yelled.

He looked up and tried to focus on where my voice was coming from.

"Yeah, I said it!" I told him.

"What you say, am I too young? Shee..it!" he responded before exhaling enough smoke to cause him to squint his eyes.

"I seen what you was doing over there and I think you too young to do that, too! If I knew your mama—"

"Say what? How old is you?"

"Why you need to know that?"

He laughed as he stepped off the curb and into the street, walking in my direction. "Aw, man." He shook his head. "You live right there?"

"Maybe..."

"Maybe? You all of a sudden mysterious or something? What's your name, girl?"

"Leesha."

"Cool. What up, Leesha?"

"What's your name? And don't come over here blowing smoke in my face!"

"You be talking mad shit, Leesha. I like that, though. I'm Scottie but most niggas call me Blaze."

"'Cause you smoke?"

"Huh?"

"They call you Blaze because you smoke..."

"Oh, nah that ain't why. They call me that 'cause I can fight real good. It's a man thing. I mean, I won't hesitate to blaze on some fool if he open his mouth wrong."

"Oh, then maybe I should be afraid of you, huh?"

"The way you out here alone, talking to somebody like me shows me you ain't afraid of much, girl. Why you out here?"

Funny thing about the look in his eyes, he really seemed concerned. The way Blaze talked to me felt different at a time when I was starting to believe that every male only talked to you to see if they could get them some.

Blaze approached the entrance to my apartment building and continued puffing on his cigarette. He was always checking the street for any movement in both directions. It kind of made him seem paranoid. Maybe he was, but I kind of guessed it came along with the territory of living the way he probably did.

I studied his movements—the way he held his cigarette and smiled every time he blew smoke from his mouth. It was strange to me that he actually enjoyed smoking. I told him it was okay to sit down, but he waved me off.

"The smoke won't bother me," I told him.

"Nah, it's not that. I just like to keep standing."

"Okay."

"So, you live in this building?" Blaze asked.

"Uh-huh."

"Why I never seen you before?"

I shrugged. "I don't know. Was you suppose to see me before? I've never seen you either…"

"Aw, there you go."

"What?"

"Being smart."

"I'm not."

"It's cool. You should keep that attitude about you, Leesha. It'll probably keep niggas at a distance so they won't fuck with you, nah mean?"

"I guess."

"What grade you in? You in high school yet?"

"Yeah, I'm in high school. I'll be in the eleventh grade this fall."

"Damn, that's cool. What school you go to, Dorsey?"

I nod my head.

"Cool. Make sure you finish, too, and don't be like a lot of these fools thinking it's cool to still be going to high school when you nineteen and twenty."

"You graduate? You don't look much older than me."

"Yeah, I graduated last year from Crenshaw. I'm thinking about going to a junior college. My grades wasn't good enough to get me into a four-year school, but I didn't really care. I was just trying to get my paper and get the fuck out of there."

"You must have your own place then, huh?"

"Nah…I mean, it's just me and my older brother, but it ain't like I'm paying rent yet."

"You lucky. I can't wait to move away!"

"What you in a hurry for?"

I shrugged my shoulders again because I didn't feel like telling Blaze about Mama and Victor. I was already feeling like I said too much to this guy whom I had just met. It felt natural, but it just didn't seem right.

"Why you all quiet, all of a sudden?" he asked.

"I don't know…"

"It's cool. You don't want to tell me all your business just yet. I'm feeling you 'cause I got shit I don't need to be telling you yet, either. It's a trip, though, how we just started talking. We may have to kick it sometime…"

"Huh? What you mean, kick it?"

I started to have instant flashbacks of Jessie and his proposition at school.

"Aw, you thinking I wanna get with you? Nah, don't even trip like that. I'm just saying it would be cool to hang out and talk some more like we been doing. You seem real cool."

I started to smile with relief. It was almost uncontrollable—so much that I ended up laughing and couldn't stop.

"What's wrong with you, girl?" Blaze asked.

"Nuttin'. It's just funny."

"Oh, okay, I don't remember saying shit that funny, but it's cool to see you smiling. When I first came over here, you was trying to look all hard, but I understand that. Like I said before, you need to keep most niggas away from you, anyway."

"So, you gonna become the big brother I ain't never had, huh?"

"You an only child?"

"Yeah," I responded. For a split second, I thought, *what if?*

Then as soon as that thought went away, a yellow Volkswagen with a license plate that read "ASSHOLE" pulled up in front of the building. The license plate didn't really say that but that's what ran through my mind when I see this car. Blaze looked at me transform from happy to serious attitude.

"What's up with you?" he asked.

I pointed to the Volkswagen before the door opened. It was Victor coming over to visit Mama. I guess she had convinced his ass to drop by.

Scottie asked me if Victor was somebody to me and I squashed any notion of that possibility by frowning so hard it hurt my face. I also decided to start calling him Scottie because I wasn't feeling that Blaze name shit.

Victor stepped out of his car and immediately noticed me. "Damn, girl!" He smiled like he was happy to see me, but his expression turned my stomach in circles. He said something to me but I didn't respond. Then he walked through the open gate, brushing by Scottie who I could tell was offended that Victor didn't acknowledge him, not even with a nod of the head.

"Excuse you, playa," Scottie said.

Victor ignored him and stepped in front of where I was sitting. He reached out like he expected me to stand up and hug him like he was my father coming home. I moved to the side and told him Mama was waiting for him.

"Is that the kind of welcome I get? You know I might be moving in some-time...," he told me.

"I don't care."

"Humph."

Victor huffed and puffed under his breath as he walked past me without looking back. I watched him walk up the stairs, hoping he would trip and fall but that don't seem to ever work when I try to use my power of thought.

"I see why you got that attitude all of a sudden. Who that?" Scottie asked.

"Mama's boyfriend. I can't stand him!"

"I see that. What he talking 'bout, saying he gonna move in?"

"Mama trying to have him move in with us. I don't know why. She say they in love and she be all up on him. I wish she would wake up!"

"I can see already that nigga ain't shit. I felt like sockin' his ass in the head for walking by me like that. Being disrespectful like that ain't cool. They wonder why young fools be acting the way we do. It's 'cause older niggas set the example for being assholes. Nah mean?"

"Is that more Blaze philosophy?"

"Yeah, and you gonna always hear it, too! I get a little bit of that from my brother even though he sees shit from an older perspective, we still agree on most things. Well, we used to."

I started laughing again and it felt good. I quickly forgot about Victor while listening to Scottie go on and on.

"There you go, laughing. You gonna have to tell me which stuff is funny so I can write the shit down and make some damn money."

"Whateva, Blaze!"

"Uh-huh, whateva...What you about to get into, Leesha?"

"Get into?"

"Yeah, I'm about to go to Fatburger's around the corner. You wanna go?"

"I don't know…"

"I ain't beggin for your company, girl."

"I know."

I didn't know why I hesitated so much. It wasn't that I didn't trust Scottie. I felt weird about walking away without telling Mama I was gone. I didn't think she really cared, but because of what Grammy always taught me, it sort of sank in that I should always be respectful in that way. Grammy's words were like a heavy anchor which weighed in on any decisions I'd make. Then I heard Mama laughing and telling Victor to stop. I'd heard that kind of playing around right before I walked in on them fucking in the living room. I didn't want to go through that again so I yelled up to the open window where I knew Mama was with Victor on the couch.

"Mama! I'm going to the store!"

I waited a few seconds and didn't hear anything.

Scottie looked at me and shrugged. "Maybe she didn't hear you. Go on up and tell her. I'll wait for you."

I yelled again. "Mama!"

"Go on, Leesha! I heard you!" Mama responded without even looking out the window. It felt as if she couldn't care less what I did. She had what she wanted in Victor and once again, like she'd always done when some man was in her life, I'd become an afterthought.

"That your mama making all that noise up there?" Scottie asked.

"Uh-huh…"

Scottie could tell I wasn't too cool letting him know that the giggling woman embarrassing the hell out of me was my mama. Most guys would probably comment about it, but Scottie flashed his smile that I would soon get used to seeing. He then nodded in the direction where he wanted to walk. I got up from sitting on the steps and quickly followed. I questioned why he began walking away from Santa Rosalia Drive, which would be closer to Fatburger than going in the direction he was headed.

"No reason," he responded.

"I think you lying."

"I might need to look at something over here first, but uh, it's cool. Sometimes a brotha just likes to take a different route. Living in the 'Jungle' without a ride don't leave you with too many travel options. I just try to make the best of my shit, nah mean?"

"Uh-huh, you drive?"

"Aww, Leesha, my ass better know how to drive! You probably learn pretty soon, too. You said you in the eleventh grade, right?"

"Well, I'm about to be."

"Yeah, see, you'll be learning soon. You don't have no boyfriend or nothing, huh? I don't want no fool raising up on me if he see us walking together."

"You don't have to worry about that."

"Cool…Walk over here for a second."

I followed Scottie across Santo Tomas Drive and stood with him in front of a green and white apartment building. It was pretty much like all the buildings in the neighborhood. They're typical two-story apartments that are way too close to each other. Everybody minds their own business even though you can pretty much hear somebody's conversation through the walls or outside on the street.

Since Scottie already told me what street he lived on, I had a feeling he was up to no good. I actually didn't mind, but at the same time, I kept my distance and stood on the sidewalk with my arms folded. I watched Scottie as he walked slowly across the grass and peered up toward one of the second-floor windows. He looked toward me and held one finger to his lips. He told me to keep quiet. I don't know why. I wasn't stupid enough to bring attention to me standing in front of some apartment building where I didn't belong. The neighborhood was really quiet at the time so any noise would give off the same shock value as a fire alarm. I kept silent, but like I said, I didn't need him to tell me to do that.

I continued watching Scottie, standing with his attention solely on the second-story window. I couldn't see anything. I wondered what he was looking at and why. And then I saw him pull out something from his pocket. I couldn't really tell what it was at first until he squeezed his hand around it tightly and then opened his hand back up. He dropped it on the grass. It looked like a big stone or a rock. I felt the urge to question him, but I knew that would be a mistake so I watched him, and then I glanced up at the window. I saw a shadow of someone walk by.

"What...," I started to question, more so out of disbelief than anything else. I kind of figured out what he was about to do.

Scottie glanced at me once more. He smiled and then like a pitcher on a baseball mound, he wound up and threw what he had in his hand, straight at the window. You could almost describe the sound as nasty because it made me feel like I wanted to cover my mouth instead of my ears. But rather than freeze up and chance someone seeing me standing on the sidewalk, facing the apartment building, I ran.

I could hear Scottie's voice, some distance behind me. He sounded calm for someone who'd just thrown a rock through a window. I think he may have even hit the person.

"Leesha, hold up!" he yelled in my direction.

I stopped but only after I'd crossed the street and run into an area that was well shadowed by trees and parked cars.

Before Scottie walked toward me, he shouted in the direction of the broken window. "Get my money, nigga!"

I walked with Scottie down Somerset Drive until we got to Marlton Avenue. We walked a half-block further until we reached Fatburger, which was at the entrance of the mall parking lot. During the whole walk, I was silent and unsure of what to say. I didn't know if it was okay to ask him about what he'd done. Scottie appeared really relaxed and that made me walk at an even pace alongside him. He didn't care so I wasn't really scared, at least not anymore.

Scottie proved to be as big of an eater as he was a risk-taker. He had money so he wasn't concerned about the size of the meal. He told me, "Order what you want, Leesha, 'cause I'm about to act like I ain't ate since last year! I seen this dude eating one of these hamburgers on the bus the other day and I was about to jack that fool."

"You're crazy!"

"Nah, for real...That thought went through my mind to take homeboy's burger 'cause that shit looked so good. But then I calmed my ass down and just used that as some motivation to make money. Now that I got the money, I can get my own damn hamburger, you feel me."

I looked at Scottie in disbelief, but he was really serious about what he'd said. Not only that but he ended up buying two King Fatburgers, which are their biggest, and he got a large soda to wash it all down. Me, I just ordered one burger and some fries. I barely ate all of it so I wrapped it up to take home. Since Mama don't care if I eat or not, I could warm my leftover burger and eat the rest later.

After we finished eating, Scottie asked if I would chill with him for a while. I got nervous behind his request—at first.

"What do you mean, go home with you?" I asked.

"Nah...Leesha. There you go, again."

"How am I supposed to know what you mean?"

"'Cause I'ma tell you what I mean."

"Okay."

"It's simple. I was talking 'bout sitting here a little longer and conversating. I mean, over here you ain't gotta worry about that fool with the yellow Volkswagen. Plus, we ain't really get to talk where you could see that I ain't trying to hook up with you."

"Okay, what do you want to talk about?"

"Shit, I don't know...How you doing in school?"

"It's okay. I'm just trying to get out of there."

"You gonna wish you was back in school once you get older. School is some real shit if you in there for the right reasons."

I rolled my eyes as if to warn the world that Scottie was about to start with another excerpt from his philosophy about life.

"Aww, that's not cool, rolling your eyes. I'ma remember that..."

Scottie's feelings were hurt so I tried to reach over and touch his hand, but he pulled it away. I worried that he was seriously offended, but then he started smiling. That smile would become our connection because no matter what would be going on around us or what we were in to, once Scottie flashed his smile, the world was alright with me.

I walked home from Fatburger alone because Scottie had to do something. I was afraid to ask what that was. Scottie brushed his hand against my shoulder before telling me he'd come see me later in the week. Being that we were still just getting to know each other at that point, there was still some uneasiness about knowing what to do as we waved goodbye to each other. Not that there was something potentially brewing between us but even as friends, it was too soon to hug each other. I didn't know that then, but I sort of figured it out much later whenever the memory visited my thoughts and I needed to imagine something that would make me feel good again.

I took my time getting home because I dreaded the possibility of walking in on Mama and Victor. No telling what I might see once I stepped through the door. I hated feeling like that. I mean, it got so bad that I'd begin to envy the homeless. At least they didn't have to come home to seeing some nigga in they house that they couldn't stand.

When I got home, this time it wasn't so bad. Mama was sitting on the couch watching television and Victor was on the other end, sleeping. I glanced at him for a minute and cursed under my breath. He was lying there with his belt unfastened and his zipper was down. He had on one of those white V-neck T-shirts and his socks had holes on the bottom. Being a female, I guess my nose was extra sensitive because I could smell that nigga as soon as I opened the door. Seeing how his socks looked made me think he probably don't change them but once or twice a week.

Mama looked at me and smiled. The content look in her eyes made me stutter step. I smiled back at her. It was sort of weird. She looked happy. Her expression had me longing for those days when we used to hug each other a lot and have long talks while she did my hair. Then Mama looked away and my memories faded just as quickly. I glanced at Victor once more and noticed him turn on his side and curl up like a baby. I could see the crack of his nasty ass sticking out and that made me sick. Mama asked me a question without even looking at me. "What you bring home, Leesha?"

"Hamburger."

"I don't want to see no roaches in your room."

"You won't."

I closed the door to my bedroom before she could ask me anything else. I could hear her start to say something before I pushed the door shut. I was so happy to be in my room and away from what was to me a constant reminder that I hated living with Mama. I could hear her laughing in the distance and that was another reminder.

FAMILY USED TO MEAN SOMETHING

A ll week long, Grammy had been hinting that something special was about to go down. She'd never tell me but she would always smile about it and say that it was a step in the right direction. She'd even called me two nights before to say she wanted to see me dressed really nice that weekend.

I was like, "What for?"

Grammy put my little attitude in check. "What for?" she snapped.

"I mean…"

"Uh-huh, I know what you mean, Leesha."

"Sorry, Grammy…"

I kept my mouth shut and listened. Grammy sounded very happy—so much that she almost gave away her surprise. Then as I was talking with her, Mama picked up the other phone.

"Y'all still on here?" she asked, sounding ghetto as ever.

"Uh, excuse me but I'm talking to my grandbaby," Grammy said.

"I know this, Mother, damn. Y'all need to hurry up 'cause I'm expecting a call from my man."

"Is that right?"

Grammy didn't sound too thrilled with Mama's announcement and I don't think she cared too much for Mama's attitude, either. Their conversation got a little heated to the point where they forgot I was still on the other line. They had me cracking up because of the way they talked to each other. Grammy never called Mama by her name.

"Daughter, just who is this man of yours and why haven't you ever introduced me to him?"

"Mother, I am way too grown to worry about your opinion of who I'm seeing. Besides, you ain't never approved of any man I been with."

"That's not true!"

"Yeah, uh-huh, well you'll meet Victor soon enough. I'll bring him with me to your little get-together."

"Well, this is supposed to be just for family. I've got a surprise for everyone and an announcement to make."

"Victor is family now…"

"Excuse me? Did you run off and marry this man?"

"No, Mother. Don't get your blood pressure up."

"Don't you worry 'bout my blood pressure, daughter. You about to get a piece of my mind if you telling me you ran off and got married, again!"

"Again?"

"You heard me right…"

"Mother, the last time I got married, didn't I tell you?"

"Uh, you told me two days after the fact. Am I gonna have to wait two more days before you tell me about this man?"

"No, Mother,,we ain't married. He's gonna move in with me and Leesha, or is it Leesha and I?"

Mama snickered at Grammy and I could tell she was taking deep breaths and holding herself back. Grammy decided to keep her thoughts to herself, it seemed. It was so unlike her to back down or get quiet, but that's what she did. The way Mama ended the conversation, it sounded like she was celebrating. She probably thought she won this round between them, but knowing Grammy, she'd strike back another time. To be honest, I wanted to be front row and center when it happened.

"I'll let you two return to your conversation, but y'all need to make it quick because Victor will be calling me soon!" Mama demanded.

Grammy didn't respond. She continued talking to me as if she hadn't heard a word Mama had said.

"Leesha, make sure you dress nice this weekend."

"I will, Grammy."

Mama had finally hung up the phone and Grammy saw that as her chance to ask me about Victor and how I was doing. Her concern almost turned to panic now that she knew there would be a man living with Mama and me.

"Okay, tell me who this man is supposed to be that's coming to live with the two of you, Leesha."

"Grammy, I can't stand his ass!"

"Leesha!"

"I mean, uh, I can't stand him, Grammy."

"Leesha, I wish you wasn't around all of what my daughter exposes you to, but I don't know if we really have a choice. It's hard for me to keep you here and be responsible for raising you. Lord knows I wish I could, but I'm at that age now where you'd have to take care of me more than I could be there for you."

"It's okay, Grammy, I understand."

"Well, I hope you do understand, baby. I believe in my heart that you gonna be just fine, Leesha. Every day I thank God that you're nothing like your mother. I pray the Lord don't strike me down for speaking badly about my own flesh and blood, but the truth has to be told at some point. She is too old to still be dealing with these trifling men that ain't no good for her. And the worst part is that she's exposing you to all this. Shameful..."

"Grammy, what's the surprise gonna be?"

I didn't mean to act like I wasn't listening to Grammy, but I was getting a little tired of hearing about Mama. I wanted to find out what the big secret was. Grammy refused to give up anything. She laughed about it and quickly forgot being pissed off at Mama.

"Chile, you'll just have to wait and see. I don't give up my secrets, especially when I can't wait to see the reaction on your face. Despite your mama bringing some man with her, I do hope she comes to the party."

"Yeah, she'll be there..."

I didn't worry much if Grammy could hear the disappointment in my voice. I would've admitted to it right away if she had asked me. Instead, just like a grandmother would, she asked me if I needed money and if I'd be okay walking over to her apartment.

"Grammy, I do it all the time."

"I know, chile, and I really hate that you have to."

"I'll be alright."

"Come over by about nine a.m., baby, so you can help me set up the chairs and tables. We gonna do this party outside in the front."

"Really?"

"Yes, and it's gonna be a lot of your family showing up, too! These are folks you either haven't met before or ain't seen since you was little. You got lots of family, Leesha, and it's about time you met some of them."

"Okay, Grammy."

Meeting family didn't really excite me because even family be trippin' and actin' like you should kiss they ass. I only pretended to be excited because Grammy seemed excited. For me, meeting new family made me nervous.

Mama's huffing and puffing in the background caused my conversation to end early with Grammy. Mama had a way with getting what she wanted. It was a trick that I noticed most really selfish people do. They play the victim role and act like what they need is more important than a nation of starving children. Mama was good at that shit and when she saw me hang up the phone, she reached her hand out like I was supposed to know what she meant. Actually, I did know but I put the phone down and went to my room. She could pick up the phone herself and I wasn't about to sit and listen to her talk to Victor. I went to my room and slammed the door.

I turned on my radio and then plopped down on my bed. I felt strange for a moment, thinking about my surroundings. I looked out the window and focused my attention on the apartment across the street. There was nothing really to see and I wasn't really looking hard. I sat there, thinking and watching. I could hear Mama on the phone through my door. She was laughing. Victor makes her happy, I guess. I can't be like her when I'm on my own. She can't live without having a man in her life and that's really sad because the ones she chooses be so messed up.

I had to turn my radio up louder. I got tired of hearing Mama's voice. She was calling him sweetie pie and shit. That turned my stomach. I wanted to call Scottie and see if maybe he wanted to come with me to the party. Then I thought maybe Grammy wouldn't approve. That might put her in shock to see me bringing a guy to one of our family functions. It's not like we have very many—not anymore.

Grammy mentioned there would be family coming to the party that I hadn't seen in years. That made me wonder if my cousin Luther was coming. He's real cool but crazy as hell. I used to look up to him when I was little. It would be a trip to see him now. Mama don't like him because she says he's a thug. She don't date thugs. She's only attracted to wimps and assholes like Victor.

Luther was a true thug. He was a serious gangbanger and definitely in it for life. He'd been in and out of jail, mostly for robbery or selling weed and violating his parole, but he ain't never been caught for doing some of the things we'd hear about but didn't know if it were true. Despite all that, Luther was a sweetheart and was all about family. I was his pride and joy when I was little. I'd see so much love in his eyes until I knew that no matter when or if I'd ever see him again; I knew he loved his little cousin Leesha.

Scottie kind of reminded me of Luther except that my cousin was a few years older. I had thoughts about the two meeting each other, but then I figured it might not be cool because of a possible rivalry or something. You always had to be leery of someone's affiliation in L.A. because everybody always belonged to something, even if it was just them claiming their neighborhood.

I slept on and off most of the night and it seemed like Mama stayed on the phone forever. Every time I woke up I could hear her voice. I tossed and turned a lot and it wasn't just because of Mama. I kept thinking about the party and why it seemed so important to Grammy. I started to think that maybe she was gonna tell everybody she moving away or maybe she's sick. I would've died if I didn't always know I could walk to Grammy's house to escape the jungle I live in. Having no alternative to Mama was like being sentenced to twenty years to life. Your heart sees no other choice but to become numb because the rest of you be in total shock.

I had to wait until almost three in the morning before it was safe to use the phone. It was real quiet in the house. I opened my door and only saw a flicker of light coming from the television. Mama forgot to turn it off although I had to make sure she didn't just go to the bathroom and would come right back. I peeked inside her bedroom and found her sleeping on top of her covers.

She didn't even get out of her clothes. I guess Victor knew how to wear her ass out even over the phone.

I closed her door quietly and returned to the living room. I found the phone on the floor. It was easy because I could hear the recording saying, "If you'd like to make a call, please hang up…" Mama probably kicked it over. She don't care.

I turned the television off and sat on the couch. It was really dark except for the street light shining through the window. I dialed Scottie's number. Actually, on my first attempt I only dialed up to the seventh number and then I hung up. I felt weird calling him so late. I knew we were cool, but since we hadn't known each other that long, I didn't want to wake him up and have him pissed off. About five seconds went by. Then I decided to call him, anyway.

The phone rang twice. He answered, "Hello?"

"Scottie?"

"Yeah, who dis?"

"Leesha…"

"Hey, what up, Leesha? Ain't you supposed to be 'sleep?"

"You are, too!"

"Yo, your mind need some cultivation, girl. You need to be 'sleep 'cause you young."

"Scottie, will you stop with your philosophy."

"Just being real, Leesha, you know how I do."

"Yeah, yeah…"

Scottie didn't sound tired at all. It made me wonder if I'd called him at a bad time. Maybe he had company or was doing whatever he does so late at night.

I asked him, "Is this a bad time?"

"Bad time for what?"

"You know, for me to be calling you?"

"Oh, nah, it's cool. How you doing?"

"I'm okay."

"You sure? People don't call at this hour unless something is up. That old dude ain't over there harassing you, is he?"

"No, thank God!"

"He ain't moved in yet?"

"Victor?"

"Who else we talking 'bout?"

"No, well, I don't know because Mama don't tell me nothing. I just know that one day he will be living here."

"I hear you. It's probably something you don't really want to talk about, huh?"

"No, well, I don't know what I want to talk about. I'm all confused."

"So, you just want me to listen until you can think of something to say?"

"Why you making fun of me?"

"I'm just playing, Leesha. I tell you what…Let's just hook up tomorrow and I'll take you to a movie."

"Scottie?"

"Yeah…"

"My grandmother is having a party and I was thinking you could go with me. It's mostly for the family but I feel weird, like something is gonna happen."

"What you mean?"

"I don't know. Grammy never has parties like this and she's acting like she got some big news to tell everybody."

"You pretty close to her, huh?"

"Yeah, I don't know what I'd do if she wasn't around. If I didn't have her to run to I'd probably be constantly in the streets somewhere. She's the real reason why I try to stick with school."

"I hear you. I ain't never had anybody on the straight path that I looked up to like that except for celebrities and shit. But you know how they be trippin,' too, so it's rare to find a hero that ain't done dirt, you feel me?"

"What about your brother? I remember you saying you were close to him."

"Yeah, I look up to him, but I'm talking about someone on the level of a father figure or like your grandmother. See, she on some Maya Angelou tip. She one of those ladies you can look at and say, 'I hope I grow old and be like her.'"

"But you haven't met my grandmother, have you?"

"Nah, girl, but I'm just saying…"

"I know. I'm just teasing."

"Aw, what's up with that? I'm trying to make a point here."

"I know. Sorry 'bout that."

"Yeah, well anyway, appreciate your grandmother 'cause not many of us can say we got one like yours."

"Are your grandparents still living?"

"I only know the ones on my mother's side. They breathing but they ain't living. They just sit around waiting for that Social Security check and then look down on a brotha trying to do his thang."

"You mean they don't like how you make your money…"

"Basically, but I can't worry bout outside opinions because that'll just F-up my whole process, you know?"

I tried not to push the issue too much about Scottie's grandparents. He had that sound in his voice that had me feeling like if I asked him anything else he might hang up on me. I'd discovered something that caused Scottie to become very guarded with his words. It was strange to hear because Scottie is usually so carefree and don't give a shit when he's talking. I mean, I never get the feeling that anything bothers him, but I guess I was wrong about that. Scottie don't even jump if a car backfires. I do. I'm halfway ducking behind cars as soon as I hear a loud noise. I'm not trying to get hit by anybody's stray bullet. I see on the news every night about somebody being an innocent victim.

Scottie and I stayed pretty silent over the phone. I felt bad about bringing up the subject of grandparents. I worried about what he was feeling, but I was too afraid to ask. I tried to break the silence by tapping on the phone and playing some music. He finally said something when I started singing.

"Aight, Leesha…," Scottie said as if he were about to warn me about something.

"What's wrong?"

"Your singing, girl…You over there ruining my thoughts, for real!"

"What you thinking about?"

"What we was talking about."

"I didn't mean to say something that bothered you."

"Nah, it's cool. I gotta deal with that shit sometime. So far, me and my brother been cool with just keeping to ourselves and forgetting that we got grandparents. Only time we get together with them is when they call, talking about they need us to do something that old folks can't do."

"What do you mean?"

"Just some heavy shit...You know, painting, carrying some stuff...One time me and my brother went over there thinking our grandparents needed us to do something, but we ended up just playing cards with the old man."

"Your grandfather?"

"Yeah."

"Maybe he was feeling lonely and trying to reach out to y'all?"

"I don't know. With me you gotta make your intentions known 'cause I got too much I'm dealing with in my own life. I can't be deciphering hidden messages, you feel me?"

"Scottie, I'm just saying—"

"I know what you saying, girl. To be honest, I thought about the same thing. Like maybe old dude was reaching out, but as soon as we got into the card game, he started in on us."

"What do you mean?"

"Ah, you know! He started criticizing us pretty much for just being young and blaming the problems he sees on the nightly news on us like we the ones that committed the drive-bys or started the riots or some shit like that. My brother just focused on playing cards until he seen me start to get pissed off. He can usually pick up on it."

"What's your brother's name? You never told me before."

"Charles Anthony Franklin. He got one of them proud-ass names that make you want to announce the shit in every hospital waiting room!"

I laughed. "Scottie, you funny! You gonna introduce me to him one day?"

"What, you trying to give my brotha some play, girl?"

"Eeew! No way!"

"Damn, girl, I forgot you a youngster."

"Whatever..."

"Yeah, whatever...So, how you feeling now, Leesha?"

"I'm okay, I guess."

"You can't be guessing about that. What's up with this party you sort of semi inviting me to?"

"Semi-inviting?"

"Yeah, you kind of hesitating about it like you think I'ma come there and be all drunk, ghetto and acting a fool. You heard that song, 'Act a Fool' by King Tee? That's my joint!"

"Well, you have me kind of worried now!"

Scottie laughed. "You trippin'…I'm just playing with you, but seriously, you inviting me, for real or not? I won't be offended if you changed your mind."

"Yeah, I really need somebody with me because I'm almost afraid to go. I don't like surprises when it comes to this family. It's like surprises usually mean bad news to me."

"I hear you."

"Grammy seemed excited when she was telling me about it, but I just don't know. I have a bad feeling about something."

"It'll be alright. What time is it gonna start?"

"Well, she wants me there in the morning so I can help her set up."

"Then you better give me directions or an address or something. She don't stay too far from here, huh?"

"No, over in Leimert on Forty-second Street."

"Cool, just give me the exact address and I'll be there."

"I was kind of hoping you would go with me in the morning."

"Say what? You talking about getting up early on a Saturday morning?"

"Yeah, and if you do, Grammy probably won't mind too much because you'll be there helping us out, too."

"You buggin', Leesha."

"Come on, Scottie. You know I would do it for you…"

"That's 'cause you know I would never ask you. That's like the best sleep in the world on a Saturday morning. The bed be all warm and ain't nobody going to work so you don't hear car doors slammin' outside or females walking all hard on the pavement in they high-heel shoes—"

"Scottie, you notice all that?"

"Hell, yeah! That shit always be waking me up!"

Scottie had me laughing so hard I thought I was gonna pee on myself. I hadn't ever felt that good, especially while sitting inside a place that I hated so much. Talking with Scottie was my escape from the reality of being disgusted with where I lived and the reasons why I wanted out.

As soon as I had begun to plead again with Scottie about getting up early to go to Grammy's place, I could hear keys jingling at the front door. At first I tried to play it off in my mind like maybe one of the neighbors had come up the wrong steps. It's happened before. However, I was fooling myself trying to think it was someone other than who I suspected it to really be.

I heard the keys drop to the floor and then I heard the sound of a man's voice cursing. That sound put fear in my heart because I quickly guessed who it was. I dropped the phone, ran to the front door and looked through the peephole. Then I thought to myself, *Mama did it!* I cursed her under my breath and looked in the direction of her bedroom. I wanted to run in there and ask her why after possibly slapping her a couple of times. I checked the peephole again and caught a glimpse of exactly what I didn't want to see. It was Victor. Then I turned to look at where I was sitting on the couch and didn't realize that I had left Scottie on the phone. I ran and picked it up.

"Scottie, you still there?"

"Uh, yeah, I'm still here. I probably should've hung up, though. What's up with that?"

"Scottie, I have to go. I think Mama gave Victor keys to the apartment."

"She gave that nigga what?"

"Keys to the apartment!"

"Man, Leesha, you need to do something about that fool."

Then before I could say anything else to Scottie, Victor had opened the door and stepped inside. "Well, if it ain't my future stepdaughter…How you doing, Leesha?"

He'd sounded as if he had one too many forty-ounces and smelled like he'd peed on himself. I had a look of disgust. I stood there like I needed to protect myself in case Victor came closer to me.

"What you doing up so late?" he asked.

"Mama in her bedroom so you need to go in there," I told him.

I didn't see any need in me answering to that nigga like he was my new daddy. I didn't respect his ass at all. As always, I wanted to see him stumble and fall so I could laugh and feel like I'd gotten some kind of justice, but that don't never happen when you want it so badly.

As I stood there watching Victor stumble around and look at me like he was crazy, I could hear Scottie's voice on the phone. I was holding it close to my shoulder before moving it closer to my ear. Scottie was getting kind of angry.

"Leesha, what's up, girl? You need me to come over there now?"

"No, but I better get off the phone. Are you going with me in the morning?"

"Damn, Leesha, are you gonna be mad if I don't?"

"No, I won't. It's okay."

"I'll be there around 11, how's that?"

"That's fine. I better go now..."

"You sure that's aight?"

"Yeah, I'm sure."

"I'ma be there then. What that nigga doing now?"

"He just standing and looking at me."

Victor began to get a little agitated since he knew I was talking to someone about him. He stepped forward, a little bit closer to me. I really couldn't move much further because of our L-shaped couch behind and to the side of me.

"Who the hell are you talking to? I can't even see why your mama let you be on the phone at this hour. Where that bitch at?"

"You call my mama a bitch?"

"Nah, I ain't mean that. My ass is too tired to be fooling with you, anyway with your spoiled behind. I need to get some damn rest!"

I watched Victor walk toward Mama's bedroom and I wanted to throw something at him. I still hadn't hung the phone up with Scottie so I told him what Victor had called my mama.

"Damn, Leesha, you need to be somewhere else, girl. That fool ain't right and no telling how he gonna be one of these days when your mama not around. That's when you need to call me up so I can come over there and blaze on that fool. He don't look like he can do shit no how. That little muh-fucker...I'm telling you, I shoulda socked him in his head that time."

"I gotta go, Scottie."

"Why you sounding like something is wrong, Leesha. Is he doing something?"

"Mama in there sleep and he just walked into her bedroom, dropped his pants and now he laying on top of her like some dog. I don't even want to see what Mama does because she probably gonna act like it's okay for some drunk nigga to be on top of her... I gotta go."

"Hold on, Leesha. Where you going?"

"I can't go nowhere, really. I'm just gonna go in my room and lock the door until it's time for me to go see Grammy."

"Oh, aight, but I'ma see you tomorrow, right?"

"Yeah."

After I hung up the phone, I took one last look in the direction of Mama's bedroom. Mama had turned over and was holding Victor in her arms like she was happy to see him. I wondered how a woman could hold a man in her arms who thought of her as nothing more than a bitch. It turned my stomach and took away the ounce of respect that I had left for Mama. I was sick of her and him.

A FAMILY REUNION

I didn't get much sleep knowing that Victor was in Mama's room for his first official night of living with us. I kept tossing and turning, trying to keep myself awake in case that liquor in his system made him brave enough do something crazy like come in my room. Nothing like that happened, but I probably only slept for three hours.

I was so anxious about Grammy's party that I decided to get up. It was only seven so I had plenty of time. I figured getting up so early meant I could get ready before Mama and Victor even thought about waking up.

Every step I took through the apartment was a careful one. I didn't want to make any noises. I kept looking behind me, checking around corners and listening out for any creaking noises coming from Mama's bedroom. My oversensitive nose was getting the best of me, too because as I walked into the kitchen, I could smell Victor. His urine smell was everywhere.

I couldn't find anything to eat except for dry cereal. We didn't have no milk and since Victor probably don't drink it, I doubt that I'll ever see any more unless I buy it myself. I decided to pass on getting breakfast because sitting at the table for any length of time would set me up for possibly another encounter with either Victor or Mama.

I brushed my teeth and took my shower really fast. I felt like I had to be on guard the whole time. My only semi-safe haven was my room. I felt a little more at ease once I was inside behind my closed and locked door. As I got dressed, I wondered what Grammy's party was gonna be like. I pictured in my mind all the family I'd see because everybody loves Grammy and if they don't love her, they at least respect her. I hoped Mama showed that same respect and didn't embarrass herself and everybody else. Somehow I doubted it, though. I thought this party would be something to remember for a long time.

I left the apartment before Victor or Mama woke up. I decided to respect Mama by leaving her a note telling her that I went to Grammy's. I didn't care if she read it, but I also didn't want to hear her mouth if she decided to look for me and noticed that I was already gone. I took my time walking. Once I made it to Stocker Street, I noticed how quiet everything was. It made me think about Scottie. His ass was probably still asleep and there I was walking outside with the morning sun causing my eyes to get all watery. None of the stores were open. The mall parking lot was completely empty except for a few cars parked near the IHOP.

When I reached the corner of Crenshaw and Stocker, I noticed only a couple of wig shops open. I ain't never seen nobody go inside, but it seem like those same shops been there probably before I was even born.

Once I crossed into the Leimert Park area, it took no time to get to Grammy's apartment. There were already two tables sitting in front of her building with white tablecloths covering them. Grammy must've got up at the crack of dawn to start preparing for the party. Then, as I was about two apartment buildings away, I saw Grammy coming outside carrying a box and placing it on one of the tables. She looked to the side and instantly smiled when she saw me. I waved as soon as we made eye contact and then I picked up my stride. She gave me a big hug as only grandparents can and then she started telling me how excited she was about the surprise she had for me.

"Leesha, I couldn't sleep a wink last night! Chile, when this day is over I'm gonna need to go on a vacation because preparing for a party feels like work to me. Goodness!"

"Why you couldn't sleep, Grammy? You excited or you had to cook all night?"

"I cooked a little bit, but mostly I'm just anxious for today to be done with. I ain't about to cook all the food. I told the family that this is gonna be a potluck celebration so all those that's bringing food need to bring it on as early as possible. We got some hungry folks in this family so I don't want nobody complaining about not getting enough to eat."

"Grammy, if I invited somebody and they came, would you get mad at me?"

Grammy brushed off the table and took a few of the contents out of the box. Her hesitation to answer my question made me nervous. She wiped her forehead. "Leesha, you have a boyfriend you been keeping secret?"

"No, ma'am. Scottie is just a really good friend. Kind of like an older brother to me because I feel like I can talk to him about anything."

"That's good because you always need somebody your age to talk with. I hope he ain't nothing like some of these other young folks walking around here with pants sagging and showing no respect for anybody."

"He's nice, Grammy."

"Uh-huh, well, I guess it's alright. What got me mostly worried is that man your mama bringing over here. Leesha, I just don't know what's gotten into her."

As I noticed the disappointment in Grammy's face, I decided not to tell her that Victor had moved in. It's a big difference between Mama mentioning that he might move in one day and him actually living with us. Most of the time it seemed like Mama was using that as a threat because she can be a bitch sometimes like that. Mama is worse than the kids I go to high school with. She got so many trifling ways about her that you'd forget she was in her late thirties. I never really paid attention to her exact age. I never really cared. It's not like knowing it would make any difference in my life.

The more I stood there thinking about Mama, the angrier I started to get. Grammy tapped me on the shoulder a few times to get my attention.

"Leesha, are you gonna stand there looking silly or are you gonna help me prepare for the party?"

"Sorry, Grammy."

"That's okay, just help me with these spoons and forks. We need to set up everything so folks can grab whatever they need. I'm not about to do anything else once everything is set. All I want to do is enjoy the party and pray that everything goes alright."

"So, is my surprise inside somewhere?"

"Leesha, I'm not gonna tell you anything about your surprise. It'll happen soon enough."

After we set up all the plates, knives, forks, spoons, and napkins, I followed Grammy up to her apartment. She started pointing to all these different things she wanted me to take downstairs, but I was steady looking left and right for some kind of specially wrapped gift. I didn't see anything. Whatever my surprise was, Grammy had it truly out of sight.

She asked, "Can you carry more, sweetie, or you gonna take that downstairs and come back up?"

"Huh?" I got busted. She knew I was visually searching for my surprise. Grammy pretended to be losing patience with me. I could tell because she laughed at me while she was telling me what to do.

"Leesha, take that downstairs before you get a hernia from carrying all those things. Now I know you anxious to see what I got for you, but you gonna have to wait, young lady. I want everyone to be a part of this special occasion."

"Okay, Grammy…"

Even though I'd understood that the surprise Grammy had meant a lot to her, I was getting sick of not knowing. I didn't have any patience whatsoever. The only way I could get over waiting was if I had something to preoccupy myself with—something other than setting up chairs and stuff for a party that I wasn't really excited about.

My prayers were soon answered once I heard a familiar voice shouting my name at the top of his lungs. I almost wanted to run for cover because the whole neighborhood could probably hear my name echoing down every street inside Leimert Park. I started to cover my ears to make the point I was embarrassed behind somebody shouting my name out so freakin' loud!

"Yo, Leesha! I don't know why you trippin' like that! You better uncover your damn ears, girl. I'm 'bout to squeeze you to death so give your cousin a hug!"

The person talking all that madness was none other than my cousin Luther. He looked so different. He was much bigger than I remembered him. All that time in prison and everywhere else he'd put a ton of weight on his body. It wasn't all muscle, either. Luther had gotten big, but as he hugged me, I could feel the strength in his arms and chest. He almost suffocated me. Luther hugged me like he hadn't seen me in one hundred years. It did sort of feel like it'd been that long.

As soon as he let me go, I spoke before he got the idea to hug me again.

"Hey, Luther, it's been a long time, huh?"

As much as I looked forward to seeing him again, the reality of Luther actually standing in front of me was almost more than I could stand. I needed to take a moment to get used to his huge presence. Luther laughed and smiled. He could tell I was shocked, not to mention nervous and out of breath.

"You surprised, cuz?" he asked.

"A little bit…"

"You ain't think I was gonna be here?"

"I wasn't sure. Grammy didn't really tell me who was coming. She just say I can expect a big surprise today."

"I heard that. How your mama doing? Where y'all stay at now? Still over there on Buckingham?"

"Yeah, we still there…Mama at home right now."

"Cool. I ain't seen her crazy ass in a while, shit. But look at you getting taller and lookin' fine as can be, cuz! You better watch your little ass, though. Ain't nobody trying to push up on you yet, is it?"

I kind of shrugged off Luther's question. His enthusiasm had me on guard, flinching every time it looked like he was gonna try to hug me again. I didn't know why I'd felt so strange about seeing him, but I figured I needed to get used to seeing how much he changed before I could really feel comfortable. Nothing seemed to bother Luther, though. He was too thrilled to see me and he really went crazy when Grammy came walking down the steps.

"What up, auntie! Woof-woof!" Luther was raising his hands and barking like a dog. The shit was embarrassing but like I said, this was a new Luther that I needed to get used to.

"Boy, I can hear you from upstairs, even with my door closed. What you down here making all that noise for?" Grammy didn't seem to have any effect on calming Luther down.

"Aw, auntie, what you talking 'bout? I'm just happy to be with family. Y'all just don't know. I mean, it's been how many years since I seen my cousin Leesha?" Luther looked in my direction. "Leesha, when we see each other last?"

Luther looked serious after he'd asked me that question, but I didn't know the answer. I wished I did but after a while of not seeing someone, time becomes hard to count. Grammy told Luther that there was a little bit of food upstairs and that was like music to his ears. He excused himself and left us to finish setting up for the party. Grammy found the trick to quiet him down. He just needed to be pointed in the direction of food.

I looked at Grammy and asked her about Luther. "He seems so different now..."

"Luther?"

"Yeah...I feel bad because I kind of backed away from him."

"Sweetie, Luther just happy to have his freedom. Plus, I'm sure he hasn't seen you since you were little and now you in high school and time just flying by. You gonna be grown before you know it. Luther just excited to see his little cousin. He'll calm down in a minute."

"Yeah, I just feel bad not knowing what to say to him. Mama never talks about Luther so I don't know where he's been or where he lives at—"

"Honey, Luther the same as he always been. He finds his way to trouble like it's his calling in life, but that don't never take away the love he has for his family. That's why I will never turn him away. Now, I know he done some things that make me unhappy and I pray that I never hear the worst of it, but I'm still here for him."

"You right, Grammy."

"Don't you worry, Leesha, you have all day to talk with Luther and I'm pretty sure he'll understand how you feeling."

Grammy gave me a hug and softly said, "Love you." She lit up my heart and took away the shame I was feeling. She always knew how to do that. Seems like that kind of ability only comes along with being a grandmother. I doubt Mama have those skills when she gets older. Victor got her head so far up his ass, she ain't gonna learn shit about life. And if he gone one day, she probably gonna find another fool to pick up where he left off. She always has in the past and probably always will.

I watched Grammy as she disappeared back into her apartment. Like always, she'd given me one more smile to remember until she returned outside. I basically had no idea what to do. I felt like my special trip to help Grammy was a waste of time because she had everything set up already. Still,

I was happy to be away from Mama and Victor. I really didn't want to spend my Saturday morning looking into the eyes of a man whose direction in life is the nearest bottle of alcohol.

Grammy used to tell me stories about men who love alcohol too much. She'd say that they had the devil in their veins. She didn't respect men who sought courage by deadening their natural God-given talents. I don't know how to feel about that because I seen guys having fun and it so happened that they had drinks in their hands. Then I watch television and they show people with wine all the time like it's good for you. A drink be like a natural extension of your hand, especially at a party. But I know Grammy is right because after a while when they start drinking too much, at least where I come from, everything gets ugly. I seen people in my neighborhood fighting and then not too far from them would be a forty-ounce. Then you look at the person left standing and notice how he can barely focus on what he'd done. He'd be just as surprised as you that his best friend was lying in a puddle of blood, face down on the sidewalk. I seen shit like that even before I reached the tenth grade. Maybe all that I'd seen was like sipping on alcohol. I'd grow to not really care about something that wasn't right, especially when it had nothing to do with me.

Another hour went by and I found myself really getting bored. Grammy stayed inside, still cooking whatever food she'd bought for the party. Plus, I think she felt a little guilty about requesting that everybody bring something. She ain't as demanding as she tries to be. Grammy loves to take care of everybody.

Luther didn't come back outside, either so I ended up going inside to see what he was doing. I wanted to make up for not really talking to him. I figured it would be a long time before anybody showed up to the party so that made it perfect for me to visit with him. I couldn't see my family being so enthusiastic about coming over so early in the day, anyway.

When I stepped inside Grammy's living room, she quickly held her finger up to her lips. She told me Luther was asleep. I believed her, but I wanted to see with my own eyes. I don't know why, but I did. I walked into Grammy's bedroom and there he was, snoring and lying face down on her bed with his shoes still on. Luther was so big he covered most of Grammy's bed. He didn't bother to get under the covers. He was sprawled all over the top. Then as I stood in the doorway, he turned over. His snoring never missed a beat. His perfectly white T-shirt was wrinkled now. He might not like that since he seems like the type to be proud of his heavily starched, white T-shirts.

I continued to look at Luther and imagine all that he'd been through. I saw a couple of scars on his right arm, as well as tattoos on both forearms. They were done with only black ink and it made me think that maybe he got those while in prison. I looked at his hands and wondered what he'd done with them. What's the difference between the hands of someone who's taken a life and someone who's helped to bring a life into this world? I thought about that sometimes and yet I didn't really know the answer. Grammy tells me a man's hands say a lot about him, but looking at Luther's didn't tell me nothing. Maybe you have to live a long time and meet a lot of men to know the difference.

Luther never woke up while I was staring at him. He's probably used to sleeping despite knowing there were others in the same room. Something he picked up from his life behind bars since he'd been in and out pretty much all his life.

Grammy cleared her throat behind me as if to say she needed something so I left Luther to his snoring. Grammy didn't really want anything. She told me not to disturb my cousin because it wasn't too often that he could get a peaceful sleep. That left me with nothing else to do but go back outside. Before I went, I spotted Grammy's can of sour cream and onion Pringles. I snatched it off the dining room table even though she'd warn me not to eat too much and ruin my appetite.

"I'm cool, Grammy," I told her.

"You cool? Listen at you, young lady. Chile, you worry me, but I know that kids aren't the same as when I was young."

"No, Grammy, and parents ain't the same neither."

Grammy quickly went silent after I'd said that. I was kind of being smart with my remark and at the same time a little bit spiteful. However, my spite wasn't directed toward her at all. I thought about Mama when I'd made the remark. I went outside and left Grammy to her thoughts. On this day, when Grammy seemed so excited to have her party, nothing to me felt like it needed celebrating. I sat on one of the folding chairs and wondered when this day would change for the better.

I was so happy to see Scottie when he came walking up the street. I felt like a proud younger sister, waving at him like he couldn't see me the first time I tried to get his attention. He saw me, but he kept his non-excited stroll intact, trying to play off that he might've been happy to see me, too.

"You could smile a little bit," I told him as he approached.

He gave me a sort of half-smile.

"What up, Leesha? You see, I showed up early and everything. Got a fresh new white tee on and if you need some help moving something around, I'll do that, too."

"That's okay, I think everything is pretty much set up now."

"Cool...What time is the party gonna start?"

"I'm not sure. This is the first time I ever been to a family party. I mean, the way Grammy is all excited, I guess it's gonna be a lot of people up in here. I'm kind of nervous since she's talking about having a surprise for me."

"Forget about being nervous, shit. Maybe you got a cute cousin or auntie that I can fool with."

"I don't know about all that..."

"Uh-uh...You trying to slow a playa down, ain't you?"

"Whatever."

"Yeah, whatever...Why you nervous about the party?"

"Because everybody's gonna be looking at me when Grammy brings out her surprise. I don't know these people at this thing except maybe a few of them."

"Uh-huh, anyway, Leesha..."

Scottie laughed as he glanced around at all the party decorations. "I don't see nothing on the table yet. What's on the menu?"

"I don't know. Grammy said she expects everybody to bring something to the party."

"Is that right? Want me to run to the liquor store?"

"No, but I can tell Grammy that you offered."

Scottie smiled as if to say he wouldn't be too disappointed if I didn't tell Grammy he offered.

"Why you come so early?" I asked him.

"I felt bad about turning you down last night. Plus, with that nigga showing up, I was really feeling bad. Nothing happened, right?"

"No, but with him in the other room, I had a really hard time sleeping."

"That shit ain't right, Leesha. Wish I could do something to help you out."

"I know, thanks."

"Who dat?" Scottie asked as he spotted Luther coming outside.

Simultaneously they looked each other up and down. I got nervous really quick because they both had that look as if there might be trouble should either one say something that the other might not like. I quickly stepped in by introducing them to each other.

"Hey, Luther!"

"Yeah, Leesha..." Luther responded while still glancing at Scottie from head to toe.

"I want you to meet Scottie. He's a really good friend. Kind of like my older brother, always watching out for me..."

"Is that right? Then you must be aight if you watch out for my little cuz..."

"Yeah, I try to look out for her...What up, playa?" Scottie greeted Luther.

"I can't call it...," Luther responded.

Guys talk funny to me. Like they try to be all macho and shit. Both Scottie and Luther stood across from each other acting like they were trying to protect their manhood. If they looked real hard, they'd probably feel like mirrored images of each other. Scottie was dressed in his oversized white T-shirt over some black khakis and Luther was pretty much dressed the same way except he had on baggy jeans and just looks older.

At this point I hadn't known all of what Scottie been through, but between the two, you could definitely tell that Luther seen a lot of things that he probably had nightmares about. I've always been tempted to ask him about what he's done in his life, but he probably wouldn't tell me. All I can rely on is hearsay within the family. Mama hates him so I know she be lying when she tries to tell me something. Grammy always asks God to help Luther after she speaks about him. I be wanting to know every little detail.

"I hope some of them niggas show up with some food soon 'cause my ass is starving like a muh," Luther said as he rubbed his big stomach.

"I heard that!"

Scottie added his two cents, which seemed to give Luther reason to smile. I was wondering why Luther was still hungry, but from the size of his stomach, I could tell it took a lot to fill it up. I wanted to remind him that he had just eaten, but I kept quiet.

I noticed an instant connection between the two so I stopped worrying that they might start some kind of gang war in the front yard of Grammy's building. In fact, I started to get a little jealous because it wasn't too long before they were talking so much to each other that they seemed to forget about me completely.

"I wish we had some dominoes up in here 'cause talking to you young blood got a brotha feeling really at home!" Luther said.

"I heard that but I got a little something we can mark this occasion with. You smoke?"

"Yeah, I do but I gotta be cool on that shit. My PO even hear about me smoking some weed, I be right back in jail, dawg."

"Aw, for real?"

"Yeah. I be getting tested every week for that shit, too."

"Damn, they sweat you real tough when you on parole, huh? My brother went through that shit for a long-ass time."

"Where he do time at?"

"Chino."

"For real?"

"Yep. He did his three years and then almost a year of probation. They used to sweat him all the time. Poe-Poe was stopping him almost every day 'cause they know him around where we stay at. It got so bad that he just stayed at home most of the time. I would have to do some runs for him and that's how I eventually got put on and learned the game."

"I heard that. Y'all got your own little set-up then, huh?"

I couldn't believe how Scottie and Luther completely blocked out any realization that I'd been sitting next to them. I was literally feeling like a fly on the wall. They talked so openly that I was scared I'd hear things they didn't want me to hear. I didn't think it was safe to interrupt them. Luther seemed impressed by the way Scottie spoke. He seemed to respect him the more he listened. I kept on listening, too, and prayed they wouldn't regret anything I might overhear them say.

Scottie put his bag of weed back in his pocket and then answered Luther. "Yeah, we got a little sumpin-sumpin set up," he said with a hint of pride in his voice.

"You be careful with that then, young blood. I used to be deeply involved with all kind of shit, but now I keep thinking about what I was doing before all that. I don't know if I qualify for that OG status now, but I feel like I'm a veteran of the war, coming home with all kind of shit broke off into me."

"I hear you. Shoot, I always thought niggas in the hood take it just as hard as them fools fighting over in them countries."

"That's true but when you survive as long as I have through all this, you wake up every morning trying to figure out where your life went to. I can remember riding bikes and having races down the street. We had this one nigga named Papa who used to be so fast on his bike that fools started coming from all the other neighborhoods to see if they could beat him. He was racing against mini-bikes, dawg! You hear me? It would be Papa peddling his bike against some nigga with a mini-bike and you know those things had motors so... I'm telling you, man, Papa was the shit!"

"That's cool. I don't remember nothing like that around where we stay at."

"That's 'cause you young and things ain't been the same for a while now."

"That's true. That's why I used to always like to talk with my brother about the old days. He probably the same age as you."

Luther laughed. "Old days?"

"Yeah, it ain't been that long, huh?"

"Nah, not really. What your brother do now?"

"Aw, man, my brother ain't the same now. Being at home like he was all that time changed him. He kind of stopped being a man. All he do is sit around and don't do shit but drink and smoke weed. He just ain't right no more..."

"Damn, I hear you."

Luther watched as Scottie went from having so much pride to looking like he'd lost hope in someone who he'd looked up to for a long time. Scottie never told me much about his brother and I could see why. I wanted to say something to him, but it seemed as if nothing really needed to be said. Even Luther kept quiet and it seemed like that was the best approach.

The first car pulling up had about five people. I didn't recognize any of them but one of the girls caught Scottie's attention. He looked up and got over his sadness real quick. "Damn, you know them, Leesha?"

"You mean her, don't you?"

"Whatever…"

"No, I don't know them."

"Leesha, you need to start hanging out with your family more often."

Luther laughed at both of us. "Yo, I know them niggas," he said as a heavy-set man stepped from behind the steering wheel. He had a dark complexion and a seriously receding hairline. He wore a light gray sweatsuit and seemed to smile as soon as he'd seen Luther stand.

"Yo, what's up!" Luther yelled out.

The man greeted Luther by holding up an unlit cigar. "L-dawg!" he shouted and focused on lighting his cigar as the others filed out of the car. I didn't recognize any of them, but they all seemed to pick up on Luther's excitement.

Luther walked over to hug the woman who got out of the front passenger's seat and then he went around and hugged the big man in the sweatsuit. Scottie couldn't take his eyes off of this one chick wearing a pink jean outfit. She was cute but her outfit needed to be spray-painted a darker color because that shit was way too bright for me.

"Why don't you just go talk to her? Damn," I told Scottie.

"I am but I got to make sure my approach is tight. I can't just step to her now with them other people all around. They probably her parents, nah mean?"

"I can't say. I never seen them before."

"Yeah, I know."

"Forget you."

"Uh-huh, I'm gonna have to end up introducing you to your own family, Leesha."

"Funny…"

Then as soon as Scottie got up the nerve to approach the girl in pink, Mama and her asshole pulled up in his yellow Volkswagen. I recognized the sound of his car even without looking. When you hate someone really bad, you can always sense when they close by. Scottie turned to look at me because he spotted Mama and Victor, too. It didn't stop him from going to talk to that girl, but at least he was concerned enough to look at me. Luther was mister happy-to-be-reunited so he was waving to get my attention.

"Leesha, ain't that your mama?" he asked.

I looked the other way. Cars were starting to pull up left and right so I turned my back on all the family greeting going on. I went upstairs to let Grammy know that people were arriving. She was still cooking although when I walked inside, I found her standing near the dining table, talking on the phone. She got all quiet when she saw me. It made me feel like her conversation had something to do with me. Grammy had never acted like that before with me around.

"What's wrong?" I asked.

She shook her head as if to tell me nothing was wrong and then she gestured for me not to say anything, but I did, anyway. I was already pissed off behind seeing Mama and Victor so I didn't care about anything else.

"Grammy, it's a whole bunch of people down there now!"

Grammy had a frown on her face. I had interrupted her on purpose while she was on the phone. I knew that wasn't cool, but I also knew exactly what I was doing. I was already prepared for what was coming when she got off the phone.

"Leesha, couldn't you see I was on the phone? Chile, you must be picking all that up from your mother because I know you didn't learn that here."

"Mama downstairs now. You can meet her man, Grammy."

"Is that all you have to say?"

"I don't know what else to say."

"Leesha!"

Grammy had so much disappointment in her voice that I felt like there was no turning back. Knowing that Mama was outside with Victor and the whole surprise thing really had me tripping. I didn't even care if I might've made Grammy so mad that she'd take her surprise back. At least all the stress of not knowing would go away and I wouldn't have to even think about all these people that I had never met before. Grammy grabbed some of the food that was wrapped and ready to go. She looked at me with sadness in her eyes.

"Is it too much to ask that you bring those vegetables and bowl of corn downstairs for me?"

I didn't answer Grammy, but I walked over to the table and grabbed as much as I could carry.

She thanked me and then went outside. I followed behind and the first thing I noticed was that a party had truly begun since I'd left. Luther was talking all loud and telling everyone old stories. He was having a good time and everyone else seemed to be loving him right back.

Scottie had his own party going on with that girl in the pink jean suit. Whatever he said to her seemed to work because during the ten minutes that I'd been standing there watching them, she never took her eyes off of him. Scottie saw me, but I don't think he wanted to interrupt his flow. Pretty in pink didn't even seem to mind when Scottie was blowing smoke all in her face. I'd kind of hoped that he wouldn't light up no cigarettes while at Grammy's party, but folks kept coming in so she couldn't really pay attention to what everybody was doing. Grammy's attention was on making sure the food was on the table.

I wanted so much to not be at the party but with Luther around, that was next to impossible.

"Yo, Leesha! Come on over here, cuz!"

As soon as Luther said that, all eyes were on me, including the ones I hated the most. Victor was looking at me and gulping down whatever was inside his paper cup. I could tell by how hard he swallowed that he had some liquor in it. Mama was sitting right next to him wearing some really tight dress. It fit her tight like silk. I couldn't believe she was looking like a wannabe hoochie. I felt ashamed that people knew I was her daughter. How did people know? Because of Luther's big mouth. He was introducing everybody like somebody appointed his ass as the announcer of ceremonies.

When I walked over to the table where Luther was, he put his arm all over my shoulders and introduced me to everyone sitting at the table. He started with that big man in the gray sweatsuit.

"That's Uncle Buddy, Leesha. Next to him is his wife, Carolyn. Me and Buddy go way back to when I was a youngster."

They both said hello to me at the same time. Carolyn looked over at Mama and kind of raised her eyebrow as if quietly questioning if that was really my mother. Luther finished with the introductions. Uncle Buddy had three daughters. They were Terry, Shanae, and Valerie. Terry was the only one of the three who spoke to me. She was older so she wasn't trying to look me up and down like I was some ho in competition. Shanae looked at me like that, and Valerie, in the pink jeans, was too busy kissing Scottie's ass.

Victor came over and introduced himself. He stumbled all over his words. That liquor probably had convinced him to take a chance because Luther looked at Victor like he was crazy.

Victor said, "Hey, y'all, my baby ain't had a chance to introduce me to the family yet so uh yeah, check this out. I just wanted to say that my name is Victor."

"What up, Victor?" Luther greeted him. "You get enough to drink, homeboy?"

"Uh-huh, yeah, I got some. The food is really tasty, too!"

"Glad you enjoying yourself, homie."

The tone in Luther's voice sounded as if he wasn't impressed with Victor. Victor was leaning all over the table and standing behind Shanae. I think she really felt uncomfortable because whenever Victor spoke, he brushed against her. He was probably sneaking a feel, but all he got was her back.

"Hey, Lynette, how long you and Victor been together?" Luther asked. "You never told me about him before."

Lynette is Mama's name and I ain't heard nobody say it in a long time. Victor don't hardly use it and Grammy speaks to her without really saying her name.

Mama answered, "We've been together a little while now." She looked embarrassed, maybe even shy about answering. She couldn't have been proud to claim that nigga as her man.

"Is that right? He treatin' you good?"

Victor tried to answer for her. "I always treats my baby girl good..."

"I wanna hear Lynette say it, homeboy."

"He treat me good, Luther."

Mama answered in a hurry because I think Luther picked up on Victor being an asshole. Everybody was kind of looking at Luther's expression and praying that Victor would sit his ass back down.

A few more people walked up to the party and that took all the attention off what was going on. Luther was the first to speak. "Who y'all supposed to be?" he said as they walked through the little gate before entering the front yard area.

Everybody kind of laughed at Luther. He'll say pretty much anything and get away with it because he's so big. Everybody knows he been in jail so nobody tries to talk back to him, but the laughter sort of eased the tension and probably made those people feel more comfortable.

It was two women and one man. The man asked about Grammy. Something about him seemed so familiar to me. Mama looked up when he spoke and asked him why he was at the party. She was acting like he was her ex-boyfriend or something. Victor got kind of mad and asked her if she knew that man. She didn't say nothing. That man just winked at her and then walked up the stairs to find Grammy. He was dressed really nice and smiled even though you could tell he was uncomfortable. The two women were dressed nice, too. They followed behind him until he told them to wait at the bottom of the stairs. When he did that, they became the center of attraction because nobody knew who they were.

"Mama, you know him?" I asked as I walked over to her table.

She didn't answer me, either. She looked the other way like something was wrong. She looked nervous. She even pushed Victor away like she was really upset about something. Scottie came over to ask me what was going on. He nodded his head as if to tell me to come closer so we could talk in private. I teased him about his pretty-in-pink girlfriend, Valerie.

"So, that girl finally let you go for a minute, huh?"

"Valerie is cool, but I can't do too much with her parents all up in the mix, you feel me?"

"Yeah, Scottie, whatever…"

"This party is a trip, Leesha. What's up with that dude that just walked in? You know him?"

"No, but I think Mama knows him. She's acting weird about seeing him. Look at her."

"That's what I'm talking about. Maybe she knew that dude before you was born. Dude got some nice clothes and was smiling like a damn movie star or something."

I shrugged. I didn't know what to say to Scottie, but my ass was just as curious as him. Then I got kind of frustrated because I looked at Mama and she was drinking out of Victor's cup like she needed it badly. Victor was smiling.

"Hold on, Lynette!" he whispered real hard. "See there, now I'm gonna have to refill this up, woman!"

Victor got up and walked over to the table with the alcohol. Mama was wiping her chin and looking to see if she had spilled anything on her dress.

I was disgusted and even more frustrated. I spoke softly to myself, but Scottie heard me. "That bitch…"

"Say what?" Scottie laughed.

"She make me sick sometimes…"

"Who you talking about?"

"Mama."

"Why, what's up?"

"Can't you see how she's acting? Look at her all nervous…"

Then before I could finish my thought, I'd worked myself up to the point where I wanted to scream. But instead of doing that, I shouted to get Mama's attention and I got everybody else's, too. "Mama!"

She looked at me like she'd seen a ghost. Her eyes were all glossy, but she had them opened wide. She waited for me to say something, but seeing her sitting there looking vulnerable made me feel sorry for her. Scottie was still standing next to me so he rubbed my shoulder and kept asking me if I was okay.

"I'm alright," I responded although I wasn't.

Then as soon as I turned to look at Scottie, I saw Grammy from the corner of my eye. She'd come back outside and that man was standing behind her.

He was looking at me and smiling like he wanted to say something. Scottie stepped in front of me like something was about to happen.

"Yo, Leesha, remember when you told me about your father the other day?" he asked.

I looked into Scottie's eyes and instantly connected with what he was trying to warn me about. Then I looked over his shoulder and Grammy had already walked up behind us.

"Leesha, come here, sweetie," Grammy said.

I swallowed really hard because I already knew what she was about to say. Something really strange but familiar lingered in the air around us. As that man stood behind Grammy, I could smell the scent of his cologne. It was the very same scent that I'd always search for whenever I would go to the men's cologne section in the department store. I only did that because it was my way of connecting with the father that I never knew. When I was a baby and felt the strong hands of a man, lifting me up and bringing me close to him, I remember what he smelled like. I can never picture what he looked like, but I do remember his scent. He'd leave it behind on my skin or in my clothes whenever he'd put me down. One day that scent faded away and never returned until I found it in a fancy bottle many years later.

As I stood in front of Grammy, waiting for her to introduce me to this man that couldn't seem to stop smiling, I heard Scottie's voice to the side of me.

"Oh shit..."

And then I heard Luther. "Yo, Lynette!"

Then Mama came and almost knocked me and Grammy down when she passed by us. "What the hell are you doing here? Nigga, you came to see your daughter after all these years?"

Grammy reached for Mama.

"Stay the fuck away from me! Is this the surprise you had for Leesha?"

Mama lost her mind and pretty much every last bit of respect she had from Grammy.

"Lynette, you better watch how you acting up! You should be ashamed of yourself. Is this how you are around my grandbaby? You're drunk. Your man over there is drunk. Now you need to sit yourself down because I've had it up to here with your behavior!"

I was afraid Grammy might have a heart attack from being so angry. Her whole face was frowned to the point where her eyes were about closed.

"Did you hear what I said?" Grammy asked Mama.

Mama put her hands on her hips like she didn't care. She dared Grammy to do or say anything else to her. I looked at the man who Grammy was about to introduce me to. He didn't seem nervous but he was uncomfortable. He was kind of smiling and slowly reaching toward Mama. He was trying to get Mama to calm down.

Luther came over but he didn't do nothing but talk shit. "Y'all is crazy up in here! This ain't how this party should be going. Y'all need to chill."

Grammy's guest of honor finally reached over and touched Mama's arm. That didn't help the situation because she went off again.

"Nigga you don't need to be touching me! You need to take your ass back to where you came from 'cause we been fine all these years without you!"

Luther asked, "Who is this dude?"

"This is Leesha's sorry-ass father and he needs to take his ass out of here!" Mama said.

I could feel everybody at the party take a deep breath and hold it for a few seconds. Grammy had tears in her eyes from being so embarrassed and hurt behind the way Mama was acting. I looked at that man, my father, and seen his smile disappear. He didn't know what to say or do. He wouldn't look at me then. He stood there and did what everybody else was doing. We all waited for somebody to say something, but nobody really did. I walked away and stood at the bottom of the stairs leading to Grammy's apartment. Scottie walked over and stood beside me.

"You aight?" he asked.

Before I answered, I looked at everyone and watched as they all separated slowly from one another. The party was ruined and Grammy stood in a daze. Mama went back to her table. Victor came up and hugged her. They sat down and started drinking again.

"I don't know what I'm feeling...I'm gonna go upstairs," I told Scottie.

"You want me to come up there with you?"

"Yeah."

"Okay."

Scottie followed me upstairs and into Grammy's apartment. As soon as we sat on her couch, I began wiping the few tears that had escaped from my eyes. I didn't want to cry too much and have him thinking that I actually cared about what had happened. Scottie understood, though.

"Leesha, that shit would get to me, too. I've been to some parties that get a little wild, but what your mama did wasn't cool at all."

"She's stupid. I really hate her sometimes."

Scottie held my hand. It was sweet because he looked uncomfortable doing it.

"Some surprise I had, huh?" I said.

"It surprised the hell out of me! You gonna talk to him?"

"I don't know."

"He don't seem like a bad dude, but then again, he might've just fixed himself up for the party, nah mean?"

"I guess. I don't know because the only person that's told me about my father is Grammy and that wasn't too long ago. I mean, I even had to ask her what my father's name is."

"Your mother never talk about him?"

"Never. I got used to it, though, so I never even ask about him. I don't even know if he sends her money or not."

"Shit, by the way she was acting, I doubt it. Sounded to me like she hates that nigga. I mean, sorry about that."

"It's okay. I know what you saying. I wish this day never happened. I know Grammy wanted this to be something really special and I hate that she's probably feeling so disappointed now."

"Yeah, your grandmother seems cool. I don't know what she thinks of me, but she seems aight." Scottie smiled. "Damn, I sure wish I could smoke up in here. Your family make a nigga need some nicotine in his system."

"Forget you!"

Scottie laughed.

"And don't you dare smoke in Grammy's house."

"I'm just playing, Leesha. It's cool, but yo, I think eventually you gonna have to talk with your old man. I mean, you told me he lives in D.C., right?"

"Yeah, that's what Grammy said."

"That's a long way to be coming out here to see somebody. I mean, even if he did get himself together just for this day, you gotta respect that kind of effort, you feel me?"

"I guess so but it's not that easy to just be okay with everything."

"I hear you. Still, maybe you can use this chance to say what you feel. Curse his ass out if that's what you want to do. But you never know, he might be cool and at least you'll know you got somebody that'll be there for you. You know…your own flesh and blood."

"Yeah, I guess so…"

And before I could say anything else to Scottie, it was him, my father. He had come upstairs to see me or maybe Grammy sent him up to talk to me.

"Knock knock," he said while standing in the doorway. "I hate to interrupt. How are the two of you doing? That was quite a scene out there, huh?"

Scottie stood. "What's up, man?" He greeted my father.

"H-hello…"

Scottie turned to look at me. "Listen, Leesha, I'll be outside so just holla if you need me. I won't leave until you say everything is cool, aight?"

I nodded my head. "Thanks, Scottie."

"No prob."

Scottie brushed past my father and out the door. I could hear him walking downstairs. I listened to each step as if I'd really wanted him to turn around and come back. I wasn't sure what to say to this man who stood before me. At least he wasn't ugly or dirty. He was actually nice looking and as Grammy said, he loved to smile.

"You mind if I come in and sit down. It feels a little awkward standing here in the doorway," he said.

"Yeah, you can come in…"

"Thanks."

"You're welcome."

He walked in and sat on the couch.

"That's a nice suit," I told him.

"You like it?"

"It's nice. I don't see many men wearing suits around my neighborhood unless somebody is going to church. Seem like not too many people do that either, though."

"You like where you live?"

"It's okay. It's not the worse place."

He shook his head as if to agree with me. He looked like he really didn't know what to say, either. It felt like he was trying to fill in all the dead space with the same questions he'd probably ask anybody he just met.

"Listen, Leesha…I'm your father, but if you want, you can call me William."

I responded by shrugging. I really didn't feel like I needed to call this man anything. If I wanted to say something, I felt like all I needed to do was start talking and if I didn't have shit to say, I would keep my mouth shut.

"What's the shrug mean?" he asked.

"Huh?"

"You shrugged your shoulders and I was wondering what that meant."

"I don't know. It's nothing…"

"Nothing…Okay."

He started rubbing his hands as if they were cold. I watched him struggle. I could see tiny beads of sweat on his forehead and temple. That suit wasn't a good thing to wear inside Grammy's warm living room. I noticed him trying to move his neck around.

"So, Grammy invited you here?"

He seemed relieved that I'd asked him a question.

"Grammy? Yes, your grandmother invited me here. I heard from her about a month ago and before that a good friend of mine told me that she was trying to contact me. We stayed in touch for a while after you were born but then… I don't know. I guess I just got too busy…"

"Why you haven't tried to call or show up sooner?"

"It's a long story."

"There's a short answer for everything…"

He smiled and looked at me as if he were impressed about something. "What grade are you in now?"

I didn't smile back. "I'll be in the eleventh this fall."

"Ain't that something?"

"So, why haven't you tried to call?" I asked again.

"Leesha, during the first year that I was away from you, I tried to call every week. Your mother wouldn't talk with me nor would she allow me to see you. This opportunity had come my way in D.C. and I couldn't pass it up. Before that, I couldn't find anything in Los Angeles or anywhere in California for that matter. So when this job came up in D.C., I took it."

"You couldn't take us with you?"

"Your mother wouldn't go. She said D.C. was too far from where she grew up. I tried for weeks to get her to change her mind, but she wouldn't. I felt like she wanted me out of her life, anyway and I'm not so sure she was happy with the pregnancy in the first place. That first year of your life I thought everything was good. Your mother and I got along really great. She seemed to accept that she was a mother and even though we struggled to pay bills, we kept dreaming and thinking about how really nice it was gonna be once we both had decent work and could take better care of you."

"So, what happened?"

"I'm not sure I even know the answer to that. After you turned one year old, your mother started to change. She complained constantly about being tired of staying home all day. She started to lash out against me. I'd come home and nothing would be cooked. All she had on the table was empty cans of baby food that she had fed you. Then if I asked her where was dinner, she'd get angry and throw whatever was close by her, right at me. I've been hit in the head by many of your baby food cans. I don't suppose you remember any of this, huh?"

"No, I don't..."

"That's understandable. I really couldn't expect you to."

"I don't know. It still seems like you could've done something to see me, especially as I got older. I mean, I'm almost out of high school now! You're telling me about when I was one year old?"

"Yeah, time got away from me, Leesha. There's no real excuse I can give to you. All I can do is find ways to apologize and I realize that might not be enough, either."

"It just seems like if I was truly important to you, it wouldn't matter what Mama said. You would've just found a way to see me. I'm learning all the time that if there's something you want, you find a way to take it…"

"Wow, is that what you've learned?"

"Yep."

"I don't know if I agree completely with you. I'm hoping that the things you want out of life, you put in a little hard work and earn it for yourself."

"Is that what you were doing all these years before you finally realized you had a daughter?"

"I always thought about you, Leesha. Not a day went by that I didn't."

I turned my head and looked toward the front door. I wanted to leave, but I couldn't get my legs to move. I couldn't stand up. Part of me was telling myself to stay and listen to this man while the other half was saying, *fuck him! Time is up!* I could feel his ass staring a hole in the side of my face, waiting for me to say something.

He cleared his throat. "Leesha, maybe this is a bad time—"

"Are you for real? A bad time?"

"Leesha, I don't know what I can say to you to erase all the years that I wasn't a father to you. If there's a way, maybe you can help me do that!"

"I can't help you do shit."

"Excuse me?" He held up his hand and closed his eyes for a moment. "Wait, I really don't want us to get angry at each other."

I turned to look at him. Those beads of sweat on his forehead had increased in number and he seemed very anxious. His struggling didn't bother me. I wanted to see him feel even worse. I stood up.

"You're leaving now?" he asked.

"I need to get back to the party and see how Grammy is doing."

"Oh, the party…Yes, of course."

"Uh-huh. It's kind of rude not to be outside where all my real family is at."

"Okay, well, I hope we can talk again, Leesha. I'll be here for a couple more days."

I interrupted his *hope-we-can-talk* speech. "Let me ask you something...," I said.

He nodded.

"Do you know what it feels like to grow up wondering what your father looks like? I was a little baby when you held me and the only thing I remember about you is how you smell."

"How I smell?" He smiled.

I walked and stood near the front doorway. My arms were crossed and I had no expression whatsoever on my face. I looked at him and continued to talk.

"You wear a cologne called Drakkar, don't you?"

"Yes, I do, how did you know that?"

"As soon as I was old enough to go to the store by myself, I would go to the men's cologne section, trying to find the scent that I remembered from when I was a baby. It probably sounds stupid."

"No, not at all, Leesha. And so, you found it, huh?"

"I found it and for a long time I would go to the store just to smell it because it reminded me of these big hands that used to hold me when I was a baby. After a while, the lady at the counter gave me free samples. She thought that I was trying to save up one day to buy that cologne for my father. She didn't know that all I was doing was remembering what it felt like to be loved by a parent. At night I would smell those samples and then imagine what my father looked like and how he sounded."

"Leesha..."

"Mama never talks about you so I had to make up my own father. Someone that always let me know everything would be alright."

"Leesha, I am your father and if you let me—"

"No you're not!"

Before he could say anything else, I walked out the door. I almost stumbled down the stairs. The tears in my eyes made my eyesight blurry so I stopped before I reached the bottom step. I didn't want to go outside and have everybody see me crying. I tried to wipe my eyes, but I don't think that helped so instead of going outside with the others, I sat down on the bottom step and waited. I waited to feel better. I waited for the tears to stop building up, but they wouldn't.

I'm not sure how much time went by, but I sat on that bottom step for what felt like forever. I cried a little bit, but mostly I fought back as many tears as I could. I fought hard. I cursed myself for letting things get to me. I hated feeling weak. Scottie seen me wiping the last of my tears.

"Damn, Leesha, I was about to come up there and see what's up. What you doing sitting on the stairs? How long you been here?"

I shrugged and avoided making eye contact with him.

"Wait, hold up," Scottie said. "You crying?"

"A little bit."

"Why you crying?"

"I don't know. I'm mad, mostly."

"Things ain't go well with your father?"

"He tried to explain what happened, but it's been too long. I can't just accept some man that shows up one day trying to be Daddy."

"Damn, Leesha, I hear you. You left him upstairs?"

"Yeah, he still up there."

"I found out them two ladies he came with is his wife and sister. They was asking me about you, but I wasn't feeling the whole vibe of giving them your life history, nah mean?"

I continued to wipe tears from my eyes as I began to smile at the way Scottie was talking. As usual, he comes up with a way of explaining things to me that would make me laugh. I couldn't stay too angry with him around.

"Yo, what's up? Why you laughing now?"

"I'm laughing at you, Scottie."

"Whatever. But check this out. I mean, them ladies was talking to me like I was your boyfriend or something. I had to put a stop to that 'cause that little honey Valerie was sitting close by. They was about to blow my whole game talking about me and you like that. Then they started asking me some personal shit like your school background and if you're a nice person. I had to laugh at that one!"

"Why, what you tell them?"

"I don't remember what the fuck I said. I think I was too busy laughing."

"'Cause they asked if I was nice?"

"Yeah!" Scottie imitated the sound of one of the women's voices. "She was like, is Leesha a nice person?" He teased while imitating someone speaking proper English.

"I'm always nice to you!"

"Yeah, whatever…Yo, that shit was funny to me. But anyway, you okay now? You still wanna stay or you wanna go somewhere else?"

"Is Mama still here?"

"Your mother, yeah she still out there. Your grandmother and your cousin had to stop her a couple times from going upstairs. She was buggin', too! Talkin 'bout 'that nigga better not try to take my daughter'! Your mother be straight going off sometimes! That dude she came with fell asleep, though. He got his head on the table with an empty bottle right next to him."

"I don't know if I should leave yet."

"Why you say that?"

"'Cause of Grammy…She wanted this to be a special party and it seems like nothing went right."

"That's true. I don't know, Leesha. Your grandmother is strong. I really couldn't tell if all this bothered her personally. I think she worried about you, but at the same time, she was still trying to make sure everybody had a good time."

"That's why I can't leave yet. I think she'll want me to stay and talk to her. I know she'll be disappointed that things didn't work out with her surprise, but I just can't forget so easy."

"Nah, I wouldn't forget either…I feel what you saying. Speak of the devil…" Scottie noticed my father coming down the stairs.

I stood up to get out of his way. He stopped as soon as he approached where I was standing. He reached out to touch my arm and I only looked at him. He stopped short of actually touching me, but I could feel his hand brush against the fabric of my clothes.

"Well, Leesha, I'm gonna go check into my hotel downtown. As I mentioned to you upstairs, I'll be in town for a couple days. Your grandmother has my number and knows how to get in touch with me. All you have to do is say you want to talk and I'll come to you."

"We already talked."

"Yes, we did and I hope it's not the last time."

I didn't respond. I watched as my father took a deep breath, said goodnight, and walked down the stairs. Scottie and I followed behind him at a distance to see if he really was leaving. We watched him and occasionally he'd look back at me and try to smile, but that did nothing for me. His wife and sister waved in my direction so Scottie waved back for the both of us. I didn't know them so I didn't feel like I needed to respond.

"You okay?" Scottie asked.

"Yeah, I'm okay, why?"

"'Cause now he's gone and uh, I'm just making sure you don't regret what happened."

"Nope. There's really nothing to regret for me. We talked enough for me to see that I don't need to be worried about him. I made it this far without him so who cares!"

"Oh okay, well, I'm just checking."

The party lasted for a couple more hours, but things weren't the same. Mostly everybody looked at each other and ate quietly. Luther was still the life of the party, but even he knew there was nothing he could say or do to change the effect of what had happened. Mama didn't say a word, either. She kept staring at Grammy and then she'd glance at me. She sat next to Victor while he slept the whole time. I think she was afraid to wake his ass up and let everybody see how stupid he'd look trying to shake off all that liquor in his system.

I walked over to Grammy once she finally stood still. Despite all that went wrong with the party, she kept her cool and never sat down to relax.

"Grammy, why don't you eat something?" I asked her.

"Chile, I can eat anytime. I don't have much of an appetite as it is, anyway."

Grammy's look on her face worried me. I felt like I was the reason she hadn't eaten. "You're not eating because of me, huh?"

Grammy stopped what she was doing and looked at me. "Sit down with me, chile."

"I really didn't mean to mess up your surprise party, Grammy. It's just that I don't know that man and uh—"

"Leesha, it's okay. I'm saddened by what occurred here, but I do understand how you feel. Maybe I should've done this a different way, but I thought a nice family reunion atmosphere would be perfect for bringing you two together. Somehow I forgot about your mother and how she's changed, and maybe I was being a little selfish in wanting this to go as I planned. Sometimes what we want we can't always have. We have to put it in God's hands."

I had trouble writing off disappointments like Grammy always did. She'd tell me to place it in God's hands and I would nod my head in agreement but deep down, I didn't really take it to heart. I believed that as long as Mama was trippin' over Victor, shit would never change. And unless I felt like I could forgive my father for not being around, then that situation wasn't gonna change, either. I believe in God, but I ain't always so sure he knows what's going on in my life.

I looked at Grammy and smiled. I held her hand and tried get her to smile. She did. She laughed, too, because that's the way she is. She can move on and get over all the stupid stuff that happens.

"Chile, I'm not gonna let all this worry me. Don't you ever think your grandmother can't handle herself." Grammy released my hand, stood up and went back to picking up empty plates and napkins that had blown off the tables. She was steady cleaning up and nobody really paid attention.

"Grammy, let me do that," I told her.

"Thank you, baby."

Scottie started to help me, but he complained about it at the same time. Somehow I knew he would. Scottie was always there for me.

"Yo, this ain't cool, picking up trash off the ground. I don't be doing shit like this on the real!" he said.

"You don't have to help, Scottie."

"Aw, you trippin', Leesha. You know you was gonna ask me to help you out so I'm just reading your mind."

"No, I wasn't gonna ask you."

"Yes, you was. Stop playin'!"

"No I wasn't."

The more I teased Scottie, the more trash he picked up. His arms were full of trash because he was trying to be the man of the hour, picking up everything in a hurry and then asking Grammy where he could throw the stuff away.

"Thank you so much, Scottie. Please take it over there." Grammy pointed to a trash can next to some bushes.

"Cool, thanks," Scottie said. Then he looked at me and smiled. "See, somebody appreciate a nigga's efforts."

"Whatever."

"Uh-huh, I got yo whatever, Leesha."

Scottie was too funny but because of him, we had the party cleaned up even before everybody left. First ones to leave were Uncle Buddy and his family. They seemed really cool even though I smelled like cigar smoke after Uncle Buddy gave me a bear hug. His daughters never really spoke to me. They were real quiet and probably couldn't wait to leave. They managed to take a lot of food home with them. Grammy ended up running out of aluminum foil behind them wrapping up so many plates of food. Uncle Buddy's wife, Carolyn, was the worst of them. She almost took Grammy's crock pot. She tried to promise that she'd bring it back, but Grammy had us cracking up behind what she said. She told Carolyn, "Chile, I don't know you!" and we all laughed.

Luther got all excited, repeating what Grammy said and running over to hug her. "That's why I love this family. Y'all be speaking y'all mind!"

Carolyn didn't seem too offended, but she didn't say much after she got busted. I could tell she was embarrassed, though.

As Uncle Buddy and his family were grabbing as much food as they could, Scottie was in the corner, feeling on Valerie. She was smiling from ear to ear in her pink jean outfit. I wanted to tell him to get away from that girl, but I know he'd probably accuse me of being jealous so I left it alone. I watched him get his last-minute mack on.

Scottie moved in close to Valerie. He kept checking to see if anybody was looking. I was but I didn't see anybody else looking at them. Then Scottie kissed her to see how she'd respond. He kissed her lightly on the side of her left cheek, close to her mouth. Valerie didn't seem to mind. She turned, closed her eyes, and leaned in to Scottie. I could see that chick's tongue go right into his mouth. I couldn't believe she was so bold with her family so close by. I think even Scottie was shocked because he stepped back and checked to see if anybody had seen what happened. He saw me looking and shrugged his shoulders as if to say the kiss wasn't his fault. Whatever...I turned around.

I took my attention off of Scottie and Valerie and found Mama trying to wake up her man. I walked over to their table with no expression on my face. I could hear Uncle Buddy and his family saying their goodbyes behind me, but I kept looking at Mama. It was a trip to watch her plead for Victor to wake up. If it was me trying to wake up some drunk fool, I would slap his ass in the back of the head and then tell him he needs to find somebody else. Mama kept kissing Victor on his head and saying "baby" this and "baby" that.

"Yo, Leesha!" Luther called out to me.

I turned to look. "Huh?"

"Come on over here and give me a hug. I'm about to take off."

I walked to him and he met me halfway. I looked into his eyes and it brought back memories of hanging out in his parents' backyard and the times we went to Disneyland together. I used to love it back then because it would be me and him, running around that park like we lost our minds. Back then Disneyland seemed so big, but now it's a trip how small it looks.

"Hey cuz, it was really good to see you. I'm sorry we didn't get to kick it for too long," he said.

"Yeah, maybe next time."

"Aight, cool."

I wasn't sure what else to say to Luther. I'm pretty sure he was disappointed that I didn't really talk to him that much. I felt bad about it, but I can't just talk when I don't have much to say.

"Aight, later, cuz."

"Bye, Luther."

Luther walked over to Scottie and shook his hand. I was glad they got along really well. Then Luther said goodbye to Mama, but she was still trying to wake Victor up.

"Take care, Lynette!" Luther shouted.

Mama waved without even looking.

"Mama, why don't you just pour some water over his head?" I told her.

"Leesha, shut up, shit."

I could hear Scottie reacting behind me. "Damn, that ain't right."

I turned to look at Scottie. "You wanna leave now?"

"If you ready, we can go."

"I'm way past ready!"

Most of what needed to be cleaned up had been taken care of so I walked over to Grammy, gave her a hug, and then left out the front gate with Scottie. I didn't even bother saying anything to Mama. I figured she'd have plenty to say to me whenever she got me alone next time. I know how she is and I know what to expect.

Scottie and I walked back over to our neighborhood. I didn't want to go home and be waiting on Mama to walk in so I asked him if we could hang out at his place. I didn't really expect him to say yes but he surprised me. He was cool about it.

"I won't laugh if your place is all junky," I told him.

"Shit, I ain't worried. We don't keep no messed-up place, girl."

"Now this I gotta see!"

"Well, you don't see me trying to stop you, do you?"

"Uh-huh, whatever, Scottie."

When we got to Scottie's apartment, he looked up and down the street like he needed to check if somebody seen us before we went inside. He and his brother lived on the first floor of their building.

"Why you checking around, you ashamed to be bringing me home with you?" I asked.

"Nah, I just like to uh, nah, it's just a habit, that's all."

"Okay."

"Listen, ain't too many people ever come home with me and since we ain't like that, I don't want nobody getting the wrong idea."

"What you mean, like that?"

"I think you know what I mean, Leesha. Quit playin'."

"Maybe if they think we like that, nobody will bother me."

"What, you think I got that kind of pull in the neighborhood?"

"You just might, Scottie. I don't know what you be doing."

"Anyway, we here now so let's go inside."

"Okay."

I looked over Scottie's shoulder as he turned the key to open the door. Not only was I looking to see if his place was clean, but also I was trying to see his brother. For some reason I felt nervous about meeting him. The way Scottie talked about him, it seemed like his brother was a loner and probably mean.

When Scottie opened the door, the first thing I smelled was strawberry incense. I almost laughed about it, but I didn't want to offend him or his brother. I kept following slowly behind, matching Scottie with every step he took. I felt like we were trying to eavesdrop on somebody. Scottie tried his best to keep quiet like he wanted to make sure every room was safe to enter. Then before we could enter the hallway from the living room, I heard a voice that kind of sent chills down my spine.

"What up, nigga!"

Scottie and I both turned around at the same time. I tried to play off that the voice scared me, and Scottie acted like he hated we'd been discovered.

"Hey, bruh, how you doing?"

"You know how it is, just chillin'. Who's that right there?"

"This is Leesha. She's cool."

"Is that right?"

"Yeah."

Scottie's brother had a dark complexion made darker by the fact that there were no lights on in the living room and the shades were closed. Scottie noticed, too.

"Why you got it all dark up in here, bruh? You saving on electricity?"

"That's some funny shit, nigga. You trying to be cool around your new ho. I can see she kinda young, too."

"Like I said, Leesha is cool so watch how you trying to talk to her."

Scottie's brother laughed. "So, what you trying to say?"

"I ain't trying to say nothing."

"Yeah, you trying to tell me I'm not suppose to disrespect the ho."

I watched as Scottie bit his bottom lip and acted very agitated. He kept balling his fist up and then releasing it. I could hear him breathing like he wanted so badly to either say something or attack his brother. Scottie took a deep breath and then stepped behind me. There was a lamp near the wall on the right of me so he turned it on. That's when I was able to get a good look at his brother. My first impression was one of bitterness. His brother looked angry, mean, and like he didn't give a fuck about life—period. The incense that I smelled was burning right next to him. The edge of it was stuck in the wall. He was sitting in a little love seat; I guess you would call it, with his legs stretched out.

Scottie seemed to cool off a little bit after he turned on the light. His brother didn't look like he could do anything to Scottie if they ever got into a fight. Scottie was much bigger. Scottie tried to change the mood a little by teasing his brother.

"Yo, Charles, I see you got the incense burning and the lights low, so maybe we interrupting something up in here?"

"Ain't nothing to interrupt, homie. It's just me, my pipe, and these four walls. I ain't like you no more. Out there in the world, bringing home young hoes and shit."

"Man, you ain't right."

Scottie brushed off his brother's comments and then grabbed my arm. He pulled me in the direction of the hallway.

"Nice to meet you, Leesha," his brother said.

I kept looking at him as Scottie pulled me away. I didn't feel anything for Scottie's brother. I didn't even care about him calling me a ho.

Scottie took me to his room and closed the door behind us. He threw his keys down on the bed and turned on his stereo system. My eyes seemed to first focus on his keys and then I looked around his room. He had a couple posters of women on the walls. They looked like strippers or something.

I asked him, "Where you want me to sit?"

Scottie still looked agitated, but I'd gotten his attention with my question. "What you mean?"

"You know, where should I sit?"

"Aw, hold up. You ain't never been over a dude's house before, huh?"

I tried to lie, at first. "Yes, I have!"

"Nah, Leesha. How you gonna ask me where should you sit? You don't see no chairs in here or nothing else. I mean, it might look kind of funny with you sitting on the floor and me up here on the bed, but you more than welcome to sit down there."

"I don't think so. Your floor looks nasty!"

"My floor aight!"

The carpet in Scottie's room was a dirty-looking light gray color. It looked like it hadn't been changed in thirty years. It had all kind of black spots on it and maybe at one point it used to be shaggy carpet. Now it was flat and hard.

"I ain't sitting on no floor, Scottie."

"Then you gotta sit on the bed. You ain't trippin' off of what my brother was saying, are you?"

"I don't like being called a ho but no, I ain't trippin'."

"Good 'cause that fool is just high. He stay that way and don't do shit anymore. If he wasn't my brother, I would blaze on that fool and beat his ass down. He ain't the same no more, but I still gotta respect that he's my brother, you feel me?"

"I don't know. He's sad looking to me. It's like he's just there. How did he get like that?"

"He gave up. Last time he got out of jail, he told me he had a really rough time on the inside and then things wasn't no better on the outside. Plus, after a while, he got lazy about finding a job and then started to become his own best customer, nah mean? He got on that pipe and now what you see is that fool's life. He'll sit in that chair, smoke, stare at the walls, and talk shit whenever he sees me."

"Seem like he should just go out and do something. He looks so skinny sitting in that chair that I thought he might be paralyzed."

"His mind is paralyzed, but I can't trip off that anymore. My brother gotta want to help himself. I already tried that shit. It's up to him, now."

"Yeah, that's true."

"So, you gonna just stand there, Leesha, the whole time we're here?"

"No, I'll sit down after you go get me a chair."

Scottie laughed. "Hah! You trippin'!"

"Your bed don't look clean to me, either."

"Aw, that's cold. Hold up. What if I get you a towel to sit on? Then would you sit on my bed?"

"Why can't we just go outside? I feel strange being in here and your brother out there."

"Aight. Let me get my boom box and a couple of tapes. Hold up."

Scottie went inside his closet and pulled out one of those huge radio and cassette players. He had to literally pull it across the floor when he first took it out. Then he started shuffling through his cassette tape collection. He threw the tapes that he wanted to listen to on the bed.

"I can't go a day without listening to this right here!" he said as he held up a tape by King Tee.

"Do you listen to anything else besides King Tee?"

"Aw, Leesha, you don't understand."

"Yeah, yeah. I guess I gotta listen to your music."

"What you want me to play, some Janet Jackson?"

"Play something that ain't all about gangbanging!"

"You really trippin' now, but that's funny. I'll find something for you 'cause I ain't selfish like that. But I still gots to listen to some King Tee and some WC and the Maad Circle."

I shook my head. I ain't never thought of Scottie as typical, but as I watched him search through his music collection with pride, I could see just how much he had in common with every young brotha in L,A. I wasn't mad at him, though. It was cute.

"King Tee the great!" Scottie yelled like he was all excited.

BITTER PILLS, ONE
AFTER THE OTHER

I was happy that summer had finally ended and it was time to get back to school. I was in the eleventh grade now and old enough to handle a lot more shit than I used to. I learned a lot over the summer, hanging out with Scottie and going through more crazy stuff with Mama, Victor, and my so-called father. He went back to D.C. with his ass between his legs. I didn't like him once I finally got to talk to him again. He seemed kind of fake to me. It was like he was just happy to see that I turned out pretty. Now he wants to claim me like I got a million dollar trust fund waiting when I graduate. That smile of his didn't do nothing for me. I think I may have taught him how *not* to smile, now. I even asked him why he always doing that, but he played like he didn't hear me.

My father looked like he does alright where he lives. Like maybe he makes good money. It's nice to know he got a wife and ain't an alcoholic. He told me his sister lives in Long Beach and that was a good way to stay in touch with him, if I wanted to. I just shrugged it off. I told him that I would think about it but couldn't promise anything. I still can't accept him not ever trying to see me all these years. It doesn't matter what Mama said or did to him. He should've still tried and kept on trying because real fathers don't ever give up.

Going to school was my safe haven every day because once I got home I always had to be on guard. I'd always have to keep watching out for Victor and his sneaky, drunk ass. Then I'd have to do battle with my mother. Ever since that party, she's been on me like we bitter enemies. She talks to me like I'm stupid and looks at me like I'm evil. There's nothing I can do but either take the shit and be quiet or treat her the same way. Since I was living with her, I had to bite my tongue and keep quiet. It was hard, though. Mama would say things that had me feeling worthless. I'd have to swallow really hard and listen. I'd get so angry that I would have headaches that lasted all through the night. You'd think I was on my period the way I be looking every night. My face would be all frowned up. The only way I could feel better is if I either called Scottie or just go sit outside.

By this time, Scottie had enrolled in college. I was happy for him because that's something he wanted to do for a while. He was proud of himself because he was taking classes over at West Los Angeles College and doing his homework in the library. I really liked seeing him excited. After about a week of going to school, I teased him about it. I asked him if he was tired of going already.

He was like, "Are you buggin'? I'm lovin' this school stuff. I even got a fine-ass teacher in my Biology 101 class. I mean, homegirl turns me the fuck on and it's a trip because the class is biology." Scottie laughed.

"I do not want to hear about some teacher you wanna fuck!"

"Yo, Leesha, I even get to use the library whenever I want to, you feel me?"

"What's so special about that?"

"'Cause it means I don't have to go home and be around Charles. When things ain't cool around you, it's hard to really elevate your mind. I can't study when my brother is sitting in the dark, smoking that pipe and talking shit. You know what it feels like to constantly have someone on your back, talking negative shit all the time? Even if my door is closed, I can still hear his ass."

I knew exactly how Scottie felt. I'd had my own negative environment that I had to walk into every day when I came home. Just as soon as I'd reach my street, turn the corner, and see my apartment, I could visualize exactly what I'd find once I opened the door. I mentioned it to Scottie after I'd called him to see if I could come over. He said it was a bad time, but he still talked to me for about an hour to make sure I was alright.

"What happened?" he asked.

"The same old thing…"

"Something to do with Victor?"

"Yeah...and he don't ever stop!"

"Stop what, Leesha? He ain't touched you, has he?"

"Nope, not yet. I mean, he always talking about sex or saying something that sounds sexual. He don't always say it straight out, but I ain't stupid."

"Yeah, but what happened this time?"

"It's just the way he talks to me. When I opened the front door, he was sitting on the couch like always..."

"That dude must time that shit so he can be sitting there when you come home..."

"I think so, too. That's why today I was like, shit, can't you just stay in Mama's room?"

"What did he say?"

"He didn't say anything. He just started licking his lips and sticking his hand in his pants. He looked nasty, plus what I hate most is that I can always smell his ass when I come home. He don't never have any windows open so it be all musty up in here. I don't know why Mama puts up with that."

"You should ask that nigga if he ever takes a bath!" Scottie laughed.

"I almost did one time but the thing is, he's always using my bathroom instead of the one in Mama's room, so sometimes I be seeing his piss all over my toilet seat. If he drop something on the floor, he don't never pick it up. I'm feeling like they both wanna see me go crazy."

"Who?"

"Mama and Victor!"

"Damn, Leesha, it's a trip what you have to go through."

"Yeah, I wish I had someplace else to go."

"Aw, gurl, you making me feel guilty now..."

"Why would you feel guilty?"

"Because I can't just have you come stay with me."

"Thanks but that would feel kind of strange to me."

"Ain't you ever gonna stop thinking I look at you like that?" Scottie laughed.

"That's not what I'm talking about. I don't know. I just want to have my own place."

"You will, Leesha. Just wait a couple more years and then see what happens. But hey, come over tomorrow after you get out of school. I should be home early. You get out at three, right?"

"Yeah…"

"Cool, be at my place around four and we'll hang out."

"Okay."

"Cool, I'll see you then."

"What you doing now, Scottie?"

"I told you, I've got some things to do…"

"Yeah, whatever…I'll see you tomorrow, then."

"That's right."

When I went over to Scottie's place, something strange happened. On the way over there I came across this knife in the streets. It gave me a really funny feeling. I'd seen two cars, one after the other drive right over it. There was a lady on the other side of the street walking with two little kids and she didn't pay any attention. She looked over at me but never glanced at the knife. I stopped to look at it. I thought about picking it up and throwing it away somewhere, but I just couldn't bring myself to touching it. I remembered Grammy one time telling me that if I've seen something that could do folks harm, more than likely the damage been done already. That's how I feel whenever I see a knife laying out in the streets like that. People don't just go around dropping them.

This particular knife had a light-wood-colored handle and the blade had some spots on it, but I couldn't tell if that was blood or not. I decided to kick it across the street and move on. It was really giving me a bad feeling. I kicked it twice until it ended up under a parked car and out of sight for anyone walking by, especially me.

When I got to Scottie's place, I knocked several times. There was no answer. I was about five minutes early so I waited on his steps. I could hear the floor creaking inside his apartment like someone was there. And then moments later, his brother had opened the door and was standing there with a background of darkness behind him. I never realized before how skinny he was and then again, I had never seen him out of his chair neither.

I was surprised to see him without a pipe in his hand. This time he had a cigarette. He was taking puffs after every time he'd say something. My guess is that Scottie probably picked up his cigarette habit from watching his older brother.

Scottie's brother started to act a little agitated like I was bothering him. I think he noticed that I wasn't trying to come in so he copped a little attitude about it.

"Well, uh, I'm not about to stand out here and keep you company so you might as well bring your little ass on inside. I'll leave the door open just in case you don't want to walk so close to me."

He laughed as he walked back inside like some evil man relishing the fact that he could tell he made me feel uncomfortable. The air inside the apartment was so filled with the scent of smoke and incense that I knew as soon as I stepped inside, it would get all in my clothes, my hair, everything.

Scottie's brother sat down in his favorite chair. He watched as I searched for a comfortable place to sit. There was a couch near the wall, but I could barely see the fabric on it because the room was so dark. I started to feel around just in case I might sit on something strange.

"You always keep it so dark up in here...," I said.

"I pay the rent here so I keep it how the fuck I want to."

"I'm just saying..."

"There's a little light over there next to the couch. You can turn that one on. Did my brother ever tell you my name?"

"Yeah, he told me."

"Good."

"Do you remember my name?"

"Yeah, I remember your name, shit...," he responded angrily.

"Why you so mad all the time?"

His only response was blowing as much smoke as he could into the air and looking at me as if I weren't really there.

"Charles?"

"Huh?"

"Nothing...Did Scottie say he would be late coming home today?"

"How the fuck I know! We don't check in with each other. That nigga could be out with some other ho. You like Scottie, don't you? I mean, you all young, got attitude, but you ain't shit. What you know about my brother, Scottie Franklin? Shit, he going to school thinking that's gonna make him somebody."

"Me and Scottie are just friends. You know, if I'm bothering you, I can wait outside. It stinks up in here anyway!"

Charles laughed. "It stinks? I'm about to light my pipe just as soon as my stuff gets here. That's when it's really gonna stank up in here!"

"Do you ever leave this place?"

"Why you worried about it?"

"I'm not worried. It seems like you always sitting here in the dark, smoking on your pipe, talking shit. It ain't cool to be calling me a ho, by the way..."

Then just as I was getting up the nerve to tell Charles off, there was a really hard, frantic knock at the door.

"Charles!" a nervous female voice called out.

Charles struggled to his feet. He looked like he smoked crack for breakfast, lunch, and dinner. That's probably why I wasn't really scared of him. I felt like if it came down to a fight, I could kick his ass really easily because he was skin and bones. The lady continued to say his name outside the door.

"Charles...Charles..."

He looked at me and smiled. "You better pray you don't end up like this ho. All she good for is sucking dick and bringing my shit."

I didn't respond but I felt really low. I wondered if anyone seeing me outside the apartment assumed that I was a crackhead or a prostitute.

Charles opened the front door. I had to adjust my eyes to the light coming in from outside. The woman who called out his name looked as bad as he did. She wasn't even big enough to block the light from coming through the opened door.

He asked her, "You got it?"

"Yeah, yeah, it's here!"

"Then give it up. Don't be trying to hide shit like the last time."

"Baby, I wouldn't do that..."

Then the woman seen me sitting on the couch. She seemed embarrassed. She tried to fix her hair. "Who's that?" she asked.

Charles was too busy checking every pocket in the woman's jacket to hear what she'd asked him.

She yelled, "Hey, girl, who are you?"

Before I could answer, Charles told her to shut up. I still responded, but I said my name softly. It was a trip to watch two crackheads trying to deal with each other. Then as Charles was checking the contents of that lady's purse, Scottie walked up.

"What's going on?" he asked.

"Your lady inside waiting for you…," Charles responded.

"My lady?"

Scottie looked inside, saw me on the couch, and smiled. He didn't smile big, but I knew he was pleased to see me. Then he took another look at his brother. "You should take that shit inside, man."

"I would if your young ho wasn't in there."

"Yo, I told you about calling her a ho."

"Yeah, well, she in the way…"

"She ain't never in the way but we leaving so you don't have to trip no more."

Charles seemed as if he were frozen by Scottie's words. He didn't say anything. He just looked at Scottie as if he were looking at a young boy becoming a man. Maybe he realized that Scottie wasn't gonna take his shit anymore. Or maybe his little mind wasn't quick enough to think of something to retaliate with. Scottie peeked his head back inside the apartment.

"Yo, Leesha, let's go…"

I wasted no time getting up from the couch and walking right toward the front door. I brushed past all three and made my way outside. I felt like I could finally breathe again. Scottie said a few more things to his brother, but I wasn't close enough to hear. I stood in the walkway, waiting. It took longer than I hoped for, but once Scottie came up to me, he apologized for what went on.

"My brother keep that shit up, I'm gonna have to move somewhere. I mean, would you want to be around all that?"

Scottie was talking away and walking as fast as the words came out of his mouth.

"Can we slow down?" I asked him.

"Sorry 'bout that. But yo, that shit ain't cool. I seriously gotta think about my living arrangements."

"Scottie, what else do you do to make your money?"

"Say what?"

"What, I'm not supposed to ask that?"

"You never asked me before..."

"I'm just curious."

"I can't tell you too much, Leesha. I just hustle to get by and at the same time, I'm trying to put some money away for the future, too, nah mean?"

"You have a bank account and credit cards?"

"Nah, but I have a connection that keeps my money clean until I can come up with legitimate ways to show how I'm making it."

"What if I asked you to show me how to make some money?"

"That ain't gonna happen, though, is it?" Scottie said as if to warn me of trouble.

"I don't know."

"Leesha, what's up? What you been thinking about?"

"Nothing...So, where we walking to, the mall?"

"Did my brother say something?"

"No, he didn't say anything. Where we going, Scottie? Stop worrying... Your brother didn't say anything and I won't ask any more questions."

"We going to check out that new movie with Jada Pinkett."

"You mean with Allen Payne and Treach?"

"Whatever...You heard about that movie?"

"Yeah, *Jason's Lyric?*"

"Yep..."

Scottie and I spent the whole two hours, watching the movie in silence. There were a few scenes that really affected me, but I tried my best not to give myself away. I wondered if Scottie felt the same things. Several times I looked over at him. I could see his left eye jumping around as though he sensed I was staring. He never turned his head to find out for sure. He was playing the same game that I was. He was being tough or maybe what he saw on the screen didn't really affect him the same way. I couldn't tell but for sure it was doing something to me.

The first scene that got to me was seeing Jada and Allen by the pond. He was washing her feet and then later on they made love. I've never felt someone's body up against mine like that. I've never had someone so into me that nothing else in the world mattered. That shit affected me, but then I turned it off because that's like allowing somebody to control your feelings. It helped that the sistah in the next scene made jokes about it. Scottie and I laughed pretty easily, but sharing any other type of emotion seemed like it was off limits for some reason.

Then toward the end of the movie came the part where the brother of Allen Payne's character shoots these guys in the house and then chases Jada into the bedroom. My heart was pounding like crazy. I couldn't resist saying something.

"I hope he doesn't kill her..."

"That's some crazy shit what he just did, though!" Scottie responded.

I couldn't tell if he was serious or actually responding to something that he wished he could do.

Then Allen Payne's character came into the scene and this movie seriously had me bugging. Still, I played it cool. I watched and I tried to anticipate what was gonna happen. Actually, I could figure it out pretty easily so I closed my eyes, hoping Scottie wouldn't look over at me and think I was scared. Shit, only thing I was scared of was him seeing tears rolling down my face because I felt what was happening on the screen. Even though me and Scottie were semi-close by this time, our emotional boundaries didn't really feel defined, at least not to me they didn't.

Then a gunshot blast echoed inside the movie theater. I could hear other people reacting in front of me, to the side, and to the rear, but I didn't feel any movement from Scottie.

I asked him, "What happened?"

"He shot her. Damn, I didn't expect that shit to happen."

"Whew...this movie was good, huh!"

"Hold up!" Scottie said as he leaned forward.

"What's wrong?"

"How they end up on a bus together? Her ass just got shot, point blank range in her chest!"

"Don't take it so serious, Scottie. It's just a movie."

"Yeah, whatever…They just trying to throw a happy ending on there 'cause they afraid to keep it real. That's bogus!"

"Can we go, Scottie? The movie was good to me."

"Yeah, let's go. That ending was whack, though."

Scottie teased me during most of the walk home. He said he could tell I didn't want to see Jada get shot. He said it was nice to see I still had a soft spot in me.

"I know you try to be hard, Leesha, but on the real, not everything is so easy to brush off like it's nothing," he told me.

"What about you?"

"What about me?"

"You brush stuff off all the time…"

"Yeah, I probably do, but that's a lot better than losing my mind from reacting to all the craziness that goes down."

Scottie went into one of his usual pep talks that he'd give me just before we'd say goodnight. He told me that I needed to stay strong and not let my situation at home affect me at school. As easy as that came out of his mouth, I wondered how I'd do trying to accomplish it. I get angry as soon as I go home. I think Scottie and I had that in common. He had issues with his brother and Mama was only giving me about five seconds of eye contact each day. Quality time had become a childhood memory.

I felt really good in the eleventh grade because somehow, I had a handle on all my studies. No matter what they threw at me in math, English, or science classes, I aced that shit. When I wasn't hanging with Scottie or locked up in my bedroom at home, I was at school, studying what I needed to know. I started having nightmares of what life would be like if I got held back in my last two years. I pictured myself going crazy at home with Mama and Victor and being some old-ass adult, going to continuation high school or taking sewing classes to fill up my "me" time. I wasn't about to be like that. Scottie always kept reminding me how he'd kick my ass if I messed up in school. I know he'd be playing, but it's cool to have that kind of support. Mama don't even ask me how I'm doing in school. I gotta pry shit out of her to get her to say something.

Most times she just snaps back at me and then I'll just turn and walk away.

Mama still asks me about once a week if my father has called. It's been so long since Grammy's party that I'd pretty much forgotten about him trying to reunite with me. I let that shit stay in the past where it belongs. Mama don't believe me, though. She thinks I'm keeping secrets. She says that's something I inherited from him.

"Your daddy always kept secrets from me. That's why he ain't here being a man or a father!" she'd say.

That's when I'd usually turn my back and walk away. But before I'd walk out the room completely, I'd say the same old thing. "Sorry, Mama, I ain't heard from him."

That's when I can see her waving me off like I don't know what I'm talking about. I don't understand why she even asks me anything if she can't accept my answer. Mama act like a silly bitch most times, anyway.

One typical day at Dorsey High seemed a little different from most. Weather-wise it was the same. I'd hate waking up because it was always so cloudy in the mornings. Gray skies made you think it was still too early to get up and when you got to school, you felt really lazy until it burned off and the skies were blue again. This day was no exception but in all those classes that I'd been acing before, I went completely blank on. The worse example was in English when I had to recite a poem. I got up in front of the class and froze up. My mind was like pockets of air colliding with each other inside my head. The teacher wasn't giving us any second chances. We either had to know the poem by heart or take an F. I didn't care about the reaction of the other students. Most of them fucked up on purpose because almost everybody hated the assignment.

I tried to shake it off before the next class. I even searched for somebody to talk to. I didn't have any real friends in school. I got so desperate that I talked to this one girl who I didn't even like. She was in my physical education class. Her name was Hazel Farlice. All the guys liked her and the gym teachers checked her out, too, because she had the body of someone much older. She had that kind of figure where either she was gonna keep what she had or just balloon and get fat. In the hallways, I could always overhear the boys talking about how they wanna get with her.

I stopped to talk to Hazel right after third-period class let out. She was sitting by herself, looking through her lunch bag.

I approached her. "Hazel, what's up, girl?"

"Leesha, hey…"

"Mind if I sit with you?"

"No," she said as if saying that word was completely new to her.

I sat down but I didn't say anything at first. I kind of pushed my hair back and took deep breaths.

"You okay?" she asked.

"Yeah, why?"

"You seem bothered…"

"I don't know. Today just feels really strange."

"Maybe you're going through um, your…"

"Nah…nothing like that, girl…This is the first day in a long time where I felt just as uncomfortable as I did back when I first came to this school."

"Why?"

"That's just it, I don't know!"

"Something must be wrong because we never really talked before."

"What, we talk in gym class!"

"Not really, Leesha. We might give each other looks or say a quick hello, but we never sat next to each other and talked. I never been sure that you even like me."

"Oh, sorry about that…I've been keeping to myself this year. I used to get into so much trouble before that I don't even want to come close to messing up again."

"Yeah, I remember hearing about that fight with Janina. That gave you a reputation for a long time and then you started hanging out with that guy that everybody says is in the Crips gang."

"We not friends no more…That was all last year, Hazel. When it comes time for me to graduate, I'm gonna run as far away from here as I can. I don't even wanna come back to those reunions they have when everybody is all old."

"Yeah, I guess. Why do you feel so uncomfortable all of a sudden?"

"I wish I knew…So, umm, what do you do when you leave from here every day, Hazel?"

"Go home, don't you?"

"Yeah…I guess I just thought you always had some place to go."

"Some place to go?"

"You know, maybe you got a boyfriend or something."

"Oh, no, my parents kind of strict about that right now. If I like a guy, he has to come see me because my father would leave work and hunt me down if I was hanging out with some guy."

"And you ain't never tried?"

"Why would you ask me that?"

"You're the one person everybody talks about in gym class and in the hallways. You don't hear that shit?"

Hazel started to bite her lips. I wasn't sure why I was sweating her, but it was better than trying to figure out what my problem was. She looked just as uncomfortable as I was.

"Leesha, I've almost been raped a couple times at this school so I don't know what you heard, but it…"

"Hold up, Hazel…You been almost raped?"

"Yeah, these guys don't care around here. They just wait for you to be alone and then they try to take advantage."

"If that was me, I'd find somebody to kick they ass."

"It wasn't you, Leesha, it was me. And, I don't have any thug friends."

"Yeah, whatever…"

Hazel stood up and grabbed her things.

"What, you leaving now?" I asked her.

She didn't respond but she acted as if she were gonna burst into tears behind being so angry.

Hazel took a deep breath. "Leesha, I thought we were gonna just talk regular. Why you have to be so hard and say stuff like that?"

"Like what? You can't be trippin' forever and letting some fool have control over you. You gonna run home from school every single day?"

"I'm not running, Leesha!"

Hazel's eyes went from one tear to an overflowing well. She held all her things tightly against her chest and looked around to see if anyone noticed her crying. I felt bad so I reached out to her but she pulled back.

"Hazel, I'm sorry…Damn, girl, I don't know what I'm saying. I'm just trying to get through my own craziness. I'm not trying to bring you down, too. Maybe it's a new habit of mine. You know, treat somebody else like shit even though I'm the one with the real problem."

Hazel listened and seemed to relax her arms a little bit. She glanced at the bench as if to suggest she might be willing to sit back down.

"Come on, I didn't mean anything bad. Plus, I have this friend that I hang out with that just talks shit all the time. It sort of rubbed off on me and I have to remember when to stop being like that."

"Boyfriend?"

"Not like that…He's just a friend. You might think he's a thug and there's probably a lot that I don't know about him, but he's always cool."

"What school does he go to?"

"He just started going to West L.A."

Hazel seemed very curious, acting like we were homegirls and I was about to tell her about some older guy I might be in love with. I started to laugh at her.

"Why you laughing, Leesha?" she asked.

"'Cause of how you all excited now…Scottie is like a big brother to me. I ain't even thought about seeing somebody or even met someone I like, yet."

"Okay. Hey, I have to go now…"

"So, we cool now? I didn't mean to get you down."

"Yeah, I'm fine. I'll see you later in gym class, okay?"

"Okay, Hazel…"

She ran off to wherever she was headed to and I stayed right there at that outside lunch table. I felt like my whole day was screwed up so I decided to skip my fourth-period class, home economics. I didn't care about missing it because our regular teacher was out sick. Plus, there were so many kids hanging out in the hallways and on campus that it seemed like the school didn't care about forcing anybody to go to class. They were just happy not to see a bunch of kids walking up and down the streets.

Since it was early in the day, I took a chance and called Scottie from the payphone near the cafeteria. He didn't answer but his brother did.

"Is Scottie home?" I asked.

"Who is this?"

"Leesha…"

Charles started to laugh. "You just all on his jock, ain't you? Why you can't find some young dude at the high school? You want you a thug, huh?"

"Can you just let me talk to Scottie?"

I tried not to let Charles bother me. I knew that if I got angry, he'd only laugh and keep talking a bunch of trash.

"Hold on, here that nigga now…," he said. Then I could hear him saying something to Scottie probably as he handed the phone to him. "Yo, you need to tap that young ass, young blood. Don't let that shit go to waste!"

"Man, give me the phone! I told you about that shit. Why you gotta be such a fuckin' hardhead?" Scottie responded and then answered the phone. "Hello?"

"Scottie, it's me, Leesha…"

"Hey, what up? Where you at right now?"

"School…"

"Okay, I was fixing to say…What you doing, skipping class?"

"Yeah…"

"Aw man, what's up with that? Hold up, I'm walking to my room."

I listened and could hear Scottie tell his brother to shut up. Then I heard a door slam shut.

"Scottie, you there?" I asked.

"I'm here. I just came into my room 'cause Charles be trippin' for some reason whenever I talk to you. I don't know what's up with that fool besides too much crack in his system. So, you alright? What's up?"

"I've just been feeling strange today. It's like nothing is going right."

"It's called a bad day, Leesha. Stop trippin' and go to class."

"Whatever…"

"I know you think you fine and everything, but even the fine girls have bad days, too. You still human…You probably need to get you a boyfriend. I seen how you was looking during those love scenes in that movie."

"You crazy...I wasn't looking at nothing! A guy right now would be too much trouble."

"When is the last time you had a boyfriend?"

"That's none of your business."

"Why you wanna say it like that?"

"Honestly? I've never had a boyfriend."

"Damn, for real?"

"Never...I've always had someone in the family to hang out with. Growing up it was always Luther so I just never really missed hanging out with a guy like that, you know, as a boyfriend."

"Yeah, but Leesha..."

"Scottie, didn't you used to tell me how I got to keep these guys at a distance? I forget how you said it, but you know what I mean."

"Yeah, I said that but as fine as you are, you can pick and choose who you want. You should get you one of them really smart dudes at school. You know, somebody that's gonna grow up one day and be running shit at IBM or something."

"Whatever, Scottie..."

"You think I'm playing but I'm actually serious. It's all about choices, Leesha. You don't wanna be nothing like your mother just like I don't wanna be like my brother. You seeing all this shit play out so make sure you don't repeat your mother's mistakes."

"What about you?"

"What about me?"

"What choices you making?"

"I'm out here doing what I gotta do, Leesha. I'm going to school 'cause I got future plans to really go legit but at the same time, my hustle has gotta stay strong, you feel me?"

"I'm not sure, Scottie. You sound like you do some other things that I don't know about..."

"I do, Leesha, but you don't really need to know."

"Why?"

"You just don't. Go to class, girl. I have to start getting ready for school, my damn self."

"Okay, so talk to you later?"

"Yeah, okay."

Scottie always had me wondering what else he did besides sell a little weed in the neighborhood. That one time when he threw the rock through the window and screamed for his money showed me another side of him. He takes risks like a true thug. That kind of excites me, I can't front. His suggestion about finding me a smart boyfriend doesn't appeal to me as much. And like I told Hazel, there hasn't been anyone around that I like. Maybe I was hanging out with Scottie too much. Maybe that kept me from even giving somebody else a second thought. It was something to think about; me having a boyfriend. Scottie was right about that movie, though. I did look and that scene had me tingling all over.

My last class each day was physical education. I liked that about my schedule. I could always end my day taking it easy if I wanted to. Sometimes I would take my showers here so I wouldn't have to worry about going home and taking one while Victor was lurking around.

Hazel Farlice also had P.E. for her last class of the day. She approached me with all smiles on her face. She seemed more at ease about speaking to me so I didn't bust her bubble by giving her strange looks. I wanted to but I remembered how choked up she'd gotten when I started teasing her about all the talking behind her back.

"Hey, Hazel, what you all smiles about?" I asked her.

"Nothing...You feeling better, Leesha? What happened after we talked?"

"Oh, my day was shitty but I'm cool now since the day is pretty much over. I called Scottie and he teased me. He said I'm just going through a regular bad day."

"Maybe you are. I mean, why do you think anything different?"

An image of that knife that I'd seen in the streets flashed through my mind. I didn't want to tell Hazel about it, but the thought kept me silent for a moment. My mind was drifting off and Hazel was steady talking.

"What you think about that?" she asked.

"Huh?"

"Haven't you been listening to me?"

"Uh-huh, I'm glad the day is over. too!"

"That's not what I was saying. You weren't even listening to me."

"What did you say?"

"I'm thinking about changing my style a little bit. Maybe start wearing my hair in braids and just be different, somehow. My parents will probably try to kill me, though."

"Oh, you don't need to change anything, Hazel. You should be glad you have two parents that care and that pay attention to you. At least you don't go home having to watch your back all night and argue with your mother every time you see her."

"That's what happens with you?"

"Every day…"

"Why?"

"'Cause my mama is stupid and she got an asshole for a boyfriend."

"Leesha, the way you talk sometimes is really something. I wish I could be more like you where I don't care what others think."

"I don't know. I don't want anyone having control over me. I like controlling my own shit. That's the one thing that I respected about Janina with her fake ass. She was in control, especially when it comes to the guys that always tried to hit on her."

"Janina…I haven't seen her in a long time. Does she still go to school here?"

"I think she got her wish and transferred to Palisades High so she could be near all that money."

"I guess. Hey Leesha?"

"Yeah…"

"You think we could hang out? I think it would be cool if you came over to my house."

"House…where you stay at?"

"Up in View Park."

"And you going to Dorsey?"

"Yeah. Dorsey has a lot of good programs and even some internships with those movie studios. That's what I want to get into someday."

"What, you wanna be an actress?"

"No, I want to do screenplays and maybe be a director."

"Your parents should've sent you to private school. You could probably have a better chance at doing that stuff because those studio people send their kids to private school, too."

"Maybe so but my father wants me not to forget where I came from. He went to Dorsey, too, and he says it's the kind of school that will keep me grounded in reality plus give me opportunities to achieve what I want. So, I'm here!"

"And, you told him about almost being raped?"

"No way!"

"Why not?"

"My father would be down here so fast and probably try to have me point out who did it!"

"What's wrong with that?"

"I like going here now and that kind of attention would mess things up for me. I've got one more year after this and I want my senior year to be really good."

"I hear you, girl. I just think it's kind of cool to have a father who cares like that."

"Where's your father?"

"D.C."

"Oh..."

"Yeah, I just saw him over the summer, too."

"You went to visit him?"

"No, he came to this party that my grandmother had."

"Oh cool. You two hung out while he was here?"

"Nah, I told him he needed to take his ass back to D.C."

"No you didn't!"

"Yes, I did."

"Why would you say that to your own father?"

"'Cause he ain't been a father to me since I was two years old. I don't even remember his ass. I didn't even know his name until a few months ago."

"Oh, I'm sorry. You think you'll ever talk to him again?"

"I don't know. He has a sister out here and he told me I could always go there if I ever wanted to get in touch with him. I guess he knows Mama will be all on my ass if she knows I'm contacting my father."

"That must be really hard, Leesha."

"I don't know. At this point, I don't really care. I'm just trying to hurry up and graduate, get me a good job, and get the fuck away from Mama."

"You going to college?"

"I guess. I mean, my grades are really cool right now. I'm surprising myself with how well I've been doing. I guess I could go to college."

It was a trip how well Hazel and I got along. In one day we'd become pretty cool with each other. My opinion of her changed even though I still thought of her as a good chick who was kind of naïve about a lot of stuff. Her desire to be friends seemed pretty sincere and she didn't look down on me just because I didn't have what she had.

Hazel acted all concerned when we started talking about our fathers again. Actually, she's the one who brought up the subject. I was trying to watch for the gym teacher because we were really supposed to be either walking or running around the track with the other students in the class. I didn't care what kind of grade I got in P.E., but I did want to at least pass.

"Leesha, where does your father's sister live?" Hazel asked.

"She lives in Long Beach."

"Oh, that's not too far."

"Shit, it's far enough to me. Probably what, an hour away?"

"Yeah, but I was thinking that if you ever want to go, I can get one of my parents to take us…"

"Us?"

"Yeah, I'd go with you just for support…"

"That's okay, Hazel. I can't see myself going anytime soon."

"Okay. Well, class is almost over. Let me know if you ever want to hang out together, Leesha."

"I will, thanks."

"Okay…See you tomorrow!"

Hazel walked away as if she were disappointed by me not accepting her offer. I get defensive whenever someone tries to offer too much help right away. Hazel was cool but I had problems with letting anyone else know more about me, privately. I could already picture Hazel trying to come over and then be able to see how I live. Was I ashamed of Mama and where I lived? Yes, I was, and I didn't want Hazel and her perfect life coming anywhere near my street.

When I got home from school, Victor was in his usual spot. He waved at me and watched as I walked into the kitchen. He had a half-smile on his face and was sucking on his teeth. The noise was annoying, especially because I couldn't stand his ass.

"Why don't you grab me one of those beers in there, baby…," he said.

I pretended I didn't hear a word.

"I was talking to you, Leesha."

My heart started to beat rapidly as I noticed the tone in Victor's voice change. I started to wonder if maybe he'd already had too much to drink and I was gonna have to fight his drunk ass.

"No wonder your father all the way on the other side of the country. He got a daughter that don't know how to mind folks. You need to have your ass beat, girl. Your mama probably didn't discipline you at all and now you think you the shit 'cause you pretty and getting older. Shit, what you doing over there in that kitchen? You don't know how to cook!"

I glanced inside the refrigerator and as usual, found nothing but cold cuts, lettuce, and cheese. Mama would only bring home enough food to make Victor's dinner each night. Her ass was coming home nights to fix gourmet meals for that nigga and spending a grip just to buy all that shit. Then he would wash it all down with a forty-ounce and fall asleep on the couch after that. Now that Victor was living with us, he took full advantage over Mama's weakness to have a man close by.

I stood over the counter making myself a sandwich while Victor continued to attack me from behind with words that bounced off the walls and landed in that part of me that wished I could do more than just imagine him dead. I was cool as long as he remained on the couch. I kept my eyes focused on the bread as I spread Miracle Whip on each slice. Then I ripped open the package of ham and placed one slice on top of the bread, followed by a little lettuce.

"You making one of those sandwiches for me? I'm still waiting for my beer. I know your ass heard me the first time!" Victor said.

After I finished making my sandwich, I placed everything back in the refrigerator and pulled out the bottled water. That's all we had to drink. I'd usually have to stop by the liquor store if I wanted something other than water, but I didn't have any money. Victor stood up after I poured my glass of water. I could see him out of the corner of my eye, which almost caused me to knock over the glass as I reached to pick it up.

"You got a hearing problem?" he asked. "I said do you have a hearing problem? I've been saying shit to you the last ten minutes and you ain't responded yet!"

I looked at Victor standing with both his arms to his side and his chest sticking out. He had on a dirty white T-shirt over some faded dark-blue pants that looked like the kind mechanics wear. He had no shoes or socks on his feet so as I glared at him up and down, I noticed his crusty-looking toes. The sight of him fueled my angry response. I couldn't hold it back any longer.

"Fuck you!" I told him.

My face was all frowned up like I was daring him to do something.

"Say what? You better turn your ass back around and get my beer. That much I know!"

"You need to leave me alone! Who you think you are?"

"You keep talking shit, I'm about to show you in a minute!"

I glanced over at the counter to see where I had left the knife that I used for making my sandwiches. If Victor was to make a move on me, I was gonna grab it and try my best to use it on him.

"Yeah, that's right. You need to back up and get my beer 'cause I ain't letting you leave this room without showing some respect."

I swallowed hard. I tried to psyche myself up for the possibility that I might have to stab this man. I wasn't about to fetch his beer and then get close enough for him to grab me.

Victor took a couple steps forward and I backed up against the counter. He smiled and pulled up his sagging pants.

"Uh-huh, see, all you have to do is bring me my beer and we wouldn't have to go through this. I told your mother I would teach you some discipline," he said as he inched his way forward with one more step.

I reached slowly for the knife while keeping my eyes on him. I could feel the coldness of the steel. It was slippery because I'd touched the blade part where it still had Miracle Whip on it. I found the handle and gripped it tightly. I waited for Victor's next move. Then as he stepped forward once again, very slowly, Mama's bedroom door opened.

"Are y'all arguing out here? What's all that noise?" Mama asked.

"Mama, you're home?"

"Yeah, Leesha, I'm home. Now, what's going on out here?"

I looked at Victor to see if he was gonna answer Mama. He didn't and neither did I, but I kept my grip on the knife until he turned around and walked back to the couch.

"Anyway, you two need to keep it down 'cause I'm on the phone with the hospital. They want me to come down there, but I ain't hardly think it's necessary," Mama said.

"Why you talking to the hospital?" I asked.

"'Cause your grandmother is there acting like she can't breathe all of a sudden. She ain't never showed no signs of high blood pressure before and now all of a sudden she's feeling dizzy. She just being a little drama queen, that's all."

"I'll go see her!"

"How you gonna get there?"

"I'll take the bus."

"It's too late to be riding the bus way over to Cedars-Sinai. If she still in the hospital this weekend, Victor will take us to visit her. Ain't that right, sweetheart?"

"I sure will, baby...," Victor responded.

I looked at Mama in disbelief. I was fearful that something could happen to Grammy while she was in the hospital.

"Can I talk to Grammy?" I asked.

"I don't know about tonight, Leesha. You can try tomorrow."

I grabbed my sandwich and glass of water. I left the room without even so much as uttering another word to Mama. I could hear Victor snickering and I could see him from the corner of my eye, smiling. I closed my bedroom door behind me and locked it. I was in for the night and had no intentions of leaving unless I desperately had to go to the bathroom because I couldn't hold it any longer.

I ate my sandwich and stared out the window. I started to hate my window because at this point I was getting much too old to always be locking myself in my room. The view of my street was the same as any other night. And if I stuck my head outside, I'd see the same people hanging out in the same places.

After I ate my sandwich and drank my water, I waited for about an hour before I'd poked my head out the door. As always, the television was still on, but I couldn't see if Victor was still on the couch or not. I wanted to use the phone. Victor took it from my room because he's always using it. Mama has the other phone in her room.

I pushed my bedroom door open and left it that way while I turned around to pick up my empty glass. When I turned back around, Victor was standing there with a big grin on his face. This time he was walking around with only his T-shirt and boxer shorts on. He had ashy legs and he stood there with his arms folded, acting like I was supposed to know what he wants.

"What's up, young lady?" he said softly.

"Nothing..."

"Where you going to?"

"Living room..."

"Is that right? Well, I'm in there watching something."

"So..."

"Don't start, Leesha. We don't want to wake up your mama."

"If you try something, I will—"

"Try something? What am I supposed to try?"

"You're blocking my way, Victor. You need to move!" I said as I pushed my way past him.

"Shush! It's cool, Leesha. I'll move out your precious way. Girl, you are getting fine as can be with all that long hair..."

I could feel Victor's nasty thoughts reaching out toward me like a thousand hands pulling at my clothes. I looked back at him and he was still standing in front of my bedroom door. He had his hand on his crotch. His eyes were focused on my ass. I felt like throwing my glass at him. I wished Mama could see how her man acts when she's not in the room, but she'd probably blame me before she'd even think about him being wrong.

I placed my glass in the kitchen and then walked over to the living room area in search of the telephone. "Where's the phone?" I asked Victor.

"It's over there somewhere, but your ass don't need to be using the phone at this hour. Ain't you got school in the morning?"

"Don't worry about it!"

"Hey, you need to lower your damn voice…Why you hate me so much?"

I didn't respond to Victor's question. I continued to look for the phone. Victor had newspapers and magazines scattered all over the place so I was picking stuff up as I searched. When I picked up some of the newspaper I noticed the carpet was wet. Then I'd seen an Old English bottle laying on its side underneath the paper and figured out why.

"Don't you know you spilled some beer over here?" I asked him.

"Say what? I ain't spilled no damn beer. You trippin' now."

"Where did you hide the damn phone at?"

"You better watch how you talk to me! You just in high school and I'm old enough to be your father."

"Yeah, but you ain't my father…You don't even work, do you?"

"I got laid off but I might have something lined up pretty soon at this glass-making company."

"That'll be perfect for you since you know so much about bottles."

"At least your young ass got a sense of humor, I see. Why don't you sit down and just talk to me 'cause I ain't going nowhere. You might as well get used to me living here."

"That's alright."

"Who you calling at this time a night, anyway?"

"I can't call nobody until I find the phone."

"It's over there behind the couch."

Victor pointed to a section of the couch that I hadn't searched yet. I looked behind it and found the phone off the hook. It was all greasy and slipped out of my hand the first time I tried to pick it up. I could hear Victor laughing, but I wasn't so sure if it was because I dropped the phone or for some other reason.

I turned to look at him and could definitely tell what was on his dirty mind. I decided against using the phone and returned to my bedroom.

"Where you going now?" Victor asked.

"Where does it look like I'm going?"

"You ain't nothing but a little bitch..."

"Fuck you..." I responded before walking into my bedroom.

When I turned to check Victor's reaction, he started to walk toward me like he was gonna do something so I slammed my door shut and locked it. After a few minutes, I could hear Mama asking what was going on. Then I heard someone trying to turn my doorknob just before Mama spoke outside my door.

"Leesha, was that you slamming your door?" she asked.

"Yeah, that was me!"

"Unlock this door!"

"Tell your man to leave me alone!"

"I'm not gonna tell you again, unlock this damn door!"

I walked over to the door, unlocked it, and then returned to my bed. I sat there waiting for Mama to open it. I waited for her to come in and defend that asshole she calls her man. I could hear Victor saying something but I couldn't tell what. It sounded like he was talking about me and knowing Mama, she believed anything that man said.

Mama opened the door once she and Victor stopped talking. She opened it slowly until she found me staring directly at her. Mama seemed a lot calmer than when she was telling me to unlock the door.

"Leesha, Victor told me you were upset because he wouldn't let you use the phone. Who you trying to call at this hour?" Mama asked.

"Nobody..."

"Uh-huh, well, does this nobody have a name? Is it that person I saw you with at your grandmother's party?"

"Who, Scottie?"

"I don't know his name…"

"How's Grammy doing?"

"Was you trying to call the hospital?"

Having a conversation with Mama was a struggle. She and I just kept answering each other with questions. She wasn't hearing what I'd say and I damn sure didn't care what she was talking about. It was clear that Mama placed Victor before me and what's worse, she showed no concern about Grammy being in the hospital.

"I'd like to go to sleep now…," I told Mama.

"Well, you need to start being nice to Victor, Leesha. I'm tired of coming home and hearing him complaining about how you show him no respect. That man treats me good."

Victor stood behind Mama, smiling and winking at me. I could see he loved every word of what she was saying. He was proud that he had Mama wrapped around his finger. Her heart continued to keep her from recognizing she was in love with an asshole. I wanted to slam the door in her face, too, just like I'd done to Victor. Instead I folded my arms and waited for her to finish talking. I rolled my eyes constantly and wanted to throw up when she started telling me how good Victor could be for us.

"You give him a chance and you'll see he could be the man your father never was," Mama told me.

After she'd said that, I almost lost my mind. I stood up and reached for the door.

"Is you crazy?" Mama said.

She looked where my hand was, gripping the edge of my bedroom door.

"If you think I'm gonna let you slam the door in my face, you must be crazy! I see now what Victor was talking about. When your grandmother gets better, I'm gonna talk to her about you staying over there unless you change your ways. I can't be having you disrespecting Victor and acting like you grown. You don't pay no kind of rent up in here! You getting too old to be acting like some spoiled brat. What you got to say?"

I looked at Mama really hard. My eyes started to tear up because I was so mad. She stood there waiting for me to respond to her. She looked like she was smiling because she knew that she'd gotten to me. Victor's smile was more obvious. I took another look at him standing behind her. That's when I started to talk without really thinking. My eyes were half closed because I was frowning so much. I just said what I'd felt.

"Victor is an asshole, Mama, and he don't think shit about you…He just using you and turning you into a—"

Before I could finish, Mama slapped me. It wasn't too hard because I was standing so close to her but I felt the tips of her nails travel from my forehead on down beneath my eye. I could feel a sharp pain as if she'd scratched me deep enough to break my skin. I touched my face as Mama shouted at me.

"Don't you ever let me hear you curse like that in my damn house! Who the hell do you think you are? Huh? Girl, I feel like slapping you again! You better close your door and stay your ass in your bedroom…"

I looked at my fingertips and there was blood. Mama had scratched me not only on the top of my cheek, beneath my eye but also just above my eyebrow. She reached for the doorknob and pulled the door shut. I could hear her talking to Victor until another door slammed and then I heard nothing but muffled voices. She'd returned to her bedroom and it sounded like Victor was with her. I sat on my bed, allowing the blood to trickle down my face. I didn't have a mirror in my room so I only imagined what I looked like and I didn't care. It wasn't just blood trickling down my face. It was tears, too. I stayed angry and even fell asleep that way.

I awoke the next morning, still in my clothes with my shoes on my feet. When my eyes focused on the clock that sat beside my bed, it read nine o'clock. I was supposed to get up at six in order to be ready for school. I was way past late. I felt like I didn't even have time to change clothes. I was still feeling angry over Mama slapping me and how she defended Victor. I didn't want to leave my room let alone go to school. I sat back down on my bed wondering if I should pretend to be sick. Pretending would be easy because Mama never checked on me anyway. With Victor in her life, I was on my own. I had to make sure I did whatever was necessary to get to school. If I didn't see school as a way to get away from Mama, I'd probably never go, but I'd die if I had to spend too many more years living with her.

It was strange not hearing any sounds on the other side of my bedroom door. I figured that Victor would at least be trying to bother me because I hadn't left for school yet. I didn't even hear any noise coming from Mama's room. There I sat within the four walls of my bedroom trying to guess what was going on outside my door. I didn't like that feeling. It was as if I were afraid to leave my room. That very thought gave me reason to stand up, open my door, and walk straight into the living room. When I looked around there was no Victor. And when I walked towards Mama's room, the door was open and I could tell no one was in there either. I had the place to myself and I was happy about that. I could get ready for school in peace and not have to watch my back. Something didn't feel right about it but I wasn't gonna trip. Then I thought about calling Scottie but I knew he'd spend most of the conversation asking me why I wasn't in school.

Being home alone for a change was addicting. I turned on the television, kicked off my shoes, and then went into the kitchen to make me something to eat. There wasn't much to choose from so I made some eggs and fried some bologna in the pan. I had the place smelling like breakfast time, for real. I was smiling and just loving what felt like freedom to me. I fixed my plate and poured a glass of water. Then I walked over toward the living room area with my food in hand, excited because nobody was around but me. That's when Mama and Victor walked in.

Mama looked at me with a cold hard stare. She didn't say anything. Her eyes glared at me and for a quick second she glanced at the plate in my hand before walking to her room. I watched her and wondered why she didn't say anything. Mama went straight to the phone in her room and started to call someone. Then Victor stepped in front of me, blocking my view.

He asked, "Why you ain't in school?"

I didn't answer him. I stepped to the side so I could see what Mama was doing. I put my plate of food down and walked in the direction of her room. I wanted to get close enough to hear what she was saying.

Victor went about his usual business. He changed the channel on the television to *Jerry Springer* and then went into the kitchen to get a beer. He mumbled something as he stood there opening the bottle.

"Hey babygirl, sorry about your grandmother..."

"What did you say?"

"I don't know how she felt about me but she seemed like good folks, you know. Life is too short, ain't it? Shit..."

"What are you talking about?"

"Oh, uh, you should probably ask your mother..."

I frowned at Victor like I wanted to kick his ass. It was a lost cause trying to ask him anything because once he stopped talking, he started drinking. He returned to the living room and to his favorite spot on the couch. He even started eating my food. I turned to look at Mama and she was steady talking on the phone. She seemed to have an attitude about something. She didn't look upset like something happened to Grammy. She was acting like she was upset behind some money. I could overhear her telling somebody they crazy for asking her to pay something.

I walked closer to Mama's bedroom, hoping she would let me hear what's going on, especially if it had to do with Grammy. As soon as Mama looked up and seen me coming close to her door, she stood up and slammed it in my face. I turned to look at Victor but he was acting like he didn't hear a thing. I really didn't want to ask his ass anything so I waited by Mama's door and listened as closely as I could.

"Your mother might not like you trying to listen through her door like that," Victor said as he noticed what I was doing.

"I don't care. It's not like you telling me anything."

"Yeah well, you gonna find out. That's something you need to hear from her, not from me."

"You already said something! Forget it...I don't even know why I'm trying to talk to you."

"Humph...You little bitch. I'm glad you ain't my damn daughter."

"Fuck you..."

"Watch your damn mouth, Leesha. I told you about that."

"Why, what you gonna do, huh? Huh?"

"Girl...don't you...You testing me and you need to stop..."

I waved Victor off like everything he said meant nothing to me. I wished that he did try something just so I'd have a reason to try and scratch his eyes out or kick him in his nuts. Being so close to a man who I hated so much did nothing for me but constantly make me angry. I looked at him and wished that he would choke on his beer.

Mama swung her door open and almost knocked me down when she came out of her room. She went straight over to Victor and acted as if I wasn't even in the room.

"They broke asses thinking I'm rich like I can just pluck some damn money out the air!" Mama said to Victor.

"What's wrong, baby?"

"These niggas that call themselves family trying to have me pay for most of the funeral. I ain't got that kind of money! They better figure something out 'cause I can't be giving them money I don't have!"

I walked up behind Mama and asked her what was going on. She acted like she didn't hear me at first. Then I touched her shoulder and she pulled away as though she didn't want me touching her.

I asked her, "What funeral you talking about, Mama?"

She looked at me hard and said, "For your grandmother, that's what funeral..."

"I thought Grammy was okay. She in the hospital getting better—"

"People die there, too, Leesha. Now leave me alone while I figure out what to do."

"Mama, Grammy is dead? You supposed to know what to do because you're her daughter!"

"You better get away from me with that, Leesha. I really don't have time to go through some drama with you. Your ass is supposed to be in school anyway. You ain't sick or nothing. Why you ain't in school?"

I looked at Mama in total shock. She didn't seem to care about losing her mother. Her only concern was money. She made me feel like I didn't need to care about her either. I looked at her like some strange woman who didn't give a fuck about anyone but herself. The only thing important to her was feeding her out-of-work, alcoholic boyfriend. She kept asking me about school and I just turned my back on her and walked into my bedroom. I wanted to cry so badly but I didn't want Mama seeing me with tears in my eyes. I didn't want to give her the satisfaction of knowing that losing Grammy made me feel as though I'd died myself.

I put on my shoes, walked back into the living room, and headed for the front door.

Mama turned to look at me. She stood with her arms folded. "You better be taking your ass to school!"

I walked out the front door and didn't even close it behind me. Mama yelled at me as I made my way down the stairs.

"Close the damn door next time! You ain't grown!"

I never broke my stride as I walked through the front gate. I pushed it closed, making it slam twice as loud as it normally did. I could hear the sound echo down the street, traveling in the direction that I began to run. I wasn't going to school. I was running to Grammy's place as a last hope that maybe this was just a bad dream. I kept telling myself that. That's when I began to cry. I cried as I ran up the street to Santa Rosalia. I cried as I ran toward Stocker Street. Tears streamed down my face as I ignored the "don't walk" sign when crossing a very busy Crenshaw Boulevard. I heard someone ask if I was alright but I kept running and didn't respond. For some reason, Grammy's apartment building seemed so far away this time. I started to tire and my legs got really heavy but I didn't want to stop. The pain in my legs got the best of me but luckily by that time I didn't have much farther to go. I could see Grammy's apartment and for some reason I began to smile. I had an ounce of hope left in my heart.

Once I reached the top of the stairs and began knocking on Grammy's door, that ounce of hope began to disappear. I probably knocked more than twenty times. I called out to Grammy hoping I'd hear her voice. I wished she was on the phone and couldn't come to the door right away. The only thing is, Grammy never kept me waiting. She'd put down the phone or stop anything she was doing if she knew I was at the door. I stopped knocking and sank to my knees. I sat by the door and remained there for hours, thinking about Grammy and wishing this day had never come.

The cold air from outside reached me at the top of the stairs where I still remained hours later. After a while I stopped crying but I could feel the stiffness in my face from all the dried-up tears. I sat there listening to the occasional car passing by or the footsteps of an unknown person walking down the street. I felt cut off from the world being up in the stairwell, hidden from sight. I didn't know what to do. My mind was a complete blank and my heart weighed a ton.

I heard footsteps approaching the bottom of the stairs so I leaned forward to see who it could be. I prayed that it wasn't Mama. I thought about her possibly coming over to Grammy's place acting like everything now belonged to her. I was gonna fight her about that but then I'd seen who it was and I was relieved. It was my cousin Luther, pulling up his baggy khakis, and walking up each step carefully.

"Hey, Luther…," I said to let him know I was there.

Luther hadn't looked up as he was walking up the stairs until I'd said something.

"Leesha?" he responded.

"Yeah, it's me."

"What you doing here, cuz?"

"I couldn't believe what happened. I wanted to think it was just a bad dream. Can you tell me that I'm only dreaming and Grammy is somewhere running late, trying to get home?"

"Shit, I wish I could say that, but it is what it is…This ain't no dream, Leesha. They say she in a better place now. I hope that's true."

"You don't believe she is?"

"You know me. I'm thinking that place is better now because of her! It's hard for me sometimes to believe what they say about God and heaven."

"You okay, Luther?"

I noticed a look in Luther's eyes that I'd never seen before. He seemed more than just heartbroken over Grammy. He looked worried as if something else were about to happen.

"I don't know, cuz. What happened to Grammy is really messing with my head. But she lived a good life and that ain't something that I can always say about myself, nah mean?"

"You grew up differently, that's all."

"Yeah, but we still got choices. I don't know, I'm just trippin' and tryin' to figure this all out. I ain't been myself lately…"

"What do you mean?"

"Well, it's like this…I mean, have I ever told you about some of the shit I did before?"

"We never been able to talk about it, Luther."

"True dat…I been in jail and we ain't seen each other in a minute. But I'm saying like this, I've done some shit, Leesha, and I know I probably sounded all proud at the party when I was talking to homeboy."

"You mean Scottie?"

"Yeah, I don't know what he been into. I can tell young dude just be hustling a little bit but me, I put in some work that wasn't about money. It was about being the strongest and feeding off hatred for niggas 'cause they was in a different gang or came from a different hood. Shit like that didn't make us no money. We wasn't helping our families. We was just destroying each other and ending up on the news every night with the same headline about another drive-by in South Central L.A."

Luther had a lot on his mind. He seemed angry and I didn't want to chance interrupting him with too many questions. His voice echoed inside that stairwell. I wondered why he wanted me to know about his past and what it had to do, if anything, with Grammy. I didn't ask. I just continued to listen.

"My life ain't changed much, Leesha," Luther said. "I'm still walking these streets worried about when my number is gonna come up. Sometimes I even be thinking that it's safer to be in jail than it is out here. At least in there I pretty much know who I need to watch. Out on the streets it could be anybody and at the same time, something could pop off while I'm with family, nah mean?"

"Have you ever shot anyone, Luther?"

He nodded his head.

"When did that happen?"

"Shit, it's been a few times. I ain't never been arrested for it, but I've done some things…It's a trip to think about it now but I've been having nightmares lately, just like I did back in the day when it happened."

"I used to ask Grammy if she knew about the things you did, but she wouldn't say much. She always told me that no matter what, she loved you and that was the most important thing to her."

"Yeah, she was real and she always showed me love. I remember I came to her two days after—"

"After what?"

Luther paused, rubbed his face nervously, and frowned as if he were about to say something that was hard to confess.

"I'ma be real with you, cuz…," he warned. "When I came to talk to your grandmother, it was because I needed her love in a way to make me feel like I was human. I mean, I had killed three dudes and never got caught for it."

"What do you mean, you killed them?"

"Straight up…about two weeks before that these same niggas rolled up on one of my homies and when I saw them, it was payback time. I ran up on them with my nine pointed straight at the first one closest to me and pulled the trigger. All three of them was sitting at this food place on Crenshaw and Sixty-seventh Street. They couldn't really move 'cause they was sitting at one of those tables where the bench is connected so if you kinda big, it's hard to get out of them muh-fuckers."

"And you shot the other two?"

"Hell yeah! They legs was locked underneath that bench and plus they was scared so it wasn't much they could do. Then my ass was pretty much unconscious and reacting on adrenaline so after I shot the first dude a couple times, I shot the other two one time. Bam…Bam! Then I stood there for a second and I think I shot one of them again but I'm not sure. That shit happened so quickly and like I said, I wasn't really thinking, I was just… shit, I don't know."

"Nobody saw you?"

"I didn't really care, Leesha. Maybe somebody did but they just ain't said nothing, at least not to the police."

"Wow, Luther…Grammy never told me about that…"

"Nah, I wouldn't expect her to. Plus, she didn't really let me tell her the whole story. She just knew that what I wanted to tell her had to do with taking a life. All she did was give me a hug, told me she loved me, and prayed that none of what I did would ever catch up to me. I don't know, cuz. Now that she's gone, I'm feeling like her prayer gone with her, too, you know?"

"No, I don't understand…"

"It's hard to explain but I just feel it right now…"

Luther and I sat on the stairs for a little while longer. I didn't really know how to feel after he'd confessed to me about what he'd done in his past. The worst part was thinking that he'd probably done more. But despite what Luther told me, all I wanted was to be able to wake up from the bad dream and see Grammy smiling again.

Luther said, "I hope I ain't got you scared of me now…"

"No, I was just thinking."

"About what?"

"I'm still wishing this was a dream."

"I feel you. You probably gonna be thinking like that for a while."

"Why did you come over here?"

"I thought somebody else might be over here from the family. I don't know where the rest of them meeting up at so I just figured that it would be here. I think your mama probably the only one with a key but I'm not sure. She say anything to you?"

"Mama don't care about Grammy…"

"Why you say that?"

"'Cause she don't!"

"She tell you that? Come on, Leesha, that's her mother…"

"Mama was over there cursing somebody out on the phone talking about she didn't have the money for the funeral."

"Damn, who was she talking to?"

"I don't know."

"I'll have to talk to Lynette. You talk to your father since that party?"

"Nope."

"Why not?"

"What for?"

"'Cause you probably should. I don't know what went down in the past but you never know; you might need that dude."

"That's okay…"

"Oh, okay cousin. I tell you what. I'm gonna go find a phone so I can call a few folks and see what's going on. I mean, I talked to Uncle Buddy's wife, Carolyn, but she didn't know much. You remember her, right?"

"Yeah, I know who you talking about."

"Uncle Buddy know some peoples over at Angelus funeral home so he probably trying to get things together. I'ma see if I can't get in contact with him. I'll be back. You gonna be here for a while?"

"I guess so, maybe…"

"Okay, well, I'ma come back anyway just to see if you still here. If not then you be careful going back home, cuz, alright?"

"I will…"

Luther walked down the stairs and took one last look up at me. He waved and then left me there to go find a pay telephone. Most likely he would have to head back up to Crenshaw. I listened to his footsteps as he walked away and then I got up. I didn't feel like sitting in front of Grammy's apartment any longer. I felt like it was time to go back home and see if Mama was gonna say something about Grammy or ask me where I've been.

When I got halfway down my block, I saw what looked like Scottie, standing in front of my apartment. I could faintly tell it was him by the way he was pacing and smoking a cigarette. Then he stopped and noticed me coming up the street. I was glad he didn't yell out my name because I didn't want Mama knowing I was close by. Scottie waved and walked toward me. He took one last puff from his cigarette before he approached. His face appeared out of the cloud of smoke he exhaled, and as usual, he had a big smile.

"What's up, Leesha?" Scottie greeted.

"Hey…"

"You okay?"

"Yeah, I think so."

"I heard about what happened from your mother. She seems kind of pissed though, but she did tell me that your grandmother passed away."

"Mama don't care. She mad because she might have to help pay the funeral costs."

"Oh, okay. When I was trying to ask her about you, she just gave me straight answers and was talking like she frustrated about something. I didn't go inside but I could see that dude chillin' on the couch. He still ain't working, huh?"

"Victor, no he don't work. I thought I was gonna have to stab him this morning."

"Say what?"

"I don't know. He was talking shit and walking toward me like he might do something so I had this knife in my hand and—"

"Damn, Leesha, that shit ain't cool...I didn't know your situation was like that."

"I'll be alright..."

"Where was you at just now? You coming from school?"

"No, I didn't go."

"You heard about your grandmother and couldn't concentrate on school, huh?"

"No, I had a hard time getting up this morning. I was up really late last night because of...Scottie, can we just go somewhere? I don't want to talk about Mama and Victor right now."

"Where we gonna go to?"

"Over your place...I don't even care if your brother is there, let's just go."

"Alright, bet, let's go."

Scottie and I walked to his apartment. We didn't say a word to each other the whole time. I think Scottie wasn't sure what to say, especially after I reached for his hand and held it. I could feel a little nervousness in his grip. It was like he was unsure if he should even be holding my hand.

When we made it to the front of his apartment, he let go and sort of looked in both directions of the street he lived on. I wondered if he were concerned that someone might've seen us holding hands but I didn't ask him. Scottie opened the front door and once we stepped inside, I was surprised to see that his brother wasn't sitting in darkness like he usually did. But then I heard a noise coming from the bathroom.

Scottie asked, "Hey bruh, you in there?"

"Yeah, I'm in here. What, you gotta go?"

"Nah, just checking."

Scottie looked at me. "That nigga probably in there smoking. Let's go in the room."

I followed Scottie into his bedroom and like the last time, he went straight to his stereo system.

"I hope we not gonna listen to King Tee again…," I said.

"Nah, I'm gonna put on something cool. Plus, you may want to talk about your grandmother. I want you to know that, well, you know, it's cool to cry if you want to."

"Scottie, I been crying all day. I'm tired right now."

"Okay, so, chill on my bed right there while I get us something to drink. You cool with some orange soda?"

"Yeah, that's fine."

"Alright, I'll be back in a sec."

I sat on Scottie's bed and leaned back. I looked around his room. I didn't really pay much attention to it the last time I was there. Scottie wasn't a junky person at all. I laughed at the music he had playing. It was the Force MD's "Love Is A House." I like that song. I remember watching the video all the time on *Video Soul*.

Scottie had mirrors on his closet doors and in the reflection I could see some magazines under his bed. I reached down to look at what he liked to read.

"Ooh Scottie!" I said out loud.

He had some *Players* magazines. He also had a whole bunch of *Jet* magazines, but I was mostly curious to look through his *Players* collection. I felt strange as I turned each page. Maybe strange isn't the word. I felt a tingling sensation going through my body. I skimmed through the pages as fast as I could. I unconsciously crossed my legs while wondering what Scottie felt when he'd look at these naked women in his magazines.

"Yo Leesha, what's up? What you doing, gurl?" Scottie asked as he stood in the doorway of his bedroom holding a liter bottle of orange soda and two glasses.

Magazines went flying everywhere! All the ones that were in my lap and on the bed were now scattered all over the floor. Scottie watched as I nervously tried to pick everything up. He closed the door behind him, placed the glasses he held on top of his television, and began pouring the soda. He didn't even pretend like he was gonna help me pick up the mess I made. He glanced at me a couple times and shook his head.

"Yo, I hope you gonna put those back where you found them."

"I will..."

"Here's your soda. I wish I could offer you some chips or something but we ain't got shit in the kitchen. I'm the only one that really be buying anything and I ain't had no kind of time with school and being out there trying to make ends. My brother don't do shit so you know how things are..."

"Scottie, it's okay."

It really bothered Scottie that he couldn't do more for me. It sort of made me feel a little bit guilty because there I was having fantasies about him, but he was still treating me like I was his little sister, worried about me having something to eat.

"So, what's up, Leesha? You done fooling with my magazines?"

"I wasn't doing nothing to your nasty magazines."

"I saw you, Leesha. For a long time you didn't even notice I was standing there. You'd probably still be looking if I didn't say nothing."

"Whatever, Scottie..."

"Yeah, I got your 'whatever,' Leesha. You just make sure you put it back the way I had it."

"I put them back the way I found them. Don't worry."

Scottie handed me one of the glasses of orange soda that he poured. He smiled and gestured for me to sit back down on the bed. "Let's talk 'cause I know it ain't cool losing your grandmother."

"I don't know how I'm supposed to feel anymore," I confessed, letting Scottie know that I wasn't as tough as I pretended to be. I took a sip of the soda and then put my glass down on top of his dresser.

"I hear you."

"Luther came over to Grammy's while I was there."

"Your cousin? That's cool...How's he taking it?"

"He's sad about it. I don't know. Luther seemed kind of down and I'm not so sure it only has to do with Grammy."

"Maybe he just reacts different than you."

"Well, I know that, Scottie!"

"I ain't trying to put you down or nothing. I'm just saying that maybe what happened got Luther thinking about his own life. People always be getting that 'life is too short' feeling when somebody close dies. You know how it is."

Scottie's voice sort of blended in with my own thoughts. My vision was almost completely blurred as I stared straight ahead. I thought about Grammy and pictured her lying in that hospital bed, dying. I never got to see her and I worried that it was my fault. Mama didn't say much so I assumed that Grammy would be okay and I could just go whenever. I hated that I did that. I hated myself. I continued sitting on Scottie's bed. I closed my eyes and cried, hoping that the tears wouldn't escape. I couldn't hold back what I was feeling.

"Yo Leesha...," Scottie said.

I heard him but I didn't respond.

"Hey...thought you wasn't gonna cry no more."

Scottie sat beside me, nudging me and trying to get me to respond to him. I kept my eyes tightly shut and my body just as tense. Scottie put his arm around my shoulder and kissed me on my left temple.

"Yo Leesha...I'm feelin what you going through. Ain't much that I can say except that I've been through some similar shit. I mean...uh, you know, life ain't no joke! Seems like the ones you love the most, leave the quickest. And then the ones that fuck with you all the time be livin' forever! Sometimes I be wishing that God could come down and tell a nigga why that is. But on the real, Leesha...I'm sorry about your grandmother and I know that this pain gonna be with you for a long time."

I took a deep breath but kept my eyes closed. I didn't want to open them. I was almost afraid to. I felt a little better with Scottie holding me next to him. I leaned closer into him and rested my head into his chest. Scottie brushed my hair with his hand and kissed me on the forehead. It felt good.

"Hey...check this out, I guess I never really told you much about my parents. We was pretty tight. Pops always smiled when he seen me and my mother loved me like I was her only child. I think that shit was so obvious that it fucked up Charles. That's why he got all that jealousy inside of him, which makes niggas weak, you know..."

"What was your mother like?" I asked. The sound of my voice was like a scratchy whisper.

"Mom's?"

I nodded my head while still leaning against Scottie's chest.

"Leesha, Mom's was beautiful. Her smile used to have me feeling like there wasn't nothing I could do wrong. She would just smile at me for no reason. I think I be trying to replace that smile sometimes..."

"I don't understand."

"These females I be messin' with...I think I'm always trying to get that feeling back, but deep down I know it ain't never gonna happen. That's a trip, huh? I ain't never told that to nobody so make sure you don't slip and say some shit about what I just said."

"I'm not gonna tell anybody, Scottie."

"Bet not!"

"Whatever..."

Before I could say anything else, Scottie's pager went off. I could feel the reaction in his body and I could tell right away that he wanted to check to see who was paging him. Scottie played it off for a few seconds and then he loosened his arms. That was my cue to lift my head from his chest.

"Sorry about that, Leesha. I gotta see who this is."

For a split second I remembered what Luther said about Scottie. He's a hustler and does what he has to do to get by. Scottie's expression when he looked at his pager was strange to me. He looked angry and when I asked him what was wrong, he maintained his angry silence. It took a minute before he finally looked at me and realized that I'd actually said something.

"Say what?" he asked.

"Nothing. You want me to leave? I don't mind."

"Nah, not yet. This can wait. I gotta make sure you alright, Leesha. You my homegirl and shit!"

"What else do you think of me as?"

"Say what?"

"Nothing."

"What you thinking about? Why you ask me that, Leesha?"

"Scottie, I'm just trying to um…"

Once again Scottie's pager went off and I was glad it did. It kept me from saying something that could make things weird between us and I really didn't want to chance causing some distance between me and Scottie. I was probably trippin' behind the death of my grandmother, anyway.

"Yo Leesha, this shit might be important," Scottie said, referring to his pager.

"It's okay. I need to get home and see what Mama gonna do. I hope she ain't still complaining about the funeral. If she is, I can't stay there tonight."

"Oh yeah? Well, page me if you ain't staying home."

"Okay, I will."

As soon as I got back home and opened the front door, Mama came into the living room. She stood there with her hands on her hips. She looked angry and on the edge of talking some major shit. I didn't see Victor so I was happy about that.

I asked her, "Where's your man at?"

"Watch your mouth. You really think you grown, huh? I don't know where you learn to talk like you do but I'm here to tell you something, Leesha, you need to quit! I will beat your ass!"

"I'm going to my room. Is that okay?"

"No, we gonna talk about your little funky attitude."

"You sound like you trying to perform for your man, Mama. Is he listening on the other side of the door or something?"

"Girl, I'ma…," Mama threatened as she held her hand up.

I could see the seriousness in her by the way she bit down on her bottom lip. Mama lunged forward but I moved out of the way.

"Come here, girl!"

Mama chased me around the living room and stopped as I entered the kitchen. I was feeling like this was a repeat of the drama I had with Victor, but despite the shit that existed between me and Mama, I had no thoughts about using a knife on her. Mama just stood there. She sounded like she was out of breath. I think she was tired from being so angry more so than chasing me around.

"I'm too old to be dealing with this mess. You want to stay in this house, that's fine. But until you move, you better watch how you act," she said

I paid no real attention to her threat. I brushed it off. I had a smirk on my face. I asked her about the funeral, which to me seemed way more important than worrying about how I was acting toward her or that asshole Victor.

"When is the funeral, Mama? I talked to Luther today."

"I don't want to talk about it."

Mama started to walk toward her bedroom. I stepped in her path before she could move any further.

"Why not? You just gonna let Grammy's body lay up somewhere and not be taken care of? Don't you care?"

"Leesha, are you gonna help me pay for the funeral? Do you know how much that shit be costing these days? I ain't got that kind of money!"

"That's all you ever worry about besides feeding your man. Mama, you ain't right!"

"I ain't right? Listen at you! I'm about to slap you in a minute but you lucky I'm feeling so tired. Did that sorry-ass Luther say he gonna help pay for your grandmother's funeral?"

"Do it matter? We ain't really talked about it but I'm sure he will—"

"Uh-huh, well I talked to your Uncle Buddy and some of the others and they acting like I should be handling everything. Shit, they calling here asking if I need anything like they gonna come by and bring some damn food or something. But they ain't talking about paying for the funeral. You got some sorry-ass family, Leesha. I hope you don't turn out to be the same way."

I looked at Mama and thought to myself that the only sorry person I'd seen in my family was her. I didn't respond to her comments. I moved out of her way so she could go on to her bedroom.

Before she was able to close the door behind her, the phone rang. I watched as she picked it up and answered. I walked over and stood in her doorway, hoping that it was some news about Grammy. She deserved better than to have her body not taken care of. That's when I seen Victor sleeping in Mama's bed. I knew his ass was somewhere close by. He was sleeping on his stomach with his body half covered and snoring like crazy. He had Mama's bedroom smelling musty and she don't seem to care. I thought, *what's wrong with her?* And then I continued to listen to her talk on the phone.

"Say what now?" she asked. "Uh-huh, okay. Well, it's about time! When is it? Okay, good. Now y'all can stop calling me all the time!"

Mama hung up the phone. She turned to look at me. Her eyes were empty and her expression, cold. "See, your grandmother wasn't no stupid woman. She had insurance. The funeral will be on Thursday and now everybody can just leave me the fuck alone. I'm tired of dealing with this."

Mama slammed her door shut and I felt nothing for her frustrations. I couldn't understand her behavior or why she seemed to have no feelings about Grammy's death. The only thing that could make Mama so cold would be if Grammy treated her the same way she now treats me. I can't imagine Grammy ever being like that. I think Mama come to be the way she is because of her own life and because she don't ever take the blame for anything she does. She ain't in control. She just selfish, that's all.

Thursday came pretty quickly. I didn't bother to ride with Mama and Victor to the funeral. Scottie came and got me. He borrowed somebody's car. It was an old Volkswagen that backfired a few times as we drove down the street. I was glad that the funeral home was only ten minutes away.

"Why you slouching down like that?" Scottie asked.

He noticed the look on my face. I tried to play it off as sadness but I was slightly embarrassed riding in the car with him.

"You trippin'. This car could be the shit once it's fixed up. I'm just borrowing it, though. I ain't trying to roll in this. It's too small. I needs a car with some room in it."

"Yes, Scottie…"

"Anyway, how you doing?"

"I'm okay. This don't feel real to me. It's like, so quiet now. Like the world just went silent."

"Yeah, that's how I felt when I lost my parents. It's like a big ass hole is in your life and now you got to figure out what to do. It's a trip, for real."

Scottie drove down Victoria Avenue because he said it would be easier to pull up in front of the funeral home that way. I think he was taking his time and maybe trying to see if I was okay. But no matter which route he took, we arrived in no time flat. Scottie gave me a look of concern and asked if I wanted to wait or go inside right then. I didn't see very many cars outside. Maybe the funeral was gonna be a private one with only a few family members.

"Let's go in now," I said.

"Okay. You have to get out on my side, Leesha. That door don't work from the inside."

I laughed. It felt good especially because I knew how I'd feel once I stood inside.

This time as we walked, Scottie reached for my hand instead of the other way around. We walked slowly inside and were greeted by a lady dressed in black. She smiled but didn't look like she meant to. She talked all quiet and I could hear some scary-sounding music coming from one of the rooms.

"Who are you here for?" the lady asked.

I swallowed really hard. I didn't want to say Grammy's name. My heart began to panic. I didn't want to imagine Grammy in a place like this. I started squeezing Scottie's hand really tightly.

"Come here, girl," Scottie said while pulling me in close.

I began to cry. I couldn't hold it in any longer. I'd been fighting it for so long, especially while I was around Mama. I never seen nor heard her shed a tear for Grammy. I thought about that as Scottie held me tightly. The mere image of Mama not crying gave me the strength to stop the flow of tears coming from my eyes.

I felt another hand rubbing my back. It belonged to the woman dressed in black.

"Are you okay? Can I get you anything?" she asked.

I turned to look at her and then shook my head. I felt okay inside Scottie's arms but I worried how I might hold up during the funeral.

"Hey, ain't that your grandmother right there?" Scottie said while pointing to a picture in front of a door.

"Uh-huh, that's her."

"Uh, that's her grandmother. We here for her funeral," Scottie said to the lady.

"Okay, well, services have already begun so let's walk in quietly and find you a place to sit."

"Are there a lot of people inside?" I asked.

"Well, it's not a large room but there are quite a few people already inside. I'm sure your grandmother was a very loved woman."

The lady walked over to the door and opened it slowly. She poked her head inside before opening the door all the way. She guided us with her hand and pointed to an area where there was room to sit.

Scottie whispered, "You gonna go up there with your family?"

I could see Uncle Buddy and his family in the front row and a few people who I didn't know but had seen during holidays. I didn't answer Scottie's question. I held on to his hand and sat down beside him. He gestured for me to lean against his shoulder. I did for a minute as I listened to someone speaking about my grandmother. It was an elderly woman talking into the microphone saying how much she enjoyed their friendship. I was happy to see some people around who actually loved Grammy.

"I wonder if your cousin is here?" Scottie asked.

"Luther?"

"Yeah."

I glanced slowly around the room as everyone quietly listened to the elderly woman speaking. I noticed people smiling and some wiping away tears. I didn't see Luther anywhere.

"I don't see him or Mama..."

"Damn, your mother ain't here?"

"No, I don't see her."

Scottie looked around in disbelief. It bothered him too how my mama was acting toward Grammy's death. Maybe it brought back memories that had something to do with his parents and his brother. Something about his reaction made me feel like he and I shared that sort of thing in common. Mama don't care about Grammy and his brother could care less about their parents.

"Oh, there she go...Leesha, she over there with dude."

I looked in the direction that Scottie's eyes were focused on. It took me a couple seconds before I could see where she was. The person sitting next to her had moved slightly forward, blocking my view.

"You see her?" Scottie asked.

"I see her…"

I turned back around and stared at the floor. I could feel Scottie's eyes on me but he didn't say anything. I listened as another speaker was introduced. I toyed with my hands and thought about Grammy. I closed my eyes and tried to listen to her voice. I remembered when she would tell me to close my eyes and find peace. She used to say that women in today's world needed to do that more often because women always trying to be everything to everybody else. I tried to find peace because I was pissed off and sad at the same time. And for some reason, what Grammy used to say wasn't working for me. I couldn't find peace at all. I only found anger and bitterness.

I opened my eyes and looked toward the front. I could finally see Grammy lying in her casket. Only her face was visible to me. She had a peaceful smile. I didn't like that they had a lot of makeup on her. Grammy never really wore any. She was beautiful without and always encouraged me not to wear too much. She would have me laughing, talking about women who wear too much makeup. She especially hated to see young women with dark lipstick.

She would say, "Life is already hard enough so a woman shouldn't be making herself look like a wolf cookie knocking on death's door!"

Grammy was funny like that but I knew that her main thing was to always instill in me what it took to be a lady. Without Grammy, I'd have to find my own route toward womanhood.

All the speakers had finished and the pastor began to give his final eulogy. He said he'd known my grandmother for twenty years. I remember seeing him visit her a few times. He said some beautiful things about Grammy. I looked over at Mama to see her reaction. I was thinking that maybe she'd stop being an asshole if she heard something nice said about her own mother. I couldn't see anything different in Mama at all. I'd begun to block out the sound of the pastor's voice. Something inside of me seemed to change. It was like a cold chill swept through my entire body as I looked over at Mama and then glanced one more time at Grammy lying in the casket. I could feel Scottie reach for my hand but unlike so many times when I welcomed him doing that, this time I pulled away. Scottie looked at me but he didn't say anything.

I began to notice more people in tears. The sounds of sadness was deafening to me. I wanted it all to stop. I clutched my heart because I wanted it to stop, too. I didn't want to feel anything any longer. I stood up and walked toward the back. I leaned against the wall with my arms folded. I was standing so that I could get a good look at Mama. Scottie stayed in his seat but he kept looking back at me.

He whispered hard. "Leesha, where you going?"

I didn't respond. I just kept staring at Mama. She had no tears in her eyes. All her attention was on Victor. She was over there adjusting his tie, which looked like a loud reminder as to when he last wore a suit. Mama didn't know it but she was giving me the strength not to cry or feel in a room filled to capacity with love and sadness. Everyone in the room expressed their feelings for Grammy. Everyone but Mama…

The people sitting next to where I stood asked if I wanted to sit down. I shook my head. I'm sure they could sense my growing attitude. Then one of the ushers came over to me and asked me to take a seat. It was another female dressed in black. She held out her hand in the direction of where everyone sat but I refused.

"I'm leaving," I told her.

I looked at Scottie and gestured for him to come with me. He stood up and followed me out the door. I took one last look at Mama and she was rubbing on Victor's face.

"What's up, Leesha? We leaving?" Scottie asked.

"Yeah, I need to get out of here! Grammy ain't coming back. She's dead!"

Scottie didn't say a word and neither did I as we drove back to the neighborhood.

"Where you wanna go?" he asked.

"You can drop me off at home."

"You sure?"

"Yeah, I'll call you."

"Okay."

When Scottie pulled up to the front of my apartment building, I said a quick goodbye and gave him a look that read: "I don't want to be bothered." Scottie understood. He let me out of the car and stared at me as I walked away. I could feel his eyes watching my every step.

"Leesha!" Scottie called.

I kept walking but I raised my hand and waved goodbye. I wasn't feeling like talking to anyone, not even my best friend. I walked up the stairs, entered the apartment, and went straight to my bedroom. I locked the door behind me and climbed in bed where I stayed for hours. The only light inside my room would come from the outside, through my window. Eventually, that light disappeared as I lay in darkness with tears streaming down my face and anger floating inside my head. All I could think about was how Mama's been acting since Grammy died and what my life would be like from this point on. I'd have no one who could replace my grandmother and I'd have a mother who I couldn't stand.

Hours later, I was awakened by the front door slamming shut and keys banging on the table. Mama and Victor had come home. They both sounded drunk because they were loud. I put my head underneath my pillow to drown out the sound but it didn't work. Mama was laughing so loud and Victor was calling out her name over and over like she couldn't hear him.

"Lynette!" he shouted really loud.

I didn't hear Mama respond.

I got up from my bed and walked over to my door. I put my ear close to where it opens hoping that I could hear what was going on. I couldn't really tell what was happening but I could hear a lot of bumping around like somebody walking really hard. Mama was still laughing. I could really tell then that she had had too much to drink.

"Lynette!" Victor shouted again.

Then I heard a slap and a scream.

"You hear me saying your name! See what you made me have to do!" Victor said.

I didn't hear Mama say anything and I found myself not wanting to know whether she was okay or not. I leaned my head against the door and continued to listen. After a while I could hear some whispering.

"Come on, you okay…," Victor whispered. "You can't be acting like that when I'm trying to talk to you."

I opened my bedroom door just enough to be able to see what was going on. Victor was helping Mama up from the living room floor. She was half naked with only the bottom half of her dress on. Victor tried to rub her face and Mama barely had her eyes open. It was pathetic to see them. Mama had reached a new low in my eyes. I hated her for how she'd handled Grammy's death and then to know that she loved an abusive, alcoholic man made me feel nothing inside. Victor walked Mama over to the couch and then let her collapse face first where he normally would sit, drinking his beer and watching TV. Mama looked like she was passed out and I watched as Victor walked slowly toward her bedroom and went inside. It seemed like the roles were reversed this time. Mama would be passed out on the couch and Victor would sleep in the bedroom.

When I felt like it was safe to step outside my bedroom, I walked into the living room. First I looked over toward Mama's bedroom to make sure Victor wasn't standing there or possibly about to come back. I didn't hear any noise coming from there and the door was closed so I took my chances.

I walked over to where Mama was lying face down in the couch. Her arm had fallen to the side and her hand was on the carpet. She really looked out of it. Her mouth was open and drool was coming out. I turned around because it got to me, seeing her like that. Then I turned back and knelt beside her. I looked at Mama and wondered how she got to be the way she was. How does anybody become who they are? That's a question that finds me because I'm always seeing the effects of when people done some wrong shit in the past.

I sat next to Mama and looked at her. I tapped her a few times just to see if maybe she'd open her eyes and look at me. I got no response. Then something came over me and I felt like this was as good an opportunity as any other time to say what I'd wanted to say. It didn't matter if she could hear me or not. I just needed to say something to Mama in her presence.

"Mama, you may not believe this but I love you."

I waited to see if maybe Mama heard me but she didn't budge one inch. I got kind of mad at that point. I pulled her hair, lifting her head up off the couch slightly. That didn't seem to affect her either so I let go.

"Mama, I can't believe how stupid you are. I ain't never gonna be like you and have some asshole for a boyfriend. You can't even see what kind of man you have. You waste all your time trying to please him and you don't even care about your own daughter. You don't even care that your daughter thinks you ain't shit. I can't wait to leave your ass behind, but I'm always gonna come back just to show you that I can do better. I'm thinking I should get in touch with my father just to piss you off, shit!"

No matter how much I said or how loud I got, it didn't seem like Mama heard me. Her eyes didn't even flutter and I was getting so frustrated that I was inches away from trying to scratch Mama and do anything I could to her while she was passed out.

I gave up trying to talk to her. I sat beside her and thought about the things I'd said. I was serious about leaving. I don't know if I'd come back to show off but I can't see myself leaving Mama and not ever seeing her again. I don't know. She may want me to do that and if that's the case, I would.

I started to think about my father. I thought about his sister who lived in Long Beach. Like maybe I should visit her and see what that side of the family is really like. I don't know. None of that shit probably matters anyway. What could he do for me out here? I definitely ain't going to no Washington, D.C. to see somebody I don't really know. He left me when I was a baby so how is he gonna act now? I'm not about to go find out. I'd rather stay my ass right here in L.A. for now. I don't know why I even thought about him.

I looked back over at Mama and she was still in the same position. I saw Victor's coat laying on the floor so I picked it up and placed it over Mama. I couldn't tell if she was cold or not but it just seemed like the thing to do. Then before I could back away from her, I noticed some vomit coming from Mama's mouth. It oozed out slowly and made me want to throw up, it was so nasty.

I tried to wake Mama up. I shook her a couple times before the smell of her vomit caused me to back away.

"Mama, get up!" I yelled.

I had to be tough and forget about the smell. I didn't want Mama choking on her own vomit so I tried to make her sit up. Mama mumbled and tried to resist but that just let me know she was awake at that point.

After I was able to get Mama to sit up, I rushed to the bathroom to get a hot towel. When I came back into the living room, mama had vomited some more, all over herself. I cleaned her up with the hot towel and fought her attempts to stop me the whole time.

"Mama, I'm trying to clean you up!" I yelled.

Mama mumbled, "No, get away from me."

I managed to clean the vomit from her mouth, but she still had some on her chest where it had dripped down to while I was in the bathroom.

Mama had me smelling nasty by that point. I was swallowing hard to keep from gagging. I could feel a lump in my throat and it wasn't from something emotional. I ain't no fucking nurse. I can't take being so close to somebody that vomited. The shit was nasty!

"You don't want me cleaning you up, Mama?" I asked her.

"No, no...Get away from me," she grunted, with her eyes still closed and a heavy frown on her face. She looked like a spoiled, overgrown child.

"Cool."

I threw the wet towel in her face and stepped away from her.

"Clean your damn self up then!" I told her.

Mama turned her face to the side and let the towel drop in her lap. That's when I noticed the bruise on her face, given to her by Victor when he slapped her.

"Mama, you let that man slap you?"

I touched her face and she swiped my hand away.

"Ow! Don't...touch...me."

"And you say you love Victor?"

"Wuh you talkin' 'bout...Be quiet, Lee...sha."

Mama's speech was seriously slurred, plus she could barely keep her head up or her eyes open. I had to stop her from falling to the side a couple times. After a while I gave up and let her ass fall over.

"I ain't never seen you drunk like this before, Mama."

Mama waved her hand at me. "Leave me...a...lone."

I did just that. I left her alone and then the phone rang. Mama wasn't affected by that either. She didn't budge. I answered it and it sounded as if Victor had picked up the phone at the same time.

"Who the hell calling at this hour?" Victor asked.

"Yo, is Leesha there?"

It was Scottie on the other end. Hearing his voice made me happy even though I hadn't planned on talking to him anytime soon. I really wanted to work through my feelings on my own but I couldn't just ignore his call.

"Scottie, I'm here," I said.

"Hey, you alright?"

"I'm fine...hold on for a second. Victor, can you please get off the phone? Your ass needs to think about what you did to Mama, anyway."

Victor didn't say anything but I could hear him breathing into the phone. Scottie asked, "What's going on, Leesha? What he do to your mother?"

"I'll tell you in a minute, Scottie. Victor, do you hear me?"

I still got no response from Victor so I put down the phone and walked over to Mama's bedroom. I opened the door and found Victor asleep with the phone laying right next to his mouth. That's why I could hear his ass breathing so hard. His familiar musty smell had me wanting to hurry up and close the damn door. I took the phone away from him and hung it up. I returned to the living room to talk to Scottie.

"You still there?" I asked.

"Yeah, I'm here. So, what's up? What's going on?"

"Victor slapped Mama tonight. She in here on the couch, passed out."

"Damn, is that right? Maybe she feeling bad about your grandmother."

"I doubt that, Scottie."

"You never know, Leesha. I mean, when niggas be trying to deny what they feel, they always try to deaden that shit some kind of way. My brother was the same way when our parents died. He did so much weed and alcohol that night it was crazy. I ain't never seen nobody get as fucked up as he was. He only stopped because he was passed out."

"Did he tell you he did it because of your parents?"

"Nah, he ain't never gonna admit to that shit. Your mother probably won't either. She just gonna get up and act like everything is cool. But you said old dude slapped her? What was that about?"

"I don't know. All I know is that I was in my bedroom at the time and I heard it when it happened. Now he's sleeping in Mama's room and Mama out here on the couch. She vomited, too! I cleaned her up as much as I could. She didn't want me touching her, though."

"Damn. I hate that you have to go through that."

"Thanks."

"So, what was up with you earlier? I mean, I thought I did something wrong. Like I didn't say the right words or hug you at the right time."

"Huh?"

"Don't act like you don't know what I'm talking about."

"I don't."

"When I dropped you off, you gave a brotha some serious cold shoulder. You gotta tell me what's up 'cause I ain't into reading minds."

"It wasn't you, Scottie. I was just mad because of how Mama was acting at the funeral. That made me so angry, Scottie. And now, I feel different about everything."

"What you mean, different about everything?"

"I'm not sure. That's why I just wanted to come home and think. It's like I feel like I gotta change in order to survive and get through everything."

"So, we still cool or are you trying to get rid of me, too?"

"We're cool, Scottie."

"A'ight then…So, you need a ride to school in the morning? I'm gonna have the bug for a couple more days."

"I guess so. I haven't even thought about school."

"Yo, what happened to your cousin? I didn't see him at the funeral."

"I don't know. I was thinking about that earlier. Luther loved Grammy so much. He's been worried that because she's dead, something might happen to him now."

"For real?"

"Yeah…I think it's kind of silly but I would never tell him that."

"If that's what he's feeling then—"

"Not you, too, Scottie...You believe in that, too? Is that a street thing or something?"

"Is what a street thing?"

"You know, believing that a loved one can take their prayers to the grave with them."

"That shit could be real though, Leesha. I understand what he's saying even though I ain't never really look at things like that. Your cousin been around so you gotta respect that."

"I don't know. I am worried about him but not like that. I don't think nothing is gonna happen to him. I'm just thinking he might be out there drunk, too. I hope I don't be like that."

"Like what?"

"Like drinking all the time just cause something bad happens. I mean, what the fuck? I'd rather cry or stay by myself..."

"Yeah, I hear you but like I said, niggas would rather deaden the pain than to feel some real shit."

"What did you do when your parents died, Scottie?"

"I can't really say. I mean, my mind goes blank when I think about it. It's just like what you said about feeling empty or like the world seems so quiet all of a sudden. To me, it's like feeling shell shocked. You walk around in a daze trying to figure out what happened. I ain't in a daze no more but I know that shit affected me subconsciously."

I thought about what Scottie said and wondered how Grammy's death would affect me. Knowing that she was no longer around for me to visit was a realization that always brought tears. And when I didn't cry, I got angry and silent. I wanted to curse anyone in my path. I had to find a way not to think about Grammy and that was hard because when I didn't think about her, I was thinking about Mama.

"Scottie, I have to go," I said.

"Damn, what's wrong?"

"Nothing, but I'll call you if I need that ride."

"A'ight...Let me know, okay?"

"I said I would!"

"Whoa, girl, I'm on your side. I feel your pain but yo, don't let it stop you from living and doing what you gotta do."

"Goodnight, Scottie."

"A'ight then…"

Grammy once said some words to me that I let fly right by. I didn't really want to understand it because I brushed it off as some old folk's philosophy.

Grammy said, when her sister died it was like a chain had been broken. The family grew apart and only visited on holidays or when tragedy occurred.

About a week after Grammy's funeral, I'd heard that Luther got into an accident. Nobody would really tell me what happened or how bad he was injured. Nobody would tell me anything, really. I hate when they do that shit. I had to go and find out for myself. They only told me that he was taken to Daniel Freeman Hospital. I rode the bus there and then two hours later, all I can remember is coming home with no feeling in my heart.

My head pounded inside like drums against the wall. The pounding was slow and methodical as if it were leading up to something. There was nothing I could do to stop it. I closed my eyes and sat down on the couch in the living room. No one was home or at least that's what I assumed since I didn't see or hear anyone.

Closing my eyes didn't help much either. It only made me relive the reason for my head wanting to explode in the first place. I couldn't cry and I didn't understand what I was feeling or what was going on inside of me. All I could do was sit there and take the pounding. Take the cold chill, traveling through my body. Remember the hollow hallways of that hospital and the constant chatter of doctors and nurses. Why couldn't they just tell me when I first asked them about my cousin? Instead, I had to find out for myself. I had to walk around listening, asking, and even eavesdropping until I could find out what happened. I did this for almost an hour before I'd finally hear a couple doctors talking about Luther. One of them said his name as if he were talking about a statistic instead of a man. That got my attention. That was the reason for me listening to their conversation.

The doctor who spoke was Asian and he was talking to a black doctor. The

Asian doctor looked like he'd seen way too many victims in his lifetime. His outfit was wrinkled and he appeared as if he hadn't slept for days. The black doctor looked no better and he acted all jittery like he had a million things to do at once. Maybe he did. People were coming in and out of that emergency room like crazy. But no amount of distraction or confusion could keep me from hearing the two doctors talk about Luther.

They didn't seem to notice me. They didn't notice how everything they'd say ripped into my heart. They couldn't imagine that they had me feeling as if someone were slowly slicing up my insides with a razorblade.

"Multiple gunshot wounds to the face and chest, injury to the stomach. Injury to the colon…diaphragmatic injury…liver injury…," the Asian doctor said.

He spoke as if everything was routine and it probably was. But for me, everything he said tore me apart.

"Luther, no!" I said out loud.

The two doctors turned their attention toward me, standing with my arms folded and bending over as if I were in pain. When I noticed that they were looking at me, their expressions spoke loud and clear.

"Miss, are you related to the patient?" the black doctor asked.

I nodded. "Kind of…," I said.

"There was a police officer here looking for family members of the victim. He had a few questions. Routine stuff…I'm not sure when he'll be back. I believe we have his card in the chart so you may wanna—"

"How about Luther, is he okay?" I interrupted.

"He's stable for the moment but he suffered a great deal of trauma to multiple areas of his head and body. There's even a wound to the base of his skull. I'm afraid Luther will need a great deal of rehab before he can leave this hospital. Are you his sister?"

"No. I'm his cousin."

"Well, we need to speak with either his parents or someone, umm…"

"I just want to know if he's gonna be okay."

"Uh, we believe he'll make it but we're never too sure, especially with wounds of this magnitude. If he pulls through, his life will definitely not be the same and rehab will take a very long time."

I listened to the doctor and folded my arms against my body tighter. He reached out and placed his hand on my arm but I could barely feel his touch. I felt as if all my movements were in slow motion and my speech was slurred.

I asked, "Did they say what happened?"

"No details were given…All we know is that it appears to be a gang-related incident. Unfortunately, we get this pretty much every day so we as doctors try to save lives and not really question how it happened."

The black doctor gently squeezed my arm and the Asian doctor smiled. They both walked away and I waited. I stood in the same spot that they left me in for probably another thirty minutes. That's when the two doctors walked out of the emergency room, looked in my direction with expressions that I once again could read before they'd speak. I didn't want to hear anything they'd have to say because I already knew. I didn't need for the black doctor to come to me with his sorry look trying to explain anything. I could see it in his eyes. I read the Asian doctor's lips just before he went back inside the emergency room.

"Okay, you tell her," is what he had said.

I didn't need to be told. I already knew. I could feel it. It was about the only thing I could feel. I held my hand up.

"No," I said.

I walked away before the black doctor could come over to me and then I ran home. The pounding still remains. The cold chill infects my body with memories of what those two doctors had said about Luther. My heart is put to rest by the numbness. All I want to do is sit on the couch and hate because I can't cry no more. Hate seems like an emotion that goes hand in hand with feeling numb inside. If I cry, that's a little too close to love. I didn't want to feel love. Love gets taken away too easily. Love makes you lose control. Love shuts you off from the world because when you lose it, you feel as I do…nothing…

LOVE EQUALS
A LIFETIME FOOL

I stopped speaking to Scottie for a long time. Phone calls to him went from once a week to once a month and then I stopped. I felt as if I needed to find my own way. Scottie was like a crutch instead of a shoulder. I leaned on him without thought. I leaned on him because I love him and he's the only one I can truly count on. I was still feeling like that sort of love for someone would only mean they wouldn't be around for very long. Like maybe something would happen to Scottie as well.

Time sort of flew by after that. I made myself officially a loner and started doing shit by myself. My relationship with Mama stayed the same but I didn't care. I was happy mostly because I'd be a senior in high school soon and after that I could possibly think about leaving home.

Mama and Victor were still together but by the time summer rolled around again, their relationship seemed a little different. They were always so quiet. I'd come home and mama would be in the kitchen either cooking or sitting at the table alone. She'd be smoking a cigarette or in her space, a million miles away in her own mind. And then I'd see Victor on the couch, in his spot watching TV and drinking a beer. I could walk in and stand in the middle of the living room for a half-hour and neither would look up or show any signs that they gave a damn.

"Hello!" I'd say before going to my room like always.

I wouldn't get a response from either one.

One night I shocked Victor because I actually came out of my room to talk to his ass. I don't know what was going through my mind except maybe I was feeling alone. I'd already been battling my conscience because I wanted to call Scottie. The fact that I hadn't called him in so long was a hard habit to break. I didn't want to dial his number and then act all normal like we'd been talking all along. Scottie is too real to let some shit like that pass. So instead, I tried to see if I could have a conversation with Victor.

Mama was in her bedroom and Victor was sitting in the kitchen. When I saw him, I couldn't resist saying something sarcastic. "I can't believe you're sitting somewhere other than on the couch! Wow!"

Victor gave me a half-smile and then told me to shut up. He wasn't serious. In fact, I think he liked that I'd said something to him. I could look in his eyes and tell something different was going on between him and Mama. I cared but I didn't care because despite me wanting to talk to him, I still didn't like Victor.

I walked over to the kitchen table and sat across from him. Victor looked over at me with a confused frown on his face.

"You okay?" I asked.

"Shit. You sitting across from me and asking if I'm okay? I'm wondering if you came over here to do your mother's dirty work for her."

"What you talking about?"

"You mean you came over here on your own?"

"I don't see nobody pushing me over here."

"What about your mother?"

"What about her?"

"Maybe she told you to talk to me about something…"

"I hardly talk to Mama. Seems to me like we all have our space and we all just come and go."

"Yeah, something like that."

Victor smiled bitterly and then took a sip of his beer. His eyes returned to the *Ebony* magazine he had in front of him. I didn't realize he was reading something because he had one arm covering one page while slumped over the other page. Maybe his eyesight was poor or he was embarrassed to be seen reading something. I couldn't tell.

"What you reading?" I asked to get a conversation going.

"This nigga getting paid all kind of money for some shit like this!" Victor said.

I had no clue what he was talking about until I glanced at the page that seemed to get him all upset. His ass was jealous, that's all. He was looking at an ad with Michael Jordan eating a hotdog.

"At least he doing something positive and working."

My comment only agitated Victor more.

"I don't give a fuck. Shoot, I'm working, too! They gonna come knocking on my door asking me to do a commercial? Hell nah!"

"I think you gotta do more than just work part time at a glass-making place, Victor."

"We make bottles and it's a good job. Once they hire me full time, I'm gonna be straight! I won't have to put up with no kind of shit, especially from no woman talking about I ain't there for her…shit."

I watched as Victor took yet another sip of his beer, although this time he kept drinking until the can was empty. He stood up, went to the refrigerator, and got another beer.

"Why you like drinking so much?" I asked.

"Shit, I don't know. Why you ask me that?"

"'Cause I'm curious…I mean, you do it like it's the best thing in the world."

"You probably be out there drinking with your friends, too. How you gonna ask me why I like it so much."

"I ain't never drank no beer. I'm not interested."

"Well, if you want to try some, I won't tell your mama. I'll keep quiet, young lady, I promise." Victor laughed.

I knew he was teasing me but I didn't care. Victor wasn't really able to get to me anymore like he used to. I watched as he sat down slowly. He returned to his magazine and started flipping through the pages. He seemed nervous with me watching him. By the time he got to the last page, he looked like he didn't know what to do with himself. Victor turned to the side and stared toward the living room.

"You miss your spot on the couch?" I asked sarcastically.

Victor sipped his beer and pretended as if he didn't hear me. He cleared his throat and then asked me a question that seemed especially deep because it came from him and it sounded intelligent. "What you plan on doing with your life?"

His question caught me off guard so much that I didn't answer for a while. Then he looked at me as if he were truly waiting for my answer.

"What, you ain't heard me?" he asked.

"I heard you. I'm not sure yet."

"You need to be sure. I know you don't like me and we never talked before but I know you smart, Leesha. I hope you don't waste that shit and at least try to do something with your life."

"I ain't worried about that."

"Uh-huh, well you need to be worried."

"Why, you got some advice for me? What have you done with your life?"

"Now you sounding just like your mother. Shit. I've done my best and ain't no woman gonna make me feel ashamed about myself. Y'all think you know everything..."

Victor sounded bitter and the more he talked, the more I could tell things weren't good between him and Mama. Actually, I could see that shit regardless if he said anything or not. I sort of tuned him out as he spoke. The sound of his voice went to the back of my mind and I thought about his earlier question: What was I gonna do with my life? I was so hell-bent on moving out on my own that that became the only real goal I was reaching for. Anything beyond that never got any serious thought. The only thing I was qualified for was entry-level fast food and retail stores. Victor brought me back into the conversation by asking me about Scottie.

"What did you say?" I questioned because I'd only heard him mention Scottie's name.

"I ain't seen him lately. You two fall out with each other? That was your boyfriend, wasn't it?"

"Who you talking about? Boyfriend?"

"Shit, I don't remember his name! That young brother you brought to your grandmother's funeral. He always with you...I ain't seen you with anybody else..."

"He ain't my boyfriend; he's just a friend."

"Okay, well...I ain't seen him."

"He around..."

Victor returned to staring in the direction of the living room and I stared at the table. His questions about Scottie hit a sour note with me so I raised my shield, which even an asshole like Victor could recognize. He didn't know what else to say and I didn't want to talk anymore. We both sat there in silence. It was uncomfortable and for the moment, I preferred it that way.

I stood up from the table and went to the refrigerator. I looked inside and it was empty as usual. I cursed and slammed it shut. Victor snapped out of his intense stare and looked at me.

"Damn, girl, shit...," he mumbled.

"There ain't never anything in this refrigerator. At least when Mama liked your ass, there was some food in here," I said to be spiteful.

"You always talking like you grown so take your ass and buy some food!"

"Who you talking to?"

I gave Victor a cold hard stare. We went at it like two kids on the street, acting like we were gonna do more than talk shit. I knew Victor was only talking and I was doing the same thing.

"I tell you what, Leesha," Victor said. "Go to the store and I'll even give you a little money so you can get me something, too."

"Yeah, right...What you want besides beer?"

"I don't know. Get me some, uh, some chicken. You know how they have them small rotisserie chickens that be nice and brown? That shit always look good. Get me one of those and some chips or something to go with it."

I stuck my hand out. "Where's the money?"

Victor handed me a twenty-dollar bill.

"You sure that's enough?" I asked.

"It better be! I got about ten more dollars in my pocket and that shit gonna have to last till payday."

I rolled my eyes and started toward the front door.

"You wanna take my car? I don't know if you drive yet, do you?" Victor asked.

"I'm learning..."

"Your boyfriend teaching you, huh?"

"I don't have no…Forget it."

"You going to Ralph's, right?"

"Yeah."

"That's right around the corner so I doubt you get stopped between here and there. Take my car."

Victor threw me his keys. I caught them and kind of stood there thinking if I should or not. I walked out the front door with his keys in my hand and walked right past his yellow Volkswagen. I walked a few more steps before my curiosity told me to turn around and go back. I walked back to Victor's car, unlocked the door, and sat inside. I put the key in the ignition and then tried to start the engine. It wouldn't work. I tried several times before realizing his car had a stick shift. I'd never driven a stick before. I got out and slammed the door shut. I looked up toward my apartment and noticed Victor watching me from the window. I gave him the finger and he laughed. Then I started walking to the grocery store.

When I got to Ralph's, I went straight to the section where they had that chicken that Victor wanted. I took care of that first so I wouldn't forget about it. Then I thought about going to where all the potato chips were but since he didn't tell me what kind, I walked right past that aisle. I was like, *fuck him*.

After that, I focused on getting what I wanted. Victor's twenty dollars was more than enough for his chicken so I figured I could put his money together with the little bit that I had saved up so I could get something good to eat. I must've walked down every aisle trying to find something, but nothing really appealed to me that wasn't junk food. I started thinking I would settle for something I could warm up and get some chocolate donuts for dessert.

As I was walking down each aisle, I noticed this guy walking slowly behind me. I could tell he was checking me out and trying to follow without being noticed. He wasn't very good at it, though. He didn't look like the usual guys that try to hit on me. He didn't look ghetto or even thuggish. I pretended to search for some nail polish so this guy could walk closer and I could get a better look at him. He fell for my trick and stood right behind me, pretending like he was searching for something. The only problem was that he was looking at something that I seriously doubt he came to buy. He was cute and had me laughing to myself. I decided to bust his bubble and let him know he'd been caught.

"Is this your first time trying to buy tampons?" I asked him.

"Huh?" he responded before his embarrassment kicked in.

"You trying to say hello to me or you really seriously trying to buy some tampons?"

"Oh, uh, yeah..."

"Yeah, what?"

"What was the question again?"

The guy had me cracking up and at the same time he was so cute. He seemed shy and slightly nerdy even though he was dressed from head to toe in hip-hop gear. I could hear him cursing quietly as he realized his first impression wasn't happening like he probably wanted it to.

"You could've got your mack on better if you had approached me sooner," I told him.

"It's no sweat..."

He tried hard to brush off his embarrassment but everything he did back-fired on him. I tried my best to hold back my laughter. I didn't want to hurt his feelings even more. It was hard, though.

"What's your name?" I asked.

"Treyvon, why?"

"I wanna know what to call you. I mean, you didn't follow me over here for nothing, did you?"

Treyvon didn't respond. Instead, he stood there trying to adjust his baggy jeans and eye me up and down like he was cool, but he only came off as being uncomfortable.

"Don't be looking at me up and down like that...," I said.

"Shit, oops, I mean, um...Sorry about that."

"It's okay. My name is Leesha, by the way, just in case you wondered."

"You are like the finest girl I've seen—ever. Hope you don't mind me saying that."

"Thanks, Treyvon. Is that why you were following me? What if I had a boyfriend?"

"Do you?"

"No, but what if I did?"

"I don't know. I guess I might get my ass kicked if he's bigger than me. You probably have a boyfriend. Girls like you don't ever be single."

"Girls like me?"

"Yeah, really fine…"

I shrugged my shoulders and pretended to go back to searching for some nail polish to see what else Treyvon would say.

"What school you go to, Leesha?"

"Dorsey."

"Oh yeah, that's cool. You like it?"

"It's alright. I'm just trying to graduate and get out of there."

"I heard that. What you gonna do after that?"

"I don't know yet."

"Really?"

"Why you say that like you're surprised, Treyvon?"

"I don't know. You just um…"

"I'll probably go to college. Maybe go to West L.A. so I can at least be doing something while I try to decide. I got a friend that goes there. I don't know what Scottie's taking but he says he likes it."

"Scottie? That's your boyfriend, huh?"

"I told you I don't have one."

I started to walk slowly down the aisle. Treyvon seemed nice but I didn't want to spend forever in the store.

"Leesha, you mind if I walk with you?"

"You can if you want."

"Thanks."

"So, what school you go to, Treyvon?"

"I'm in a private school."

"I've always wondered what that was like."

"It's okay, I guess. I like that they have a lot of drawing and art classes. That's what I'm into."

"You draw good?"

"I think so. I'm looking into schools back east so I can really learn different things. I want to one day create my own comic book series."

"You make money doing that?"

"Shoot, you can make a lot of money doing that!"

"Drawing cartoon characters?"

"Not just cartoon characters but comic book characters. Mine is gonna be called Political Ninja. He's gonna be able to fight like Bruce Lee but be like a revolutionary or something. You know, be for the people."

"Sounds kind of silly to me."

"Nah, it's gonna be cool."

"I'm happy for you, Treyvon. Do you work?"

"Not really but sometimes I get a little money for doing murals and painting that stuff you see on store windows. I did a couple of those beauty shops on Crenshaw. It's cool and it's a good way to practice."

"That's nice...Listen, I need to get home."

"You need a ride, Leesha? I can take—"

"We just met. I can't have you knowing where I live already!"

"Oh...well, how about I drive you to your street? I could let you off at the corner."

"No, I'll walk but I'll tell you what."

"What's that, I talk too much?"

"No. I'll give you my phone number."

Treyvon rubbed his hands together like he'd hit the lotto and was about to get his cash. I ripped off a piece of a magazine as we stood in the checkout line.

"You have a pen?" I asked.

"I always got something to write with."

Treyvon reached into his left pocket and pulled out a black ink pen. He handed it to me and I wrote my number for him.

"Okay, here you go."

Treyvon was smiling from ear to ear and kept moving like he couldn't stand still.

"You okay?" I asked.

He nodded his head and smiled again. I paid for my food. All I'd gotten was my chocolate donuts and that chicken for Victor. I couldn't decide what I wanted and talking to Treyvon really took away my appetite.

By the time I made it home, Victor was sitting on the couch in his normal spot. He was asleep and didn't hear me walk in. The smell of his chicken was talking to me. I opened the container and ran my fingers over the juicy skin. Then I licked off the tips of my fingers. I was so tempted to just tear into it. That's when Mama opened up her bedroom door and stared at me. The sound of her voice scared the shit out of me. I thought I was busted but Mama didn't know that chicken was for Victor.

She said, "Somebody named Treyvon or something like that just called you."

"Treyvon? He called me already?"

"I don't know about no *already* but yes, he called you. Who is this Treyvon person?"

"Nobody…"

"Uh-huh, well then you shouldn't be giving out your number if he ain't nobody. I hope his ass ain't gonna be calling here in the middle of the night all the time. Make sure you tell your little friend I said that, too."

Mama turned to walk back inside her room, but then she took a second look at the chicken that I had sitting on the table. "You buy that?"

I nodded my head. That's how I answered her when I wasn't being completely truthful.

"Humph," she responded.

When Mama closed her door I felt like I had to take a bite of Victor's chicken. It smelled way too good and I figured that by the time morning came or whenever he woke up, Victor would have forgotten all about his chicken.

Victor was right about rotisserie chicken tasting so good. I tore off one of the legs and sunk my teeth into it. I closed my eyes and savored the flavor. My hands were all greasy and then the phone rang. I stopped chewing and tried to be as quiet as possible. Victor turned to the side but his eyes were still closed. The phone kept ringing. I thought Mama would've picked it up but she didn't. I glanced at her bedroom door wondering what was she doing and why wasn't she answering the damn phone. Victor's eyes opened up by that time. He glared at me and then he glanced at the chicken in my hand.

"Is that mine?" Victor sat up. "Wait a minute, that's my damn chicken! Why you eating my chicken, Leesha? You gonna spend my damn money and come home and eat my chicken?"

"You over there 'sleep!" I said in defense.

"But I gave you the money to buy the chicken for me! I didn't tell your ass to come home and eat my food. You probably trying to keep my change, too, huh? How you gonna eat my chicken?"

"I only ate a little bit..."

"A little bit? Look like you already ate half of it. Them chickens ain't that big. You better pay me back for that shit."

"I'll give you your money. All you can charge me for is a leg. That's all I ate. Shit."

"There you go with that bad-ass mouth of yours. You ain't grown enough to curse or eat chicken that don't belong to you. Give me the rest of my damn chicken!"

"I'm not serving you. That's Mama's job!"

The phone stopped ringing while me and Victor was going back and forth about his stupid chicken. Maybe that was Treyvon trying to call me back. I wasn't sure how to feel about him calling me so soon. I thought he would at least wait until the next day but I guess I had him so excited that he couldn't wait.

I put the plastic top back on Victor's chicken and grabbed some water out of the refrigerator. I took my box of chocolate donuts and headed for my bedroom. Victor watched me the whole time. He looked half-drunk and half-asleep but I guess nothing could prevent him from keeping an eye on his chicken.

By the time I closed my bedroom door, the phone rang again. I opened the door back up and walked into the living room, hoping to answer the phone before anyone else did. Before I could get there, Victor had answered it already. I could hear him trying to figure out who was on the other end. He didn't sound too happy to hear whoever it was. I started to think that maybe he was talking to somebody that had been messing with Mama.

"Is that for me?" I asked Victor.

He held up his hand as if to tell me to be quiet.

"You want me to tell Mama that's for her?" I asked to see if it really was for her. Victor frowned. "It's real late. You shouldn't be calling at this hour any damn way!" he told the person on the phone. "I could just hang up on your ass."

I began to sense that the call was really for me so I reached for the phone. Victor tried to lean away but I managed to grab part of it. I tried to pull the phone away from him, but Victor was definitely stronger than me. He pushed me off of him and I fell to the floor. My first reaction was to jump right up and kick Victor in his leg. I couldn't tell at first if Victor was shocked by what I'd done or if I really hurt him. He held on to his leg and grimaced in pain. I couldn't resist smiling but at the same time, I kept an eye on him in case he tried to do something else. I picked up the phone and before I answered it, I had to say one last thing to Victor.

"Next time you need to give me the phone!"

Victor was too busy holding his leg and probably didn't listen, though I did hear him mumble the word "bitch" a couple times.

I finally spoke into the phone after I'd disappeared inside my bedroom. "Hello?"

"Hey, baby gurl..."

"Who is this?"

The voice on the other end sounded familiar but I wasn't sure enough to guess who it could be.

"This is your father. I think I let enough time go by before I contacted you since you can't seem to get in touch with me."

"That's what you good at, isn't it? You let time go by..."

"Leesha, listen..."

I hung up the phone before he could say anything else. I stood up and looked out my window, wondering why that man called me in the first place. Hearing his voice instantly made me feel confused inside. I'd pretty much gotten over that I'd seen him that time at Grammy's party. He was no longer an issue for me because so much time went by that I stopped thinking about him.

The phone rang again and I picked it up before it could ring twice.

"Hello!" I answered angrily.

"Leesha, listen to me and please don't hang up."

"Why are you calling me?"

"Because I'm your father and you're important to me."

"When did that happen?"

"What do you mean?"

"Me becoming important to you?"

"That's not fair but I understand why you feel that way. I want you to listen to what I have to say. Maybe by talking over the phone it'll be much easier than it was when we saw each other. I know that was probably uncomfortable for you but me and your grandmother thought it might be a special way for us to sort of reconnect."

I listened to my father speak and I had a hard time believing anything he said. There were too many years that separated us and that was a wall that was hard to knock down. What made me listen to him more than anything else was the fact that he'd mentioned Grammy. I found myself wanting to know more about what she may have said or shared with him so I could somehow hear her voice again.

"I was really sorry to hear when she passed away. Leesha, your grandmother was a special lady and I can never thank her enough for always keeping in touch with me over the years. She always wanted to make sure that I knew what was going on with you. Maybe that doesn't mean much to you, but I hope you know that I never stopped caring."

"Did Mama have a restraining order on you?"

"Restraining order?"

"Yeah! That's the only reason why a parent would have to stay away from their child."

"Leesha, I know it's hard to understand. I have trouble figuring it out myself how I could allow your mother to separate us for so long."

"Why are you calling me?"

He paused for a long time and I didn't try at all to make things easier for him. All I wanted to do was to make him feel sorry for not being around. I didn't care that he'd become frustrated behind my resisting him trying to come back in my life.

"Leesha, I'm not gonna disappear this time. I'm gonna keep trying until you sit down and talk with me face to face."

"Where are you now?" I asked.

"I'm in D.C. right now."

"That figures. Did you try to come to Grammy's funeral?"

"I didn't know about it until a few days after."

"You plan on coming out here anytime soon?"

"That depends on you, Leesha. I'm willing to take this at whatever pace you feel comfortable. For now, I ask that you visit with my sister in Long Beach."

"What should I do that for? You tried to get me to go there before. I don't wanna see your sister."

"Leesha?"

"What!"

"Just go sometime. Allow my sister to show you the other side of your family. You have two parents and you need to know my side of the family just like you grew up learning about your mother's side."

"That's because they were around..."

"I know this, Leesha, but give it a chance."

"I'll think about it."

"Please..."

"I have to go."

"Leesha, do it for us."

I hung up. I didn't want to hear anything more from my so-called father. He wanted me to visit his sister so badly that it made me feel uncomfortable. I kept thinking that I'd go over there, something would happen to me, and then I'd wake up with a headache in Washington, D.C. He sounded desperate enough to do some shit like that. I'm not about to go over there and get my ass kidnapped.

The next morning came and mama was immediately on my ass. She had me feeling like it was a weekday because as soon as I came out of my bedroom, there she was. She had that same funky look I'd see on her face almost every day, especially if I overslept on a school day.

Mama seems like she's always uptight and frustrated. When I came out of my room, I had just gotten off the phone with Treyvon. He called me a little before seven in the morning, which pissed me off at first. But then, I started to enjoy talking to him. Having somebody so into me was kind of a trip. It reminded me of my old enemy, Janina Parrish, and how she used to have so much control over guys who liked her silly ass. Treyvon gave me the same kind of attention over the phone, but Mama ruined that good feeling as soon as I stepped into the living room.

"Were you just talking to your father again?" Mama asked.

"How you know I was on the phone?"

"'Cause I heard it ring and Victor had to go into work early so I knew it wasn't him that picked it up. He told me about the call you got from your father last night."

"Yeah, so…"

"What did that nigga want this time?"

"Just to talk, that's all."

"His ass must've had a lot to say since he ain't been around in years."

"He says it's your fault he wasn't around."

"My fault? Next time you let me talk to his trifling ass—"

"I don't know if there will be a next time. Mama, I'm trying to finish school and do what I have to do. I'm not trying to worry about my silly parents."

"Hold up!" Mama yelled as if she didn't like what I'd said.

She'd gotten so agitated that her upper lip started quivering. Mama stepped a little closer.

"Victor told me about how you try to talk like you grown all the time."

"I don't care what Victor says."

"You don't care? Where you getting this attitude from? Is this what you learning from your boyfriend or you got some little niggas at school teaching you this?"

"I don't have a boyfriend. And, any attitude I have, I get from you, Mama. With you and Victor as role models, how do you expect me to talk?"

"Don't give me that shit, Leesha. Just, just go, okay? Just go…"

What I'd said seemed to affect Mama. For once she got quiet and didn't lash out like she normally did. I actually felt a little sorry for her. I walked over to the front door and started to leave without saying a word but that didn't feel right for some reason.

"I'm going to hang out with Treyvon. That's who I was talking to just now, Mama. It was Treyvon, not my father."

Mama didn't respond but I could tell she'd heard me. She looked the other way and didn't say anything. It was strange to see her that way, but I guess I'd gotten the best of her.

Treyvon let me choose the place where we would meet. I told him that we could hang out and talk at the Der Weinerschnitzel hot dog stand. I always liked hanging out there because you could watch the cars go by on Crenshaw Boulevard. I had to walk to get there but it's not that far from my neighborhood. In fact, I'd walk right past the funeral home where Grammy's service was held. The memories made me get sad but I snapped out of it about a block and a half later. That's when I saw Treyvon already ordering his food. I guess he was hungry and didn't feel like waiting. I didn't bother him about it too much because I figured with me walking, he probably was waiting for a long time.

"Treyvon!"

"Hey, Leesha!"

"How long you been here?"

"Not too long...ten minutes at the most."

"And you couldn't wait for me?"

"Sorry about that. But hey, check this out. I brought a blanket and I ordered five hot dogs so we can have a little picnic. What you think?"

"That's cool. Let me get something to drink, though."

"I'll get it for you."

I smiled for two reasons. One was that it was really nice to have somebody trying so hard to make me happy. And two, Treyvon was showing me that he had some money and didn't mind spending it. I made a mental note of that.

Treyvon spread the blanket underneath the tree. It was a trip trying to have a picnic with cars zooming by. Treyvon had a car but I didn't feel like going anywhere else. The spot underneath the tree was perfect.

"What's that?" I asked Treyvon.

He'd pulled out a black journal from his backpack.

"I carry this everywhere I go in case I get an idea for something to draw. My parents used to always tell me that if I don't use the talent that God gave me, I'll end up losing it. I don't ever want to stop being able to draw so I keep a journal with me all the time."

"That's cool. I wish I had a talent like that."

"Maybe you do."

"I don't think so. It doesn't bother me. I'm smart so that's probably all I need."

"You mind if I draw you, Leesha?"

"Draw me?"

"Yeah, do you mind?"

"I guess not. Go ahead."

Treyvon excitedly turned to a blank page in his journal. As he flipped through the pages, I'd seen sketches of all sorts of things. I wondered if I'd see another girl's face in his book. For a second I thought I'd discovered that Treyvon was really a playa and used his talent to impress females. I didn't see any other girl in his journal, though. I guess I was the first but then again, how many journals did he really have? I didn't ask, but I thought about it.

"You don't have to pose or anything. Just act naturally."

"Humph…"

"What's that for, Leesha?"

"What's what for?"

"You look mad."

"It's nothing. Thanks for the hot dogs."

"You're welcome. I hope you're okay with me sketching you."

"It's cool, I guess."

Treyvon started to sketch very lightly. I watched him closely. His hand moved really fast. I was curious to know what was going through his mind. He bit down on his bottom lip as if he were making a special effort to really concentrate on what he was doing. It made me self-conscious about how I looked. I tried to sit up straight with perfect posture. I fixed my hair several times.

"Leesha, just be yourself and act normal. No matter what you do, I'm still gonna draw your face the way I see it, know what I mean? It's like I've already captured you in my mind. I have photographic memory."

"Then why you need me posing for you?"

"I don't really. I need you to be yourself so that if I put certain expressions on your face, I'll be able to know if I'm really drawing this to look like you."

"Whatever."

"Leesha, what makes you tick?"

"What are you talking about?"

"You seem so defensive and mad a lot."

"You trippin'."

"See?"

"I'm not defensive. I just don't really know what to say."

"That happens a lot when I try to draw someone. It's the same way with cameras. People freeze up or they open their eyes too wide. People who draw have to be even more patient than a photographer. I can't just snap your picture a second before you blink. I have to remember everything."

"You have a lot of friends, Treyvon?"

"Nah, not really."

"That's 'cause you always trying to draw niggas!"

"Dang, Leesha! How you get like that?"

"Like what?"

"Hard."

"Whatever."

"You are so fine. I don't think anybody would ever guess you talk the way you do."

"I don't worry any more about what people think, Treyvon. I just have to be me and do what keeps me happy. You should do the same thing and try to pursue your dreams. You seem like you've grown up right. You probably spoiled and get everything you want."

"I don't know, I guess so. My parents are cool. Dad is sort of like an ex black hippie—"

"A black who?"

"Hippie…"

"I don't even know what that is."

"That's some sixties stuff. He comes from that time when the Vietnam War was going on, Black Panthers, and Jimi Hendrix. My dad still listens to that stuff. It kind of influences me, too, because Hendrix was real creative. Sort of like Prince. You like Prince?"

"He's okay. I like his slow songs and I seen *Purple Rain* on video."

"What kind of music you listen to, Leesha?"

"Whatever is on the radio or bump'n down the street...I don't know, shoot."

"I bet you like Tupac."

"What's wrong with that?"

"Nothing."

I glanced down at Treyvon's journal and noticed an image that looked exactly like me. As we were talking, he'd sketched an outline of my face really quickly and had begun sketching my body as I sat across from him with my legs crossed. It was a trip to see. It even made me smile but I turned my face away from him so he couldn't see me.

"What's wrong, Leesha?"

I frowned. "Nothing is wrong, why?"

"I don't know. The way you turned away from me had me thinking I said something you didn't like."

"No, it's cool. Finish what you were gonna say about your parents."

"Oh, well, my dad always jokes about today's music. I mean, I listen to Tupac, too, but mostly I listen to a lot of the East Coast hip-hop. I'm really into the culture and being that I draw and want to do my own comic book series, I try to learn from that graffiti stuff that they do back East."

"We got graffiti artists out here."

"Yeah, I know but it ain't the same. I mean, they try to lock up graffiti artists out here but back east, they celebrate that stuff. You got them subway trains that's fully loaded with graffiti art and nobody gets arrested for it. Out here they act like all you doing is tagging walls with gang stuff. It's more to it than that. Remember that dude named Chaka? His name was all over L.A. and he became a legend and a nuisance. Then he got locked up. They shut him down and killed his creativity."

"You are too nice to do graffiti. You're trying to tell me that you write on walls and billboards?"

"Yeah, I've done a few. I'm even working on a mural underneath this bridge downtown. It's so well hidden that nobody knows about it, though. I'll probably finish it in a month or two. I don't know. Now that I met you, it may take longer."

"Why you say that?"

"I'd kind of like to add your picture to the mural. I hope you don't mind that? I mean, it's gonna look cool!"

I thought for a moment. The silence between us had Treyvon looking nervous. He stopped sketching me and drank his soda. He kept looking at me and clearing his throat. I looked away and smiled once again. I thought about my picture somewhere on a wall and the idea was pretty cool.

"You gonna show it to me when you finish?" I asked him.

"What do you mean? Show you what?"

"This mural you're talking about?"

"Oh! Yeah, you know it!"

Treyvon was all excited. He didn't know what to do with his hands so he returned to something more familiar as he laughed to himself and kept smiling at me. Treyvon picked up his journal and continued sketching. He added more details but he never tried to show me what he was doing. I glanced at what he'd done every time he'd look down. It was a trip to watch him because he didn't look at me that often. It was like he said. He'd captured my image in his mind and that's all he really needed.

Me and Treyvon didn't hang out for very long. I wanted to get back home and be around the house for a while. Something about the sadness in Mama's eyes made me wonder what was really going on. I'd seen that look before. It comes and goes with the ending of each relationship she's in. I could feel the door closing on her situation with Victor. It looked all too familiar to me.

When Treyvon dropped me off, I thanked him for a really nice time. It was cool. It was different for me because he had me feeling like a kid again. When he pulled up to the front of my building, I waited to see what he would do. I wondered if he was gonna open my door but he didn't. Then I waited to see if he was gonna try to kiss me. He acted like he wanted to. He even tried to ask me if it was okay but he stuttered so much that he gave up. I smiled and patted him on his leg. I know he hated that but there would be another time. I don't give freebies. Niggas got to earn every inch and every minute where it concerns me. Even though Treyvon is a sweetheart, him being nice don't give him no exceptions to my rules. Treyvon blew his horn and drove away. I frowned at him for making all that damn noise and then I went upstairs to check on Mama.

When I opened the door, she was nowhere in sight. I didn't bother to call out to her because I'd seen her keys on the kitchen table. I could hear her coughing in her room as I walked over to the TV and turned it on. Coughing was a good sign that she was at least breathing but something felt funny in the air. It was silent and the house didn't smell like stinky socks. I started to wonder if I was dreaming. Usually after being home for five minutes, Victor would appear out of nowhere to talk shit to me. He wasn't around.

I put my things in my room, took off my jewelry, and changed clothes. I felt a new sense of freedom knowing that Victor wasn't around. I could relax and enjoy some television all by myself for a change. I felt like celebrating. I walked to the kitchen and took my time looking through the refrigerator. I was shocked to see that there was no beer inside but the amount of food was still the same. There was hardly nothing except some stuff to make sandwiches. I was cool with that because I didn't have to worry about Victor bugging me to make him one, too.

I got a little bit too relaxed on the couch after a while. I mean, I was sitting in front of the TV, cracking up. I got tired of hearing about the O.J. trial on just about every channel. The only thing else on was *Seinfeld* so I watched that. It was funny. I got so into it that I didn't realize Mama was standing in the living room looking at me. I only noticed because she cleared her throat.

"Mama, you scared me!"

"What are you doing?"

"Watching television. This is the first time I've been able to in months."

"You probably need to be in your room studying. Ain't nothing on TV that you need to see."

"Mama, don't start!"

Mama had that look on her face like she was about to talk non-stop shit to me. I thought I'd get a break from her for once while she was in her room feeling sorry for herself. She stood there, not really looking at anything but sort of drifting off. I could tell she had a lot on her mind, but she didn't think too hard because she'd snap back to reality and say some funky shit to me.

"How many boys you sleep with so far?" she asked.

"What?" I laughed.

"Did I say something funny? I don't know what you be doing out there. I ain't seen that young man you used to hang around with in a long time. Now you got some other boy calling you."

"Mama, I ain't slept with nobody and I ain't seen Scottie, just because—"

"You two broke up?"

"He wasn't my boyfriend. I told you that before."

"Yeah, well, something must be wrong. You was always together."

"What about you and Victor? You was always together, too!"

"Humph."

Mama returned to her silence. I guess she wasn't ready to talk about Victor yet. It would take more prying for me to get her to open up about it. That usually meant I had to make her mad. That's how me and her communicated. Piss each other off and somebody is bound to say something. I think she tried to beat me to the punch by changing the subject and talking about my father.

"How many times this week have you talked to that nigga?" she asked.

"Who you talking about?"

"Your father, that's who!"

"Why you hate my father so much? I mean, I don't like him either but my reason is obvious. What's yours, Mama?"

"Don't you worry about that, Leesha. You wasn't even born yet when your father started showing me what kind of man he is, so you don't need to know what happened."

"Something must've happened. Maybe I should just ask him."

"Yeah, you probably talk all the time, anyway. You planning on going out there to see him?"

"No."

"Then why is he calling you so much?"

"Mama, he don't call me that much. You be thinking that he does. I told you that last time, it was Treyvon on the phone."

Mama's anger and sadness was easy to pick up. She kept going on and on about my father when deep down I think she was worried about me leaving her. As much as I wanted to leave, it had nothing to do with my father. I wanted my own place. I thought to myself that if things were different between Mama and Victor, she probably wouldn't give a damn where I went to. I wouldn't be missed at all. The only time I get most of her attention is either when she's mad or in between assholes like Victor. I'm like her cure for when she gets bored. I know she'll find another man soon and it'll be the same old thing because Mama's habits never change.

Mama came over and sat beside of me on the couch. She picked up the phone and started to dial.

I asked her, "Who you calling?"

"Your father."

"What for?"

Mama stopped and then sighed heavily. It was the first time in a long time that I had seen her cry.

"Why you crying?"

She didn't say anything. She held her head up and looked at me. Tears streamed down her face and she looked mad. I watched her, wondering what she was about to do or say. She was sitting there, holding on to the phone. She didn't finish dialing my father's number but she still had the phone off the hook. I could hear laughter in the background from the *Seinfeld* show but I kept my eyes on Mama. She was still crying but she hadn't made a sound. She looked so angry that I could imagine her tears felt like hot boiling water dripping down her skin. She stood up with the phone still in her hand. She kept staring at me.

"What's wrong with you?" I asked her.

That's when Mama threw the phone at me. I was lucky that I put my hands up or it would've hit me in the face.

"Why you do that?" I shouted as Mama walked past me and headed back to her bedroom.

"You call your father and tell him he can come get you! If you want to go live with him, that's fine by me!"

"I told you I ain't going nowhere!" I screamed back at her.

Her response was the slamming of her bedroom door. I screamed out one last word to her before our apartment became engulfed in silence.

"Bitch!"

I sat in front of the television, scouring and thinking about how much I hated my mother at that point. My arm was sore from when I blocked the phone from hitting my face. I rubbed my skin and thought about making a phone call myself. I didn't want to call my father but I was curious to call his sister in Long Beach. Maybe hearing her voice might help me. Maybe she knew what happened back in the day to make Mama so angry at my father. I had to go to my bedroom and search for the phone number. I'd written it down the last time I talked to him, but I had an attitude about him giving it to me so I couldn't even remember what I did with it. The more I searched for the number, the more the idea of calling began to fade away. I couldn't find it. I went to bed. Mama and I both seemed to feel like shit on this night and I'm pretty sure that if anyone walked into our apartment, they'd have felt the same way.

I sat thinking about Mama in school all day long. It's a trip how me and her acted toward each other. What's even worse is that I got used to it. I don't even know how it got that way or why. One day I got older and realized that she and I argue all the time. And once I got the nerve to talk back to her, nothing has changed between us since. The only thing that seems different now is the sadness in Mama. I'd seen her get over others before with a deep sigh and a shoulder shrug. It seemed to be on a much deeper level this time. Maybe she actually loved Victor. Maybe she got used to always being there for him. I don't know what she saw in that asshole. People like him never stick around and Mama should've known that.

I got through my day at school by keeping to myself and not really saying much in class. Usually, I was always first to raise my hand when a teacher would ask a question. This time I would look around and wait for somebody else to answer. If the teacher called on me, I'd speak up but I wouldn't smile or show any kind of interest in the question. When I walked out of my third-period class, I remember Mr. Carmelo asking me if I was okay. I looked at him but didn't really answer.

"See you tomorrow, Leesha," he said.

I waved goodbye and dragged myself down the hallway until I got to my locker. My mind was so gone that I even forgot my combination for a minute. I leaned my head against the locker and told myself to get it together. I never really did, but I did have a nice surprise waiting for me outside the gate when I got out of school.

When my last class ended for the day, I was so relieved. I walked with my head down, contemplating every step I took. I wondered what kind of mood I'd find Mama in when I got home. I was so deep in thought that I was caught completely by surprise. Treyvon was waiting outside the gate holding flowers in his hand. I didn't really see him until he stepped right in front of me. I was about to give him a piece of my mind about a split second before I noticed the flowers.

"What up, Leesha!" Treyvon said.

He was all happy and standing proud. He pushed the flowers in my face like some little boy giving a girl flowers for the first time. "Here, you surprised?"

"Uh-huh. How did you even know how to find me?"

"I got lucky, plus I was asking everybody and yelling out your name. One person told me what your last class was, so here I am. I would've come to your apartment if I didn't find you here but none of that matters now! You like the flowers?"

"Yeah, they're nice. Thanks. What time you get out of school? You must've drove fast over here."

"Yeah, I drove kind of fast but I've been planning this since last night. I bought the flowers early this morning and then kept them in my car. I got out of school early. I got it like that!"

"Oh, you do, huh?"

"Nah, just playing. We had a test today and as soon as we finished, we got to leave. It was easy so I did it as fast as I could."

"You sound so excited, Treyvon."

"I am! Let me give you a ride home."

"Okay, but relax a little."

"I'm cool. I'm cool."

"Uh-huh, you don't look too cool."

"Well, Leesha, I like you a lot."

"I can tell but you're embarrassing me with all that jumping around and talking so fast."

"Oh, sorry about that. I just never really been into a girl before like I am with you. I want you to like me and see that I'm a good guy."

"Go slow, Treyvon. I'm not trying to get serious with anybody. I think you're cool, though and I appreciate the flowers."

"You think I'm cool, huh?"

"Yeah, you're cool."

"That's a start. A good start, huh?"

"Yeah, it's good."

"Great."

Treyvon was trying real hard to do all the right things. We walked to his car and then he opened the door for me. He held the flowers while I got into the car and then he handed them back to me. I smiled. I liked being treated like a lady. It was different for me. I wasn't really sure how I felt about Treyvon, though. He's cute and all but too nice for me. I wasn't gonna tell him that. I figured why not enjoy the things he does for me? I already let him know that I wasn't trying to get serious so that pretty much says that there are limitations to our situation. I wasn't sure that Treyvon understood that but, oh well.

Treyvon took me to Fox Hills Mall. I looked at him like he was crazy, driving me so far from home. It's really not that far but he had me wondering what he was up to.

"Why we come here?" I asked.

"Oh, um, I thought it would be a cool place to take you. They got some cool stores up in here."

"I been here before, Treyvon. You ain't the only one that gets around."

"Oh. Well, we can eat here, too, if you like."

"Okay."

Treyvon was the gentleman once again as he ran around the front of his silver Acura. It was nice to ride in a car where both doors opened. I could definitely tell that Treyvon was never without money in his pocket. His parents probably made sure of that regardless of if he worked or not.

We started walking toward the entrance of the mall. We'd parked by Robinson's-May department store. I looked at Treyvon walking next to me so happy. He had a serious bounce in his step. I was walking with my arms folded, tripping off of him. I kept my arms that way because I didn't really want him to try to hold my hand. He seemed like the type who would do that.

Treyvon stepped in front of me so he could open the door as we entered Robinson's May. I noticed he wasn't carrying his journal so I made a comment about it.

"I thought you said you always carry your journal, Treyvon."

"Oh shit, I forgot! You mind if I run and get it?"

I laughed. "No, if it's that important to you, I'll wait."

"Cool. I'll be right back. I sketched something that I want to show you later."

Treyvon literally ran back to his car. As I waited for him to return, a couple of guys walked by trying to get my attention. They both were older and were probably around the same age as Scottie.

One of them spoke and the sound of his voice instantly made me smile. It was really deep and he had that look about him that seemed kind of thuggish. "What's up, young lady?"

His walk was so cool. He told his friend to hold up. They both stopped in the doorway. I wasn't sure what to say. I wanted to hear this guy speak some more and at the same time I was trying to look out for Treyvon.

"You waiting for your man or what?" the thuggish guy asked.

"No, I'm waiting for a friend."

"That's cool."

I overheard his friend commenting that I was young. They both was looking me up and down. I could hear warning signs in my head saying I didn't need to be fucking with these guys. They was sizing me up and trying to see how stupid I was. That one guy looked really good, but I wasn't about to get my ass raped by some older nigga no matter how fine he was.

"Nice talking to you," I said as I noticed Treyvon about to enter the store.

The thuggish guy looked at Treyvon and laughed. "Aight, nice talking to you, too."

Treyvon walked over to me and said, "You know that guy?"

"Nope. He was just trying to talk to me, I guess."

"You like guys like that, huh?"

"What do you mean?"

"You know…thuggish-type guys."

I shrugged my shoulders. "I don't know. He's okay, I guess. Let's forget about him. I'm kind of hungry right now."

"Cool, let's get something. I'm hungry, too."

Treyvon continued with his bouncy walk and I kept my arms folded. I probably looked like I wasn't interested but it was more like I felt weird being with him. He's cute, he's tall, and from what I could tell, he had a nice body. It's just that he acted slightly nerdy despite that he wore some cool clothes.

We bought some hamburgers from the A&W place inside the food court. Treyvon straddled his chair in front of me, sitting like most guys tend to do. I guess he was trying to be cool or something. I just rolled my eyes.

"What's wrong?" he asked.

"Nothing. What did you want to show me?"

"Show you?"

"Yeah, you said there was something you sketched, remember? You smoke weed or something?"

Treyvon laughed. "Weed? Hell nah! Why you ask me that?"

"'Cause your short-term memory is whack!"

Treyvon smiled. "No, I remember. I was gonna get around to it. You know, I have a friend that smokes a lot of weed and he forgets, too. He been smoking for years! He always brags about it, too, and then five minutes later, he'll forget what he said."

"You actually know somebody that does weed?"

"Why you say it like that?"

"'Cause you don't seem like you hang out with anybody that might do something that's not considered a good thing."

"Nah, Robert might be a little dense but he's cool. He's not a drug addict or anything like that. He has some strange mood swings, but we just joke with him because he looks like he's forty going on fifty-something. His skin is all jacked up."

"Well, make sure I don't meet his ass."

"Okay, Leesha, I won't bring him around."

"Thanks."

"How about you?"

"How about me, what?"

"What kind of friends you have? Do you have a best friend?"

"Yeah, I have a best friend but I don't want to talk about that right now. Show me the sketch you did."

"Okay."

As Treyvon thumbed through the pages of his journal, I found myself drifting off and thinking about Scottie. I felt a little guilty about calling him my best friend when in reality, I'd shut him off. I hadn't spoken to him in so long and it wasn't because he did something wrong. Scottie never did anything wrong. It was just me, tripping off what happened with Grammy and pushing Scottie away.

"Leesha, check this out," Treyvon said.

I didn't hear him at first. He had to wave his hands in front of my eyes to get my attention.

"Hello, you okay?" Treyvon asked.

"Huh?"

"You was gone, Leesha! What were you thinking about?"

"Nothing...I was just looking around."

"I don't think so. I mean, your eyes were open but they weren't focused on anything."

"Whatever. You gonna show me your sketch or not?"

"Yeah, that's what I was trying to do!"

"Okay, well, show me then."

Treyvon turned the journal around so that the page could face my direction. He told me to wait before I looked. He wanted me to close my eyes so he could unveil it slowly. I closed my eyes for a second but I felt weird about doing that in a crowded mall, so Treyvon covered the sketch with a napkin.

I was like, "What's the big deal?"

"I just want you to be really surprised, Leesha. I mean, this came out really good. I may have to put this one on a wall somewhere, but I'm thinking that since you gonna see this one, I need to create a new one."

"Is that right?"

"Yeah, because I want you to be surprised again."

"Well, I ain't surprised yet because you haven't shown me the sketch!"

Treyvon removed the napkin that he'd used to cover the sketch. When I laid my eyes on what he had done in his journal, I started buggin' out a little bit. I thought to myself, *how could this guy like me so much to be doing something like this?* The sketch he'd done looked so life-like.

"This looks just like me!" I told him.

"It is you, Leesha. You like it?"

"It's nice, really. I can't believe you draw this good. How long did it take you?"

"Not that long. I did most of it when we were having that picnic but then after I got home I smoothed out the rough edges. Then I sketched a few more details until I came up with what you see now."

"You need to try to do something with your talent."

"Like I told you before, I am. I'm checking out schools back east. My parents are pretty excited about it, so we'll see."

"I don't blame them. This is really good."

"Thanks, Leesha."

Treyvon blushed as I continued to check out his sketch of me. I wasn't just trying to pump him up. What he'd done was really good.

"Well, I need to get home, Treyvon. You gonna take me?"

"Of course! Why, you think I wasn't gonna take you home?"

"Nah, just playing but I really need to get home. Mama ain't been acting right. She broke up with her boyfriend so she's trippin' right now."

"Your parents been separated long?"

"They never really been together so I guess you could say that."

"Oh, sorry about that, Leesha."

"Why you sorry?"

"I don't know. I just—"

"Don't be sorry, Treyvon, unless you know what you're talking about."

"I'm not trying to make you mad, Leesha. I was trying to...I don't know what I'm trying to say."

"Let's just go. It might be hard for you to understand because your life is

cool. Your parents will be together forever and they'll make sure your school-
ing is paid for. You got it made, Treyvon."

"Is that so bad?"

"I think we should go, okay?"

"You mad, Leesha?"

"Treyvon?"

"Okay, damn…"

Treyvon had no more bounce in his step. I wasn't really mad at him. I didn't
feel like I needed to open up and tell him my life story. His life seemed perfect
compared to mine, and I felt like talking to him about Mama was a waste of
time. He wouldn't understand because his parents were together, and he
ain't never had to deal with his mother the same way I do. Only Scottie could
relate and actually tell me something that might help me. Treyvon only
reminded me of how much I missed Scottie's wisdom.

I was so happy to be home once Treyvon dropped me off. As soon as I
opened the front door, I yelled. "Mama! You home?"

I heard no answer. I checked her bedroom. Her bed was all messed up, the
closet door was open, and I'd seen a couple of her shoes on the floor. Mama
always kept her room kind of junky so I didn't see anything out of the ordinary.
I checked both bathrooms. I could pretty much tell she wasn't home but I
still had to look. I felt like her not being home was a good thing because it
meant that Mama wasn't sitting around doing nothing. Maybe when she
comes home, she'll be happy.

I took full advantage of Mama not being home because once again, I had
the place all to myself. It was a weird feeling but it was nice. The only problem
was that this time there was no food in the refrigerator and my ass was broke.
I wasn't sure what to do if I got hungry again later. I was glad that Treyvon
had taken me to get something to eat. Maybe it was a good thing that I had
him around.

A few hours went by and there was still no sign of Mama. It got to the point
where I kept the sound of the television down so I could listen out for her
keys jingling. Mama had been out late before without telling me so I figured
this was probably another one of those times. I tried not to worry about it

too, but at the same time, I wasn't really comfortable being completely alone for so long. I know I talk about moving on my own all the time, but I think it'll be different then. I'll get me a place in a neighborhood that feels a lot safer. Kind of like where Grammy lived.

On this night as I continued to wait for Mama, it was eerily quiet. The gate outside no longer slammed shut because somebody had broken it recently. They decided to remove the part that opens up. I'd gotten used to hearing that loud noise. Without it, the building seemed a little less safe. That gate was like a security alarm for us but now, anyone could walk through it and not be heard.

I stayed up until about two a.m. I knew that because I kept checking the clock every few minutes and by that time I was trying to fight off sleep. I'd grabbed a blanket and pillow and slept on the couch. I wasn't about to go to sleep in my bedroom with the door closed like I normally do. I think I only slept a couple hours before the phone rang and woke me up.

I was like, "Shit, Mama!" because my first thought was that it would be her calling. It wasn't mama. In fact, I wasn't sure who it was because they hung up after I answered. I had my eyes closed the whole time I'd picked up the phone so I was able to turn right back over and go to sleep.

The phone rang again a few minutes later and this time the person said something. It was Victor on the other end, sounding like his usual self. His voice was scratchy and he acted like I should be happy to hear from him. Then all of a sudden the tone of his conversation changed. He was acting like he needed to tell me something that I might want to hear. He was right in that I needed to hear it, but he was wrong about me wanting to hear what he said.

"Leesha, you need to go get your mother out of jail."

"Huh?"

"Yo mama in jail, girl. You should probably get her ass out unless you don't care. I'm just telling you this 'cause that's how I am. Personally, I think the bitch should rot inside there."

"Why Mama in jail? What did you do?"

"I ain't done shit! Your mama the one come over here and bust out my windows! I had to call the police on her ass. She was still going off when they came. Yo mama crazy, too!"

"How am I gonna get her out of jail? I don't have no money! What jail is she in?"

"She over there on Martin Luther King Boulevard. You know where that station is right next to the carwash?"

"Why you can't get her out?"

"I don't want to and she come over here attacking me so I'm the one that put her ass in jail. I'm through now. I did my part by telling you...bye!"

Victor hung up the phone and I had no clue what to do. I sat in my own silence for a while trying to figure things out. I didn't have any money and no clue who to call about getting Mama out of jail. I thought about calling Treyvon but that was only because I figured he had the money. But then I thought about him losing his mind trying to figure out what to do. I doubted that Treyvon knew anything about getting somebody out of jail. That's when I decided it was time to call Scottie. When I picked up the phone, my hand was trembling because I was so nervous. I was thinking that Scottie would either hang up on me or curse me out.

It was almost five-thirty a.m. so I'd begin to think that maybe Victor was right. Maybe I should let Mama stay in jail since it was almost daylight, anyway. I don't know, for some reason I couldn't do that. I mean, despite all the shit between us and how we didn't really get along anymore, I just couldn't go back to sleep and let Mama stay in jail. I had to at least try to do something. I don't know if she'd do the same for me but like I always said, she and I ain't the same, anyway.

I called Scottie and this time I didn't hesitate. I dialed his number quickly and held the phone to my ear. I was still nervous but this had to be done. It took about five rings before he finally answered. "Yeah..."

His voice was a welcome sound to my ears. I smiled when I heard it.

"Scottie, it's me...Leesha."

"Leesha? Been a while, huh?"

Scottie's voice was calm and sounded as if he was waiting to see what I'd say before he'd curse me out. I could hear him take a deep breath as if to say, *why the fuck is she calling me?* He didn't say that but I wouldn't blame him if he did.

I asked him, "Scottie, you mad at me?"

"What you mean?"

"You know. I mean, it's been a long time and I've kind of just disappeared on you..."

"Yeah, I started to wonder, you know...I was like, what the fuck? But then I figured you was just really down about your grandmother so I left it alone. Then that gave me time to concentrate on some shit that I needed to do, nah mean?"

"Like school?"

"Yeah, that's part of it but hey, I know you ain't call a brotha this time in the morning to catch up on old times. What's up?"

"Mama in jail..."

"Say what?"

"She in jail...Victor just called me telling me she busted out his windows. He called the police on her."

"For real?"

"Yeah."

"Damn, time changes everything, huh?"

"Why you say that?"

"It's a trip how things happen. I figured those two were still together and you was still trying to get away."

"Well, Mama and Victor been acting strange toward each other for the last few months. Then the last couple days he wasn't around and Mama was looking sad so I figured they probably broke up. I ain't never seen Mama take it this hard before. She shouldn't even be trippin' over that nigga."

"You got that right. So, what you gonna do about her being in jail?"

"I don't know what to do."

"Okay...I'll see what I can do. You okay with going down to the police station? I mean, we may not have to go but just in case..."

"Yeah, I'll go if you come with me."

"I got your back, you know that."

"Thanks, Scottie. I'm sorry for not—"

"Yo, it's cool. We'll talk about it."

Scottie told me to wait for him to call me back. He said he knew a bail bonds person who could get Mama out of jail. He'd used him a few times because of his brother. It was some guy named Mathew. I told Scottie where Mama was and he kind of laughed. He said he been to that station too many times. I asked him if he'd ever been to jail and he said, "almost."

Scottie called back about an hour later. I jumped when the phone rang because all I'd been doing was sitting on the couch, staring at some morning show on TV. I wasn't really paying attention, except for thinking about how silly those people be acting. I guess they act stupid like that to wake people up.

When I answered the phone, Scottie was so calm like what he'd done was no big deal. He said that everything was taken care of and that we didn't need to go to the station.

"How she gonna get home?" I asked him.

"After they process everything, Mathew gonna bring her home."

"Thanks, Scottie."

"No prob."

"But hey, what about money? I mean, I don't have anything to even go to the store with right now."

"Leesha, it's cool. We friends for life, right?"

"I hope so."

"Cool, then whenever you got the cash or you just wanna do a brotha a favor then you do it. I got your back and I think you got mine, too. And don't be thinking I'm talking about sex 'cause we ain't like that, aight?"

"Okay."

Scottie read my mind before I could even say anything. He did have me thinking that the kind of favor he was talking about was sexual. To be honest, I thought about it, too. I didn't know how I was gonna repay him for what he'd done for Mama, and it seems like the only other thing that people want besides money is sex.

I continued to talk to Scottie while waiting for Mama to get home. It was as good a time as any to catch up and see what'd been going on in his life. Sometimes Scottie had me laughing and other times I wondered how deeply he was involved in his illegal activities that he didn't tell me about.

I asked Scottie, "How's school?"

"Aw man, school is real cool but after the semester ended, I had to stop."

"Why? You always preach about staying in school."

"True, but things got too tight with me supporting my brother, paying the rent and shit like that. Plus, opportunities came up to where I needed to explore some things. I've been coming home at crazy hours so I knew school would be affected by that. I ain't the type to do some shit halfway, you feel me?"

"I don't know what you mean."

"I'm talking about school. That's way too important for me to mess around and not take it serious. So, I had to take this semester off, but I'll be back probably next fall."

"Then what have you been doing? You never tell me things, Scottie. You know I ain't gonna tell nobody."

"I don't know, Leesha. Sometimes it's hard for me to tell you or anybody else what I do because the more niggas know about your hustle, the easier it is for shit to go down the wrong way. I don't want nothing coming back on me that I can control by handling my business in a smart way."

"You don't think you could trust me?"

"Yeah, I can trust you but I'm just saying that's how I am."

"What else you do besides sell weed? You a gigolo or something? Am I gonna see you over there on Santa Monica Boulevard?"

"Aw, you got jokes! You ain't never gonna see me over there. I don't care how much money they make. I got some guidelines to my hustle."

"You're funny, Scottie, and you really take it that seriously?"

"I got to, Leesha. It be some dangerous stuff going on out there so it ain't all fun."

"Then why do you do it?"

"Why you asking me these questions?"

"Because I wanna know! I think we've been friends long enough for me to ask you stuff."

"Maybe so, but I still need some time before I tell you everything."

Scottie's defensive tone warned me that I should switch gears and lighten up the conversation. It was a trip how much he actually didn't say to me, but I could read between the lines. I could tell that everything Scottie had been doing lately wasn't legal.

I asked, "Scottie, you have a girlfriend?"

He laughed. "Say what? Where did that come from?"

"What you mean, where did it come from?"

"First, you was trying to question me about my moneymaking and now you trying to see who I'm messing with."

"Is that a secret, too?"

"Nah, ain't no secret. Ain't no lady in my life."

"Why not?"

"Aw, you trippin', Leesha. Why not? Because it just ain't happened."

"You don't date or nothing?"

"Damn, girl!" Scottie laughed.

I could've sworn he sounded like I was making him blush. I didn't think it was such a big deal me asking him about any girls in his life, but his reactions made me think that there was a shy side to Scottie "Blaze" Franklin.

"What's wrong with my question?" I asked him.

"Nothing is wrong. It's cool…um, maybe I should be asking you, though! Shit. It's been a while since I seen you so maybe you been kicking it with some dude."

"I asked you first, Scottie. You can't just throw the question on me."

"Yo, Leesha…I ain't got no girlfriend and nobody that I'm interested in. I been hanging out at the strip club whenever I need to rub on some booty and uh, a few days ago, I kicked it with this prostitute that had it going on!"

"I don't know if I wanna hear about that."

"Well, you asked."

"Yeah, but I mean, a prostitute?"

"Ain't nothing different about her except her situation in life. She struggling and using what she got to get some money. I hope she don't get caught up 'cause right now she fine as hell, but sometimes sistahs stay in that game too long."

"What do you mean?"

"They stay in it too long and forget why they started doing it. They lose sight that it should be temporary and only for the money. They get caught up and start messing with the drugs and alcohol. They meet up with the wrong niggas trying to pimp them. All kind of things be happening on the streets, you know that."

"And what if I said I wanted to do that?"

"I'll beat your ass, girl! You need to do what you doing and stay in school graduate, and find yourself a fuck'n career!"

"But you was talking like it was okay a second ago."

"Leesha, that's different…Don't be thinking about doing some shit like that. I'm serious…"

"Whatever…"

"Uh-huh…"

"What if I want to strip? You know somebody at that club that could get me a job in there?"

"You buggin' out, girl!" Scottie laughed.

"What's wrong with working at a strip club? Don't they have waitresses in there?"

"For them other hoes, it's cool, but not for you. Plus, you too young for that shit…Them waitresses just be there waiting until they get the nerve to hop on stage. I don't want you doing that shit, Leesha. You got choices right now. Why you thinking about this stuff?"

"I got the body for it and I can dance."

"What body? Shit. It's a trip that I don't even look at you that way. But uh, I think you just trying to mess with my mind. You need some money or something?"

"Yeah…"

"I'll give you some, aight? You don't need to be working at no strip club. You got me worried like I'm gonna need to watch what you be doing. I used to kick it with this girl that works at Sears. Maybe she can hook you up with something there."

"I'm okay. Listen, I met this guy that seems really nice. I don't know. He's cute—"

"Say what? So that's why you ain't called me in a while, huh?"

"No, I just met Treyvon not too long ago…"

"Trey who?"

"Treyvon. He's sweet. It's crazy how much he likes me already. It kind of scares me sometimes because I be thinking he gonna be camped out at my door all night and follow me everywhere I go."

"That's cool. You got you a nice muh-fucker instead of a thug. That's good."

"I don't know about all that. Treyvon is nice but we ain't going together."

"Uh-huh, well I hope you ain't trying to hook up with a thug. You been seeing anybody else or is Trey the only one?"

"I haven't met anybody else. Hold up, Scottie, I hear somebody walking up the stairs."

"It might be your mother."

"Oh shit!"

"What happened?"

"Somebody just knocked on the door really hard. You hear it?"

"Yeah, I hear it. Go check it out, I'll wait."

"Okay, wait...You hear that? Somebody said my name and I don't know who that was."

"That might be Mathew bringing your mother home."

"Scottie, can you come over here?"

"Aight, I'll be there in a minute."

Scottie hung up and I walked quietly to the front door. I jumped every time the person knocked on the door. I was feeling like in any minute, they was gonna kick it in. I looked through the peephole and could see a man but I didn't recognize him. His voice was powerful when he called my name.

"Leesha, open the door!"

I finally spoke up. "I don't know you! What do you want?"

"I brought your mama home."

"Are you Mathew?"

"Yeah, that's me."

I opened the door carefully. This man named Mathew was big, light-skinned and had a baby face, but his voice was so powerful that it echoed even when he tried to speak softly. I only saw him standing there until he gestured to his right. That's when I'd seen Mama looking tore down. Her clothes were ripped and her hair was all messed up. She had both her arms crossed like she was trying to cover up her cleavage. She kept her head down as she stepped inside the apartment. Mathew followed behind her and asked me if he could use the phone. I told him yes and then I watched mama as she walked over to the kitchen table, pulled out a chair, and sat down. She started crying and holding her face. I wasn't sure what to say or do. I stood there and she didn't look at me one time.

When Mathew hung up the phone, he said goodbye and wished me well. I was thinking he was gonna ask me for money but maybe that's why he made that call. Maybe his office told him that everything was taken care of.

After he left, I closed the door and sat down on the couch. Mama was still wiping tears and pulling at her torn clothes.

I asked her, "Mama, you okay?"

She didn't answer.

"Mama?"

"I heard you, Leesha. Just leave me alone for a minute."

"Leave you alone? You was in jail!"

"Leesha, I told you to leave me alone!" Mama shouted.

She looked in my direction and that's when I noticed how badly her face had been bruised. Mama's right cheekbone looked like somebody had punched her and her right eye was bruised, too. She didn't look in my direction long enough for me to see the rest of her face.

"How you get them bruises? They do something to you in jail?"

"Leesha, shut up, please. I have to sit here and think a while."

Mama started rubbing her temples as if she had a serious headache. I guess taking somebody's fist will do that to you. She wouldn't tell me what happened so all I did was sit there. I watched her rub her head and wipe away tears. I wondered what was going through her mind but she didn't seem to care about telling me anything.

When Scottie arrived, Mama and I still hadn't talked. Scottie walked inside and the first thing he did was say hello to Mama.

"What's up, Ms. Tyler? Remember me?"

Mama turned around and glanced at Scottie. She didn't say anything. She looked him up and down and then went back to holding her face in her hands. Scottie had a smirk on his face as if to say, *fuck you, too.* I walked him to my room and when I turned around to close the door, I could see Mama staring really hard at me. I felt like I could tell what she was thinking, but at the same time, I didn't really care.

Scottie asked, "What's up with her?"

I shrugged my shoulders. "Can I have a hug?"

"A hug, my ass..."

"What, you not gonna give me one?"

"Yeah, come here."

Scottie squeezed me real tight and it felt good. I closed my eyes and smiled. I think Scottie noticed how much I was enjoying the hug because he pulled away before I wanted him to. I laughed and then sat on the bed. Scottie stood near the window.

"You can sit on my bed. It's okay."

"Nah, I'm cool. Hey, Leesha, you got me over here so early in the morning and I ain't had much sleep."

"Yeah, and?"

"I'm just saying that to let you know that right now my ass needs a smoke. I'm gonna stand here next to your window and smoke a cigarette, aight?"

"Okay."

"Cool."

Scottie lit his cigarette and I watched him for a minute. He took long deep hits off his cigarette. I thought he would start choking but he didn't. He loves to smoke. It was like what you see when people smoke cigars. They act like they appreciating the finest-tasting wine when to me, all they doing is filling up they lungs with smoke. Scottie had me coughing 'cause not all his smoke was going outside.

"Sorry 'bout that, Leesha."

Scottie's apology made it alright but I still had to ask him about it.

"Why you like smoking so much? You sure you don't be using that weed you sell?"

"Nah, I don't smoke weed."

Scottie went back to blowing smoke out the window. It seemed like his mind was miles away. I didn't get the feeling he wanted to talk too much so I didn't push my questions on him. Then he leaned his head out the window to watch a car driving by.

"You know them?" I asked.

"Nah, but that's cool how they got they ride fixed up. Plus, they bumpin' some Too Short. That shit sounds tight!"

Scottie started bobbing his head up and down until he could no longer hear the music. Then even after the music had disappeared, he still was saying some of the words from the song.

Ain't nuttin' like pimpin'... He laughed. "Too Short is funny to me."

"You so ghetto!"

"And you say that to say what?"

"Whatever, Scottie..."

"Hey, tell me about this dude in your life. Treyvon, right?"

"Yeah, that's his name."

"How many dates y'all been on?"

"I don't know if you can call them dates but he took me somewhere to eat yesterday and then we also had a picnic one time."

"You had a picnic? Damn, girl. This young brotha really trying to romance your ass, huh?"

"I guess. It was nice even though we did it on Crenshaw and not at a park."

Scottie laughed so hard that he choked on his cigarette smoke.

"You talk about me being ghetto. How you gonna have a picnic on Crenshaw?"

"We sat on that grassy area right in front of the hotdog place."

"Okay, I guess that's cool. Treyvon's a creative brotha. I'll give him that."

"He's very creative. You should see the little sketch he did of me."

"Oh yeah? So, he draws, too?"

"Yeah, he wants to do comic books or something like that."

"You got you a talented young brotha. I like that. Where he stay at?"

"Somewhere up in View Park."

"Uh-oh, so his parents got money then...nice!"

"Whatever...You just making fun of me."

"Nah, Leesha. I'm actually happy for you but I hope you don't break this dude's heart. I know how you can be sometime—"

"What does that mean?"

"You be acting hard but I also remember how after we seen that movie, you started thinking about love and shit. You remember that?"

"I wasn't thinking about love."

"Leesha, yes you was. Now you got this young dude who probably could be good for you and show you the same kind of attention like in that movie. You got a good thing so don't let the shit around you affect how you relate to this dude. You feel me?"

"I guess. I don't know, Scottie. I ain't trying to get serious with nobody. I got too much to worry about."

"That's what I'm saying. Don't be like these hardhead L.A. chicks. Don't just take advantage of dude and have him go all out trying to express his love for you, then you step all over him and tell him he ain't never really done nothing for you."

"Why you defending him? You don't even know him."

"That's true. But, I'm saying from what you telling me about him, he sounds like a good dude. Just be straight with him."

"Scottie, right now all I need is money and to hurry up and graduate."

"Then make sure Treyvon knows that. He probably gonna still try to kick it with you but at least let him know what's up."

"I will."

Scottie flicked his cigarette out the window and lit up another one. After a while it dawned on him that this was a weekday and I should've been in school. He gave me a look that was almost comical. He had to do a double-take after he looked at his watch.

"Yo, Leesha, ain't you supposed to be in school?"

"Yep."

"Why you here then?"

"With what happened to Mama, I couldn't go to school."

"You still could've gone and said you had an emergency. Your Mama look alright to me."

"Mama ain't alright. I wish she would talk to me because I think Victor beat her. I've seen him hit her before but if you look at her now, you can tell he did something. The police should've arrested his ass, too."

"Yeah, I'm surprised they both ain't in jail. Niggas getting thrown in jail left and right for even thinking about hitting a woman, especially after that O.J. shit. By the way, did I tell you I was thinking about doing that Million Man March?"

"Doing what?"

"You ain't heard about it?"

"I think so but I didn't really pay attention."

"I got the money to go but I ain't never flown before so I'm kind of bugged out over that."

"When is it?"

"October 16th. I got a few months before it happens but I'm trying to prepare for it."

"That's nice, I think. I don't know much about it."

"Yeah, it's gonna be a trip to see a million black men. I hope something comes out of it. But to be honest with you, I don't think people care like they used to. I mean, this is gonna be all about marching and bringing us together but I'm thinking, we just gonna be cool for a couple days and then those that already have everything gonna continue to have and those that do what they gotta do, gonna keep hustling."

"Why is it just men?"

"'Cause we need to get our shit together, don't you think?"

"I guess but you need to take Mama with you, too."

"You buggin', but anyway, I didn't mean to cut you off about your mother. I should probably leave so you can talk to her. You should be in school, though—for real, Leesha."

"I'll go tomorrow."

"Uh-huh."

I walked Scottie to the front door. We both looked around, wondering where Mama was. Then I heard her walking around in her bedroom so I breathed a sigh of relief.

"I was about to say," Scottie mumbled.

We both had the same fear that maybe Mama had walked out the door.

"Aight, Leesha. I'll talk to you later. Call me if you need anything. I gotta go home and see what's up with my brother. He's trippin', too."

"Okay, thanks for everything...again."

"Aight, later."

Scottie and I hugged and then I closed the door gently behind him. When

I turned around, I could see Mama pacing back and forth inside her room. I started to wonder if maybe she was on crack or something. She seemed all jittery like she couldn't sit still. I walked over to her bedroom door but I didn't say anything. I kept watching her. She couldn't even sense that I was there. She was too busy being spaced out and thinking about whatever it was she was thinking. I knocked gently on her door. That was the first time I'd ever done that before.

Mama turned to look at me. "Yes?"

"You okay, Mama?"

"Do I look okay? I was in jail last night after Victor had me thrown in there. His ass should've been in there. The police wouldn't listen to me."

"What happened?"

"They believed everything Victor said. They kept telling me to shut up. That's all I heard, over and over. Shut up! Look at my face. They didn't say shit about that!"

"Mama, why you go over there in the first place?"

"I did everything for that man. I let him move in here and I spoiled his ass. Now he say he tired of me and moving on like he had enough."

"Mama?"

"Leesha, please leave me alone."

"Mama, why you acting like this over Victor? You ain't never been like this before."

Mama didn't answer me. She walked into her bathroom that's connected to her bedroom and shut the door. I didn't bother to try to talk to her anymore. I left her to herself. I didn't understand why she couldn't get over Victor. I wanted to hurt that man for what he did to Mama and at the same time I wanted to curse her out for the way she was acting. Mama stayed in the bathroom and I sat on the couch keeping an all-night watch like a security guard, jumping at every little sound. I worried that Mama would try the same shit all over again and go see Victor. I couldn't watch her all the time but I was for damn sure gonna keep her from being stupid, two nights in a row.

SENIOR DANCE

My senior year brought with it some crazy-ass responsibilities. Mama lost her job 'cause she wasn't showing up for it. They fired her ass and she didn't even care. Of course, she didn't tell me until I had to make her mad enough to say something about it. Mama been turning herself into a sorry-ass bitch.

Most mornings when I was leaving for school, I'd be talking to her bedroom door because she'd refuse to open it. I'd have to beat on it a few times before she'd speak.

"What do you want?" she'd yell.

Then I'd tell her that I was leaving for school and she'd be like, "So, I don't care!"

"You don't care if your own daughter goes to school or not?"

"Leesha, leave me alone!"

Then I'd kick her door and leave.

One time I tried to play a little trick on her. I acted like I was leaving for school. I went out the front door and everything. I waited outside for about ten minutes and then I walked quietly up the stairs, opened the door really slowly because I had left it unlocked, and then peeked inside. I found Mama trying to make her something to eat. She looked sloppy with her robe half open and her hair all messed up. She needed to go somewhere and buy herself some new hair. I watched her for a few minutes before I said something.

"Mama!"

I scared her to the point where she had to clutch her heart. She started trying to fix her hair and pull her robe together. She wouldn't look me in the eye but she talked a lot of shit.

"What the hell do you want, Leesha? I thought you went to school?"

I told her that I forgot something, but I didn't. I just wanted to see if she came out of her hiding place after I'd leave for school.

I asked her, "Mama, why you still tripping over Victor? That man been gone a while now."

"Listen how you talk to me. Just cause you a senior now you think you can talk to me like that? You don't understand, Leesha, because you ain't been through shit like me."

"I can see that you gave up, Mama. You lost your job because you stopped going. That would be like me not going to school and then wondering why I didn't graduate. What's wrong with you, Mama?"

"Ain't nothing wrong with me. You wouldn't understand."

"What's to understand about giving up?"

"Leesha, will you just go to school?"

"Why you can't tell me what's wrong with you, Mama? It's got to be about more than Victor. I mean, I don't even see you trying to look for a new job. Are we supposed to wait here until they eventually kick us out of the apartment?"

"Leesha, I'm serious now. You need to take your smart ass to school and don't worry what I'm gonna do."

I looked at Mama's sorry ass and waved my hand at her. She didn't make no kind of sense but she had me worried about the possibility of not having a home. I was old enough to realize that if you don't pay rent, you get evicted. I'd seen and heard of that happening to other people even though some deserved to get thrown out because they was crackheads or purposely not paying rent.

I left Mama alone and went to school. Every day pretty much felt the same after that. Mama and I would have repeats of the same arguments and I would watch her look worse, day after day. That's when I caught myself doing something I didn't think I would ever do. I searched and searched for my father's number. I couldn't find the number anywhere in my room. Then I got this idea to look through Mama's phone book. At the time I was digging in her purse, looking for her phone book, she was in the bathroom smoking a cig-arette. That became her new hobby. I tried to always keep her door shut so the smell wouldn't stink up the apartment but it did anyway.

Once I found her phone book, I couldn't believe what I saw. It was the very same piece of paper that my father wrote his number on and gave to me. I looked at that thing with my mouth wide opened. I was in total shock. More than a year had gone by since I'd seen it. That had me wondering if Mama was always searching through my room when I wasn't home. I didn't ask her about it because I didn't want her giving me static about me calling my father. Shit, I really didn't want to talk to his ass but for whatever reason, I thought maybe he could help me with Mama. I was getting desperate to get her to stop trippin' and try to go back to work.

I dialed the number and got a busy signal so I waited a few minutes. I sat down in the living room and looked out the window. I tried to think about what I was gonna say but it seemed like it didn't really matter. I dialed the number again and it rang. I listened as after about the third ring, someone answered. It was a female voice.

"Hello?"

"Who is this?" I questioned with some serious attitude in my voice.

"I beg your pardon? Were you looking for someone in particular?" the lady asked.

"Yeah, I was, but who are you?"

"I think I'd need to know who you are and what your purpose for this call is before I'd divulge my name."

"Never mind. Is William Tyler there?"

"Yes he is. Who's speaking, please?"

"Leesha—"

"And what is this in reference to?"

"Would you please just get him on the damn phone?"

The lady didn't say anything but it sounded as if she'd dropped the phone. I didn't need her ass to be polite to me so I didn't much care if she was offended. I could hear some muffled voices in the background as if she was telling him that somebody rude was asking for him.

"Leesha?" he said.

"Yeah, this is Leesha…"

"Wow, this is a…Are you alright? So you kept my number, huh? This is great. You sure you're okay?"

"I'm fine. I'm calling you about Mama."

"Lynette?"

"Yeah, Mama…"

His voice got a little calmer after I mentioned calling about Mama.

"Nothing happened to her, did it?"

"No, well, she's changed a lot. She lost her job and now she's just different. I don't know what's gonna happen because I'm pretty sure the landlord is gonna come knocking on our door soon."

"What do you mean? She's not paying the rent?"

"How could she? Mama don't work no more. She don't do shit no more!"

"Leesha, your language…You need money? I'm not sure what I can do to help. Lynette and I don't communicate at all."

"Why you gonna send money now, all of a sudden?"

"Isn't that what you want? I'm not sure what else I can do. When I came to that party, it seems as though Lynette had a man with her—"

"Victor wasn't shit and now he's gone. I'm not sure why I called you. I was thinking that maybe you could talk to her or say something that would get her to stop tripping so hard. I mean, I don't understand why she acting like this and I don't think she understands either."

"Leesha, give me the address there and I'll send you some money."

"Are you gonna talk to Mama?"

"I don't think Lynette is going to speak to me."

"Can you try?"

"Leesha, it's like this…"

"Forget it."

I hung up the telephone before he could say much more. Then a few seconds later the phone started ringing. I walked out the door and let it ring. I didn't care if Mama answered it or not. If anything, that might force the two to talk. Maybe if she argued with my father that would wake her ass up. Anything is possible.

When I walked outside, I decided to do something I hadn't done in ages. I walked to Scottie's apartment. I figured I could ask him for help. Plus I wanted to see him. It didn't take me no time to get to his place. I was kind of happy about the possibility of seeing him so knocking on his door felt really good to me.

I knocked a couple times, really hard. I knocked a third time as the door swung open.

"What the fuck? I ain't seen your pretty ass over here in ages!"

It was Charles, Scottie's brother who answered the door. He looked like he had gained weight but you could still smell the smoke coming from inside.

"Charles...I see you still look the same."

"Shit. The same as what? The only difference now is that I cut back on some things and I'm eating more. Me and Scottie got a little agreement so I'm trying to change my ways."

"Is Scottie home?"

"Yeah, he in his room. I thought your ass just wanted to stand outside since you look like you scared to come in. Where the fuck you been? You two get mad at each other?"

"You still talk crazy, huh?"

"Crazy? Your ass is older now so I don't need to watch what the fuck I say. You need me to call that nigga out here or can you make your way back to his room?"

"I know where his room is."

"Nah, I'ma get that nigga for you just in case."

"Do whatever, Charles..."

"You got an attitude now? Shit. I'll be back."

Charles entered the hallway and knocked on Scottie's bedroom door.

"Scottie! Leesha out here! You want me to tell her ass to leave?"

Scottie opened his door almost immediately after Charles' last comment. He walked into the living room where Charles left me standing. Scottie smiled instantly. "What's up, girl?"

"Hey, Scottie. Can we talk?"

"Yeah, the room is kind of messed up and as you can see, I ain't really dressed for company."

Scottie was dressed in a T-shirt, some baggy shorts and had house shoes on his feet. He really wasn't expecting company.

"That's okay, I don't mind," I told him.

Charles had to say something smart since he'd seen how cool me and Scottie was with each other.

"Y'all make me sick acting like that, shit."

Scottie led me to his bedroom and closed the door behind us. His room was kind of junky. He had magazines spread all over the bed and some on the floor. It was a mixture of his usual sports and dirty ones. There was also a shoebox with the lid off. I could see he used that for his weed rather than his shoes. Scottie was rolling some while we talked.

"Excuse the mess," he said.

"Huh?"

"I see you checking out how junky I got it so just find you a spot on the bed and have a seat. I'm taking care of a few things for later tonight."

"I see..."

"Oh, the weed?"

I nod my head.

"It ain't like you don't know I be selling. Business been good, too, but tonight I got to meet up with somebody at King Henry's. We gonna shoot some pool and talk about some shit. This dude is bank-rolling these local knuckleheads that's trying to get into the rap game. He said they real tight so they might just make it. If they as good as he say then I'm gonna try to invest a little money, too. Shit, the rap game is like hustling on the street. That's why so many niggas getting into it and my ass just might be next."

"Scottie, I need money."

"You need money? Okay, cool...How much?"

"Not like that."

"Not like what, Leesha?"

"I mean, if I just wanted money I would've accepted the money from my father."

"Leesha, you ain't making sense. Either you want some money or you don't. What's up?"

"Scottie, I don't just want somebody to give me some money. I want to do something for it."

"Then get you a job, shit!"

"At my age, what's a damn job gonna pay me?"

"Shit, I don't know but at least you working and making some money. Get you a job after school and see what happens. Just don't let that shit fuck with your grades."

"Scottie, you don't understand."

"Understand what?"

"Mama lost her job and—"

"Damn, why she lose her job?"

"Because she stopped going to work. I think one day I'm gonna come home from school and find that we got no place to stay. So, I need to do something to make sure that don't happen. I don't think a little after-school job is gonna help me with that."

"You not talking about dropping out of school, are you? You can't get you no good job that way. They want to see a diploma and not just a high school one but college, too."

"Scottie, get me a job at that strip club."

"You crazy!"

"Why not?"

"You gonna dance on stage and have niggas throwing dollars at you?"

"I don't know. Is that the only job for females in them clubs?"

"They have waitresses, too, but we already talked about that…This club I go to sells alcohol and you too young right now for that, anyway."

"I could pass for older."

"They'd be after me if they found out you was too young. I ain't about to mess with them fools. I know a couple people that work there but I don't know like the owners and shit."

"Do all of them serve alcohol? I bet those girls make a lot of money."

"I don't care how much they make. I ain't about to get you into that shit. You gonna have to think of something else, Leesha."

"I'll sell some of your stuff then."

"You fuck'n crazy. I don't know if you just messing with me right now or what. You ain't never done no shit like this and I wouldn't be looking out for you if I tried to bring you in on what I do. I don't think so. Just, you know… get you a part-time job and before you know it, your mother be working and everything will be cool. Plus you a senior now so it won't be long before you'll be in college doing your thang. Don't even trip over this money situation. I'll hook you up."

"Scottie, it's okay. I'll work something out. If I can't, then I'll ask you."

"You sure?"

"Yeah…"

"Aight now, Leesha. Don't all of a sudden go into hiding and I don't hear from you. You ain't mad at me, right?"

"No, Scottie. I understand and I know you just being protective."

"Yeah, but don't be playing, Leesha."

"I'm not. It's okay, I promise…"

"Aight then, what else you been into besides trying to look into some illegal ways to make money?"

"I haven't been looking until I saw this stuff on your bed, Scottie."

"So, you trying to say that I'm a bad influence on you?"

"No, that's not what I'm saying. I just want to make some money, that's all…"

"You need to keep your hustle inside them books. That's all you need to do, Leesha, for real! That's some real talk, you listening to me?"

Scottie gave me a real hard, serious look. He kept staring at me like he wanted me to promise him I wouldn't do something crazy to make money. There wasn't anything else I could think of to do. I couldn't see myself going out on my own to do what Scottie did. I needed his help if I was to ever do something that I could get arrested for. I promised Scottie I wouldn't do anything so he would stop looking at me so hard.

"Damn!" I said.

"Shit, Leesha, I'm just making sure."

I gave Scottie a reassuring smile and continued to watch him roll more joints and fill up different size bags with weed. Scottie looked like he planned to do a lot of business in the near future. He was scraping up every bit of the weed he had. He opened one of his dresser drawers and pulled out another large bag. That's when I noticed some small rocks.

"You sell that, too?" I asked him.

"Yeah, but not too much, nah mean? I don't have a whole lot of time to make the shit so I've been going in on it with this dude. He'll make it and I'll sell it. We split fifty, fifty but I don't like doing that too much because it means I got somebody out there that I don't trust who knows too much about what I do."

"Well, it's like a partnership, right?"

"Yeah, but it ain't like he my brother. I mean, Charles might be an asshole but when it comes to the two of us doing shit, I can trust him completely."

"Maybe you should stop selling that then."

"Eventually I will. That's why I'm looking into different investments. I don't like not being able to open up a bank account under my real name or have credit cards. Shit, one day I wanna know what it feels like to own a Platinum card. I'll be the shit, walking into them stores and taking out my card."

"And then you gonna go in debt!"

"Shee-it. I know how to handle my funds. I aint never gonna fuck that up once I get mines."

"Whatever..."

"Yeah, I got your whatever...You just concentrate on school, aight."

"You don't have to worry, I will."

On my way back home I thought about Treyvon. For some reason, the thought of getting money from him didn't bother me as much as taking it from my father or from Scottie. I didn't know why at the time. Maybe it was my own sort of hustle. Looking back on it, I know that's what it was because it was fun. I got a little thrill out of it. I did what I needed to do to have Treyvon feeling obligated to spend some money on me.

When the weekend came, I called Treyvon and told him to come over.

I said, "Meet me in front of my apartment around twelve-thirty, okay?"

He was all excited and telling me how much he looked forward to seeing me. He sounded sweet but I kind of brushed it off a little bit. I just couldn't see myself falling for this guy. I needed to do what I had to do. Mama still had herself locked up in her room and wasn't coming out, especially if she knew I was around. I was getting kind of scared because I'd seen the phone bill in the trash along with some other mail that wasn't opened. Only thing Mama keeping is magazines and those be all over the place. Sometimes Mama don't even clean up after herself. I was beating down her door one time trying to let her know that she had one of her magazines sitting in some pancake syrup. It was bad enough that roaches be coming in from other apartments but now we was about to have some coming from ours.

While I was getting ready for Treyvon, Scottie called me. He said he didn't have any plans during the day and wanted to see if I was up to anything. I hated to say no but I had to turn down his offer.

"Why, what you gonna do today?" He asked.

"Treyvon is coming over in an hour."

"Treyvon? Oh yeah? So, you giving that young brotha some action, huh?"

"I don't know about all that Scottie, but I am gonna see him."

"Cool...cool...Y'all gonna kick it at the crib or you going somewhere?"

"We going somewhere. Ain't no way I'm gonna be sitting in the house all day. Plus Mama be in her room bumping around. I never know when she's gonna come out. She might end up embarrassing the shit out of me in front of Treyvon. I don't never hear her water running so I know she ain't taking showers. Mama probably funky as hell!"

"Leesha, you gonna make me have to apologize in a second."

"Why?"

"'Cause I wanna laugh even though I know this shit is serious, nah mean?"

"It's okay, you can laugh. Ain't no man gonna want to get with Mama. Her coochie probably all stinky and shit."

"Hold up, Leesha. What you know about some coochie? What you been doing in my absence, girl?"

"Scottie, I ain't no little girl or nothing. I'll be a senior pretty soon."

"Yeah, but what's up? You talking like you, uh...you know what I'm trying to say!"

"Scottie, I ain't had no sex, if that's what you mean."

"Oh, aight then..."

Scottie broke out into a sort of nervous laughter. It was kind of nice because of the way he's so protective of me. He tried to explain himself but he had a hard time.

"I guess I should be cool but it's a trip how I think about you. You definitely like a sister to me and besides, on the real? Leesha, you got the kind of looks that niggas go after. I mean, I told you when we first met that time about having attitude to protect yourself 'cause you were cute, but now you grown up a little more, ya know!"

"I remember our talks back then."

"Yeah well, just be careful, aight?"

"You think I'm fine, Scottie?"

"Say what? You trippin' now!"

I laughed because Scottie tried to play off the fact that he noticed me a little more than being sister-like.

"I know you my big brother," I teased. "You can be honest with me. I won't try to accuse you of nothing."

"Yeah, well, like I said, you look good now, Leesha. You almost got that Indian look to you with the long hair and brown skin. I'm talking about that Middle Eastern Indian look, nah mean?"

"I think so. Anyway, I'm sorry we can't hang out today. I gotta get ready for Treyvon."

"Listen at you! I thought you wasn't really into this young brotha."

"I like him, Scottie, that's all. He's sweet..."

"Yeah, okay. I'ma keep checking on you, Leesha."

I laughed to myself after I hung up the phone. Scottie sounded so suspicious of everything I was telling him. He made me feel like I was up to no good. The thought of Treyvon coming over began to excite me.

I got ready in a hurry after taking a shower. I threw on some stretch jeans and a shirt that I like to tie at the waist. I had a nice stomach so I didn't mind showing it. One day I was thinking I might get a tattoo put on it somewhere. Mama called me a tramp one time when she seen my stomach out. I laughed and told her she was jealous. Then I watched her tired ass go back in her room.

Treyvon showed his age when he came over. He didn't walk up the stairs and knock on the door. He stood outside and shouted my name.

"Leesha!"

I was like *what the fuck!* But I didn't say that to him. I said it out loud while I was looking for one of my shoes. I couldn't find it so I put on some black boots. They look big on me but they make me look taller. I liked that.

"Leesha!" Treyvon shouted again.

I poked my head out the window and told him to be quiet.

"I'll be down in a minute. Hold up."

When I got downstairs, Treyvon was looking all excited like he couldn't stand still. He gave me one of those bashful smiles like he figured it would lure me into giving his ass a hug. I did. I hugged him and he started laughing.

"Why you laughing?" I asked him.

"Oh, nah…I mean, that felt good."

"You need to stop being so goofy and just relax, Treyvon."

"What you mean, goofy?"

"I'm playing. Where you taking me?"

"I was thinking about taking you to the movies and if you don't mind, I'd like to take you to the one in Century City."

"Century City?"

"Yeah, you ever been?"

"Nope."

"How about Westwood or Universal City?"

"Why you trying to make me feel bad, Treyvon? You want me to tell you that I've never been very far outside my neighborhood? I'm not trippin' about that so why should you?"

"Leesha, I didn't mean anything by it. I feel good about being the one to show you these places, if you let me."

"Let's take it slow. We gonna eat in Century City, too? What is it, a mall?"

"Yeah, it's an outdoor mall. It's pretty cool. My parents used to take me there all the time but now I go by myself since I'm driving. They got some cool stuff there although it's nothing like Universal City. You should let me take you there next time."

"I might."

I have to admit that I really liked Treyvon's silver Acura. I found myself wanting to drive it. I was tempted to slide over into the driver's seat and demand that he let me drive his shit. I even lied to him and told him that all my boyfriends let me drive their cars.

"How many you had, Leesha?"

"How many I had? I didn't say it like that!" I frowned, thinking Treyvon meant something else by his question.

"No, Leesha, I didn't mean it like that. I was asking how many boyfriends you had."

"Let's just drop it."

"Okay. You mad?"

"Treyvon, don't start. Listen, I'm gonna call you Trey because saying your full name all the time is whack."

"Okay, cool. Just don't shorten it when you're around my parents. They'll get real mad about that."

"Why does it make them mad?"

"They think Trey is a gang-banger's name. I started calling myself that after I saw *Boyz N the Hood*."

"Oh, you stupid!"

"Why you laughing? Did you see that movie?"

"Yeah, I liked it."

"You probably liked Ice Cube the best."

"Yeah, but only 'cause he reminded me of my cousin Luther. Are we gonna miss the movie you taking me to see? We standing here talking and shit. I'm ready to go!"

"Yeah, we better get going. It won't take long to get there, though."

Trey opened the passenger side door and waited as I carefully sat inside. He had me feeling like a prom queen with all the attention he was giving me. I kind of laughed at him when he got in the car because he made sure to buckle his seat belt and adjust his seat perfectly.

"I don't remember you doing all that the last time I rode in your car," I told him.

"Oh, yeah...My father drove my car earlier today. I'm still trying to get my seat back the way I like it."

"You always talk about your parents. I guess that's a good thing."

"Yeah, we're kind of close."

"I wouldn't know what that feels like," I mumbled.

"Huh?"

"Nothing."

I stayed pretty quiet during most of the drive on the way to the mall. I was doing some major sightseeing because all the streets that Trey drove down were so unfamiliar to me. He took me down Pico Boulevard, past Doheny and all the way to this street called Avenue of the Stars.

"That's a weird name for a street," I said.

"Yeah," Trey responded nonchalantly.

"Well, it is to me, anyway."

"Sorry about that. I guess I'm just used to seeing it."

We continued driving down Avenue of the Stars until we reached the mall. Trey seemed to be very proud. He was acting like he was finally among his own kind. As we walked around, he was showing me where he goes to buy his video games. I didn't really care but I only smiled and acted interested so that he could feel like he was doing something special. I walked most of the time with my arms folded, but I could sense he wanted to hold my hand.

When we got to the area of the mall with the movie theater, the lines were pretty long. I was buggin' out that there were so many black people around. I figured Trey was bringing me to see the same movie they was gonna see. I looked up at the board and noticed but one black film.

"We going to see *Higher Learning?*" I asked.

"Yeah, you mind?"

"Sounds good to me. I was thinking you were taking me to see something dumb."

"No, Leesha, I would never do that."

Once we got inside and found our seats, Trey excused himself so he could go get us some popcorn. I had to tell him to loosen up. Trey seemed so nervous and acting like we was on some kind of important date. He was making me nervous!

"Relax, Trey," I whispered to him.

"I'm cool."

I watched the people crowd into the theater while Trey was getting our food.

It was a trip. I was used to going to see movies at Magic Johnson's theater where it gets a little rowdy sometimes and mostly it's black people. I'm kind of spoiled by that.

The theater filled up pretty fast and I was getting an attitude. I lost count on how many people I had to stop from sitting in the seat next to me. I started to look around for Trey. He was taking forever. I know I'm not good at being patient, but I was feeling really out of place. I sat there with my arms folded, looking around and staring down anybody who tried to look at me. I guess you could say I had a habit of folding my arms.

Trey finally showed up with two hotdogs, a large popcorn, two sodas, and some Junior Mints in his hands. He looked like he wanted me to give him props for his effort.

"Did you get me anything?" I joked.

Trey laughed all loud and was smiling like he was the happiest fool in the world. I looked at him like he was crazy but he was cute. I waited for him to sit down, not realizing that I was supposed to offer to help him.

"Um…Leesha?" Trey said softly. "Can you grab the soda so I don't spill it?"

"Oh yeah, my bad!"

Trey had a smirk on his face and then shook his head.

"What's wrong?" I asked.

"Nothing. You like Junior Mints?"

"Yeah. Is one those hotdogs for me?"

"Of course. You can have both, if you want."

"No, one is cool. Thanks."

"No prob."

Five minutes after Trey sat down, the lights dimmed and they started playing that tired-ass *LA Times* commercial.

"Why they always show the same shit?" I asked Trey.

I didn't even pay attention to how loud I spoke. This lady in front of us turned her head to the side and I could see her right eye moving around. I could tell she was trying to look at me. She should've just turned around and told me to shut up. Trey looked uncomfortable so I decided to be cool, sit through the boring commercials, and try to not say a word.

I whispered, "Did you bring any mustard?"

"No, you want me to go get some?"

"No, that's okay."

I really didn't care about having anything on my hotdog. I was mostly trying to get Trey to say something. It was hard keeping quiet. I quickly learned that he had manners unlike Scottie who would be cracking jokes and talking like he at home until the movie starts. Scottie is usually quiet through the movie unless something unbelievable happens. Scottie's habits have rubbed off on me because now I think I'm like that.

About halfway through the movie I could feel Trey's leg against mine and then I noticed his fingers tapping constantly on the top of his thigh. We'd finished all the food and popcorn. I stopped drinking my soda because I didn't want to have to go to the bathroom. The movie had gotten pretty good. Trey's leg knocking up against mine started to annoy me. I could tell he was trying to give me a hint that he wanted to hold hands but I wasn't trippin' about that. I was busy watching Ice Cube. Busta Rhymes had me laughing because he was so wild. Those white boys in the movie kind of scared me with all that racist talk. What they were saying was so true, though. I was wishing that Scottie was sitting next to me 'cause I know he would have had something to say. I looked over at Trey and he was still trying to figure out a way to get me to hold his hand. That kind of bothered me but I stayed cool. Well, I kind of stayed cool.

"Later, okay?" I told him.

"Okay, sorry about that…"

After the movie was over, Trey walked me around the mall a little bit more. He wanted to take me over to this other area that was across the street but I didn't feel like going. He said that when he gets old enough, he wants to hang out at this place called the Century Club.

"A lot of rappers and athletes go there," he said.

"Yeah, and?"

"I don't know. It might be fun. Probably get an autograph or something."

"I don't think they'd want to be bothered."

Trey had a smirk on his face. I sort of guessed that was his look whenever somebody says something that he doesn't like or agree with. I wasn't trying to hurt his little feelings but I didn't really care about some nightclub and who goes there. I had other things on my mind like figuring out how I was gonna get some money. I looked at Trey and I didn't know if he could read my mind or if it was a lucky coincidence that he'd be walking alongside of me, counting his money.

"Why you doing that?" I asked.

"Just checking how much I have in case you wanna go somewhere else and do something. I was thinking about Santa Monica. We could go to the pier out there and play video games or maybe go on some of the rides."

"No, maybe next time...I'm feeling kind of tired, plus I probably need to get back home ,anyway. I've gotta check on Mama."

"She sick?"

"No, but she's been really down 'cause she lost her job. I'm not even sure if we gonna be able to stay where we are. She been out of work for a long time."

"Really?"

Trey put his money in his pocket but he kept looking at me like he was trying to decide something. I continued to talk about Mama so that Trey would feel sorry for my situation. I could tell it was working. Trey kept his hand in his pocket, probably gripping that money he'd been counting.

"I might have to find me a part-time job. I really don't want to work at some place like Fatburger. I'd really be embarrassed working at the movie theater. I can't see myself doing some shit like that, but I know I have to figure something out. Mama don't look like she's gonna be working anytime soon. Scottie had mentioned he knew somebody at Sears one time, so I might go for that. I don't know..."

"Wow, Leesha. Maybe I should give you this," Trey said as he handed me his money.

"I couldn't take that."

Even though I was refusing him, I grabbed the money right away. I was glad he didn't pick up on my eagerness to take it.

"It's cool. I mean, I get an allowance from my parents, plus I make extra money painting those store windows. Remember I told you I do that?"

"Yeah, I remember."

"So see, I'm cool. I'd rather give this to you because if you have to leave your apartment, that could mean I wouldn't be able to see you."

"Thanks, Trey. That is really sweet of you. I'll have to make it up to you some-time. I hope you don't mind me not going to Santa Monica with you tonight."

"No, it's cool. I was gonna spend most of this money on you there, but now it seems like you could use it more."

"That is really sweet."

I kissed Trey really quickly on the lips and he loved it. He started smiling and looked like he was feeling really good about himself. I didn't want to be so obvi-ous by counting the money he gave me, but it stayed on my mind the whole drive home. I wondered how much he'd given me. I tried to sweet-talk him a little bit after that to make him feel good and for my own selfish reasons. I was secretly hoping that wouldn't be the last time he'd do something like that for me.

On the way home from Century City, I flirted with Trey a lot. There were times when he was taking his eyes off the road so I had to tap him on the side of the head and tell him to watch where he's driving. Then I realized how quickly he'd fallen for me when I teased him about not wanting me to be forced to move out of my apartment.

"So, if I had to leave, you'd really miss me, Trey?"

"Yeah, I would. I'd probably go crazy trying to find out where you are."

"That's sweet but I'm not the only girl in the world. You're a good-looking guy, you're very talented, and you gonna go places with your drawing. You should even think about painting and becoming an artist or something. You could be famous. Then when you go clubbing, all the women will be rubbing up against you!"

"What about you?"

"What about me?"

"Nothing...I don't know. I'm thinking about changing my plans to go away to school."

"Trey, what are you talking about? Changing your plans?"

"I don't know. Leesha, it's like this..."

Trey struggled with what he wanted to say but to me it sounded like he was changing all his future plans 'cause he liked me. That really bugged me out, but I tried to act like I was flattered and play the shit off.

"Trey, you need to pursue your dreams. I mean, when you showed me that drawing of me, I was so impressed!"

"Yeah, well wait until you see the one I did of you that's on that wall."

"You seriously did that?"

"Yeah! It's not finished yet, but I'm working on it. You can already tell it's you but I need a couple more weeks on it."

"Trey, you always do this with the girls you meet?"

"Never done it before, Leesha. I really like you, that's all."

"I've never had a guy so into me. I don't know what to say."

Trey and I got really quiet during the final ten minutes of the ride home. I was speechless at that point and trippin' off how much he liked me. I even contemplated giving him his money back, but I really needed it. I glanced at Trey a few times and he kept his eyes forward. He seemed like he was deep in thought and only raised his head occasionally to check the rearview mirror. It got a little uncomfortable. The car seemed smaller inside because I felt a little tense, worrying about what Trey was thinking. I wondered what was going through his mind and I felt bad about him possibly changing his goals in life because he got a thing for me. It gave me a serious guilt trip, but I found a way to brush it off. I thought about my situation at home with Mama. I thought about making sure we didn't get evicted so I'd have a place to stay until I was able to move on my own. I couldn't worry about this nigga being all into me. I like Trey but I gotta worry about me, first.

When I got home, Mama was peeking through her bedroom door. I could barely see her but once we made eye contact, she closed her door. I shook my head and went on about my business. I was through trying to figure out what was wrong with her. My mind was mostly on the money that Trey had given me. I was curious to see how much it was. I couldn't believe how easily he gave it up and to be honest, I liked that a lot.

There I was standing in the middle of the living room, feeling proud of myself and counting this boy's money. I laughed out loud and didn't realize that I had an audience of one, checking me out. I sat down on the couch, still unaware that Mama was watching me until she said something.

"You selling drugs?" she asked.

Mama scared me a little bit. I ended up dropping some of the money on the floor.

"That's a lot of money for somebody with no job. Since I'm not working now, you gonna be bringing home drug money? Maybe you're out there selling your coochie…"

"Mama, you trippin'. I ain't sold nothing."

"Then how you get that money?"

"It was given to me."

"It's probably drug money. You get it from your hoodlum friend?"

"I don't know any hoodlums. Trey gave me this money, Mama."

Mama didn't say anything else. She turned around and walked back to her bedroom. I watched her disappear behind her closed door. She'd spend so much time alone in her bedroom that I'd begin to wonder what was in there that kept her so content. I yelled out to her to see if she'd respond.

"Mama!"

She didn't respond at all. I yelled several times. Then I told her that I was gonna pay the rent this month, thinking that might get her to show her face. Nothing happened so I finished counting the money I had. It came out to be two hundred and fifty dollars. That wasn't enough to pay the rent but it was a good start. Before I went out with Trey, I didn't have any money at all.

I sat for the longest time on the couch, thinking about Trey and what he'd done for me. It made me smile because I felt like Janina. Even though I never seen her after that time I kicked her ass, I still thought about her. I still wanted to have the same kind of control she had. Trey was sprung over me and as I sat on the couch still holding the two hundred and fifty dollars, I thought about the next time I'd have him do something for me. I stayed up all night thinking about it. The television stayed on the same channel because I wasn't really looking at it. I had it on with the sound turned down. I was thinking. The only thing that took my attention away from my thoughts was the occasional noise outside and whenever I'd hear Mama bumping around in her room.

I loved to keep the window open. When it got really late, I could hear sounds from far away. It was like I could literally hear a conversation way down the street and I'd hear the noise from Crenshaw Boulevard, too. Funny thing, I'd never really gone outside before when it was late. I started to get very curious about it. I wondered what would happen if I went outside and walked to Crenshaw at night. I felt like at this point I could pretty much do whatever I wanted to. Mama didn't care. She'd seem to celebrate whenever I left for school or went anywhere. I got the feeling she comes out and throws herself a party when I'm gone.

I found myself restless and bored. I continued to think about walking to Crenshaw to see what it was like at this time of night. Actually by now it was morning. I'm talking like three o'clock, which isn't that bad but with me being a female, I don't know. Going for a walk seemed a little risky but it's that risk which made me want to go really badly.

I looked at the clock and then I glanced at the television. I took deep breaths while anxiously trying to decide what I wanted to do. Going to sleep wasn't an alternative for me. I was too wired to lie down and close my eyes. If I did, they would pop right back open and I'd only be staring at the ceiling. I was making my decision slowly as curiosity took over my consciousness. I started to get dressed and then I'd stop to think about what I was doing. I'd hear little sounds and whispers coming through the window. Those sounds only fed my curiosity even more so I put on my shoes, grabbed my coat and the keys to the door. I walked outside, right into the uncertain darkness of my neighborhood in the wee hours of the morning. Every step I took was like asking myself if I should or if I shouldn't. I was looking around in all directions as I literally crept down the street.

It was a little bit cold outside. I kept my hands deep inside my pockets and my coat zipped all the way up. I celebrated when I made it to the corner of my block without anything crazy happening. I celebrated quietly with a smile. Then I worried slightly because I could see shadows in the distance as I looked in the direction of that liquor store that everybody hangs out in front of on Santa Rosalia Drive.

I kept an eye on the shadows, making sure they didn't move in my direction. I walked slowly but carefully. I tried my best not to look or act too much like a female because I didn't want to be noticed. There were no cars passing by. Santa Rosalia was empty and quiet with the exception of voices coming from those shadows.

As I continued walking down the street, I noticed the smell in the air and the wet grass. It's like I was noticing shit for the first time but the smell added to the cold chill that I was feeling. Then as I was walking, it felt like I'd walked through a spider web. I was wiping my face like crazy and brushing my clothes off for fear that a spider was crawling on me somewhere. I hate spiders. While I was lost in trying to wipe the spider web off me, some guy pulled up in his SUV. His voice scared the shit out of me because my mind was totally elsewhere.

"Yo, what's up, girl?"

He asked me that twice before I even looked in his direction. I kept walking in case I needed to start running. I felt like I had the advantage, anyway since he was in his truck and I knew my neighborhood pretty good. I could duck into dark places or run down some alleyways if I had to.

"Hey, what's up?" he continued.

I still didn't respond but I kept a cautious eye on him. He had the passenger side window of his black SUV rolled all the way down. I could see his face pretty clearly since his truck put us at eye level. He was smiling and looking at me like he was feeling lucky. He was light-skinned and had on a football jersey. I still didn't respond to him but I noticed him getting a little anxious as I picked up the speed of my stride.

"You gonna talk to me or what? You need a ride; you dating, girl?"

I started to walk faster. I weighed my escape options in my mind. I figured if I crossed the street and ran into the mall parking lot, I might be taking a chance because he could easily catch me in that wide open space. My other options were to run down one of the streets on the right of me or run in the opposite direction of where I was walking. I didn't like my last option because it meant I'd be running right into those dark moving shadows.

I was scared. My heart was beating like crazy. I stopped looking at the guy and focused on what I was about to do. I kept my eyes pointed straight ahead.

"I know you getting tired of walking, girl. Why don't you get in so we can talk!"

His voice started to change. He began to speak with anger. I figured it was time to run and that's what I did as soon as I approached Somerset Drive. I was off and running. I never ran so fast in my life. I didn't even look to see if he was following me, but I could hear the sound of his truck revving up until my heart thumping and heavy breathing drowned out everything else around me. I was gone. I cut through the grass in front of this one apartment building and noticed they had a very dark stairwell. I ran inside and sat in the darkness. I could see the street from there and if I needed to, I could take off running again if I saw that guy approaching.

Moments later I could hear the sound of someone driving up very slowly. It was that guy again. I could see him looking around but he couldn't see me. He stopped and seemed to be looking in my direction but I still didn't feel like he could actually see me. I sat with my knees to my chest, hugging my legs tightly and trying not to move one inch. It started to feel like a waiting game. It was as if he knew I were somewhere close by because he stayed right where he was. Then my heart sank to the ground as it appeared that he put his truck in park and turned the engine off. He lit a cigarette and sat. This was really strange to me, but I felt like I had the advantage as long as it was dark. During this time in the wee hours of the morning, most apartment building lights are off so that made the streets even darker. I was okay. But if this guy was crazy enough to wait for a couple hours, he'd be able to see me easily because it would be daylight.

An hour went by and I'd had about thirty minutes to go before the sky would light up enough to reveal where I was hiding. My heart pretty much sank to my feet, especially when I'd seen that guy get out of his truck and lean up against the passenger side door. I worried that he knew exactly where I was. He was facing in my direction. That blew any plans that I'd had of making a run for it. In my frustration, I cursed out loud and then I worried that he might've heard me. This was the first time in a long time that I'd pray and think to myself how badly I wished I were home.

The stairwell around me began to reveal itself as the sky slowly lit up. I could hear the sounds of birds chirping and cars driving by in the distance. Just like always during this time of the morning, Los Angeles was slowly waking up. I was wishing it would stay the fuck asleep because I truly feared what might happen once that guy seen me.

I don't know if I was just lucky or what but I noticed his eyes were closed even though he was leaning against his truck. I figured the sight of him dozing off was my best opportunity to sneak away. My eyes were getting a little heavy, too, but fear kept me awake.

As I stood up and slowly began to make my way outside, I'd heard some noise behind me coming from the top of the stairwell. I saw a couple of people walking quickly down the stairs. They looked at me and then looked away quickly. They seemed in a hurry to get where they were going. I was, too, but watching them made me look away from what was supposed to be keeping my attention. That was a mistake that seconds later I would regret and eventually pay the cost for. That guy was no longer standing near his SUV. Instead, he was standing right in the path that I'd chosen to sneak away.

"What's up, girl? You gonna talk to me now?" he asked with a giant grin on his face.

The fact that he waited for so many hours scared the shit out of me. Anybody that's chasing you and is willing to wait must have nothing but bad thoughts going through they mind.

"You gonna talk to me or what? I didn't wait all this time for some bullshit. You should've said something to me when I first approached you. I hate bitches that be doing shit like that."

The more he talked, the more I could see his eyes start to flare like he was getting angrier by the second.

"I don't know you, so what do you want?" I asked.

I pretty much pleaded my question to him, hoping that he'd have some sort of sympathy and let me go.

"I'm only in high school...," I pleaded.

"I don't give a fuck! You old enough to walk the streets at night like a damn prostitute. That makes you fair game, girl. Shit, I don't know what you trying to pull."

I glanced around hoping I could use the fear traveling inside my body to run away before this guy could stop me. I didn't do a very good job of looking around without him noticing me. He grabbed my arm and started to pull me toward him.

"What, you thinking about running? You looking around like somebody gonna help your ass? I don't give a fuck somebody sees us!"

"Let go!"

"Let go? Bitch, I don't give a fuck!"

He started to pull and shake me around like I was nothing. He started roughing me up and talking to me like I was his woman.

"Bitch, you should've come to me when I first approached you. Now you trying to act like you can't talk to me?"

His shaking me quickly turned even more violent as he pushed me down to the ground and kicked at my legs.

"Stop! I don't know you! Stop!"

I screamed over and over, hoping somebody would look out their window and call the police. I prayed for somebody to drive by and see what was going on. I didn't hear a sound around me. All I could hear were the angry words coming from this man I didn't know as he continued to kick my legs.

"Get up!"

"No, stop!"

Back and forth he traded angry words with my own defensive, unanswered screams for help. Nobody came to my rescue and none of my prayers were answered. This strange guy didn't seem to get tired at all. He kept on going until he reached down to pull me up to my feet. He had both my arms pinned against him but I tried kicking him in the legs. All that did was make him even angrier. The force of my kick caused him to loosen his grip. My legs were too sore and beat up for me to run. I tried but I only ended up falling to the ground on my face.

He kicked me again. "Bitch!"

I tried to ball up so that I could absorb the blows. I didn't know what else to do or if I would even live to see another day. So many thoughts went through my mind. Fighting with another girl was easy but defending off some crazy guy was something all together different. I had no defense but to take whatever was gonna happen and hope it ended quickly.

"How you feeling now, huh? What you got to say!" he shouted.

I flinched whenever he raised his voice, fearing that it would be followed by a hard kick to my body or to my legs. I had tears running down my face but I didn't cry out loud. I no longer pleaded because I wanted to save my strength. I was basically waiting for him to do the worse to me and maybe knock me unconscious so I wouldn't see or feel anything.

He stood there breathing heavily behind me. I lay on the ground in a fetal position, waiting for something to happen. I kept my eyes closed and I'd pretty much relaxed my body. My face was wet from tears, sweat, and the dew coming from the grass. I could even feel ants crawling on me. My skin itched but I was too afraid to move even a little bit. I kept as still as I could.

The strange guy started to laugh. "I bet your ass never thought some shit like this would happen, huh?"

He moved closer. I started to flinch again.

"Nah, I ain't gonna kick you," he said as he started to rub his hand along my back and down my legs.

"If you would've come talked to me, none of this would've happened. I told you, girl. See, and ain't nobody even come out here to help you."

He continued to rub my legs and then he reached to pull my arms away so he could run his hands over my breasts.

"You must get a lot of attention in school with a body like yours, huh?"

The more he touched my body the more I cried. This time he could hear me sob. His hands all over my body made me feel disgusted, especially with me lying in the grass and him all over me. He started to pull at my shirt and I didn't know what to do. He had one hand on top of my head, holding me down. The sound of windows breaking behind us caused him to stop what he was doing.

"What the fuck?" he shouted in the direction of his truck. "Nigga, that's my ride!"

He pushed off of me in an effort to quickly get to his feet. I tried to get to my knees, but I was in so much pain that it was hard to move. I was able to turn and look to see what was going on. When I focused on the guy and his truck, I cried—this time because I was happy. Scottie was standing in the distance. He'd broken the front and side windows of that guy's SUV.

Scottie didn't say much but I could see his eyes, and only I could tell what he was about to do. That guy had no clue. Scottie was always good at removing his emotions from situations that needed him to do the worst possible thing to someone. As that guy approached Scottie, his curses were quickly silenced by Scottie's fist to the side of his head. He went down and Scottie began kicking him.

Scottie called, "Leesha, you okay?"

I could barely answer. I struggled to get up and that only fueled Scottie's anger.

"Motherfucker!" I could hear him shout as he stomped his foot on top of that guy's face. It was as if his head crushed against the pavement. I could see blood oozing from his nose. Scottie kicked him a couple more times and then dragged him by the collar across the front yard and to the side of the apartment building I was hiding in. Once Scottie had dragged him completely to the side of the building, I couldn't see them anymore. Two seconds later I heard two loud noises. I didn't want to believe what I'd heard but I knew what it was. Scottie came out from the side of the building and ran over toward me. He didn't look scared at all. He seemed more concerned about me. I was scared for the both of us, but at the same time I was happy to see him.

Scottie lifted me to my feet and tried to help me walk. I had a hard time so he lifted me in his arms and carried me instead. I could feel the hard steel against his waist. I knew what it was, like the same way that I'd recognized the loud sounds. I didn't ask Scottie anything about it but I looked into his eyes as he carried me home and I knew what he'd done. The look he had, revealed what he couldn't say. He was calm about it and his anger seemed to have gone away the closer we got to my apartment building.

By the time we reached my front door, Scottie was tired and breathing heavily. I smiled. I wanted to thank him but I wasn't sure how to say it. He'd killed someone because of what they'd done to me. I didn't know what to say. All I could do was hold on to Scottie and hug him tightly. It was the first time I'd felt so helpless. Actually, it was the second time. First was getting beat down by that strange guy and then not knowing what to say to Scottie.

"Damn, Leesha, you better let me take you inside. I hope your mama don't flip out when she sees you. I'm not even sure I want to ask how this happened."

"If I tell you, you're probably gonna say it's my fault."

"It don't matter."

"You sure?"

"Yeah. We can just say we even."

"Even?"

"Yeah, we ain't gotta talk about what I did, neither, you feel me?"

Scottie nodded his head as if to make sure I nodded in agreement. I did and I understood exactly what he meant. He helped me inside and Mama was in her room as usual. She probably had no clue that I was gone. Scottie helped me to my room and gave me a hug goodbye.

"Let me know if you think you need to go to the hospital, Leesha. Those is some serious bruises, nah mean?"

"I'll be okay."

"Aight. I'ma call you later anyway."

I nodded my head and watched as Scottie walked into the living room. I could hear him close the door, leaving behind nothing but silence and curiosity behind him. I wondered what Scottie was feeling and if what he'd done had changed anything between us. I worried about him in the same way that Grammy used to worry about cousin Luther. There was something behind Scottie's focused glare as he carried me home that was neither fear nor happiness. He was unconscious about what he'd done. His only concern was getting me home.

STILL AIN'T LEFT

I came home all happy and shit. I was fresh out of high school and about three weeks into my first year in college. It was probably no big deal because I was taking courses at a junior college. I didn't have the money to get into Cal-State Dominguez where I really wanted to go. I had to settle for Santa Monica College instead. Trey actually talked me into going to SMC. He said it's a really nice school and not too far from the beach in case I ever wanted to skip class and go hang out by the water. That was the last thing on my mind because my focus was taking care of all those prerequisites so I could transfer to a real college.

My money was tight. I didn't have enough for shit because of all I was spending on rent and food. Mama started claiming some kind of disability. I don't know what she called it, but she'd been getting a check so that kept her at least running to the mailbox at the end of the month. With that money she was taking care of maybe one bill and using the rest to buy a little food and a whole bunch of cigarettes. She lucky my ass was still around because I saved us from becoming homeless.

Scottie would always beat me over the head with some speech about being one paycheck away from the streets. Then he'd start in on me, making sure I stick with school and graduate with a degree.

"Don't be trying to live check to check like all these muh-fuckers be doing. They act like dogs waiting for the master to toss they check on the floor like a bone. I hate seeing grown-ass people act like that."

Scottie would preach to me like he'd been working a nine-to-five all his life.

Fact is, he'd just started working for some kind of shipping company in Long Beach. He'd said it was legitimate work that had benefits and sometimes he even got overtime pay. I'd laugh at him because he seemed to enjoy having a job.

"Yeah, Leesha, I love going to work. I mean, I ain't given up my other hustle yet but having benefits and a place where I can go every day and put in some work is cool as hell. Plus my boss got me doing inventory because he see I'm gifted with numbers. He don't know. I just be on top of my shit, that's all. I'm used to keeping track because I do it all the time. I got to, nah mean?"

Scottie would go on and on but I'd listen because he was happy. I'd let him talk until he'd slow down and get quiet. Then I could say something without him accusing me of not listening or cutting him off. Scottie was sensitive about being heard when he felt he was saying something important.

Scottie's hustling ways sometimes got the best of him. He couldn't seem to resist fixing the inventory to show one or two less items. Then he'd come over to show me something he'd plan to sell on his own. One time he brought me this really cool jean jacket and other times he'd bring me a box load of school supplies.

"Now you ain't got no excuse about being broke and not having money for your school stuff. This shit will last you for a long-ass time!" he'd tell me.

I would be like, "Thank you, big brother."

"Yeah, whatever…"

Scottie would be proud of himself despite my teasing him. Then I'd watch as that hustler mentality came to the forefront. He had a serious game plan when it came to making money and from what I could see he was a long ways from being homeless or broke. He only had to make sure he didn't get caught and that was something that Scottie was very good at. He was also very good at avoiding questions. Whenever he would talk about his so-called hustle, I'd always be curious to know what would happen if he'd get caught. I'd asked him so many times about that but he'd avoid answering until I got on his nerves.

"Damn, girl, you know I don't think about that!" he'd say.

"Don't you look at both sides before you try something?"

"You mean, weigh the fuck'n pros and cons? Shit, I've got to keep my mind focused on making profits instead of second-guessing my ability to stay ahead of these fools."

"But what would you do if something went wrong?"

"If shit goes wrong, the game is over. My ass will be either dead or in jail. I can't afford for things to go wrong. That's why I keep my mind sharp and stay on top of everything I do. I can't trust a lot of folks with knowing about what I'm up to, and I can't really hesitate when I've decided to do something. This game can't be played with fear, Leesha."

Scottie spoke as if he didn't give a shit about my opinion, but I knew he was just speaking out with a lot of confidence. I wished I'd had the same strength inside of me as I listened to him. A lot of my own confidence had been stripped away since that incident with that strange guy. Scottie could tell how that affected me but nobody else knew. Trey would ask me all the time if something was wrong whenever he'd catch me looking a certain way. I couldn't tell him, though. The closest he'd come to knowing anything about that day is when he'd heard about a man's body found over on Somerset Drive. Trey feared for my safety when he'd heard the news and then a few days later he'd forget all about what happened just like everyone else in the neighborhood.

I ran errands for Scottie whenever he needed somebody he could trust, and he would pay me for it, too. He never had me carrying drugs but he did have me deliver money sometimes. I didn't see the difference since it was basically drug money, anyway. Then sometimes he would give me letters to deliver. That was really strange. Of course, I'd ask him about it and as always he didn't disappoint me with his response.

"I learned that shit from reading about underground organizations. My ass be paranoid sometimes about using phones, especially at home. My brother might pick up the phone and hear something I don't want him to know about. And then with these damn cell phones and beepers, no telling who be picking up on your frequencies. To me, once that shit get out over the airwaves, you fair game to get your ass caught."

Listening to Scottie was always a lesson in creative behavior. Most times I would laugh at him and then other times I'd think to myself that he must be doing something right because he'd never get caught and he'd always have money. The lines between right and wrong were sort of blurry by this point in my life. I tried to use any lessons I'd learn from Scottie and apply it to whatever I was involved in.

Trey...I knew I was doing him wrong but it was right for me. I'd saved up enough money to move out on my own after about six months of hanging out with him. I mean after a while, I no longer had to ask him for help. Trey was just giving it to me like he owed me child support. Every time we'd get together he'd take me out, we'd have fun doing whatever, and then when he brought me home he'd be like, *Here, Leesha, I want you to have this.* Trey would usually give me no less than two hundred dollars at a time. I only questioned him about it once, maybe twice, because I'd be tripping at how much money he always had.

"You always got money, huh?" I'd ask him.

"Kind of...I been stepping up my projects and taking on a lot more side jobs. I still get help from my parents even though they don't like the fact that I didn't go back east to school."

I always brushed aside his comment about not going away to school because deep down I knew it had to do with me. He usually brought it up in almost every conversation. I think he'd be trying to get me to ask him about it, but I didn't want to get into a conversation about him having deep feelings about me. I avoided hearing that shit like I'd avoid walking the streets late at night after getting my ass kicked. That memory stayed fresh in my mind no matter how much time went by.

Trey took me out this one time to some club in the Valley. I was surprised for one because I didn't really think Trey could dance. He proved me wrong. And then I laughed because this club played a lot of rap and Trey knew all the words to pretty much every song up in there. He showed me his hip-hop side and then he laughed because he told me he was a gangster on the down low.

"I hope you keep your secret to yourself?" I teased him.

I knew Trey was about as far from being a gangster as I was of becoming President of the United States. I'd seen some true gangsters, not only when

I was young and hanging out with my cousin Luther, but also as I ran errands for Scottie.

One time Scottie introduced me to a friend of his. He said they didn't really hang together much because his friend had moved south to Atlanta. This guy scared me when I first met him because of how mean he looked. He had a serious glare and some strong black hands. I always thought guys knew they were supposed to shake a woman's hand differently from a man's but Scottie's friend almost crushed every bone in my fucking hand.

Scottie introduced him with pride in his voice.

"Leesha..."

I felt like I'd hear a drum roll and see this guy walk out on somebody's stage the way Scottie was being all dramatic and shit.

"Peep this out...this is my nigga right here!" Scottie continued.

Scottie spoke as if he were preparing me for greatness. I didn't even pay attention to the guy until he sort of stepped forward and made his entrance. His smile slowly developed. It took him a while before he'd finally show all his teeth and then he'd close his mouth real fast and just look mean. His skin was dark like he grew up in Africa instead of South Central L.A. like Scottie said he did. Scottie finally told me his friend's name.

"They call him Supreme."

Then he asked his friend's permission if it was alright to say his real name. Supreme smiled as if he were trying to play off the fact that he'd tasted something bitter. The way he looked, I'd wonder if he was secretly biting into his own flesh just to get that look on his face.

"Nah, Blaze. I'm keeping my real name on the low-low from now on. I know this your home girl, but she gonna have to settle for Supreme."

"I hear you, playa. That's why I had to ask," Scottie responded.

Scottie and Supreme didn't allow me to stick around them for too long and I didn't mind. Supreme really struck me as someone who didn't allow many people into his inner circle. And then again, his inner circle probably only consisted of himself and a couple of buddies.

After I met this Supreme, I was very happy that the experience had only lasted a few minutes. I talked to Scottie later that night. He told me stories about his friend and I wasn't surprised. He basically looked like death in hip-hop clothing. Once Scottie told me that this black-as-tar-negro had skills that the CIA would pay money for, I knew right then that I didn't want to spend any quality time with Supreme.

"Have you ever done things with him, Scottie?" I asked.

Scottie hesitated before he'd answer. "Nah."

I could hear his real answer during the minute and a half silence that followed his response. Scottie seemed to look up to Supreme a little bit too much to not want to be like him. I could tell from how he'd introduced him and how he stood, almost imitating the way Supreme was standing. The only thing I couldn't tell was why he tried to act like he didn't idolize his friend. Scottie was proud of the stories that he shared about Supreme. He wanted to share some more but I stopped him. I'd get the hint what kind of person this guy was and at the time I didn't really want to hear any glorified gangster stories. So, when I think about Trey trying to bill himself as some kind of undercover gangster, that only made me want to kick his ass before he made a fool out of himself in front of someone who truly led that lifestyle. Most of the time I knew he was kidding, but even shit like that could get you in trouble.

Trouble and drama seemed to always be just around the corner for me no matter how much I'd learn from Scottie's street wisdom. His words kept me thinking, but they never allowed me to prevent something from happening.

When I got home from SMC one time, Mama had music blasting loud as hell in her bedroom. She had the door shut but that didn't matter. I was like, *Fuck! What the hell is she doing in there?*

I yelled, "Mama, why you got your damn music so loud!"

She didn't answer, probably because she didn't hear me. I slammed the front door behind me and nothing happened. She still had her music blasting.

"Mama!" I yelled again.

I walked over to the dining table. I put my keys and books down so I could grab something to drink before going to my room. Then as I stepped away from the table I tripped over some shoes. I looked down thinking that I'd forgotten to put my shoes in the closet that morning, but I quickly noticed they didn't belong to me. They damn sure didn't belong to Mama, neither.

These shoes belonged to a man and that was pretty easy to tell because Mama ain't never worn no Stacy Adams before.

I could hear Mama's laughter behind her closed bedroom door as the music faded to an end. Then I heard a man's voice.

He said, "Woman, you need to start the record over and play that shit again!"

"Why you wanna hear it...again?"

Mama's speech sounded like her tongue was in the way. She probably was either drunk or had that nigga's dick in her mouth.

"Baby, I wanna see you move like that again! You wild, girl...You wild!"

I listened to this man's voice but I couldn't recognize it. The sound was all big and husky. I looked at his shoes again. They were big, too. I imagined Mama had her a big heavy man this time instead of some skinny asshole like Victor. And then I figured, since this man was already in her bedroom, he probably wasn't shit, either. Mama don't even know how to get with a good man. Then again, with the way she looks at herself, ain't no good man want to look at her, either.

That music they'd been playing was driving me crazy. I could hear it through the walls of my bedroom. Mama and that man was talking all loud. Mama kept screaming and laughing like he was pinching her ass or something. They were playing some kind of pillow-talking song. It sounded like some old shit, probably from the seventies. The singer on that record was acting like she was having sex. I put my ear up to the wall thinking that was Mama sounding like that. Then I started to get disgusted because I knew they probably would be having sex after a while, if they hadn't already.

The phone started to ring as I was sitting on the edge of my bed listening to all the noise. It was Scottie.

"Yo, Leesha, what you up to?"

"Nothing..."

"What's all that noise in the background?"

"You can hear it?"

"Hell yeah! My brother used to play that song back in the day. That's tight. That's the kind of shit you play when you with some old school chick."

"Scottie, I don't need to hear that."

"What's wrong?"

"That music is coming from my mother's bedroom."

"No shit?"

"She in there with some new nigga. I don't even know what he look like but I can hear his voice and he left his shoes in the kitchen."

"Damn, I thought that music was coming from outside."

"Nope. And you know what? That's it!"

"What you mean, that's it?"

"I'm gonna look for me a place."

"You sure?"

"Yeah, I can't take this anymore. Mama with her silly ass needs to get her a job. And whoever this guy she's with now can help her until she does find something. Mama always doing shit like this!"

"What you talking about, Leesha?"

"Scottie, if you know you got a daughter coming home from school, are you gonna be up in the house fucking somebody? I mean, come on."

"Yeah, I know what you saying. You need help finding a place? I see rent signs all in this neighborhood. I seen a couple over there on Nicolet Ave."

"It's crazy over there…"

"Yeah, but the rent is cheap."

"I don't know. I probably be staying up all night 'cause I'll be scared to go to sleep."

"It's only a few blocks away; what you talking about being scared?"

"I'll look into it but if I don't feel right, I ain't moving over there."

"Let's look tomorrow then."

"You gonna go with me?"

"Yeah, I'll go. That way they won't be tripping about you being a young single girl trying to move in by yourself. It'll look different if they see us walk up in there together."

"I guess."

"What you up to now?"

"Nothing…I'm just listening to these fools over here. I'm about to go back outside and wait until this man leaves."

"He may not leave, Leesha."

"That's why I need to move, Scottie."

"I hear you."

During the silence between Scottie and me, I listened to Mama laughing. She was moaning like that man was touching every pleasure spot on her body. The music wasn't as loud as it was before, so I could hear Mama a little clearer and that made me want to leave even sooner. I mean, leave for good. I needed to get out of the apartment really badly.

"Scottie, you there?" I asked.

"Yeah, I'm still here."

"Listen, I need to leave."

"Hold up. I was gonna ask you if you wanted to hang out with me and Supreme. He's about to go back to Atlanta tomorrow but he wanted to hang out tonight. He asked me to bring you along. I think my homeboy kind of likes you, but to be honest, I would never try to hook y'all up."

"Then why you want me to come?"

"I'm cool with him just looking at you, but anything else I ain't really down for, but umm...I leave it up to you if you really want to go."

"Where you going?"

"King Henry."

"That strip club? I thought you didn't want me going up in there?"

"Nah, I don't want you working in there, Leesha. I mean, this is just gonna be a one-time thing and Supreme wants to check it out. You ain't even old enough to go up in there, but I already talked to them and it'll be cool as long as you ain't trying to drink."

"Okay, I'll go. Anything is better than being here."

"Cool, I'll pick you up in about an hour or so."

"Okay, I'll be outside waiting for you."

"Cool."

An hour had gone by before Scottie came to get me. Most of the time, I spent sitting outside waiting. I stood there with my arms folded like I had an attitude. I didn't want to sit down on the stairs for fear of getting my clothes dirty. I tried to dress a little bit older so nobody would question me about my age.

When Scottie pulled up, he was smiling. I smiled, too, but in the back of my mind I was wondering if he liked what he saw. Scottie blew his horn even though he seen me standing there.

"Why you blow your horn?" I asked.

"'Cause you standing there with your tight black pants on and trying to show some stomach. You look good, Leesha. Hop on in."

I got inside Scottie's car. This time he was driving a silver Cutlass. I couldn't resist making a comment. "Every time I see you now, you're driving something new."

"This ain't new."

"I never seen it before."

"What you trying to say?"

"Nothing..."

"Well, unless I come up with some major cash, you gonna be seeing me in this car for a long time."

"Are we going to pick up your friend?"

"Supreme?"

"I hate calling him that."

"Don't let him hear you say that. But uh, Supreme should be at the club by the time we get there. He said he getting a ride from one of our homeboys."

Scottie seemed so pleased when he was talking about his friend but I was kind of getting tired of hearing about him. Scottie changed the subject and started asking me about Treyvon. I wondered if he'd picked up on what I was thinking or maybe I was too obvious about not wanting to hear about Supreme. I mean I did roll my eyes and smack my lips a little bit.

"Treyvon is okay," I told Scottie.

"Y'all still hanging out, right?"

"Yeah, sometimes..."

"That's a trip that he still out here. That nigga must be in love."

"How much farther before we get to this club?"

"Aw, you trying to change the subject?"

"Not much else to say, really."

"Uh-huh, well, I hope you don't screw up that young brotha's mind too much."

"He old enough to think for himself. It ain't my fault he didn't go away to school."

"You right."

Scottie got quiet and that made me nervous. I started feeling guilty about what I'd said.

"What? You think I'm wrong for saying that?"

"Nah, I ain't trippin' about that, Leesha. That's your situation; know what I'm sayin'? That ain't gonna affect me one way or the other."

"Whatever, Scottie…"

"Listen, Leesha, it's cool. You know me; I'm all about doing what I got to do to make it. I guess for some strange reason I feel a little sympathy for that young brotha, but I got your back one hundred percent."

"You sure?"

"Hell yeah!"

"Then stop making me feel guilty about it, Scottie."

"Guilty?"

"Yeah…I know I take advantage of Trey and he still keeps doing stuff for me without really asking for anything in return. I almost feel obligated to give him some."

"Ha! You trippin' now!"

"So you're telling me when you do things for one of your lady friends you don't expect a little something in return?"

"We ain't talking about me though, Leesha."

"Uh-huh, see, you do expect something in return."

Scottie started laughing and trying desperately to avoid my question. He was looking every place else except at me. We drove down Crenshaw Boulevard, sometimes in silence. Other times we'd glance at each other trying to figure out what to say next. By the time we got to the club, we managed to avoid any conversation that might reveal what was truly going through our minds, especially about Trey. I really did feel like I needed to do something for him. What else was there except for sex?

Scottie and I walked into the club. It was like five dollars to get in. Scottie paid my way. I could definitely tell by the way the security guard patted Scottie down that they knew each other. It seemed like he was only going through the motions in case somebody was watching him. When we got inside, it was really dark. The lighting was mostly red so it was hard to really see everyone. My eyes took a while to adjust to the light and plus, I was feeling nervous. I bumped into Scottie a couple times as he was walking slowly in front of me. He looked back and laughed.

"You aight?"

I nodded my head and continued to follow behind him as he searched for a place to sit. This club was nothing like I'd imagine, though I'm not sure what I really expected. It was more like a neighborhood bar with a lot of televisions everywhere. The only thing that made the place feel like a strip club was the half-naked women walking around, shaking they ass and talking to the men.

Scottie found us a little spot near one of those television sets and then he motioned for one of the waitresses to come over.

"This place is a trip, ain't it?" he said to me.

I shrugged my shoulders and then glanced to the right where this lady was grinding up against this man in the corner. Scottie noticed me staring at them.

"That nigga over there getting him a lap dance!" Scottie said.

I watched as the lady was going through different motions. First she was bent over, shaking her ass in his face and then she sat on top of him and began grinding in slow circular motions. I was so deep into watching them that I didn't even notice the waitress come over. Scottie had to tap me on the arm to get my attention.

"She gonna have a Coke but we want some fries and maybe some of those chicken fingers to eat, too."

Scottie seemed to enjoy himself, acting like a big-baller in control of the situation. The waitress returned pretty fast with our drinks and then she was all into Scottie, telling him how good he looked. She told him to let her know if he wanted a lap dance from any of the ladies.

Scottie said, "Nah, I'm cool. I'm just gonna chill tonight with some friends."

"Is this your lady?" the waitress asked, pointing with her chin in my direction.

"Nah, but she's close to me like a sister, aight?"

"Hey girl, let me know if you need anything!" the waitress told me.

I just kind of looked at her. I felt like she was all fake trying to be so helpful. She was making me sick by being so nice. I was thinking, *when the fuck is she gonna leave?* I looked away and that's when I saw Supreme enter the club. I couldn't see his face that clear because of the lighting and his own dark complexion. But I knew right away it was him. Scottie was too busy smiling at the waitress and throwing money up on the stage. When I seen him throw a whole bunch of dollars in the air at one time, I questioned him about it because I thought he was crazy for doing that.

"Is that how you have fun?" I asked.

"Hell yeah, that shit is fun!"

"That girl can't even dance…"

"What?"

"I said that girl can't dance!"

"Yeah, so what…I ain't trying to watch no stage show."

"You gonna have her grind against you like those two in the corner?"

"Nah, Leesha. Like I told the waitress, I'm just gonna chill tonight."

"Whatever, Scottie…"

"Hold up, there go Supreme over there. He probably don't see us."

Scottie stood up and walked over to where Supreme was standing by the bar. I think he actually saw us when he came in but was taking his time coming over. Scottie and Supreme walked over to the table. Supreme was smiling as he approached. He looked like he was about to get his flirt on. I tried to give him the kind of look that would let him know he didn't need to waste his time or mine. I wasn't about to mess around with him, nor was I interested.

"Yo, what up, Leesha? How you doing tonight?" Supreme asked.

I could barely hear him over the loud music but I knew what he'd said. Scottie sat to the left of me and Supreme sat to the right, almost in front of me. He was staring and half-smiling in my direction.

"Why you looking at me like that?" I asked him.

Supreme laughed out loud and made it seem as though I wasn't worth responding to. He brushed me off and started talking to Scottie. I watched them both talking like I wasn't even there, although occasionally Scottie would touch my leg or nod in my direction. But despite that, I still felt like I was sitting there, slowly blending in with the atmosphere. The only attention I got was from my stomach growling. After the waitress brought over the food Scottie ordered, I didn't even hesitate to start eating. Scottie was too wrapped up in the conversation to notice that the strip club food actually tasted good.

Supreme leaned in closer toward Scottie. The music seemed to get a little louder or maybe there were more people inside since we'd first stepped into the club. Either way, it was noisy. I could hear Supreme saying things that he probably didn't want me to hear. Scottie mostly listened and kept a straight face. He didn't have any obvious reactions to what Supreme was saying.

"Yo Blaze, this club is aight. You need to come to Atlanta and let me take you to the ones out there! The shit gets real wild, especially if they know niggas gonna be tossing that paper!"

Supreme laughed after every time he spoke and then he smiled in my direction. His teeth reflected in the darkness because he had that silver stuff all over them or maybe it was platinum. I don't know. I hadn't really noticed it before but it stood out this time.

Scottie took a sip of his drink and nodded his head to the music. I'd wonder what was going through his mind. He seemed very quiet and didn't really say much. He was so un-like his normal self.

Supreme finished off the rest of his drink in one motion. It must've been something strong because he slammed the glass down hard and had a strange look on his face. Then he leaned toward Scottie again so he could say something.

"Yo, I'm about to step over to the bar and holla at this chick over there. She was whispering to me about a private dance. You know that's just some down-low talk for letting me know I can have that pussy, if I pay for it."

"Don't fall asleep after you hit it, though. That chick might take all your money and your jewelry, dawg," Scottie responded.

"No doubt but even fools who don't know me can tell right away that I'll find they ass if they do some disrespectful shit, nah mean?"

Scottie nodded. "I feel you…"

"I know you do. Yo, I heard about the ill shit you just did for your fam, dawg. That's the way to make shit right again. Let niggas know that it don't matter how long it take, they still can get got, nah mean?"

Scottie nodded his head slowly, sort of in time with the beat of the song. The look on his face sent chills down my spine. Supreme smiled like a proud father figure or a teacher and Scottie looked like his student. For some reason, Scottie's dark side was more noticeable around Supreme. I'd wonder what they were talking about or who they were talking about. I knew Scottie wasn't afraid to hurt or even kill somebody but watching the two talking in front of me had me feeling really strange.

"I'm telling you, man, you need to come to Atlanta. I'll even pay your way, fix your grill up like mine. Shit, we could own them streets out there!" Supreme said.

"Nah, I'm cool out here. I mean, I know I get my hustle on but I'm trying to step away a little bit, too."

"I feel you. But you know something, Blaze?"

"What's that?"

"Niggas like us got a certain talent; a certain aura about us that keeps us locked into this lifestyle, dawg. Even if you go do something where you got to give a speech up in some boardroom, you still gonna blaze on any fool that step out of line, you feel me?" Supreme laughed.

"You crazy, dude."

"Tell me I'm wrong, nigga. You know how we do!"

"I don't know, Supreme. I'm trying to do my thing and be able to put away some money legally."

"That's cool, but on the real…Niggas like us is born into this game and we take it wherever we go. Even in this club, muh-fuckers is checking us out 'cause they can tell we ain't just some regular niggas here to rub on some bootie. They see that shit, dawg. They feel that shit! It's all about how you carry yourself. I been telling you that for a long time…"

"Yeah, you have and I know what you saying."

"Aight then. You just, you know, think about what I'm saying and holla at your dawg if you want to come to Atlanta."

"I will."

"Cool, I'ma be over here talking to this female."

"Aight, I'll be here chilling with Leesha for a little bit longer."

"Cool. Be safe, dawg. Leesha, I'll holla!"

Supreme walked away with a sly grin on his face. He looked back at me and I was looking straight at him. He did exactly what he said. He walked right over to one of the strippers and started talking in her ear. She didn't hesitate to wrap her arms around his neck and start grinding all against him. I guess that's what you do if you worked at this club. I don't think I'd ever be able to get used to hugging on every man who looked my way.

As I was watching Supreme, Scottie tapped my arm to get my attention. I slowly turned my head to look at him. He was smiling. It kind of threw me off because I didn't expect to see Scottie looking at me like that. He leaned toward me. "What you thinking about?"

"I don't know."

"How can you not know? You ain't paying attention to your own thoughts, Leesha? What's up with that?"

"I don't know, I mean, I'm looking around and seeing all this stuff. Plus, your friend Supreme is a trip to me. He seems like he always got secrets and they all bad."

"Oh yeah? Well, ain't you got any secrets?"

"Not really. I mean, if I do, you know them all."

"You trying to say you tell me everything?"

"Now that I think about it; yes I do tell you everything..."

Scottie sat back in his chair and smiled. Then he turned his attention toward the stage where this girl was onstage sliding down the pole really slowly, gripping it with only her legs.

"Paradise onstage for y'all doing her first of two songs! Throw some money up there and ask this gorgeous lady for a lap dance, fellas!" the DJ said as the song playing came to an end.

Scottie seemed to like this Paradise girl. She was tall, had on some high-heeled black boots, and was showing as much ass as she could. Scottie got up, showered her with dollar bills, and she smiled. His ass seemed all happy.

"I don't see how you could do that, Scottie," I said as once again I couldn't understand the concept of throwing so much money away.

"Hey, I'm here enjoying myself and these ladies up in here trying to get they hustle on, you feel me? That's how they make money and I'm just showing appreciation for what they do. Don't knock the hustle 'cause you know you trying hard to find your own, too!"

I didn't respond to Scottie but what he said was very true. I mean, there I was kind of looking down on these females, but I needed some money my damn self. I wasn't about to become a stripper even though I did used to ask Scottie about working at this club. The trip part about it is that if I needed to, I'd probably do all kinds of crazy shit if I knew it was gonna bring me some guaranteed money.

When I got back home, the apartment was completely silent and dark. I didn't even hear a sound coming from Mama's bedroom. I looked to see if that man's shoes were still in the same place. They were gone which could only mean one thing: either he left or took his shoes in the bedroom. I wanted to knock on Mama's bedroom door but it was real late and I really didn't want to hear her say anything to me. My plan was to tell her about me moving out and then go look at those apartments Scottie was talking about. I figured I could live over there until I made enough money to move somewhere else, like to the Valley or anywhere else but over here. At least in the Valley it would be a new experience and I'd be about forty-five minutes away from Mama, which to me was like an eternity.

Morning came pretty quickly because I didn't get to sleep until close to four in the morning. The sun peered through my window like a serious wake-up call. I was tossing, turning, and feeling so uncomfortable. I knew I needed to get up so I could talk to Mama. I dreaded that shit. I didn't want to hear her mouth or anything negative that she might say. I knew she'd probably say some shit to piss me off and ask me how I'm gonna pay my rent. Shit, I'm paying ours so she didn't even need to go there, anyway.

I had a hard time getting out of bed. I felt so lazy and wanted to lay there but when I'd heard the front door slam shut that got me to my feet real quick. I opened my bedroom door enough to see what was going on in the living room. Mama was standing there looking tore up as usual and fumbling through her purse. I didn't see any sign of that guy she was with so I opened my door all the way.

"Mama!" I said.

Mama dropped her purse and looked at me like I was crazy.

"Leesha, you scared the shit out of me! You need to make some kind of damn noise before you start hollering. Shit. Made me drop my purse."

Mama bent over to pick her purse up and all the stuff that fell out of it. I noticed a bag of weed, some tissue, and some loose dollar bills.

"You smoking weed now, Mama? What you do, go out and buy you some just now?"

"Shut up, Leesha. I'm your mama so you don't need to be asking me shit about what I do, you hear me?"

"Mama, why we can't talk normal to each other? You used to have yourself together, but you changed ever since Victor left you and Grammy died. You acting this way because of Grammy?"

"Leesha, you need to leave me alone—"

"Leave you alone? I'm just trying to figure you out, Mama. Before I leave out of here I want to know why you let yourself go down so much."

"Well, you don't need to waste your time, Leesha. You should take your ass to school now and leave me alone. I'll be fine."

"I ain't talking about school, Mama. I'm moving out of here."

"You ain't going nowhere. Or what, you got you some nigga to move in with? Is that why you moving out?"

"I'm moving because of you, Mama, and no, I ain't moving in with nobody. I'm not like you. I can do shit without a man."

"Whatever, Leesha…You go on and do whatever. I ain't got time for you or your shit. You wanna move, then move! Fuck it, just move!"

I watched as Mama walked to her favorite hiding place. She slammed her bedroom door and I'd had my answer as to how she would feel about me moving out. Mama didn't care one bit. How could she when she could care less about herself.

I remember when Grammy used to tell me when somebody's heart is filled with resentment, there won't be any room for understanding. The only thing they gonna see is what they don't have and they only want you around as long as they see you going down with them.

That was a hard pill for me to swallow, having a mother who resented me but at this point, I didn't give a fuck just like she didn't. It was way past time for me to go. I felt like Mama was done with me and as much as that hurt me inside, that was the best motivation for me to move on without looking back. I was done with Mama, too.

MONEY GETS THE GIRL

Scottie came through for me, big time! I was about to move into one of those funky-ass apartments on Nicolet Avenue when he told me about this place in the Valley. He said it was gonna cost me a grip but he didn't have a problem with helping me make the rent each month. I looked at him thinking I might have to do him some kind of special favor.

"You trippin', Leesha. I don't know how many times I gotta tell you we ain't like that. You ain't some ho that I'm trying to keep on the low low somewhere. You my homegirl...You like my sister, nah mean?"

"I'm just teasing you, Scottie."

"Yeah, well, I saw the look on your face when you agreed to take that apartment on Nicolet. I could tell you were scared. You can't fool me even though I give you your props for trying to be hard and stick to your decision to move out. That's what I like about you."

"Yeah, whatever...I was ready to move in, but I'm very happy now so it doesn't matter anymore."

When Scottie first brought me over to see my new place, I was smiling like it was Christmas day and I had a real mama spoiling me with a lot of presents under the tree. The apartment had really clean white walls, a nice kitchen, and even a balcony. That's what really had me smiling. Plus, I could see Ventura Boulevard in the distance and if I wanted to, I could walk to 7-Eleven and not worry about somebody trying to mess with me. I didn't have to worry about stepping over drunks, either if I wanted to go inside the store. I told Scottie he should move to where I was but he brushed me off.

He said, "this is too far away from everything I do."

"You mean, too far from your illegal activities…"

"You know what I'm saying, girl. Don't make me start talking about that dude, Treyvon. I know how you get quiet every time I bring that name up."

"Whatever…"

"Uh-huh…"

Scottie was right. Every time we talked about Trey, I'd end up getting quiet. It was really hard for me to talk about him with anybody. I could snap my fingers and Trey would show up whenever I needed. I'm always doing that—snapping my fingers. Trey never complained about it so I never stopped. I had him come over on the second night in my apartment. He called in sick from his janitor job at the hospital to be with me. He had no clue what I had in store for him, but the cool thing was that he brought plenty of food over to stick in my empty refrigerator.

"Damn, Trey, why you do that?" I asked.

"I figured since you probably had to pay first and last months' rent, you might not have any money left over for food."

Trey was always thinking and trying his best to keep me happy. He didn't seem to mind when I would tell him about Scottie helping me out, too. I don't think Trey really paid much attention when I'd talk about anyone else besides him. He'd get really happy whenever the conversation had to do with just us.

When Trey came over with the food, he sat on the floor and leaned against the wall. I didn't have any furniture yet but I did have a television and plenty of blankets to sleep on. That was about it. My apartment would get really cold because it was so empty. Trey made comments about me needing furniture and I would smile. After a while he started suggesting we go check out some stuff at Ikea. I smiled again but I didn't let him see me. I was preparing something for us to eat and I didn't want him to pick up on what I was thinking. I'd feel a certain satisfaction because basically, I had him wrapped around my finger. All I had to do was look like I was in need of something and he would be right there, suggesting we go get it.

I glanced over at Trey. He was watching TV and sitting there all content and happy. He doesn't ever complain about shit when he's with me. To me that's almost abnormal for somebody to not complain about anything. I was baking some chicken so I placed it in the oven. I was making noise, banging pots and pans. Trey still didn't say anything. I banged a couple pans together while looking straight at him. Still I got no reaction.

I asked him, "You okay over there?"

"I'm cool," he responded.

"Trey, don't you ever get upset about anything?"

"Like what?"

"Anything. Like don't you ever vent about something or someone? I know you've heard me complaining about everything from no money to Mama and her tired ass. I can't even remember you ever complaining to me about anything."

"Oh, nah… I don't really have much to complain about. I'm cool with what I'm doing. My parents complain about me but I don't have any problems with them. I guess when there's something bothering me, I just escape into my painting, you know? It's like I have an outlet for when things get me down. Most people don't so they have to complain. Not that I'm saying anything is wrong with that."

"You sound like Scottie now…"

"What do you mean?"

"Scottie always have some philosophical reason why things are the way they are."

"Oh, well I didn't mean to sound like that. I was just always told that I have an outlet that keeps me you know, content about things. That's why I can do other jobs like at the hospital without feeling down about it."

"It's okay, Trey. I was sort of wondering why you're so cool with everything. Like no matter what's happening, it doesn't affect you."

"I don't know. I feel like I'm gonna be okay no matter what because I have my painting. That's all…"

I let Trey go back to watching TV while I checked on the food. I felt good about cooking for him. It was my way of actually doing something for him, for once. I could tell he wasn't really thinking on that level, but I was feeling like I needed to do something or Trey might stop trying. Dinner wasn't the only thing that I'd plan to serve him. I was gonna make him my first and he didn't even know it.

I'd been planning this for a long time in my mind. Scottie was always teasing me about thinking this way. He says it comes from some kind of mentality that women have today. Like we can use what's between our legs the same way we might use an American Express platinum card. I personally think it's better than a damn credit card and it's accepted all around the world without hesitation. Some niggas is so desperate they wouldn't even mind if it was funky and left a bad odor on they dick for life.

I knew Scottie was looking out for me like a big brother but nothing could change my mind about Trey. The thought of having sex with him came natural to me. It just seemed like something he and I should do. I could basically see myself as the one in control so I didn't worry too much about Trey trying to be rough or lose control of his mind. I couldn't imagine him being anything other than his usual self, trying to please me.

I sat down on the floor right next to him. He looked over at me and smiled when he felt my body next to his.

I asked, "What are you watching?"

"This sports show. They talking about the Lakers."

"Oh…I hope you're hungry. I'm making some chicken and maybe some broccoli. That cool?"

"Sounds good to me."

I wanted to laugh at myself because there I was, talking to Trey all calm and sexy. My voice was so soft and yet, I couldn't tell if he was picking up on it or not. He seemed kind of ho-hum in his response to me. I guess I wasn't direct enough or maybe he was being shy.

"Maybe after dinner we can do something," I told him.

"What you mean, like go to a movie or hang out somewhere?"

"No, I mean…you know!"

Trey shook his head as if to say he wasn't sure what I was talking about. He didn't pick up on the hint I gave him with my eyes traveling down to his crotch or when I massaged his leg with my foot.

I whispered, "Come on, Trey, you know what I'm talking about."

Trey smiled but he didn't say anything. I could see him swallow really hard and then he nervously watched my fingers slowly traveling up his inner thigh. He stared at my mouth as I slowly leaned in toward him for a kiss. He closed his eyes before I reached his lips. It was a cute reaction.

"You probably expected this, huh?" I asked him teasingly after we'd kissed.

"No, but I've always been hoping for it."

"Why you ain't tried to make it happen?"

"Leesha, I never want to have you pissed off at me so I couldn't take that chance."

"Okay, well...are you mad at me now?"

Trey laughed. "No, not at all."

"Cool then, let me do it again." I kissed him lightly. "And again..."

One soft kiss after another had Trey taking deep breaths and blowing them out when I allowed him to breathe. I placed my hand between his legs and found him hard as a rock. I kept kissing him. He seemed defenseless and that turned me on. That was like a green light letting me know it was okay to proceed and even if I didn't get that reaction, I would still keep on going. This shit was feeling good to me. I don't know if Trey could tell. He was lost in the moment and only reacted with the movements of his body and the sounds of pleasure coming from his mouth.

I climbed on top of Trey and rubbed against him like I'd seen one of those strippers doing when I went to the club with Scottie. I don't know how it felt to them but for me his stiffness sliding against my pussy had me aching. This was supposed to be my first time but it didn't feel like it. At least not at first, it didn't. Rubbing against Trey felt so good that the motion in my hips surprised me as much as it did him. But I got tired of play fucking so I reached down and unzipped his pants. Then stopped long enough to remove the black leggings that I was wearing underneath my oversized shirt.

I didn't waste any time getting back on top of Trey but that's where my excitement got the best of me. I wasn't thinking but he was. Trey told me that he didn't have a condom.

I smiled. "I do..."

Trey seemed to enjoy the way I placed the condom on his dick. I think I got lucky that I did it right. After that, I slid down on top of him a little too fast for comfort and that shit hurt.

"Shit!" I shouted in pain and then I laughed at myself.

It hurt, it was painful, but I was so wet and turned on that nothing could stop me from getting mine. What started off as me wanting to give Trey a little something to thank him turned into me wanting to be in complete control and get me some! I moved my hips in circles, climbed up and down like a wave and grinded as deeply as I could once I got used to the pain. Trey was saying my name in shock and responding to me with breathless words that came out like he'd reached the end of his life.

"Leesha...," Trey said before clutching tightly to my shoulders.

I could feel a burning hot sensation between my legs and I knew it was him. I smiled and kept moving my hips with deep, long strokes. I didn't stop until Trey's grip loosened and his stiffness grew soft. I didn't really get mine like I wanted to, but I was very satisfied by the outcome. Once again, I was in control and that made me feel super sexy.

I lay next to Trey all night listening to him snore and watching the dark sky outside. I opened the sliding glass door leading to the balcony so that some fresh air could come in and chase away the smell of sex that filled my living room. Plus I love cool air at night and Trey was completely out so he didn't feel a thing. I got up a few times during the night because I couldn't sleep. The first time I got up was so I could remove the burnt chicken from the oven. Trey and I never did eat. I'd forgotten completely about the food cooking in the oven.

I got up for the last time around four in the morning. I had a lot on my mind after having sex with Trey. I needed to talk to someone and as always that person ended up being Scottie.

"Yo, what's up, Leesha? I guess I don't have to tell you what time it is, but you always calling a nigga at some crazy hour anyway..."

"Whatever...I need to talk."

"Why you sounding so quiet?"

"Hold on."

"Why I gotta hold on?"

"Shh...I'm gonna close the door."

"Ain't you alone? Why you gotta close the door? You acting real strange over there."

"I just need to close the glass door. I'm outside on the balcony."

"Hold up. This is only your second night at your new crib and you already got somebody over? That's some shit that I would probably do!" Scottie laughed.

"Shut up. Trey is over here, that's all."

"Yeah, and he over there kind of late, too! What's up with that?" Scottie teased.

"I invited him over for dinner."

"Uh-huh, you ain't even need to say nothing 'cause I already know what's up. So, why you calling me? You feeling guilty now?"

"No, I'm not feeling guilty. Not about that, at least."

"Then what's up? You still ain't told me."

"You haven't given me a chance yet!"

I took a deep breath before I could begin telling Scottie what was so heavy on my mind. I glanced over at Trey still sleeping on the floor. I didn't have to worry about him overhearing me, so I figured it was safe to talk comfortably with Scottie.

"Scottie, I want to show you something tomorrow. I've been meaning to have you take me over there but I've been putting it off."

"Take you where? What you talking about?"

"There's this mural that Trey did of me downtown. It's really beautiful but it's crazy to have some guy feeling like this about me and I'm not really feeling the same."

"What you mean?"

"I mean, I like Trey. He's really cool and sweet. He's so talented but he ain't somebody that I would get serious with. He's just Trey to me. You know what I'm trying to say?"

"Nah girl, you got me sitting here clueless."

"Shut up, Scottie."

"Nah for real, Leesha. I understand a little bit but I'm also wondering why you keep seeing dude or umm, do you ever plan to let him know how you feel and don't feel?"

"I don't know. I want to tell him but I also feel like I need him right now. If I say how I really feel, I know it'll mess everything up."

"Mess it up for who?"

"You know…"

"Leesha, I'm listening to what you saying and in a way, we've had this talk before. All I can do is have your back, nah mean? I can't judge you on this. I know you keeping this dude around 'cause of what he does for you more than anything else."

"I like him, though!"

"Maybe you do but be real about it."

"What you mean? I am real about it—"

"You real with me but not with dude…"

"I can't right now."

"I know, but one of these days you gonna have to."

"I will."

"Yeah okay, so anyway, what's up with this mural?"

"I'm gonna show you. It'll be my first time seeing it finished. I've seen it half done but he told me he finished it now. I also wanna talk to you about something else."

"What's that?"

"Just something I've been thinking about."

"Damn, Leesha, you been doing a lot of thinking, huh? What's this about?"

"Just wait until I see you, Scottie. I'll tell you when we go look at the mural."

"So this is like a surprise then, huh? You got a gift for a nigga? Y'all females don't be giving brothas shit but more drama!"

"Scottie, will you stop! I'm serious."

"Aight, I'll pick you up at what time?"

"I wanna do it soon, like about eleven."

"Damn, you got me up at four in the morning and now you want me to be at your crib at eleven?"

"Please?"

"Okay, I'll be there but this surprise better be real good. Is dude gonna be there? He going with us?"

"No, I'll wake him up soon and have him leave."

"Okay, see you later."

"Thanks, Scottie."

Daylight came around an hour after I got off the phone with Scottie. I woke Trey up around that time and told him I had something important to do. I lied. I told him I had a job interview that I needed to go to. I wanted to get him to leave without too much drama or suspicion. Trey looked a little tired from sleeping on the floor, but he was cool about leaving.

I tried to get some sleep after Trey was gone but that didn't happen. I would close my eyes for about thirty minutes and then wake up thinking I'd overslept. I didn't want to still be asleep while Scottie was knocking on my door. Having Scottie take me downtown was very important to me, not only to see the mural but to tell him about my plan. I knew he was gonna be shocked out of his mind and then he'd probably wave me off like I lost mine. Maybe I had but I'd been thinking about this for a couple weeks. I'd even dreamed about it a few times. I guess when you think about something enough, you end up watching it play out in your head when you sleep.

About two weeks before I'd moved into my apartment, I did a little errand for Scottie. I deposited some money for him in this bogus bank account he has with B of A. I don't know how he set it up but he usually will have me make the deposits for him. When I went to the bank, I noticed an armored truck sitting outside. My eyes were so fixed on the truck that as I was walking around it, I bumped right into the guard standing with his gun at his side. It was embarrassing but I think mostly for him. I started to think, *if I was a criminal I could take him easily.*

The guard and I both laughed but I kept looking back at him as I entered the bank. I think he was also checking me out so that let me know I could get the drop on his ass just because I'm a female. His partner was exiting the bank at the same time I was going inside. He was holding the bag of money and I couldn't shake the thoughts that ran wild inside my mind. I tried to laugh about it and think of myself as one crazy chick who probably seen way too many movies. But the thing about it; I felt like I could seriously take that money if I had maybe one other person helping me.

Ever since then I hadn't been able to stop thinking about that armored truck. And all I could visualize after I'd get the money is freedom. I could move and start fresh in a different state. I always heard about black folks moving to Atlanta. I ain't never been out of L.A., let alone California so I think it would be nice to start fresh where nobody knows who I am.

Scottie showed up right on time. When I opened my front door he had a big smile on his face. He looked around excited and then he laughed. He teased me because I still had no furniture.

"It's only been a couple days! How you gonna expect me to have furniture already?" I said to defend myself.

"You right, you right. I'm just laughing about it, that's all. We should go get you a couch or something, Leesha. Now that you be having guests and shit, you don't want them sitting on the floor all the time."

"Ain't nobody gonna come over here but you and sometimes Trey. That's it. So, I'm not even worried about visitors."

"Oh, aight…What you got on your mind, anyway? You know I've been thinking about that ever since we got off the phone. You messed up my sleep so don't say nothing if I start to drift while I'm driving."

"I'll tell you, soon. Let's go see the mural first."

"Damn, Leesha…"

"I'll tell you, don't worry."

Scottie had this little frustrated look on his face the whole time we were in the car, headed downtown. It took a while to get there. We got stuck in all kinds of traffic and that had me thinking. Besides trying to visualize in my mind what would happen if I tried to rob an armored truck, I'd also been watching every single high speed chase they show on the news. I got nervous because I thought about that person being me that's trying to run. I would die if it got to that point where I was being chased by the police.

Once we reached the area known as Boyle Heights in downtown L.A., Scottie finally opened his mouth. He asked me if I was sure this was where the mural was located.

"Yeah, it's over there." I pointed.

We drove over this long bridge. We could see some graffiti to the side and I told Scottie that the mural was underneath.

"Why he put it way over here? Why he didn't do it like on Crenshaw or somewhere close to where you was staying at?"

"I don't know, Scottie. Actually, I think he said he put it here because of the trains passing by. People could see it every day."

Scottie shrugged his shoulders and looked for a place to park. We would have to climb over a fence and then climb down into the area where the mural was. Once we got there, Scottie reacted before I did.

"Check that out! That nigga can paint, huh? Look at that shit!"

"It's beautiful," I said in total disbelief.

I'd seen it before it was finished and thought it was nice but now that Trey added the final touches, it looked really beautiful. I could barely feel my feet hitting the ground, I was so amazed. The expression Trey painted on my face looked so real. Trey had even drawn a white flower in my hair like that jazz lady, Billie Holiday.

"I need to have that dude paint me, too! Damn, Leesha, you need to tell that brotha to do something with his talent instead of chasing after you. I'm looking at this and I see a young dude with a solid ticket to fame, but he putting all his energy into trying to get you to love him. You my girl and all but I know you feel what I'm saying."

"I know, Scottie, but why should I feel bad? He's as old as me so he should be able to make his own decisions."

"Yeah, you right but when a brotha is real about loving somebody, he don't always see everything clearly. His mind is all messed up right now and all he trying to do is figure out what he could say or do to make you feel the same way that he does."

"Whatever, Scottie…"

"Damn, Leesha, y'all must've made some serious love for that brotha to be painting you like that…"

Scottie was talking to me almost under his breath as he stood in amazement over the huge mural that Trey had created. If it weren't for Scottie mentioning something about making love, I would've ignored his comments and kept my eyes on the mural like him. But then I thought about what he'd said and immediately got defensive.

"Scottie, what did you just say?" I asked.

"You two been together, right?"

"You mean, had sex?"

"Yeah, you know what I'm talking about!"

"Our first time was last night so I don't know what you trying to say."

"Damn, for real?"

"Yep."

"That's deep."

"I don't understand what you trying to say, Scottie."

"Yo Leesha, it's like this...I mean, the way this dude put so much detail in your face and your eyes? Damn, it's almost like he held your face in his hands and just placed it on the wall."

"So, what does that have to do with us having sex?"

"Might be just sex to you, but dude is so into you that he captured your spirit. If I never met you before, I could look at this mural and feel who you were."

"I don't know what you talking about, Scottie."

"Aw, you trippin'...I bet you do know what I'm talking about. Shit, you in shock just like me."

I knew what Scottie was saying but I didn't really want to think on that level. I couldn't because I had other things on my mind. Trey was just a friend to me and I didn't want to admit to the reality that I cared about him because of what he could do for me. I glanced over at Scottie and he was staring at me really hard. He was shaking his head and looking at me like I needed to do something.

"What!" I shouted. "Why you looking at me like that?"

"I don't know, Leesha, this is deep to me. I mean, maybe I'm getting soft or something but I feel this nigga's love for you."

"Scottie, let's sit down so I can talk to you about something else."

"What, you don't wanna talk about this right here, this painting?"

"We can talk about that later. If I don't tell you what's been on my mind lately, I'm gonna drive myself crazy thinking about it."

"You got something else going on besides this stuff with Trey? Damn, girl, you stay busy, huh? I don't never hear you talking about how good you doing in school. What's up with that?"

"Scottie, school is fine. I need to talk to you about something else."

I wasn't sure how to approach telling Scottie what I wanted to say and he didn't give me much time to think about it. He kept nudging my shoulder as we sat close to each other on the pavement, underneath the bridge. The beautiful mural that Trey had painted was in back of us, and we could hear cars passing by overhead. I figured the best way to tell Scottie what I'd been thinking was by bringing it up casually. I wanted to get him thinking about something else and then I could say what I had to say.

"So, what's up?" Scottie asked.

"You know, I can't believe you were so quiet on the way over here. Did it really bother you that I had you wait on what I wanted to tell you?"

"Nah, it's cool. I was a little tired, you know? I mean, we all got shit we don't say right away and I figure you gonna tell me what's up eventually, right?"

"What do you mean, like secrets?"

"Yeah."

"You got some?"

"Shit, maybe...but we ain't here for me to confess anything. This is about you so what's up, Leesha? How much longer I gotta wait? I mean, this must be some heavy shit you about to tell me, huh?"

"I don't know, maybe it is. It's something that's been on my mind; something that I feel I should do."

"Is that right? See, you still ain't told me nothing, though."

"I'm trying to, Scottie. It's just hard to come right out and say!"

"Damn, is it that deep?"

I turned to look at Scottie. I started to laugh a little bit because I had one of those stupid soap opera looks on my face. Not that I could see myself but I imagined that's how I looked. My mouth quivered a little bit before I could say anything, so I took a deep breath and tried to relax.

"Yo Leesha, you don't have to tell me if it's bothering you that much. I ain't going nowhere. We got time."

"Scottie, you're gonna think I'm crazy, but I'm really serious about what I'm gonna say. I mean, I've been thinking about this and I know I can do it."

"What's that? You steppin' up your game at school?"

"No, I want a new start somewhere, like in a different state. I'm thinking about Georgia. I always hear about black people moving to Atlanta."

"Atlanta?" Scottie asked in disbelief. "And you said you want a new start? What you talking about Leesha, damn…"

"Scottie, I got this idea…" I swallowed really hard and then I said it. "I'm gonna rob an armored car."

At first Scottie didn't say a word. He looked at me and then he started laughing. I could tell he wasn't taking me serious. I didn't smile and I didn't try to stop him from laughing because despite being nervous about my decision, I was dead serious.

Scottie asked me while still laughing, "Why you playing, Leesha?"

"I'm not…"

"You not playing; yeah, right. You telling me you serious?"

Scottie paused for a moment and looked straight ahead. His silence was a strong contrast to the noise of downtown Los Angeles. When Scottie finally did speak, he scared me a little bit because I wasn't expecting him to say anything for a while.

"When did this idea hit you? That's some way-out-in-left-field shit. You ain't never even been in trouble before other than at home. I thought you was gonna ask me about working at that strip club again. You straight trippin', Leesha!"

Scottie went on and on as if I lit a fire under his behind. He seemed really pissed off at me. He had a strong glaring expression on his face as if I'd already committed the crime. I glared right back at him as if to say, *Why can't I do the same shit he does?*

"Why you looking at me like that, Scottie?" I asked.

"Why? Shit, you talking about robbing an armored car, Leesha. How else would I look at you? You doing this crazy shit alone?"

"No, I'm gonna get somebody!"

"Who?"

"I don't know yet. I'm hoping you know somebody."

"Oh, now you trying to get me involved with this? I love you like a sister but I ain't trying to get you killed in some robbery, Leesha. How you gonna ask me that?"

"Who else would I ask?"

"Hold up, let me think...You blowing my mind with this shit."

Scottie sat next to me, shaking his head and rubbing his temples. He was really trippin' behind what I'd asked of him. He didn't calm down no time soon, either. He seemed really mad.

"Damn, sorry I ever told you," I said.

"Nah, hold up. I mean, you put it out there so we gonna see. You wanna do this shit, then you gotta be ready. I don't want you going to somebody else about this 'cause I know how niggas can be. You'd be in some real trouble then."

"So, you'll help me?"

"We'll see, Leesha. Let's go. I wanna take you somewhere..."

"Where?"

"Don't worry about it. Let's go. You want my help, then you need to show me something."

"Show you something? Scottie, what are you talking about?"

Scottie stood up and started back toward the fence that we climbed over before. No matter how much I questioned him about where we were going, he wouldn't say a word. He was dead serious about whatever was on his mind and I was nervous as hell. I didn't know what to think. Was Scottie gonna kick my ass or what? All I could do was follow behind him and that's what I did. I didn't want him to see how afraid I was, so I stopped questioning him and stayed silent.

We returned to the car and drove in a direction that wasn't really familiar to me. I mean, we stayed in the downtown area, but I couldn't say where I was if somebody had asked for directions. Scottie seemed to know, though. He kept looking down streets like he was trying to find a particular turn that he needed to make. I was hoping he wasn't trying to find some back alley to take me and beat me down like some gang initiation thing.

"Can I ask where we're going?" I asked.

"You'll see in a minute. You'll be aight."

Scottie's response didn't really make me feel any better. How could I be in an area that looked so rundown with trash all over the place and not many people in sight. I folded my arms and awaited my fate. I was in Scottie's hands. I had to be cool and try not to panic.

Scottie pulled up slowly into a warehouse parking lot. I didn't see hardly anyone around. There was this one guy driving a forklift and I saw some other guys walking until they disappeared inside one of the buildings.

"Why you drive over here?" I asked.

"Hold up, you'll see in a second."

"This is weird...," I mumbled.

"Hold on to this," Scottie said as he handed me a gun that he pulled from underneath his seat.

"I don't want that!"

"Why not? You talking about robbing somebody. See that truck over there?"

Scottie was testing me; I could tell, and to be honest, I was scared shitless. Mostly I felt that way because I wasn't sure what Scottie was gonna do. The look in his eyes had me feeling like he was serious. Like maybe he was about to have me do a robbery with him to see if I could do it for real.

"Why are you doing this, Scottie?"

"I want you to see what this shit is like before you throw your life away."

"I know what I'm doing."

"You don't know shit, Leesha. Look at that truck over there. You gotta be ready emotionally and you might even have to pull the trigger on one of them fools. Can you do that?"

I didn't answer Scottie. I looked in the opposite direction and sat quietly. I listened to him until his words became muffled by my own concentrated thoughts. I tried to visualize how I would react when the time came, but I couldn't see anything. I couldn't imagine doing it at all and that was strange. All I really wanted to do was to have Scottie take me home.

"I need this money...," I mumbled.

I didn't think he'd heard me but he did.

"Well, you better re-think your strategy, get a full-time job, and work you some damn overtime. You ain't ready for some shit like this, Leesha. I'm being real with you."

I shrugged my shoulders and didn't say a word. Scottie put the gun he tried to give me back underneath his seat.

Scottie was grinning. "You ain't ready, Leesha. You better think about what you trying to do."

I didn't respond. I kept my focus away from him and looked out the window. Nothing could change my mind about my decision. As much as I refused to admit it, Scottie was right about me not being ready.

When we got to my apartment, Scottie dropped me off. I mumbled my goodbye and I wasn't sure if he'd said anything or not. It was a very disconnecting feeling between us. I'm sure he felt disappointed and me, I felt really strange. I watched Scottie drive off and I stood there hoping that maybe he would turn around and come back to tell me everything would be alright. That wish never came true, but when I opened the door to my apartment, my phone was already ringing. It was Scottie, calling me from his cell phone. I smiled really big because I needed to hear his voice, no matter how it sounded.

"Hey, Leesha"

"Hey, you okay?"

"I'm good and I apologize for getting quiet on you, but you gotta feel how crazy this is for me."

"Scottie, I do know but I really need your help."

I could hear Scottie taking a deep breath as if he'd come to some kind of acceptance that I was serious about this whole robbery thing. He said he was pulling into the parking lot of a Ralph's grocery store so he could talk to me. I knew then he was about to do his usual big brother, always got some deep philosophy speech. I sat down on the floor and prepared myself to listen.

"Leesha, peep game and tell me if you recognize what I'm trying to say to you."

"Okay."

"You listening?"

"Yeah, I'm listening to you, Scottie."

"It's like this…You trying to do something that you ain't really designed for, you feel me?"

"Huh?"

I reacted as if I was preparing to stand up and defend every woman in the history of the world that I assumed Scottie was going to criticize. He quickly squashed that assumption.

"Nah, nah girl, hold up. Yo, check this out...I'm talking about this whole idea you got to do this armored car thing. I mean, that's why I took you to that warehouse because I knew a truck would be there. I wanted you to see it, smell it, and feel what it's like to be looking at one with the thought in mind that you about to rob that muh-fucker. It's a lot different than just seeing it casually on the streets when you pretty much don't even pay attention to it. That's a whole different kind of feeling right there. I wanted you to experience that and see if you still serious or if you just got caught up in some crazy-ass fantasy."

"Is that what you were doing? I'm okay, Scottie."

"Aw, you trippin' now, trying to act all calm and shit. Alright then, you play like it's no big deal, but you gonna see what happens when it's time to go through with that shit. Can you pull a trigger on somebody that's looking into your eyes? You got what it takes to do some shit like that? Leesha, you wouldn't even take the gun from me when I tried to give it to you!"

"I didn't wanna take it!"

"Wake up, Leesha...You need to think about all this shit since this whole thing ain't really your career choice. Are you ready for what's gonna happen if this shit don't work out right? Your ass should watch that movie *Dead Presidents* again! You seen what happened to them niggas?"

"Scottie, you've done worse and ain't never been caught."

"This ain't about me, though, Leesha. This is all about you. I ain't never tried to rob no armored car. I got friends locked up that have. I got some demons of my own that I wrestle with because of my past, but my experiences go way back and it's been a part of my life. Your ass just starting out and you over there talking about doing a one-time thing like this some roulette wheel in Vegas. This ain't no investment into your future, Leesha. You making a crazy-ass decision that could get you killed, girl."

I listened closely to Scottie and I knew where he was coming from. I understood everything he said, but I felt like I had to play the tough role to boost my level of confidence. I shrugged things off as if to say I had it under control. But truth be told, I could picture all the worse-case scenarios a little too clearly. Scottie didn't help by mentioning that movie to me. He and I watched it together and I remember the sadness at the end. I had to shrug that memory off and release it completely. I was always known as a hardheaded chick, so it was time to put that stubbornness to good use.

I told Scottie, "I'll be alright. I believe I can do this."

"Damn, I thought you was listening to me?"

"I heard everything you said!"

"Nah, you didn't."

"You still gonna help me?"

"Yeah, meet me at that Sherman Oaks Galleria tomorrow. It's not too far from you. I'ma bring somebody with me. You better really plan this shit, Leesha. Don't do it anywhere close to where niggas know you at. That'll be real stupid if somebody calls out your name while you trying to pull off a robbery, nah mean?"

"Okay."

"If you gonna do this shit, do it right!"

"Thanks, Scottie."

"You crazy, for real, girl."

When Scottie and I hung up, I felt good. I was relieved knowing that he would help and be there for me. I'd hoped that I could feel this same way on the day when everything actually happened. It was a weird feeling but my mind never changed. I needed to go through with this.

A DAY FOR TRUTH

I decided that Wednesday would be the perfect day. It's the middle of the week and everybody would be at work. No weekend traffic to deal with and hopefully no kids around. I found the perfect place on Magnolia and Laurel Canyon. It's in a small shopping center and I watched carefully for a few days how everything moved around there. I imagined a disruption in the typical flow of life would only cause everyone to stop and get the fuck out of the way.

Scottie told me to make sure there was a freeway close by. There is one, right up the street, actually in more than one direction. He told me to choose the one closest so if the worse-case scenario happened, I'd be able to get farther away, faster.

"You gotta hit hard, fast, and get out. Don't waste time, Leesha. Don't be trying to grab every last dollar, neither. Just get the fuck outta there!"

Scottie had been calling me every day, making sure I was still going through with the robbery and also giving me pointers. I felt like I was in bank robbery school every time we talked. I was actually glad he kept doing that because it put me in a mind state that I could do it with no problem. It gave me confidence and it made me happy, knowing that Scottie cared so much.

Most things we'd talk about had to do with the robbery, but it got a little more serious whenever we'd talk about Trey. I'd decided that I had no other choice but to get Trey involved. Scottie didn't care much for my decision, but he wasn't surprised.

"Shit, the way you got that dude wrapped around your finger, I know he'll lay his life on the line for you. You won't have to worry about his loyalty, nah mean? This is some crazy shit though, Leesha," Scottie said.

"Yep, you keep saying that."

"Yeah, and I'm gonna keep on saying it, too!"

I told Scottie about Trey's reaction to what I wanted to do.

"What he say?" Scottie asked.

"First he was real quiet and sort of looked away. Then he mumbled a bunch of questions like he could see it coming that I was gonna ask for his help."

"Dude probably wanted to run right then, huh?"

"I don't know. I guess I didn't give him a chance because I just kept talking."

"Where was this at?"

"My apartment."

When I told Trey about wanting him to do the robbery with me, he didn't say yes but he didn't say no, either. Like I told Scottie, Trey mumbled a lot of questions. At the end of the night, I basically had to assume that he would be there for me. I think we sat together in the dark for almost two hours before he went home that night. I'm guessing that Trey was in shock. I didn't want to hear him turn me down so I was cool with it being so silent.

"It's getting late..." was the last thing Trey said to me.

I walked him to the door and that was it. I waited anxiously for the next three days, hoping to hear something from him. If he said no, I wasn't sure what I'd do but on that third day, I got my answer when he called.

Trey asked, "Leesha, what's gonna happen if we get caught?"

Those were his first words. He didn't say hello or ask me how I was doing. It was real obvious that he'd made his decision because of how he felt about me. I tried not to think about that too much. I was too relieved that Trey agreed to help. It didn't matter that I'd be putting his life in danger. I had one of the major pieces to the puzzle in my hands. Now it was all about going through with everything.

The air was tense that day. Wednesday morning came and I couldn't do a damn thing for myself. I looked into the mirror and didn't know what I was doing. I tried to put on makeup before thinking to myself, *Why the fuck am I doing this?* I wasn't questioning what I was about to do. I questioned why I needed to be concerned about how I looked.

I was nervous. I was breathing in and out as if I were taking my last breaths. I kept going over in my mind all these different scenarios. I had this intense fear that Trey wouldn't go through with it. Like maybe he'd come over to pick me up and then tell me he'd changed his mind. I thought about Scottie and all the things he'd been drilling into my head, over and over again. He'd warned me about so many things to look for that I could fill up an entire book listing all of it. He'd helped me a lot but he'd also made me angry, telling me I wasn't ready.

We'd argued like crazy over this robbery and then since he knew how stubborn I was, he'd throw his hands in the air and give up.

"Do what you wanna do…" he'd say in a quiet mumble.

Scottie's worrying got the best of him, too. It was really different for me to see. I even believe he was fighting back a tear or two. It was like he was really struggling to say something and then he'd have to swallow real hard or look in another direction.

Me and Scottie; we had a verbal wrestling match going on over whether I should really go through with this robbery thing. That didn't last too long but I guess Scottie had to make one last attempt before giving in completely to the idea.

Scottie asked me about Trey. "Is he ready?"

I answered yes, but truthfully I wasn't sure. I'd only be able to answer that question after Trey came to get me. Scottie kept me on the phone for a long time. It was really funny to me.

"Scottie, I'll be okay…," I told him.

"Shit, you don't know that, Leesha. Nah, mean? You can't ever assume something like this will go smooth. You just gotta be on your game."

"You sound so worried."

"Yeah, whatever, Leesha…"

As I was talking to Scottie, I heard a car pull up outside in the front of my building. I figured it was Trey, so I walked out onto the balcony to see. I was both nervous and excited. I made Scottie hold on while I took a look. It ended up not being Trey, so I got back on the phone sounding like my spirit was wounded.

"What's wrong with you?" Scottie asked.

"Nothing…"

"That don't sound like nothing. Your voice changed since you put the phone down. What's up, Leesha?"

"I thought that was Trey, that's all."

"What you telling me? You don't think he's gonna show up?"

"He'll be here…I'm just anxious, that's all."

"Shit, you scared, Leesha. You need to be scared and thinking about what you doing!"

"I have thought about it. I'll be okay once Trey gets here and we go through with it."

"Go through with it?"

"Uh-huh…"

"You don't go through with committing armed robbery like this is a part of your growth as a woman. You trippin', Leesha, the way you sounding. I hope you be this way when the real shit goes down. Don't freeze up when you see the guard's hand go up and he try to blast you. Is you ready for that?"

"Scottie, I hear a horn outside. I think that's Trey so I better go…"

"Damn, Leesha."

"I'll call you."

"Nah, I'ma keep calling you so I can talk you out of this shit."

"Bye, Scottie."

I hated to sound so final but I really couldn't take much more of Scottie telling me what could go wrong. I already knew that. I wasn't as calm and collected as I seemed. I mean, what the fuck was I gonna do if I had to shoot somebody? I didn't want to think about that. I tried to focus on what would happen afterward when I could leave L.A. and go where nobody knew me. I could meet new friends eventually but most of all, I'd have my own place and be in a damn house instead of an apartment. That's what I looked forward to. I didn't want to hear any more what-could-go-wrong scenarios. I knew I could do this!

When Trey pulled up in front of my apartment, I got his attention from my balcony. I told him I would be right down. I grabbed everything I needed and left the apartment so fast I couldn't remember if I'd locked my door or not. That was the least of my worries on a day when if something went wrong, my ass could die.

When I opened the door to Trey's car, he had a blank look on his face. It was like he was already in that zone with no emotion and ready to do something serious. When he said hello; I could barely hear him.

"Hey, Leesha."

"Huh?"

"Hey."

"You ready, Trey?"

"Guess so."

That was about all we'd say for the first fifteen minutes of being in the car. It only took twenty minutes to get to the Bank of America on Laurel Canyon and Magnolia Boulevard. We pulled into a stall where we could watch everything going on through the rearview and side mirrors. I told Trey to park this way because of the advice that Scottie had given me. He said that if we were to park in a stall facing the bank, we might be seen by cameras and anyone else facing in our direction. Funny thing, as I sat nervously in the car with Trey, everything Scottie had warned about was coming back to me. I didn't realize I had listened to him so closely.

Trey and I didn't make eye contact for a long time. We sat in silence. I don't know what he was thinking, but my feeling was that if I'd seen any kind of fear in his eyes, that would mess me all up. I was nervous enough. I reached for my bag in front of me and opened it. I pulled out the gun that Scottie had given me. It felt heavier than ever and I almost dropped it in my lap. Seeing it in my hands made what I was about to do seem more real. I couldn't believe I was sitting in the parking lot of a bank, holding a gun in my hand. It was as if I were no longer in control of my own actions. If it weren't for Trey speaking up, I would've continued to sit there in a coma, staring at the gun in my hands.

"Leesha, maybe you should call your mom," Trey said.

"What did you say?"

"You haven't spoken to your mom in a long time and it seems like now would be a good time before we do this."

"Did you speak to your parents?"

"Nah, I can't do that."

"Why not?"

"My parents would be able to tell right away that something ain't right. If something goes wrong today, I'd rather they just hear about it."

"Yeah, well, I doubt if my mother would even care. She probably wouldn't even hear about it, either."

"Still, I think you should call her."

Trey didn't have to do much convincing to get me to call Mama. I had been thinking about that anyway. I dialed her number and got a busy signal.

"The phone is busy. She probably got a new man in her life and ain't even thinking about her daughter."

"Try again, Leesha. I think you probably need to talk to her."

I re-dialed Mama's number.

"It's ringing now," I said.

"Don't look so disappointed."

I responded to Trey's sarcasm with a smirk. I wasn't really sure what to say to Mama when she'd answer.

"Hello?"

"Mama, it's me...Leesha..."

"Oh, finally decided to call, huh?"

"Nice to hear your voice, too, Mama. How have you been?"

"I'm fine, Leesha. You just move away and forget that you spent most of your damn life with me? Is that how daughters treat they mamas now?"

"Mama, the way you act I figure you glad I'm not living with you no more. Ain't you happier now that you got your freedom?"

"Leesha, that's no way to talk to me. I see you still got that mouth on you, girl. Have you called your father? You probably talk to him all the time, huh?"

"Nope, I ain't talked to him since that last time. I could care less if I ever hear from him."

"Oh...well, are you okay?"

"That's the first time I've ever heard you say that, Mama."

"Leesha..."

"Mama, I just called to see how you're doing. Maybe we'll talk sometime, okay? I'm gonna be moving soon."

"Moving?"

"Uh-huh, out of state…Moving to Atlanta."

"Atlanta! Wait a minute. You get on my last nerve telling me stuff without some kind of warning. Girl, why you do that!"

"Mama, we'll talk again soon. I have to go now."

"Leesha!"

Mama tried her best to keep me talking, but I hung up after hearing her say my name over and over in desperation. Trey was right, I needed to call her, but at the same time I wasn't sure what it really accomplished.

As Trey began asking me about my conversation with Mama, I could hear a truck pull up behind us. I could even smell the fumes. It was so familiar to me because of that time when Scottie drove me to that warehouse in downtown L.A. I didn't even have to look in the mirror to know that the Brinks armored truck had pulled up to the bank. Trey cut himself off in midsentence and sloped down in his seat. We both watched in the mirror as one of the guards got out of the truck and went inside the bank. Trey reached down beneath his seat to pull out a gun. He told me earlier that he convinced his cousin to let him borrow it. I couldn't imagine him actually owning a gun. He then hid it underneath his jacket and waited. We both waited. I still had my gun in my lap, in plain view. If someone had walked by slowly and looked inside the car, they could've seen it. I wasn't really thinking; I was going through some very strange motions.

Trey almost looked like a zombie, he was so cool and without any signs of emotion. I guess he was ready for this. I sure wasn't. I don't know; maybe I was misreading his body language. I studied Trey more than I'd kept my eyes on what was going on in front of the bank. Trey caught me staring at him because he glanced at me when my cell phone started to ring.

Trey said, "When we do this, you probably better leave your phone in the car, Leesha."

"You think I should answer it?"

"Yeah, might be your mother calling back."

"I don't wanna talk to her."

"Well, let it ring then."

I looked at the phone number to see who was calling me and noticed it wasn't Mama. "This is Scottie calling me."

"Scottie?"

"Yeah."

"Well..."

"Let me see what he wants."

Trey let out a disappointing sigh. He turned his head to watch the armored truck. I don't think he liked the idea of Scottie calling me, but I felt I had to answer.

"Hello?"

"Leesha, where you at?"

Scottie sounded almost frantic. His voice made me frown as if someone had screamed into the phone.

He was like, "Leesha, where you at now? You there?"

"I'm here with Trey. We're...you know...We're about to do it."

"Nah, Leesha. Nah, don't do that shit. You ain't ready. Listen, I need to talk to you about something."

"Scottie, I need to do this. We're here and the truck is sitting right near the entrance of the bank. I'm thinking that once I step outside this car, I'll be okay. Isn't that what normally happens? I'll be okay. I just need to make the first move somehow."

"Leesha, come on, don't do it!"

I hung up the phone and then glanced at Trey. He was sitting there, quiet and focused on the guard standing outside the truck. The other guard was still inside the bank. All we needed to do was wait for him to come back outside with the money and then make our move.

"Leesha, we may have to kill someone, huh?" Trey mumbled.

"What did you say?"

I knew what he'd said, but it was the way he said it that placed this whole scenario in slow motion. It was as if I could see my actions before I'd even start. I could see myself walking toward the armored car, gun pointed in the direction of the guards and me squeezing the trigger. I'd keep shooting until no one was standing and God help anybody else that might get in the way or be in the line of fire 'cause I probably wouldn't stop shooting.

Trey spoke again. "The only way we can do this now is if we..." Trey turned to look at me. "We really might have to kill someone...," he repeated.

I looked down at the gun in my hand and swallowed really hard. I started to shake a little. Then a tear rolled down my face. I couldn't look up. I didn't want to look at that guard again and I didn't want Trey to see the tear. I wanted to close my eyes and somehow be able to pull this off unconsciously. But I knew I couldn't. I reached for the door handle hoping that small step would give me the confidence I needed to do this and to kill if I had to.

"What are you doing? The other guard ain't come out yet, Leesha," Trey asked.

Before I could answer him, my cell phone rang. Again, the call was from Scottie, still sounding frantic. This time he seemed more relieved, possibly because he assumed that Trey and I hadn't done anything yet.

"Leesha, you have to listen to me right now, aight?" Scottie said. "Forget about that shit and just listen to me!"

"Why are you calling me now, Scottie?"

"Listen, when you get home you gonna find a package that I left for you on your balcony. I climbed up there because I wanted to leave it where I knew it would still be at once you got home, aight?"

"What's inside?"

"That don't matter; listen to what I have to say. I put a note in there, too, so that'll kind of explain what I don't say to you now."

"What's wrong?"

"Leesha, ain't too much that I'm afraid of but right now, the one thing I can't do is say what I have to say to you in person. I've tried the last few times we hung out, but I just couldn't. Now, I have no choice and at the same time I wanna say this before you mess up your life trying to do that robbery shit."

Treyvon spoke as I was listening to Scottie. "Leesha, there they go! The other guard just came out! I think they gonna be leaving pretty soon."

"Leesha, you there?" Scottie asked.

"I'm here," I said as I waved off Trey.

"Good. Forget about that shit over there. I gotta tell you about something that went down over a year ago. It's something that I did because I had to. I mean, it's how things are when you down for your set."

"Scottie, I never really seen you involved with gang stuff."

"I keep my distance most times but I'm still connected with it. I've got friends and family that's down. I mean, it's been a part of my life forever to where it's second nature and not something I really talk about, nah mean?"

"I don't know, I guess so."

"Thing is, over a year ago I found myself in a situation where this dude that we been looking for, for a long-ass time surfaced unexpectedly. Everybody kind of knew who he was, but we couldn't get close because this dude was always in and out of jail. We all figured that if we was patient, we'd catch up to this fool once he was back in the hood."

"What did he do?"

"He killed some of my homeboys. He blasted on them while they was eating hamburgers. He did it like pulling the trigger meant nothing to him. He didn't care if anybody was around. He was just making a name for himself."

"Why you telling me this, Scottie?"

"Like I said, it took time but we all knew this dude would come back to the neighborhood and he did. The trip part about it is that I'm the one who found him, and I wasn't even looking for him at the time."

"Meaning you killed him?"

"I had to. When I first seen him, I had to play like he wasn't familiar to me, but deep inside, I was wanting to call all my niggas and tell them that that fool was standing right in front of me. Dude had no regard for the life of my homeboys. And then to see how he was laughing and eating at the same party I was at? I had to do some acting for real on that day. But at the same time, I didn't have my gun with me anyway so payback had to wait."

"Scottie, I'm really not sure what to say. I know you've done things before. You killed that one guy that tried to hurt me that time. I know there's other sides to you; I always knew that."

"So, you saying you can look past something like that?"

"I have already."

"You saying you can forgive me even though I've taken a life."

"I dont really think about it that way, Scottie."

"Leesha, could you be able to forgive me for killing your cousin?"

"What do you mean?"

"Your cousin, Luther."

"Scottie, what are you saying?"

"I couldn't look the other way, Leesha. Even though you his cousin I still had to pull the trigger.. I mean, it was a trip because we started talking about you and the whole time I was looking at him knowing that before I walked away, I was gonna smoke him. He didn't know. He was just trying to find out if we was going together. Then he started telling me some old story about you, but I didn't want to hear it. Seeing all that love in his eyes for you made the shit harder to do, so that's when I stepped back and pulled out my gun. He seen it and tried to run. I blasted on him. Shot him up a lot, too! That shit happened fast..."

"No!"

"Leesha, I had to do it!"

"Luther is who you and Supreme were talking about that night in the club, huh?"

"Yeah."

"Oh my God, Scottie! Oh my God!"

"Leesha, you alright?" Trey asked as he noticed I was trembling. "Leesha, those guards are looking over this way! I think they can hear you."

"Shit!" Scottie yelled into the phone.

"Oh my God, you killed Luther? You killed my cousin?" I screamed into the phone, over and over, "You killed my cousin!"

Moments later, Scottie hung up on me and I couldn't stop trembling. Treyvon started the car, all the while reaching over and placing his hand on my thigh in an attempt to calm me.

"Where should we go right now? I'm gonna leave because those guards look like they can tell something is up," Trey said.

I was in total shock and unable to answer or respond.

"I'm not so sure I should take you home, Leesha. I'm thinking maybe we can go somewhere and park until you feel better. Your neighbors might see you and start asking questions. I know we gotta go before those guards come over here."

I still didn't respond to Trey so he took it upon himself to pull out of the bank parking lot and drive down the street. He was talking and driving the whole time like we'd committed the robbery and needed to get away. He kept one hand on the steering wheel and the other one trying to reach for the top of my hands. I was still holding on to the gun and it was a good thing that my finger wasn't on the trigger because I was squeezing really tightly; I was in such shock. I think Trey noticed so he was pretty careful when trying to reach for my hands.

Tears streamed down my face. I stared out the window while Trey was driving. When we stopped at a light, this lady in the car next to us was looking at me. She stared and then she looked away when I focused my anger in her direction. I was hurting so deeply inside that my heart was growing cold. I couldn't feel it anymore. That's how I knew. The numbness set in so deeply that I could feel it traveling down my spine and even inside my throat. I let my body go. Even my hands felt so numb that I let the gun fall from my lap and onto the floor in front of me.

"Leesha, you okay? I'm not sure where to take you, but I'll find someplace, okay?"

Trey tried his best to say something that would comfort me but I only half listened. I didn't know what I was supposed to feel. Scottie had knocked the wind out of me with his confession about Luther. All this time I looked at him as my brother and loved him like he could do no wrong. And now I was finding out he's the one responsible for taking the life of someone so dear to me, especially during my early childhood.

I couldn't believe what I was feeling inside, but then something clicked. I'd realized that what Trey and I set out to do never happened. We were going nowhere and running away from nothing. I looked at Trey with blurred vision from all the anger and tears. I told him we needed to go back to the bank.

"I need that money, Trey!" I said.

"What?"

"We need to go back!"

"Leesha, that truck is long gone by now and so are we. I mean, we're not even that far from where you used to stay at."

"What am I gonna do then?"

"I don't know. Right now I don't think you can do anything. You need to relax and think for a minute. What happened, anyway? I mean, all that talk about your cousin being killed…"

I hesitated before I answered Trey's question. Even the thought of repeating what was now a very real nightmare filled my eyes up with tears. I didn't know what to do and I sat there wishing I could call my grandmother.

When we stopped at another red light, Trey reached over to touch my arm. "It's okay if you don't want to say nothing right now."

I didn't respond. I turned my head and continued to stare out the window. I needed to think. Getting that money was important to me. Now it felt like I had nothing and no way out. In one day my life felt like it was ruined forever and it didn't happen because something went wrong at the bank. This happened because a friend turned into someone I will hate for the rest of my life.

Trey had a stranglehold on the steering wheel. We sat in silence and seemed almost separated even though we were inside his car. He had his space and I had mine. I had a million things going through my mind all at once and yet nothing was clear to me. It was as if my life were flashing in front of me. Most of what I'd seen was memories of my grandmother and of Scottie and Luther. I glanced over at Trey and decided to break my silence. I had a hard time allowing him to see my eyes as I didn't want him to know what I was thinking.

"Luther would still be alive if I didn't invite Scottie to Grammy's party," I said to Trey who seemed shocked that I'd finally allowed words to come from my mouth.

"What do you mean?"

"That's when Scottie first met Luther. He killed my cousin."

"Why?"

"Retaliation."

By this time, Trey was driving down La Cienega just past Rodeo Road. We were only minutes away from where I lived with Mama. I thought about her as we got close to my old neighborhood. Maybe Trey could feel what I was thinking because he looked at me and asked if I wanted him to make a left turn at the next light on Coliseum Street.

"Yeah, let's go by there," I responded with no emotion.

"You okay?"

"Not really."

Trey was very careful with his words. I think he worried not only about how I was feeling but how I might react to anything that he'd say. I thanked him for being a friend and never hesitating to help me. Trey smiled and nodded his head. He turned right on Santa Rosalia Drive and we were almost there. He slowed down for the big dip in the road once we reached Hillcrest Drive.

My heart grew numb once again. I was feeling something strange inside seeing those familiar streets. An image of when that guy followed me when I went for a stroll in the wee hours of the morning gave me chills. I could hear in my mind the gunshots when Scottie killed the guy. I trembled as Trey slowed down to make a right turn on my old street. And as soon as he turned, I told him to slow down.

"Why, what's wrong?" he asked.

"Can you take me over to Scottie's? He's around the corner."

"What!"

"Please, Trey... Just, just take me..."

"After what he told you?"

"Yeah, I need to say something to him and then you can take me home."

"Say something to him? He's a killer, Leesha."

"And what were we about to do, Trey? Huh?"

"You're right. So, you not gonna see your mother?"

"No, she's just gonna sweat me and ask a lot of questions."

"You mean about moving to Atlanta?"

"Yeah."

"Can I ask you something about that?"

"We'll talk later about it, okay? I really need you to do this for me first and then I won't ask anything else of you."

"I don't mind doing things for you, Leesha."

"I know but I've asked for way too much. No guy would do what you've done, believe me!"

Trey shrugged his shoulders as if he didn't understand what I was saying to him. Maybe he did but at this point, all I could read in his body language was worry and concern. I could pretty much guess where he wanted to take the conversation. but I wasn't ready to talk about us. I needed to say something to Scottie and get the feeling I had off my chest. It was the only way I could move on.

Trey turned his car around and drove back on to Santa Rosalia. Scottie's street was only a couple blocks away. Trey drove slowly once I told him to turn right. We were only seconds away from pulling up in front of Scottie's apartment. The worst part of that realization was I could see Scottie standing in front of his building.

"Isn't that him?" Trey asked.

I nodded.

"Want me to blow the horn and get his attention? Looks like he's on his cell phone."

"No, don't. Just keep going."

"We not gonna stop?"

"Yeah, go slow and stop in front of the building."

I was so nervous that I didn't know what to tell Trey. It was strange to see Scottie not constantly looking in both directions like he'd usually do. He hadn't even noticed me and Trey pull up in front of his apartment. We sat there for a good two minutes before Scottie happened to turn around. The expression on his face changed from being totally relaxed to being in complete shock when we made eye contact. He immediately stopped talking to whomever and yelled out my name.

"Leesha! Yo!"

Scottie walked nervously toward us, looking unsure of why Trey and I were sitting there. I could hear him tell the person on the phone he'd call them back. Scottie was pulling up his baggy pants as he walked a little faster in our direction.

"You okay?" he asked, half smiling.

I didn't answer. I looked at him until he got close enough for me to say something without really saying it loud.

"I have something that belongs to you," I told him.

"What's that?"

"The gun you gave me."

Scottie stopped his forward motion and stepped back with his hands up. His left hand was empty and in his right hand was his cell phone.

"You came to use that on me, Leesha? What?"

"No, it belongs to you, Scottie, and I don't need it."

"Is that right? You gonna give me my gun back just like that, even after what I told you earlier about Luther?"

"Scottie, I don't want to talk about it. I just came to give this to you. If you can't take it from me, then I'll just drop it on the ground. I don't think I can ever see you again, either."

"Leesha, if I apologized now, would that be enough?"

"I didn't come here for your apology."

"So, you came to bring the gun back and that's it?"

I nodded.

"I have a hard time believing that, Leesha."

"Goodbye, Scottie."

I leaned out the window to drop the gun on the ground next to the edge of the curb where there was a little bit of grass. I just wanted to get rid of it and then be able to feel like every memory of Scottie could be left behind along with his gun. Of course, that would be impossible, but it was my intention.

As I leaned further out the window, the movement of the car had shifted a little more than I'd expected. Then I heard a door slam shut. Trey had gotten out and walked around to where Scottie was standing, all in one quick motion. By the time I frantically glanced around to see where Trey was, I could already hear Scottie acknowledge him.

"What up, homie," Scottie mumbled.

We all sort of looked at each other and then Scottie glanced at the gun that I'd placed on the grass. I didn't know what was really going on until the split second it took for Scottie to begin lunging forward and the simultaneous loud explosion of the gun that Trey had in his hand. Scottie cursed as he hit the ground in agony and before I could tell Trey to stop, he'd fired another shot into Scottie's body.

"Stop!" I screamed more than once. "Trey, stop!"

Trey ran back around and got inside the car.

"Leesha, I had to...I just..."

"Go, Trey! Drive away from here, please!"

I looked back at Scottie with blood pouring from his body. I could see him still moving. Maybe he was fighting to stay alive or maybe that was the natural reaction to bullets invading someone's body. Scottie appeared to be shaking. I watched as long as I could before Trey turned the corner. I even screamed in Scottie's direction.

"I'm sorry, Scottie!"

Trey drove like a mad man and kept apologizing over and over. He sounded like a little boy on the verge of losing a girl he'd had a crush on for a long time. He was whining and even crying. We both cried.

Trey was acting like he'd lost complete control until I screamed at him to slow down. I didn't want the police stopping us for speeding and then finding out that we'd been responsible for the guy bleeding to death on Somerset Drive. I tried my best to think about what we would say if somebody confronted us about the shooting. And then I realized that the gun I tried returning to Scottie had my fingerprints all over it.

"Oh my God, they're gonna come after me!" I blurted.

Trey drove past La Brea and Sycamore Avenue. He pulled into the back of a little shopping center. He parked in the middle of several spaces. I noticed everything because I so desperately didn't want anyone coming up to us to ask questions.

"What's wrong, Leesha?"

"I held that gun!"

"What do you mean?"

"Scottie's gun!"

"What should we do? We can't go back."

"Trey, I know. I'm not stupid, okay?"

"Sorry, Leesha, I wasn't..."

"Trey, let me think for a minute."

"That gun wasn't fired at all so maybe they'll just assume that he pulled it out and then got shot."

"I don't know. I think eventually they'll check out of routine."

"We can't go back, Leesha."

"Trey, you don't have to keep telling me that!"

Trey was getting on my nerves and that motivated me to begin talking about how things would inevitably have to be between the two of us. I feared telling him we weren't gonna see each other because we were a good forty-five minutes away from where I lived. Being stranded wouldn't be a good thing for someone who could be accused of being involved in a murder.

"Trey, I need to go home and be able to think. I may even have to pack and go stay in a hotel or something. I don't know. If they do find my fingerprints on the gun, then before I know it, they'll be knocking on my front door and my life would be done."

"I can take you home, Leesha. I can put you in a hotel somewhere, too. Whatever you want, I'll do for you. That's never been a problem."

"I know and I really thank you for everything. But it's time for you to think about your future, Trey."

"Leesha, I always think about our future, ya know?"

"No, you need to think about your future, Trey. I mean, seriously."

"Seriously, what?"

"Think about it...I remember when you sat me down on the grass in front of that hotdog stand. You showed me pictures that you sketched and we talked about your plans. We did this at the mall, too, remember?"

"Yeah, that was cool."

"It was nice, Trey, but why let it be all talk?"

"I still plan to do all that stuff."

"I don't think you'll ever do what you planned as long as you're so caught up in being with me. I mean, come on. I've got you trying to do a robbery and on top of that, you just killed someone. Trey!"

"Leesha, I did it for you! We'll be alright. No one is gonna care."

"I care, and that's something that I've never said in my life. I've been taking advantage of you because I didn't care. I've been hating Mama because of how she is and talking about her because of the choices she makes with men. She fucked up her life because of those choices. I thought I had everything together because I wasn't like Mama and because I believed I had control. I ain't in control. And the only thing I truly have to fall back on is my life, which right now is not that good, Trey. I don't want to bring yours down. too."

Trey looked away but I think everything I'd said made sense to him. The only thing bad about that was it slowly broke his heart and I could see it in the way he sat behind the steering wheel with his arms folded. He didn't cry but he did look as though he were completely shutting down, right before me.

"Trey, listen, you need to get back on track and become the person you were supposed to become before you met me. You are so sweet and so gifted. You need to share your gift with the world and not just on barbershop and beauty salon windows or in private with me. What you do is *amazing*. I've never seen anyone as good as you."

Trey slowly turned toward me and then stopped halfway. I could see his right eye looking downward. I tried to get him to loosen his arms, but he kept them folded very tightly. I continued to talk, hoping that everything I'd said would get him to start thinking seriously about his own life without me in it.

"Trey, I care about you and I would love to see or at least hear about you making it. I believe that can only happen if you move on. Someone will come along that actually deserves you, Trey. You need to let love find you because you're like no other man I've ever seen. You are so genuine that it's almost scary and I'm praying you remain that way despite what happened. You have to, Trey. Don't stop being you, but, make sure that when you give yourself to someone, do it when you know that person feels the same way about you."

I was feeling really strange inside. It was like, everything I was saying to Trey was sort of hitting home with me. My life was all I pretty much had so I needed to wake up and do something about it. I even felt like a lot of Scottie's wisdom had rubbed off on me and the tables were turned. There I was giving a sermon to Trey as though I'd seen it all when I was basically just getting started my damn self. I laughed quietly and relaxed for a minute. That minute didn't last long because of a loud helicopter flying above.

"Trey, I bet you that helicopter is flying around because of Scottie. I think we better go!"

Trey didn't say anything. He turned on the engine and slowly exited the parking lot. We drove down Sycamore Avenue to Rodeo Road, took a left and then headed toward Culver City. I didn't see anyone following us. No police were around even though I could hear sirens in the distance. We'd seen a paramedics truck drive by really fast. Trey reacted with no emotion. He drove as if he were in no hurry but not really slow, either. It would become the longest forty-five minute drive I'd ever experience. But I was happy that he didn't kick me out of his car after I'd basically told him, we could never see each other again.

When we got over the hill and finally made it to Ventura Boulevard, Trey glanced at me as if he were taking his last few looks. We were probably about ten minutes away from pulling in front of my apartment.

"So, we ever gonna be in touch, like maybe years from now?" Trey asked.

"I don't know. Let's see what happens. Right now I need to figure out what I'm gonna do and where I'm gonna go. That's my one and only concern."

"No thoughts about me?"

"I didn't mean it like that."

"This seems very easy for you, Leesha."

"I already explained how things have to be, so please don't make this harder than it is. Think about your future and do what you're meant to do."

"It's not that easy."

"It's not easy for me to have nothing, Trey. At least you have a start. Be a friend and let me find my own."

"A friend..."

Trey pulled up in front of my building. He kept his eyes forward and waited for me to exit his car like a limousine driver with no emotional attachment or concern. I opened the door slowly and stepped out. I shut the door, all the while looking at Trey. He never stopped staring forward. Before I could finish saying goodbye, he pulled away from the curb. He drove away without even looking back and all I could do was wave with the hopes that he'd at least see me doing that.

Trey was gone and I needed to get myself away from where someone might find me easily. Before I walked inside my building, I listened for sirens in the distance, I glanced around corners and I walked carefully like I was the poster child for paranoia. I was really scared that someone would appear out of nowhere with a badge and their gun pointed at me, but no one was around. It was all quiet except for the usual noise of traffic on Ventura Boulevard.

When I unlocked my door and went inside my apartment, it still looked as I had left it—completely empty. The place still smelled of fresh paint and I looked around as if I were about to walk away from a home that I'd lived in for most of my life. It was special to me because it was my very own apartment and I liked it a lot. It was my own space and I felt free. But standing there made me feel nervous when reality sliced away at my shortlived memories. I could hear some noise outside my window that sent me right into another state of panic. I walked slowly out onto the balcony to make sure the noise had nothing to do with my worst fears. Thankfully, it wasn't the police. It was someone unloading groceries from their car.

As I turned to exit the balcony, I noticed a package sitting near the sliding glass door. It was a box that had been wrapped tightly with two kinds of tape all over it. I had completely forgotten about what Scottie had told me. When I saw the package, I could instantly replay in my mind, the frantic sound of his voice when he told me he'd placed it there. I picked it up and took it inside. Time was getting away from me so I needed to grab my things and leave.

I placed the package on the counter in the kitchen and then went to grab some clothes and my overnight bag. I didn't need to be lugging around too much. I only needed a few things to keep me going. For the first time, I really didn't care about looking good because turning heads was the last thing I wanted to happen.

After I grabbed what I was gonna take, I glanced over at the package again. I thought about what might be in it. I figured it was probably some kind of gift that Scottie had bought me to make me feel good.

The box had so much tape on it that I got tired from trying to open it. I couldn't even tear it apart. I was feeling pathetic and nervous at the same time. I really needed to stop messing around and leave. Then I grabbed a knife from the drawer and cut my way into the box. I opened it enough so I could stick my hand inside and really pull it apart. Once I did that, I noticed an envelope sitting on top of lots of money.

"Scottie, what is this?" I asked as if he were standing close by and could answer.

There was a lot of money in the box. I thumbed through some of it all the while looking at the envelope which I'd placed to the side. I figured Scottie probably explained everything in the letter, but I was a little hesitant to open it. I was scared because of what it might say and because he was dead. I turned and leaned against the counter. I opened the letter slowly, revealing words gradually that seemed to jump off the page and create the flow of tears running down my face. Words like "love" and "hope"; words that I skimmed over before reading the entire letter as written. I breathed deeply and began:

Leesha,

I'm hoping that when you read this letter, it means you've made it home safely. It's crazy. All these years together as friends, I feel like I gotta be the one to help you out. It's cool, though, because I like the idea of making your life straight, nah mean?

Leesha, check this out. From the start and ever since you had this idea about doing the robbery, I felt like I needed to figure out how to stop you. Yeah, I tried to be supportive and teach you some things but on the real, what kind of shit is that? Friends don't let friends make stupid ass decisions and if I truly got your back and hold you in my heart, then I need to be true to that. I need to steer you away from the life that I been into.

Leesha, I've been thinking about this letter and thinking about what I'm gonna say to you. This is actually some hard shit but it's a lot easier than telling you in person. By this time you probably don't care and don't believe what I'm saying anyway because before you get this letter, I will have told you about what happened to your cousin Luther. I don't think you'll hear me if I apologize. I did what I did and it's not much more I can say other than what I'll tell you when I call.

Funny thing about writing this letter, though...A lot of other shit comes to mind. You know, thoughts that you lock up inside you because you pretty much already defined how you gonna feel about a person. I pretty much feel like I can say anything and confess everything right now because I'm gonna be leaving soon. Just like you, I'm gonna move away and start fresh somewhere. I'm gonna get away from my brother, away from all my peeps in L.A., and try to step away from you. too. That's the hardest part of this whole thing because what I feel for you ain't just brotherly love. I know; we had that kind of friendship. Me looking out for you like an older brother but as I've watched you grow and become who you are, I've found myself sitting at home thinking about you in other ways. I would be trying to shake that shit off like I just walked through a spider web or something. And nah, I ain't talking sexually. I'm talking about wanting to be with you, forever and always like a fucking Luther Vandross song. I'm talking some romantic type shit and that got me straight buggin right now!

Leesha, I write this letter to you, coming straight from my heart. I love you. girl, and it ain't as an older brother but as a man. That's some crazy shit, huh? Listen, there's some money in this package. It's about eighty thousand. Take the money and start your new life. Maybe one day when we both settle into being just regular folks, we can get together and talk. For now I would just say to handle your business and make your dreams real, aight? Do it for you and don't get caught up in what ain't necessary. Take your life to a better place and who knows, maybe I'll see you there, nah mean? Ain't no reason why we both can't make it and ain't no reason why I can't say it again; I love you, Leesha.

Peace,

Scottie "Blaze" Franklin

I dropped the letter as if I were holding hot coals in my hand. I couldn't believe what Scottie had confessed. I cursed him for telling me his feelings this way. He'd left me behind with two confessions and two reasons to hate him. It was easy to hate because I didn't have to think too hard. I could walk away from everything he and I were or could've been and not give a damn. I could continue to be Leesha Annette Tyler, a young woman who didn't give a fuck about anybody. I'd never be like Mama because no nigga had any control over me. I controlled everything. This is my life and it's all I got.

Funny thing, being Leesha ain't so easy for me anymore. My heart warmed up because of Scottie. The woman in me soared because of Trey's infatuation. I've had the best of both worlds with those two in my life pretty much supporting me while I'm in school. And now as a dead friend tells me to find a better place, I wonder if that's possible knowing full well that who I was affected more than just my own life. Trey pulled the trigger, but I'm the one that really killed Scottie. I may have even killed Trey, too.

EPILOGUE

When I arrived in Atlanta, nobody met me and no one knew who I was. I walked through Hartsfield Atlanta International Airport, holding my bag and taking steps that I felt unsure about from the moment I'd stepped off the plane. I stopped to get a candy bar and a magazine. I'd reached my destination but I didn't know where to start. I kept thinking to myself, *I'm in Atlanta, I made it!* It felt good to think about, but I still had no clue what to do or where to go first. It took me a while to realize that I was scared to even venture outside the airport. There I was, sitting as if I were waiting for a connecting flight when in reality, this airport was like my transition from the past to the rest of my life; my new life.

I was stuck for a while, sitting there. It was just me, my fears, and my future waiting on the other side of some sliding glass doors that stayed open because the foot traffic never stopped. I stayed inside the airport for a good two hours, waiting and thinking. I watched CNN on the television. I thumbed through my *Essence* magazine and kept my feet on top of my bag. That's where I had all that money Scottie had given to me—all eighty thousand of it. They questioned it back in L.A. but I'd told them right away it was all I had and I wasn't coming back. The sad look on my face seemed to convince them more so than anything else I'd said.

It was a trip to be sitting on so much money and not knowing at all what to do with it. I hadn't touched any of it except for when I packed it in my bag. I'd been using my own money, which I had enough to buy my plane ticket and anything else I needed.

Too much time had passed and I needed to take my first steps toward my new life. I walked through the opened sliding glass doors and found a place to sit outside. That was a big step for me. Then I watched as airport shuttles, rental car buses, and everybody else picked up somebody and drove off. I figured the next hotel shuttle that I'd see would be the one I would take. And about ten minutes later, a Howard Johnson's van pulled up to the curb. I stood up like I knew what I was doing and the man asked me if I was waiting for him.

"Where you coming from?" he asked as he attempted to grab my bag.

I pulled it away from him.

"Okay, I'll leave that one alone," he said.

I never answered his question. I got into the van and didn't say a word. The driver made a couple more stops before finally getting to the hotel. It wasn't very far from the airport. I didn't really care about that too much. I needed a place to lay my head and make some plans. I was scared to death not knowing what to do, but I was happy as hell to be away from L.A. I paid for three nights' stay and was finally out of my own money.

The lady at the counter told me about the continental breakfast each morning and gave me information about some kind of MARTA system.

I was like, "What is that?"

"Like a subway…You don't have one where you're from?" she asked.

"I think they're building one in L.A. but I don't plan to ever use it. I'm planning to move out here, so umm…"

"Oh really?"

"Yeah."

"Then you should definitely learn about the transportation until you get your own. Let me know if you need anything else. We'll be happy to assist you."

"Thanks."

As I turned to walk away from the front counter, the woman said something to me that really woke me up and made my situation more real. It was the kick start that I needed to begin loosening the firm grip of my past.

"Welcome to Atlanta!" she said.

AUTHOR BIO

V. Anthony Rivers is the author of *Daughter By Spirit* and
Everybody Got Issues. He has also contributed to various anthologies,
including *Sistergirls.com, Chocolate Flava, Truth Be Told* and
Love Is Never Painless. A native of Los Angeles,
he currently resides in Van Nuys, CA.
Feel free to email him at Romeodream@aol.com.
Visit the author at www.vanthonyrivers.com

If you enjoyed this novel, make sure you check out
Daughter by Spirit and
Everybody Got Issues by V. Anthony Rivers.

SYNOPSIS OF

Daughter by Spirit

BY V. ANTHONY RIVERS

AVAILABLE FROM STREBOR BOOKS INTERNATIONAL

Christian Erickson is the perfect man: sincere, handsome, intelligent, and passionate. Maiya Hightower has searched for a man like him throughout her entire life. Unfortunately, when she finally finds Christian he is already taken. Maiya reluctantly settles for a close friendship with Christian and the two of them become inseparable. In the midst of turmoil in her personal life, Maiya gives birth to a beautiful daughter Angelina, but fears that Angelina will make the same mistakes in her life that she did. Thus, she leads Angelina to believe that a man she has never shared one single act of intimacy with is her biological father. She wants Angelina to grow up with high expectations so she places Christian, who is no longer a part of her life, onto a well-deserved pedestal and convinces Angelina that he is the role model that any young man that comes into her life must follow.

Angelina becomes immersed in Christian's world through his words: books, magazine articles, and personal letters written to her mother. Even though she has never met him, she is his daughter by spirit. Maiya continues this farce for sixteen years with the help of her best friend and mother who oppose the situation, but both have been drawn into the lies to the point where they can't get out of them.

But like all things in life, whatever you do in the dark eventually comes into the light and Maiya is faced with the consequences of her actions. The only question is will her relationship with her daughter survive.

"An emotional rollercoaster, *Daughter by Spirit* will likely move you to tears. This novel is for anyone that appreciates the importance of building close emotional ties and expressing feelings to loved ones before it is too late. V. Anthony Rivers writes with sincerity and passion and is a dynamic new voice in the literary field."

—ZANE, author of *Addicted, Shame on it All,* and
The Sex Chronicles: Shattering the Myth

"*Daughter by Spirit* is a moving novel. The characters are written so crisp, the dialogue flows so nicely that you're able to follow every scene, building up to the novel's dramatic conclusion. The novel is so pure, so deep that moments within it will move you to tears and to joy. Rivers does an excellent job in pulling you into the story's dramatic plot and leaving you soulfully satisfied at the end of a fast-paced novel. I will definitely be on the lookout for future novels by this author!"

—SHONELL BACON, The Nubian Chronicles
and co-author of *Luvalwayz*

Everybody Got Issues

BY V. ANTHONY RIVERS

AVAILABLE FROM STREBOR BOOKS INTERNATIONAL

This edgy, compelling novel offers an honest portrayal of the ups and downs of everyday life as experienced by three memorable characters.

Everybody Got Issues features Avonte Douglas, Ina Sinclair, and Nakia Davidson, three employees of the successful advertising agency Montaqua Publications. As young, single, and ambitious professionals, their friendship occasionally deteriorates into a vicious cycle of jealousy, gossip, selfishness, and backstabbing. Outside the walls of Montaqua Publications, Avonte, Ina, and Nakia also endure the disappointments and failed expectations of personal relationships that, even when seemingly on the brink of success, prove to be struggles.

In this fast-paced story about friends and coworkers, V. Anthony Rivers deftly conveys the ugly realities of personal and professional relationships. Demonstrating a deep understanding of people—their ulterior motives, the emotional baggage they inevitably carry, and of course their issues—Rivers crafts a novel that is as easy to identify with as it is entertaining.

SYNOPSIS OF

Until Again

BY V. ANTHONY RIVERS

COMING FALL 2006 FROM STREBOR BOOKS INTERNATIONAL

U*ntil Again* is an epic story. It is part slave narrative and part contemporary fiction. The lead character, Julian Woods, is a young artist with a strong resistance to believing that the past has anything to do with the present. One night after agreeing to do portraits of black people living during slavery, he begins to dream about a woman named Eula and from that moment on his life changes. For a while he believes that perhaps these dreams are merely great inspiration for painting with more realism. He can travel back in time, witness their lives, and capture on canvas what he'd seen through his dreams.

Julian's simplistic explanation for why his dreams occurred would soon take a backseat once he'd discovered that, indeed, the past had a real effect on his future. He meets by chance a young woman by the name of Zena. She bears an uncanny resemblance to Zenobia: a woman from the past who becomes the focus of all his dreams thereafter. Zena, it turns out, is the great-granddaughter of Zenobia. Questions beg to be answered: Does this discovery mean that Julian has found his soul mate? Is this the real reason for the dreams that hold him captive every night?

It takes learning about five generations of black women before the truth is finally revealed to Julian. Once it is, he will discover what a blessing his gift is for a family of strong black females.

Baptiste, Michael
Cracked Dreams 1-59309-035-8
Godchild 1-59309-044-7

Bernard, D.V.
The Last Dream Before Dawn
0-9711953-2-3
God in the Image of Woman
1-59309-019-6
How to Kill Your Boyfriend (in 10 Easy Steps)
1-59309-066-8

Billingsley, ReShonda Tate
Help! I've Turned Into My Mother
1-59309-050-1

Brown, Laurinda D.
Fire & Brimstone 1-59309-015-3
UnderCover 1-59309-030-7
The Highest Price for Passion
1-59309-053-6

Cheekes, Shonda
Another Man's Wife 1-59309-008-0
Blackgentlemen.com 0-9711953-8-2
In the Midst of it All 1-59309-038-2

Cooper, William Fredrick
Six Days in January 1-59309-017-X
Sistergirls.com 1-59309-004-8

Crockett, Mark
Turkeystuffer 0-9711953-3-1

Daniels, J and Bacon, Shonell
Luvalwayz: The Opposite Sex and Relationships 0-9711953-1-5
Draw Me With Your Love
1-59309-000-5

Darden, J. Marie
Enemy Fields 1-59309-023-4
Finding Dignity 1-59309-051-X

De Leon, Michelle
Missed Conceptions 1-59309-010-2
Love to the Third 1-59309-016-1
Once Upon a Family Tree
1-59309-028-5

Faye, Cheryl
Be Careful What You Wish For
1-59309-034-X

Halima, Shelley
Azucar Moreno 1-59309-032-3
Los Morenos 1-59309-049-8

Handfield, Laurel
My Diet Starts Tomorrow 1-59309-005-6
Mirror Mirror 1-59309-014-5

Hayes, Lee
Passion Marks 1-59309-006-4
A Deeper Blue: Passion Marks II
1-59309-047-1

Hobbs, Allison
Pandora's Box 1-59309-011-0
Insatiable 1-59309-031-5
Dangerously in Love 1-59309-048-X
Double Dippin' 1-59309-065-X

Hurd, Jimmy
Turnaround 1-59309-045-5
Ice Dancer 1-59309-062-5

Jenkins, Nikki
Playing with the Hand I Was Dealt
1-59309-046-3

Johnson, Keith Lee
Sugar & Spice 1-59309-013-7
Pretenses 1-59309-018-8
Fate's Redemption 1-59309-039-0

Printed in the United States
By Bookmasters